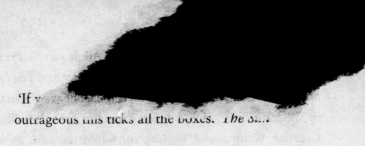

'If y... outrageous this ticks all the boxes.' *The Su...*

'This isn't a book for the squeamish or the faint-hearted
… think Bridget Jones meets *American Psycho*.' *Red*

'This darkly comic novel…has the
potential to become a cult classic.'
Daily Mail

'*Sweetpea* hits all the right buttons. A dark, twisted
read about a female serial killer with dollops of
humour, sarcasm and a lightweight approach…
keeping you gripped and on the hook, both smiling and
squirming.' Maxim Jakubowski, *Lovereading.co.uk*

'You MUST read this book especially if you
like your (anti) heroes dirty-mouthed, deadly
and dark, dark dark. ADORED IT.'
Fiona Cummins, author of *Rattle*

'This book is OUTRAGEOUS.'
Compulsive Readers

'This anti-hero is psychotic without doubt,
sexually voracious and incredibly funny.'
Shots magazine

Adult novels *Pretty Bad* ...*ter* and *The Deviants* an... ...*...peas* She was born in 1980 in Weston-super-Mare, England. She has first class degrees in Creative Writing and Writing for Children, and, aside from writing novels, works as a Senior Lecturer in Creative Writing at Bath Spa University.

In Bloom

CJ Skuse

ONE PLACE. MANY STORIES

HQ
An imprint of HarperCollins*Publishers* Ltd
1 London Bridge Street
London SE1 9GF

This paperback edition 2018

1
First published in Great Britain by
HQ, an imprint of HarperCollins*Publishers* Ltd 2018

ISBN: 978-0-00-821672-6

MIX
Paper from
responsible sources
FSC™ C007454

This book is produced from independently certified FSC™ paper
to ensure responsible forest management.

For more information visit: www.harpercollins.co.uk/green

Printed and bound in Great Britain by
CPI Group (UK) Ltd, Croydon, CR0 4YY

For Matthew Snead. From a distance,
you've been an excellent cousin.

'The odour of the sweet pea is so offensive to flies that it will drive them out of a sick-room, though not in the slightest degree disagreeable to the patient.'

– A TIP FROM *The 1899 Old Farmer's Almanac*

Sunday, 24th June
– 7 weeks pregnant

KNOCK KNOCKKNOCK KNOCK KNOCK. KNOCK. KNOCK.

So there I was, red-handed, red-faced, naked and straddling a corpse. His body is covered in my DNA so even if I *did* toss him over the balcony onto several parked hatchbacks, the evidence would lead straight back to me.

KNOCK KNOCKKNOCK KNOCK KNOCK. KNOCK. KNOCK.

'Jesus Christ police have got loud knocks. Okay okay okay okay think whatdoIdowhatdoIdowhatdoIdo?' Prison is a no no. I've seen *Orange is the New Black*. I can't do all that lesbianing. It looks exhausting.

ANSWER THE FUCKING DOOR!

'Yeah, I guess I'm gonna have to, aren't I?'

I fling on my dressing gown and tiptoe across to the bedroom door. The knock comes again and I jump a clear foot in the air.

For crying out loud, Mummy. This isn't just about you now. You've got me to think about. Answer it and tell them you can't speak to them now.

'Oh yeah they're gonna love that, aren't they? "Sorry, Sarge,

could you pop out for a couple of doughnuts while I dispose of this corpse I've been sleeping with, then do feel free to come back with your Marigolds on and have a good root around?" It's not gonna wash, Foetus Face.'

KNOCK KNOCK.

Right well that knocking is getting right on my tits now so just answer it. You'll think of something.

I'll admit, I'd have been lost if it hadn't been for that little voice from beyond my own vagina telling me what to do. I tiptoed across the cold floor.

KNOCK KNOCK KNOCK.

The words 'shit' and 'creek' spring to mind and there ain't a paddle in sight. 'Fuck fuck fuck fuck fuck fuck fuck fuck FUCK!'

Damn stupid to kill him here in the first place. What was I thinking? Must be the start of 'Baby Brain'. That's what I'm going to blame it on anyway.

Don't you lay this shit on me.

How did I think I was going to get a six-foot Australian man-child out of my flat, along the hall, down two flights, across the car port *and* into my tiny car without being seen by some busy-body with a nose for cadavers? *I've told you what to do - cut him up!* Fortunately AJ wasn't decomposing quickly – I'd drained him out over the bath before I left for the hen weekend. This slows the process down. I saw Dad do it once through a warehouse window – him and his associates, all in balaclavas.

Not just a pretty face, am I? *wink emoji*

Anyway, my heart's pounding and my mouth's all dry but the situation is what it is. There's no escape. The knock echoes once more, I take in a deep lungful of air, prepare my best 'shocked and saddened' face and open the door of the flat.

And it's Mrs Whittaker.

I let out my deep breath. Our kleptomaniac neighbour who gets more Alzheimersy each time I see her usually annoys the knicker elastic off me with her unsolicited visits, but today I could lick her bristly mouth.

'Hello, Rebecca,' she says.

My name is Rhiannon but nobody ever gets my name right. Even at school. Even when I got famous, few news editors could spell it. I get it – people are stupid. I let old Whittaker off a bollocking for the simple fact that she isn't wearing latex gloves or brandishing a search warrant.

'I'm popping into town in a bit to do my big shop and I wondered if you wanted anything. I know your young man's away at the moment.'

The implication being that I, as a young woman alone, can't cope. Bless. She's eyeballing the room over my shoulder, as usual, obviously wanting to come in and snoop for unattended *objets d'art.*

'Ah that's nice of you, Mrs W,' I say, keeping an eye out for cops on the stairs. But there's nothing and no one.

I think briefly about sending her on a mission for a Dyson noise-less power saw but feel it will garner too many questions. 'I think I'm okay, thanks.'

'When's your young man back? France, isn't it?'

'No, Holland. He's gone to watch the football.' I haven't got time to go into details about Craig's arrest and subsequent charge for the three murders that *I* actually committed so I leave it at 'Yeah, he's having a great time, seen some clogs and stuff.'

'Bet the flat's felt ever so empty without him. I know when my John died…'

She witters on for three minutes about how long it took to come to terms with her husband's passing and I'm going 'Mmm' and 'Aah' in all the right places, but my mind is going in a hundred directions. When's she going to leave? When are the police coming? Where am I going to cut him up?

As I'm standing there, a bubble emerges from my think tank.

She's going out. Her apartment will be empty for hours.

If I can drag AJ's body downstairs into *her* flat, it will leave *my* flat clear for the police. If this is my rescue boat it has some huge holes in it, but you can't look a holey old boat in the mouth, can you? So I start rowing.

'Okay I better be off to get my bus,' she says.

'Actually, I do want a couple of bits and bobs if you don't mind,' I say. 'I'll just grab the list. Come in.' She can't resist a root around my nick-knacks.

Parking her in the lounge, I retreat to the kitchen and locate the bottle of cooking oil under the sink. I break the seal and pour it down the plughole. She's pootling about beyond the partition wall, commenting on how warm it is with our underfloor heating. Her block heels click towards the record player.

'Yeah, here we go,' I say, joining her in the lounge – the empty oil bottle trailing by my side. She's nosing through Craig's vinyl, lifting out *Listen Without Prejudice* and trying to pick off the HMV sticker that had been on there since Craig bought it. She doesn't see what I'm doing.

'It's only this cooking oil actually. We've run out.'

'Rapeseed oil.' She frowns, putting George back in the stack and taking the bottle from me to squint at the label. 'Where do you get that?'

'With the other oils. If you can't find it, don't worry …'

'Oh I'll find it. I like a quest,' she says, smiling so toothily I fear her falsies are gonna shoot out of her mouth. 'I never cooked with this before.'

'It's so good for you,' I say, surreptitiously parroting the label blurb. 'I think it has the lowest amount of saturates of any other oil on the market and no artificial preservatives, and it's kind to cows and stuff.'

'Sounds wonderful,' she smiles again as I guide her back towards the front door. 'Might get some myself. It doesn't make chips taste funny, does it?'

She walks on ahead of me, right into my oily trap...

WALLOP

She goes down like a perv priest on a preschooler, but to my chagrin doesn't bang her head. I rush in and do it manually, grabbing her ears and yanking her skull back for hard contact to ensure disorientation.

'Ooh! Ow! Ooh! Ooh, what's happened? My head! Ahh, my arm! Where am I?' she gabbles on, flailing about like an upturned tortoise.

'Oh dear, it's all right,' I say, dialling 999. 'You must have slipped. I'm going to put you in the recovery position now...'

'Oh it hurts. Oof! Oww! Owwwww!'

'That's okay, pain is good. Pain means it's getting better.'

With her settled as comfortably as she can be on her side in front of the afternoon film – *Calamity Jane* – I go to my room and wrap my secret love in the sheet he's lying dead on. There's a *thump* when he hits the rug.

'What was that?'

'I dropped something,' I say to the back of her head as I drag AJ's body across the lounge floor behind her. Doris Day dances about on a counter. Crazy bitch.

Whittaker keeps trying to look back at me. 'I'm in so much pain, love.'

'Ahh lie still, Mrs W. The ambulance is on its way. You're going to be fine but you have to stay still. You could have a broken… primula.'

Could not think of the name of that bone. Damn baby brain.

It's not my fault. You got yourself into this mess.

I'm sweating like a pork chop as I drag my human fajita through my door and downstairs to Mrs Whittaker's flat, bundling it inside with seconds to spare. I hear the quick *pad pad* of shoes down the corridor and I look up to see Jonathan Jerrams careering towards me, arms out.

'Rhiannon!' he yells, barrelling into me at speed.

Old Mr and Mrs Jerrams bring up the rear, apologising in his wake.

Jonathan's my self-appointed 'best friend ever' because of something I did for him over two years ago. I saved his life. Sort of. There used to be a guy of no fixed abode who'd hang about the concourse shouting abuse at residents, tipping over bins and stealing bikes. He wore a pig mask to frighten people – I nicknamed him The Notorious P.I.G. Anyway, he picked on Jonathan something chronic because Jonathan has Down's syndrome and he could get money out of him easily. One day, The P.I.G. threw an apple core at Jonathan's head as he was coming back from feeding the ducks – one of the few solo pursuits his parents afforded him – and I saw it happen.

It's one of my rules – defend the defenceless. I had no choice.

So immediately after the apple-flinging, I strode up to the P.I.G., snapped the mask from his face and yelled 'If you don't disappear I will visit you in the dead of night and cut your *real* fucking face off.' Got spit in his eye and everything. I eyeballed him until he looked away, got onto his bike and sped off, laughing like it didn't matter. Clearly it did. We never saw him on the estate again.

For ages after, Jonathan left me presents outside my door, sent random cards and flowers, then Craig got jealous and asked him to stop. Now it's tackle hugs and proclamations of love across the car park.

'We're going to the zoo, we are,' says Jonathan, rocking to a tune only he could hear; trouser hems flapping in the breeze.

'How lovely,' I say, wiping facial sweat on my dressing gown sleeve.

'I like animals, I do.'

'Yeah, so do I. They're great, aren't they?'

The Jerramses laugh for no apparent reason.

Jonathan prods Whittaker's door with his spoony digits. 'What's in there?'

'I'm watering Mrs Whittaker's house plants. She's gone into hospital.'

'Oh dear,' says Mrs J. 'What's happened?'

'She had a fall.'

The Jerramses accept this. Whittaker's a proper Weeble, always falling over – usually in the stairwells. Most residents have had to carry her flabby arse up two flights before now. It's like a rite of passage in this place.

'Where's your dog?' Jonathan shouts, two feet away.

'Tink's staying with my parents-in-law,' I tell him.

'Do you like my t-shirt?'

He opens his jacket to reveal a *Jaws* t-shirt with a sizeable belly underneath and a bolognaise stain on the neck. Why do people who look after the disabled never dress them in good clothes? It's always cheap Velcro shoes and washed-out charity shop threads that never fit. The shark glared at me, teeth gleaming. It didn't have as many calcium deposits as Jonathan.

'Nice,' I say. 'You wear it well, JJ.'

I'm still sweating like I'm at hot box yoga even though all I'm doing is talking – meantime I have a corpse mouldering in one flat, a broken pensioner in another and a police forensics team arriving any second. It's only when I'm making my excuses I realise my dressing gown has opened and boobage is on the prowl. Old Jerrams can't take his eyes off them. I have to say, it's a big turn on when he looks up my dressing gown as I'm climbing back up the stairs.

'What are you doing, Rachel?' Mrs Whittaker calls out, scaring the crap out of me. I'd forgotten she was still there in front of *Calamity Jane*. Doris and some other tart are singing about a woman's work never being done.

Too fucking true, Doris.

'Just went to see if there was any sign of the ambulance.' I mop over the oil puddle with a bleachy dishcloth. 'You all right there while I get changed?'

'Oh yeah, you carry on love, don't mind me.'

I change my bed, turn the mattress, Febreeze the room and open both windows. When I'm changed, I go in and sit next to Whittaker and watch a bit more of *Calamity Jane* 'til the ambulance comes.

'I'll water your house plants, don't worry,' I call after her as they stretcher her into the lift. 'And I'll call Betty for you. Leave everything to me.'

It's minutes between the ambulance leaving to the police drawing up. I'm on the balcony, chewing a Dime bar. Three be-suited people – a tightly-bunned black woman and two men, one tall, blond and erect; the other like the short tubby guy in *Grease* who's about forty years too old for high school. It's then time to get into character as the wronged girlfriend of a serial killer.

I've learned a lot from watching those *Crocodile Tears* docus on YouTube. It all comes flooding back, like an old First Aid course when you have to treat a casualty. Not that I've ever had to. Or would, let's face it.

I've remembered the key points about lying to police and they are these:

1) **Strong emotional displays** – *dead giveaway.*
2) **Micro-expressions** – *Keep gestures to a minimum. Rubbing one's face denotes self-comfort/lying. Stillness/ shock are natural responses.*
3) **Shaking hands** – *good, if you can manufacture it. Luckily, my hands were shaking efficiently – the adrenaline of my frantic lunchtime running round hiding corpses and maiming pensioners.*
4) **Script** – *less is more. Any idiot who killed his wife and went on TV to beg for help in 'catching the bastard' always makes the same mistake – their dialogue is too prepared. Sandwich the lies between truths – I was on a hen weekend, Craig did call me from Amsterdam to say*

he'd been arrested, he did habitually use pot to relax.
Then the lies.
   5) **Co-operation** – *do everything they say without hesitation.*

The detective leading the investigation, DI Nnedi Géricault from the Major Crime Investigation Unit in Bristol, interviews me with DS Tubby Guy from *Grease*. The blond guy dons gloves and snoops around the flat. They have had to get a warrant which is presumably why they have taken so long to get here. Thank Fuck.

'Do what you need to,' I say, still in utter shock and bewilderment, fiddling with the solitaire on my fourth finger.

I tell them I'm pregnant and that I have high blood pressure – a half-truth so they'll treat me with kid gloves. Works like a charm.

'We'll keep it brief today as clearly it must be a stressful time for you,' says Géricault.

'I can't believe it,' I keep repeating. 'Please tell me this is a mistake.'

If there's one thing I've always been able to do well, it's cry on demand. I learnt from an early age that people soften when you turn on the waterworks – nothing too dramatic, just some light sobbing at the right moment and you're laughing.

Internally, of course.

'I've known the guy for four years,' I wail. 'I live with him. I sleep in the same bed as him. I'm having his *baby*. How the hell is he supposed to have killed three people behind my back? It makes no sense.'

'Would you like some water?' Géricault offers, motioning

to the blond in the kitchen. She has a couple of fingers missing on her left hand – the fourth and fifth are stumps. I wonder if they'll find AJ's blood spatter in the grouting. You'll only see it if you're looking for it. And this isn't a crime scene.

Yet.

'How long will this take?' I ask, glass shaking in my adrenalized grip.

DS Tubby Guy from *Grease* says 'It'll take as long as it takes.' I'm so thankful I pay my taxes to keep his ass in cheap suits.

As it turns out they stay around two hours forty minutes. They ask all sorts of questions – questions they already know the answers to, like where Craig is right now and where his van is and even questions about my dad's well-documented vigilantism.

'Craig didn't know my dad for long. He didn't know about what he did in his spare time. He wasn't one of them.'

'How can you be sure?' asks Géricault.

'I guess I can't,' I shrug. And they ask no more about it.

They say I'll need to move out for a while. I inform them that Craig's parents Jim and Elaine have said I can stay with them. They take Craig's laptop and his pot in evidence bags, some of our kitchen knives (not the Sabatiers of course as those babies were hidden in advance) and his spare tool box from the cupboard outside our bedroom.

'Some people are experts at hiding what they are,' says Géricault as they are leaving. 'You mustn't blame yourself.' She nods and holds my stare.

It's clear from this meeting that Craig's in the frame. I'm a key witness at best; the pregnant, scared girlfriend of a man who was, by day, a mild-mannered builder – by night a vicious, apex predator. They'd got the bastard.

Gordon Ramsay clap DONE.

*

So, I guess now you want to know about the old choppy-choppy? Well, it was the messiest, most nauseating thing I've ever done. God, when I think how easy it was for murderers in the olden days. All you had to do was lace someone's tobacco with arsenic or push them in the Thames. They rarely caught people like me back then – sudden death was usually down to 'The Pox'. Now you've got to do all this dismembering and fingerprint-hiding shit.

First I had to make a list for Homebase –

- *rubber gloves (1 box)*
- *plastic sheeting and/or cling film (lots)*
- *shovel (1)*
- *bleach (2 bottles, possibly 3)*
- *duct tape (3 rolls)*
- *cleaning sponges (several)*
- *electric power saw and/or bow saw (1 of each).*

How did I know what to get? My dad was a vigilante – kids pick these things up.

Then I scrubbed out rubber gloves, bleach and sponges from the Homebase list and decided to get them in Lidl so it wouldn't look like I was doing a supermarket sweep for dismembering tools. I also added Penguins, Kettle Chips, oil and elderflower pressé. Lies sandwiched between truths.

Annoyingly, Craig's power saw – a bloody expensive one he'd bought with his Screwfix vouchers – was still in his van

which is, as I write, being impounded by police in Amsterdam. I therefore had to buy a new one.

The guy I pounced upon in the masonry paint aisle at Homebase – Ranjit – was only too happy to help. I played my Dumbass Girly Girl role to the hilt, saying the saw was Hubby's birthday gift and that he 'wanted to get started on our decking pronto'. Ranjit had just the tool – a power saw. I chose the Makita FG6500S with dust guard and free goggles for two reasons:

1) it cut through wood like butter and
2) it was the quietest.

I bought my bits and pieces, got it all back to Whittaker's flat and set everything up in her bathroom. It took ages. And then doubt crept in. What if someone heard the saw? What if Jonathan and his folks returned early from the zoo? What if one of Whittaker's friends popped by just as I'm up to my elbows in Australian long pig? It was getting on for four o'clock. I needed to see what the situation was outside my own private abattoir.

I dressed in my most girly outfit, brushed my hair so it went all Doris Day and grabbed the spare set of Craig's keys. Up and down the hallway I went like the fucking Avon lady, knocking on doors asking if they'd been dropped in the lift. Only three families were in on Whittaker's floor – the gays with the cats, the couple in wheelchairs and Leafblower Ron and Shirley who were watching TV and eating haddock and mash judging by the smell.

It wasn't ideal but I had to chance it. Saw and be damned.

You can do it, Mummy. I believe in you.

When I started, I kept seeing his face flash across my mind. His eyes. His smile. The moment he told me he loved me.

I had to keep telling myself 'It's only a dead pig. The pig was a bad, bad pig' and threw a tea towel over its face when it was staring. 'I don't like being blackmailed by a lanky dead Australian pig.'

But all the while a little voice was telling me differently.

That's not a pig though, Mummy. That's my daddy.

I vomited until it was stringy water. I don't know if it was pregnancy sickness kicking in or the pervading stink of bleach or the fact that on some level I'd appalled myself. The thigh bones were the worst – I used a hammer to drive the knife down deeper to break into them. I used the saw as sparingly as possible, French-trimming the bones before smashing down through them. I ended up with six pieces. Wrapping them took longer than cutting them.

The whole process was not to be repeated. By that evening each section was tightly wrapped in cling film – head, torso, arms, right thigh, left thigh and lower legs. I packaged them in two sports bags and took it all down to my car with my other stuff – clothes and Sylvanians. Nothing else mattered.

And it wasn't just the body parts I had to dispose of either. I also had:

- *the plastic sheeting from the bathroom*
- *the shower curtain*
- *all my bed linen*
- *all AJ's possessions – including his rucksack, passport and phone*

14

I'd have to burn as much of it as I could. Somehow. Somewhere.

I didn't allow myself to cry until I was in the car and half way up the motorway towards the coast. The rain lashed against the windows. I half-wished it would skid off the road as I drove. I could barely see through my tears or the windscreen at one point.

It was getting on for midnight by the time I turned up on Jim and Elaine's doorstep in Monks Bay. I was sobbing, soaked and spent of energy. I fell into Jim's cashmere arms, ready for him to take care of me. Ready for Elaine to wash my face and make me hot chocolate and dress me in warm, pyjamas and tuck me into their spare room on the second floor and tell me everything was going to be all right.

Ready for someone else to take the reins.

Monday, 25th June – 7 weeks, 1 day

1. *People in washing powder adverts who are surprised when the washing powder gets the clothes clean, i.e. does its fucking job.*
2. *The first man who got the first woman pregnant. And the first woman who thought that was a good idea.*
3. *People who buy fake flowers.*
4. *People who make fake flowers.*
5. *Tourists in open-toe sandals – now that it's summer there are suddenly yellowing, gnarly trotters everywhere. Now I know how the Nazis felt when the Ark of the Covenant opened.*
6. *Johnny Depp.*

For just a moment the other day, I thought I was running out of items for my Kill Lists. But then lo, a new morning breaks and with it arrives a whole new bunch of thorns in my raw little side.

I gave Jim the *Gazette*'s switchboard number and left him to explain why I was off sick. I can take as long as I need. Bet they're loving this. Nothing as newsworthy as this has ever happened in that town. I can see Linus Sixgill now, creaming his genius over his by-line:

PRIORY GARDENS SURVIVOR IN SEX SLAYER SHOCK
SHE USED TO MAKE OUR COFFEE!

or

GAZETTE GIRL'S BOYFRIEND IS GAY SEX SLAYER!
WE ALWAYS THOUGHT HER COFFEE TASTED FUNNY!

or perhaps

GAZETTE JUNIOR LIVES WITH SICKO SEX FIEND:
Did she make his coffee too?

I've felt sick all day. And thirsty. And *dizzy*, like I've been stuck in a revolving door for a decade. I'm also shivery, which Elaine says is 'either a chill or pneumonia'. She is making me endless cups of tea and checking my temperature on the hour.

Either Jim or Elaine have come into my bedroom unannounced twelve times since I woke up with the doorbell at 9.58 a.m. Tink scampers in too. She hops up on my bed and makes a beeline for my face, licking it all over. She seems to love me again, even though Jim has taken over her care now.

God I feel awful. Perhaps I'm dying. Wouldn't that be ironic? What if Elaine's right and this is what pneumonia feels like? How the hell is a thing the size of a chickpea causing me so much discomfort?

You overdid it yesterday. You need to rest. I need to grow in peace.

FFS. It's talking to me all the time now. Like Jiminy Cricket but without the musical interludes.

Elaine's been in to change my sick bucket and bring in a two-litre bottle of water and a piece of dry toast. I wonder if this lot will stay down. Got no appetite at all. I don't have a hunger for anything. It's like Heil Foetus has invaded Womblandia and drenched that fire in amniotic fluid.

Ugh. I feel sick again. Every time I close my eyes, I keep seeing his thigh meat all over my hands.

Thursday, 28th June – 7 weeks, 4 day

1. *People who share Facebook posts like 'Hey, put a star on your wall to support brain cancer' or 'Post this as your status if you have the best hubby/wife/dad/hamster ever.' Stop with the whole global community thing. It ain't gonna happen, not with me in the community anyway.*
2. *Tourists with their faces in their Greggs nosebags, who walk in human chains along pavements.*
3. *People who say 'There are no words' when there's been some tragedy. There are always words. You're just too lazy to form them into complete sentences.*

Tink's barking woke me up. Jim always answers the door to spare me and Elaine and today I heard a snippet – *national* press. How they found out I'm living here I don't know, but one peek out of Jim and Elaine's bedroom window shows they're camped out for the duration.

I think about going all Tudor on their asses and tipping a bucket of piss over them but I guess I need them on my side, which is a shame because I have rather a lot of piss in me right now. And wind. And vomit.

Jim only announces callers when it's a flower delivery – and

we've had many. Sixteen in all. Jim will bring them in, vased, say who they're from – their friends, the *Gazette*, one of the PICSOs (my old 'friends', the people I couldn't scrape off), some random school friends – and set them down on my nightstand so I can see them as I'm drifting back to sleep. Then Elaine will come in, take my temperature, set down a plate of chopped banana and dry crackers and take the flowers out because 'plants sap all the oxygen out of the room'. I don't know where they go after that.

I managed one trip downstairs today to get a biscuit mid-afternoon. Saw a pile of business cards and scraps of paper on the dresser. Notes from reporters, asking for 'my side of the story.' My life with Craig Wilkins – the most vicious serial killer the West Country's ever seen. *We only want the truth*.

If only they knew the *real* truth. It should be *my* face on those front pages. *My* headlines. *I* did those things, not him. I want to stand on that doorstep and scream it: IT WAS ME. ME. ME. ME. FUCKING *ME!*

But then another tsunami of nausea sweeps my way, crashing out every other thought in my head other than 'Get to the toilet, quick.'

Not today, Mummy. Back to bed.

I'm throwing up water now. Elaine says it 'must be something in the bottles'. She's read how pregnant women drinking from plastic bottles can pass on abnormalities.

'One baby in India came out with two heads and they said that was because of bottled water.'

I don't want to split my hoo-ha so I guess I'll have to make the switch to filtered.

Sunday, 1st July – 8 weeks exactly

Ugh.

Monday, 2nd July – 8 weeks, 1 day

Double ugh. I opened the fridge to get some chilled water and screamed – on the bottom shelf was a dead baby tied up in a see-through bag. Turns out, Elaine had just bought a chicken for tea. Once seen, not forgotten.

I crawled back upstairs and into bed like the girl out of *The Grudge*.

My head is swimming and I can't see the point of doing anything. Though one of the journalists on the doorstep *did* wink at me when I went out to bring the milk in. I must look like 180 pounds of shit in a ten-pound bag but still, it was a brief boost.

Wednesday, 4ᵗʰ July
– 8 weeks, 3 days

1. *Elaine – the way she loads the dishwasher is the stuff of nightmares. Okay so I've killed people but at least I don't stack un-rinsed muesli bowls and leave them for days to dry out. It's clean-dish SUICIDE.*
2. *The woman in the Vauxhall Meriva who cut us up on the motorway.*
3. *Yodel van drivers – they are out to kill us all.*

I feel a bit better today so I've decided to go back into work before they sack me. Jim says they can't do that or there'll 'be hell to pay'. Elaine said it's 'far too early' but I was adamant and she made me a packed lunch – a superfoods salad with fresh lettuce 'not bagged because bagged salads have listeria in them.' Jim drove me, even offering to linger in town all day before driving me home again. I don't deserve them. And they don't deserve me.

As it turned out, Elaine was right. It *was* far too early. And I didn't stay long. I made a huge, unplanned boo-boo.

I'm dropped off outside the *Gazette* offices and there are two paps on the doorstep as I swipe my key card. They snap away like it's about to fall off, asking questions about Priory Gardens and

Craig. The new receptionist greets me on the front desk. She has an accent – Spanish or Geordie – and looks like the President's wife – far too glam to be a greeter. I give her three months.

I head into the main office. At first glance, everything's the same. The same faces, same haircuts. Same plate of cakes on top of the filing cabinet. Same *clink, tap, whir* sounds and aromas of strong coffee and newsprint.

Ugh, coffee. What used to be my heroin is now my abhorrence. Heil Foetus does not like coffee.

I'm not a foetus yet. I'm still an embryo until next week. Mmm, doughnuts.

That artless piss drip Linus is on the phone, leaning back in his chair, fingering his bald patch with his Mont Blanc. The subs are meerkatting at me over the tops of their monitors. Bollocky Bill's eating a doorstep sandwich, the postman's leaving with an empty sack, Johnny the photographer is getting his list of jobs from Paul. Claudia Gulper, AJ's aunt, is on her phone, but affords me the briefest of glances.

My daddy you mean. Auntie Claudia! Yoo hoo! She killed him, Auntie Claudie! You have to save me!

Anyway, nothing has changed.

Then I go to my desk.

Some five-year-old bobble head in a short skirt and a blouse that looks like it's been torn down from a care home window is sitting in my chair. My things have all vanished – my stapler with the sparkly Chihuahua stickers, my Sylvanian pencil case, the gonk on my monitor that AJ bought me, the coffee rings next to my Queen of Fucking Everything coaster. Even the coaster. The 'Rhiannon' label on my in-tray has been messily torn off and replaced with a clean one saying 'Katie'.

All eyes are on me but nobody says anything.

The handle yanks down on Ron's office door and out he struts –greasy-shiny, Cuban heels, trousers crotch-tight. 'Sweetpea! How *are* you?'

I don't know how to answer. I'm struck dumb.

'This is Katie Drucker, our new Editorial Manager. Katie's been holding the fort while you've been away.'

Katie stands up from my chair and smiles. I smell her breath before she opens her mouth. Marmite. Huge yellow teeth. In my mind, she is gaffer-taped to my chair and I'm pulling out those massive gnashers with the biggest pliers you've ever seen. 'Hi, how are you?'

'Fine thanks,' I say.

She glances at Ron who takes the proverbial ball and runs with it as fast as he can in his Cuban heels, specifically made for short-arses like him. 'So how's everything?'

'Fine,' I say again.

'Did you get our flowers?'

'Yes.'

'You poor thing, Rhiannon,' says Katie Drucker, Patronising Fucker.

'Do you want to pop in my office and have a quick chat?' asks Ron.

No, I'd like to pop into your office and see if your £500 shredder will accommodate more than five fingers at once.

And don't be fooled by the breezy tone and friendly-sounding 'pop' and 'quick'. 'Pop' in particular is a caped crusader and 'quick' its evil Boy Wonder. This wasn't going to be some brief, cosy chinwag – this was going to be a rip-your-head-off-and-shit-down-your-neck-conversation, beginning with 'we have to boot

your arse out the door' but 'how about a think piece on Craig before you do?' as a drizzle of honey on the festering shit heap.

Ron summons Claudia over because when you're a boss who's as powerful as a fart in a bag, you can't face altercations on your own. She grabs a pad and sweeps over from her desk, affording me a bright smile on the way.

'Hi Rhee, how are you, Sweetpea?'

'I'm FINE,' I say, louder, garnering two more meerkat subs to peer atop their monitors. And it's then that time does a Matrixy thing. Katie's phone pulses in her knock off Vuitton handbag beside my desk – old school Britney. The main door opens and in strides that malodorous slunt Lana Rowntree. Tight grey skirt, chunky platforms but less of a swish to her blonde hair than usual. The woman who shagged my man and sent me off down this road in the first place. A human satnav of hideous betrayal. Her head is down. My throat aches.

It's all. Her. Fault.

That's my only thought as I watch her dish out papers and glide through the office towards the sales department, like nothing happened. Like her life hasn't changed one bit. She doesn't notice me.

Doesn't see me coming.

The ache in my throat burns as I move closer to her, closer, closer –

I'm.

Not.

That.

Innocent.

I'm reaching out, grabbing a fistful of blonde, pulling it backwards. A waft of Herbal Essences flies past my face as she

goes down. I don't hear what I say. I don't know who pulls me off her. I'm pounding her face. Over and over.

Oops, I did it again.

And the next thing I know, Jim is buckling my seatbelt and the engine's running and his and Ron's voices carry through the crack in the passenger window. *Hormones. Just needs some time. Knew it was too soon.* Cameras click. Someone calls my name. *Look up for me, Sweetpea.*

And I'm sitting there, picking flakes of her blood from my knuckles.

Friday, 6th July – 8 weeks, 5 days

1. *People who tap dance – more unnecessary noise.*
2. *People who present any TV programme before 6 p.m.*
3. *Any of those design programmes about people who take a nice little abandoned barn and turn it into a soulless, four-storey gym with diamond encrusted swimming pool and a remote-control garden etc. Ugh.*

Jim's on the phone to Ron now – Lana isn't pressing charges. I listened through the bannisters. He'll come up in a minute and tell me what was said, he's that kinda guy. I've already heard what I needed, I'm that kinda gal.

*

I made the front page! **Gripper Killer Girlfriend in Office Brawl.** Jim has been trying to keep me away from the news but we walked into town earlier and stopped outside the newsagent so Elaine could go in and get her *Woman's Own*. There was a stand of papers outside.

'Come on,' said Jim, taking my arm, leading me towards the seafront.

I'm actually better at handling the attention than either of them gives me credit for, but of course I have to pretend it affects

me deeply. It blew up the week I moved in. The angle then was **PRIORY GARDENS SURVIVOR IS SICK KILLER'S GIRL**. Elaine has banned all news bulletins from the house – she doesn't want to know. Jim craves news so he has to buy his daily paper and read it in a café on the seafront to get his fix. I saw him once. The headline on his paper was **THROW AWAY THE KEY: WILKINS' SICK AND DEPRAVED ACTS SHOCK NATION** and there was a picture of Craig being led from a police van, grey blanket over his head.

I preferred that one to

GRIPPER'S GIRL IS CRECHE ATTACK SURVIVOR… and she's UP THE DUFF! One paper is calling him this year's 'Hot Felon'.

Photographers were outside the house most mornings, snapping away like a pack of North Face-clad alligators.

'Oi, Priory Gardens!'

'Oi, love, gissa quote, gissa smile!'

'Hey Rhiannon, have you seen Craig Wilkins yet?'

'Where are the other bodies, Rhiannon? Did he tell you?'

'How's he doing in prison?'

'Did you know, Rhiannon?'

'Did you help him?'

'Wossit like living with a monster, Rhi Rhi?'

That winky journalist is usually there in the throng and I noticed this morning his lanyard says the *Plymouth Star*. He has black hair, a square jaw and his smile is knicker-wettingly blinding. If I met him in a bar he'd be paying me child support.

Some fucker should.

'How are you, Rhiannon?' he asked me.

'I just want to get on with my life, thanks,' I say, opening

and closing the door once I've brought the milk in, flashing him some unsolicited leg through the dressing gown, as is my wont.

'Is it true you and Craig were engaged?' I hear as I flick the chain on.

On the days, I'm feeling up to it, I don my Victoria Beckham sunglasses, sweep my hair to one side, prepare my downcast face (not difficult – I look like a ghost most days thanks to the vom) and sashay through the melee throwing out breadcrumbs like 'I'm fine thanks' and 'I knew nothing'.

I'm just giving them what they want – they see what they want to see. Not looking past what's already been decreed – that Craig Wilkins, my boyfriend, did knowingly and wilfully murder three people in cold blood and masturbate over their corpses. That moi – Rhiannon Lewis – she of that terrible crèche massacre at Priory Gardens all those years ago, is just the naive girlfriend. Remember when they brought her out of that house, wrapped in blood-soaked Peter Rabbit blankets? How can one girl get so unlucky twice in one lifetime? It's too tragic.

When they can't get a comment from you, they shove notes through the letterbox instead. Business cards, scrawled scraps of paper, all asking for me to get in touch. I could barely read the writing on some.

One of the notes was barely legible, scrawled on a scrap of notepaper 'To my Sweet Messy House' it looked like and there was a phone number underneath. I'm thinking it could be the local mental case – he sometimes posts rants about the government and how they're trying to kill us through our tap water on his way up to the war memorial to talk to dead soldiers.

What I resent most of all about this kind of press intrusion is that all they're interested in is Craig. How *he* did it. How *he*

could rape that poor woman. What it was like for me living with a monster? How *he's* feeling about being the most hated guy in the country right now.

He's not actually. There's always paedophiles. And according to Twitter there's a guy who sprinkled his girlfriend's ashes on his Shreddies who's *way* worse.

I don't know who I am now. It's like one day I was in a couple with a flat and we had a baby on the way and the next I went into a phone box, spun around three times and now I'm Poor Little Murderer's Preggo Girlfriend – I even come with accessories: eighteen-carat white-gold solitaire on my ring finger, meek smile, washed out Primark panda pyjamas, greasy hair and slight stomach protrusion.

Jim and Elaine walk along the seafront every morning – it's their ritual. And they've allowed me and Tink to join in too. We sit on a bench with a hot drink and a bun – iced for them, brown seeded for me – and we sip and chomp in silence. Everything is small here. Small and safe. From across the estuary at Temperley, Monks Bay looks like a bucket of tiny houses tipped down a hillside by a giant child. There's no design to it at all – it's a higgledy-piggledy mess of streets too narrow to drive a Fiesta down without cracking your wing mirrors, a funicular railway, a church and quaint little B+Bs and cottages called names like The Sloop and The Brigantine.

For me, killing has been what makes life worth living. So at the moment, I'm not living, I'm merely existing. I'm like that polar bear I saw once at Bristol Zoo. Wandering back and forth, back and forth across his concrete. Safe, fed and secure but slowly going ever further out of my mind.

'Go on, love, eat your roll,' said Elaine. 'You've got to keep

your energy up. You didn't eat your Protein Puffs this morning either.'

I took one bite. Tink leapt off my lap. She knew it was coming before I did. I vomited on the sea wall. A seagull promptly ate it while it was hot.

Monday, 9th July – 9 weeks, 1 day

1. *Owner of the bulldog-with-the-ridiculous-bollocks walking along the seafront who laughed at Tink's diamante collar and called her a 'poof'.*
2. *Dentists – but hey it's FREE now I'm up the duff so screw you, Rapey Eyes Mike. That'll be £300's worth of porcelain fillings and be quick about it.*
3. *The editor of* Take a Break *magazine.*

Living with Jim and Elaine has its downsides – Jim's adenoidal symphony in the dead of night is one. Elaine's obsessive dusting is another. Other things they do irritate me for no apparent reason, like the both-getting-out-of-the-car-to-put-petrol-in thing. I just don't get it.

But the best thing about living with them is their garden. Me and Jim have bonded over our mutual love of all things green and wild. All I had at the flat were window boxes and container herbs, all of which have since died – but here there are large raised beds and espalier apple trees along the fencing, Japanese maple, flowering dogwood, large white roses that look like ladies' blouses and smell like heaven, ice cream tulips, tiny bleeding hearts. I try to name as many as I can – dahlias, camellias, blood red rhododendrons, alliums, yuccas, nasturtiums, silvery

catmint, Michaelmas daisies, deep blue larkspur. The little herb bed with lemon thyme and rosemary and soft sage leaves I can't stop rubbing along my lips —

Dammit, didn't Ophelia do that in *Hamlet*, list all these flowers? Told you I was going out of my mind.

For Jim the garden isn't ever finished – he's always deadheading or pruning or stroking a leaf like he's injecting himself with medicine. He says he could never live anywhere but England because of our climate and our flowers, though he has expressed an interest in going somewhere called the 'Carrizo Plain' in California. He read about it in the *Daily Mail*.

'The Superbloom,' he said, his eyes all twinkly. 'I'd love to see that. The desert comes alive with wildflowers – purples, pinks, yellows – only for a month or so and then it disappears. It comes when the desert's experienced a lot of rain and it's extraordinary. Oh the colours, Rhiannon!'

Jim's one of the few people I've ever met who encourages weeds too. He allows the back of the garden to grow wild for the butterflies and his shed is covered in ivy. Jim says other gardeners hate ivy because they think it throttles growth but Jim says it's terrific and 'does so much good for the ecosystem, the birds and the insects'.

He loves all plants, good or bad, pretty or ugly. Even ones that stink or the spiky ones that catch flies.

'Ivy's a tenacious little thing too,' he says. 'No matter what you do, she grows back, climbs up, there's no stopping her. There's an old wives' tale that if ivy's grown on a house it can protect you from witches.'

Gonna need a shit load more ivy then, Jim.

Went to the dentist's after lunch. There was an article about Craig in the *Take a Break* magazine – a centre page all about his fetish for gay chatrooms and gimp masks. None of it's true but since when has that mattered? I got quite the jolt when I saw him, smiling on a beach in Cyprus. We'd had sex after we took that, as the sun was going down. I'd been cut out of the picture – his Facebook avatar – it was a joint selfie originally.

Jim says we shouldn't talk to the press, despite the wedges they've offered. The *Gazette* had wanted an exclusive, being my old employers and all, but Jim said no. No interviews, no news coverage, nothing.

'You're not up to it, Rhiannon. I'm putting my foot down. We can't have you stressed so early on in your pregnancy. Think of the baby.'

I *am* thinking of the baby but I can't help thinking I'm missing out. This could be my moment. It could be *Miracle of Priory Gardens: Reloaded*. I could be on *Up at the Crack* again, eating croissants, sitting between that homeless cat who wrote a bestseller and the kid who got all those retweets for chicken nuggets. But instead I'm here. Doing nothing. Playing Best Supporting Actress – an award where nobody ever remembers the winners.

I did do one useful thing today though – updated AJ's Facebook status. It's the one of the few times Facebook's good for something – when you're stealing people's holiday photos to create the illusion that someone is absolutely *not* dead and in several cling filmed pieces in the boot of my car. There have already been some comments underneath the post, one from Claudia.

Glad you're having a great time. Bulgaria looks as beautiful as you said it would. Wouldn't hurt to ring your aunty once in a while! Love you, C XX

Need to find somewhere to bury him soon.

Jim's been in – the police are finished with their investigations at the flat so I can go and pick up the rest of my stuff. He says he will drive me – later, I said. Gonna sleep now.

Friday, 13th July – 9 weeks, 5 days

Elaine saw this flyer in the library for The Pudding Club – a weekly social where 'new, expectant and seasoned mummies get together for a natter and a cuppa and cake in mum-friendly spaces'. She suggested I go along.

The words 'natter' and 'cuppa' make me want to tear off my eyelids.

I knew it would be a load of old clit but I went along for said 'natter' and 'cuppa' because according to Elaine 'it isn't healthy to be staying in all the time on your own'. She practically pushed me out of the door.

I met the group in a lilac and white tea shop off the seafront called Violet's – *the* place to go in Monks Bay if you're a) cake-oriented b) a mum and c) have several screaming children clinging to each limb.

The scene in the café was like a *Muppet Babies* homage to the Somme.

It was a wall of noise. Screaming. Squealing. Cupcake missiles. Tiny sandwich grenades. Mini roll IEDs. Babies wailing in adults' arms or banging yoghurty spoons on high chair trays. One blonde toddler was full-body tantrumming on the carpet like she was in pain. I wanted to leave immediately.

The Pudding Club mummies were ensconced in a

somewhat-quiet booth at the back. The leader of the gang was obviously Pinelopi or 'Pin' as she preferred – forty-eight, Greek and expecting her fifth. She's got a PhD, drives a Jeep and is married to a guy called Clive who works in finance. Pin claims to have once shagged Prince Andrew but she says 'it was years ago so he probably wouldn't recall'. She presumably added this last bit in case one of us rang him to check.

Then there's Nevaeh – Heaven spelled backwards – twenty-nine, black, gay and likes to be called Nev. She lives with her wife and kids and the kids' dad Calvin which I think is the ideal family set up. If I'd have been born with three parents I'd still have one left. Nev intends to call her forthcoming twins Blakely and Stallone, presumably because she hates them. She smokes 'to keep their weight down' and calls everyone Darlin'. I asked Nev about childbirth.

'They say the moment you first look into your baby's eyes you'll fall in love but you won't – you'll just be thinking "Thank Christ that's over, get me a Subway." Seriously, Darlin'. When Jadis was born, I hadn't eaten for two days. She ripped me from earhole to asshole. My vadge looks like the Joker's smile.'

Scarlett is the youngest Pudding at nineteen. She's as vain as a WAG and cranially underdeveloped but I guess that doesn't make her a bad person. She takes a selfie every twenty minutes and thinks World War Two started with an iceberg. She's due at exactly the same time as me – to the week. I said:

'I'm envisioning a scene from that terrible Hugh Grant film as our babies come out in the delivery room and some strange foreign doctor is shuttling back and forth between our gaping vaginas like a rhino on speed.'

Nothing.

Scarlett didn't get the reference – nor did she know what 'envisioning' meant. She then asked 'Was High Grant the one in *The King's Speech*?'

Then there's the tedious one, Helen. Ginger hair, milk-white skin covered in fish food freckles, huge overstuffed bump. She is slightly cross-eyed and her chin zits look like spheres of chorizo, though of course it's *de trop* to mention either.

'Helen Rutherford,' she said, all pinched and evil. 'Nice to meet you.'

'Likewise,' I returned, more evil. She only joined in the conversation to correct some statistic or brag about how easy her last pregnancy was, how she 'breastfed Myles until school' and how tight she is cos she 'kept up her exercises.' She thinks anyone who doesn't breastfeed or give birth 'naturally' is the Devil incarnate. Helen is my least favourite pudding. In fact I hate her already.

A baby started screaming in its high chair on the next table and all of them looked at it with that same expression of 'Ahh, bless.' I was horrified. This was no place for the noise-sensitive.

There was one Pudding who wasn't as ball-achingly thick, arrogant or tedious as the others and this was Marnie Prendergast – twenty-eight, conker-brown eyes and a soft, Brontë-country accent. She's due in September but has a tiny bump so her clothes still fit. Her parents are dead too – her mum after birthing her brother (a blood clot I think but the cakes were coming) and her dad had 'some kidney thing'. Her brother lives abroad and they don't speak.

'Orphans Unite,' she beamed, clinking her coffee with my water. 'We're like Annie and that little kid she sings to in the night, aren't we?'

'Molly?' I said.

'Yeah,' she laughed. She laughed at many of my comic asides today. Nobody ever laughs at my comic asides. I liked Marnie immediately.

I liked her outfit today too – a Frankie Says Relax t-shirt, black jacket and pedal pushers. She had on black and white Vans too – like the pair I wore until Craig got paint on them. We got onto the subject of Sylvanian Families – she adored them as a child. She even still had her Cottontail Rabbit family and Cosy Cottage Starter Home, though it was 'still in the loft somewhere'. I can forgive her for that. But yeah, despite her incessant phone-checking and the Take That badge on her lapel. I'm pretty sure I've made a friend.

I asked her where to buy cool maternity clothes, not Helen's kind that looked like she'd crash landed on a chintz marquee.

'If you want to trawl threads, I'm your gal,' she said. 'I love shopping.'

'I hate it,' I said. 'But yeah we could go to the Mall or something.'

'It's a date. Let's swap numbers and I'll give you a buzz at the weekend.'

This was the only nice conversation I had at Pudding Club – the rest involved either pre-eclampsia, nipple-hardening or pissing oneself. I strained to hear most of it over all the screaming and though I laughed along and enthused about joining their antenatal classes I wasn't feeling it. I kept thinking, *Is this my life now? Is this all there is?* The one saving grace was that no one was bringing up the Craig thing.

Until someone brought up the Craig thing.

'So what's happening with the trial, Rhiannon?' asked Pin,

chewing her apricot Danish. All heads except Marnie's turned to me.

'Uh, nothing at the moment. He's due to plead in November and then I think the trial will be set for some time next year.'

Nev was working her way through a vegan brownie. Her teeth were covered in brown clods. 'What's he going to plead?'

I fiddled with my engagement ring. 'Not guilty.'

'But did he do it? Did he kill all those people?'

I shrugged. 'I don't know. It's been a lot to process.'

Marnie cleared her throat. 'Rhiannon might not feel comfortable talking about this—'

'Yeah do say if you're not comfortable talking about it, Rhiannon,' said Pin, at full volume. Pin used to be in the army so could easily project her voice like it was still fighting for attention with the landmines. Several eyes from the other tables turned to ours as she was talking. 'But you must have known something, surely.' The tiny tantrummer on the carpet started up again, furious at having her face wiped.

I smiled meekly, my Just-Your-Average-Preggo smile. 'I really didn't know anything.'

The others nodded along like they were stuck on a back windscreen.

'I saw you on *Up at the Crack* a few months ago,' said Scarlett.

'Oh, for the Woman of the Century award?' I said. 'Yeah, that was fun.'

Not.

'Yeah you had a lovely top on. Sort of peach with frills?'

'Miss Selfridge,' I informed her.

'Cool,' she said, getting her phone out and Googling it.

'Why aren't you talking to the press?' said Helen. 'Bit of a wasted opportunity if you ask me.'

Marnie sighed. 'Helen, for goodness sake—'

'No it's fine,' I said. 'It doesn't feel right. Feels like I'm selling him out.'

'Why don't you though?' asked Helen, her fish-flake cheeks pounding down her banana bread. 'He's left you high and dry with a baby on the way. You need all the money you can get, surely.' She was looking down at my engagement ring. 'That must have cost a pretty penny too.'

'I'm fine,' I said. 'My sister Seren and I inherited our parents' house—'

'He is a murderer after all. Don't you think the victims of those appalling attacks deserve some answers?'

'What victims?' scoffed Nev. 'That guy in the canal had it coming by all accounts. And the dude in the park was a –' pause to lower voice to a whisper '– *sex offender* – and that woman in the quarry—'

'What?' said Helen, all raised eyebrows and pass-ag. 'The MOTHER in the quarry who was held for weeks and tortured, then raped and thrown into a pit? She had three children, Nevaeh. Thee!

Nev shut up. Scarlett looked at Pin. Helen looked at Scarlett, snooty as a fox. My heartburn scorched my throat and my arse had begun to twitch. Pin called the waiter over for our bill. Marnie patted my forearm and mouthed 'I'm so sorry.' I think she meant it.

I turned to Helen. 'It hasn't gone to trial yet.'

'And you're standing by him, are you, Rhiannon?'

They looked at me. The waitresses looked at me. Tiny

Tantrummer looked at me. Old Me would have said something meek and non-controversial but today, I just couldn't be bothered. I could see the Pudding Club becoming like the PICSOs – bloody hard work. In a parallel universe, it might have been different. We'd have dinner parties, drink Prosecco into the small hours and bond over risqué conversation about fluffy handcuffs and fisting. Perhaps we'd have had barbecues and playdates and swapped ideas about nativity costumes in the schoolyard. But in this universe? No chance.

'Yes Helen, I'm standing by my knife-wielding, rapey-lady, torture-happy, murderous asshole of a boyfriend. Now get me a doughnut before I pass the fuck out.'

Monday, 16ᵗʰ July – 10 weeks, 1 day

1. TV *programmes about billionaires who spend millions on lampshades and ornaments and STILL find stuff to bitch about.*
2. TV *programmes about benefit cheats who buy fags, tattoos and Heineken but have 'nothing to feed their kids'. Cry me a river.*
3. *People who say 'might of' and 'could of' not 'might have' and 'could have'.*

Plymouth Star guy was on the doorstep when I went out the front to shoo seagulls off the bird table. Him and a curly-haired camera guy.

'Hey, Rhiannon. How you doing?'

'Good thanks.'

'Any chance of a couple of words for the *Star*?'

'Yeah, I've got two words that would be perfect for you.'

'Come on, throw me a bone, I've been in the job ten weeks and the most interesting thing has been Kids Set Fire to Furby in Precinct.'

'I know what it's like. I used to work for a local newspaper. Not the heady heights of crack reporting mind you – just editorial assistant.'

'So you know what it's like?' he said. 'Please. I need a scoop or they're going to fire my ass. This is a huge story and you're right at the centre.'

'Too true,' I sighed, folding my arms.

'Please? Anything I can take back to the office? You'll be getting your own side across. Some of the tabloids are saying you knew all along what Wilkins was doing.'

'I did *not* know anything,' I said. I noticed then he had Voice Memos recording on his phone. The camera guy was clicking. I calmed myself with a breath. 'Tell me why I should bare my soul to you. Give me one good reason.'

He backed away. 'I can't.'

'Why not?'

'It's my job,' he said. 'This is what I do. There isn't a good reason.'

'Come on, give me a sob story. Why should I put you through to the second round? Dad dying of cancer? Brother out in Afghanistan? Granny just too damn nuts in the nursing home to recognise your face anymore? Tell me why I should give *you* my story and not the *Mirror* or the *Express*. They've offered me shitloads more than Pleases.'

He backed away, frowning. 'I don't have anything to give you. I just need a break.' I stared him out until both he and the camera guy had disappeared through the front gate and out of my sight.

*

I have made a boo-boo – I shouted at Elaine. In fact it was worse than shouted. I jumped on the highest of horses, whipped its ass and rode it right through her. I caught her dusting around

45

my Sylvanians country hotel in the corner of the lounge and rearranging things in the rooms.

'DON'T FUCKING TOUCH THAT! WHY ARE YOU TOUCHING THAT?'

I didn't mean to say it, it just splurged out. And I know they've been good to me and looked after me and blah de blah blah, but JEEEEEZUS why can't people leave my things alone?! I'm not asking too much, am I? She'd moved the front desk into the sitting room. She'd made up the bed in the cat family's bedroom when the maid was CLEARLY on her way there to do that herself. *And* she'd taken out everything in the fridge and put it on the kitchen floor.

Nerve = touched.

'Rhiannon, I was only having a look, love ...'

I could see my mother's face in hers – *What's the big deal? It's only a few toys, Rhiannon. You're too old for toys now.*

'You weren't "having a look", you were touching things! Why can't you leave them?' My fingers were lengthening; my breathing grew sharper the longer I looked at her blank face. The room seemed to pale away and into sharp focus came the phone cord and Elaine's saggy neck. Wrapping it around again and again, pulling on it, squeezing it, that face going purple.

'I'm sorry,' Elaine blushed. 'I'm so sorry.' She sprinted from the room.

I took the hotel upstairs and shoved it in my closet, safe and sound. I knew it was too exposed downstairs but I had no room to display it up here. I had more Sylvanian stuff than I had clothes.

When I resurfaced, the house was quiet and there was a note on the hallway table – Elaine was at the church hall with her

Christian women's group for the craft fair and Jim was on the beach with the dog. I walked down there to find him sitting on the large rocks watching Tink sniffing in the rock pools. He didn't mention the Sylvanians debacle at first; he started off-topic.

'Did you look into that Airy B thing for me?'

'Airbnb?' I said. 'Yeah, all done.'

'You've done it?'

'Yeah, I'll show you later. We've had a few enquiries already. I think it's looking quite good for August.'

'Oh that's great, thank you.'

'No problem at all. It's the least I can do, isn't it?'

He smiled, looking out to sea. 'I don't have a clue about this internet lark. That place needs to start paying its way to keep the bank happy.'

See this is a lie pie if ever he's baked one. One of the discoveries I've made about Jim since living with him is that he's LOADED. He has quite the property portfolio. It's another hobby – buying up shitholes and turning them into sought-after real estate. I've seen his bank statements. He's got three projects on the go – a flat in Cresswell Terrace where a junkie melted into the floor, a five bed house on Temperley called Knight's Rest where a hoarder stashed several hundred ice cream tubs of his own shit, and a holiday cottage called the Well House on the Cliff Road which has just finished being refurbed. For years it was used as a derelict meeting place for local teens to shag and break bottles. Jim asked me to put it 'on the line' now that it's ready for holiday bookings.

That's Jim's problem, he trusts me. And I, being the gal that I am, am letting him down. I've put the listing up but once I've

shown him, I will take it down again. I've decided I need the Well House – it'll be my refuge. A place I can go anytime I want to eat and escape Elaine's factoids about hot baths causing abortions and the link between obese mothers and autism.

'Elaine mentioned you'd had a set-to about your doll's house.'

I sat down on the lower rock next to Jim. 'My deluxe country hotel, yes.'

'Bit OTT wasn't it?'

'No.'

'She was only cleaning it, Rhiannon.'

'I DON'T WANT IT CLEANED.'

'All right, all right. Cor dear, those hormones are playing up today, aren't they?' He laughed. He actually *laughed*.

I glared at him. 'You don't get it.'

'Get what?'

'After Priory Gardens, I went into a children's rehab facility in Gloucester. It was horrible. It stank of cauliflower and farts. I was lonely. One morning, my dad and my sister went on breakfast TV to talk about it and how I was doing. Seren mentioned I liked Sylvanian Families. And I got sent so many. All the shops, all the animals. Seren would bring them in for me to play with. The toys the centre provided were either chewed or dirty but these were new and *mine*. I learned to talk again using my Sylvanians. I learned to hold things again, grip things. They helped me more than anyone will ever know—'

'You don't have to say anything else—'

'—nobody else was allowed to touch them except Seren and she knew she could only play with them when I was playing as well. I used to rub the rabbits' ears on my top lip and suck the clothes. No idea why, just liked it. Mum was always complaining

48

about it – she said it made them stink. She said it was childish. I was still playing with them when I was twelve. Then one day, I came home from school and they'd all disappeared.'

'Disappeared where?'

'Mum had got rid of them. My post office, my supermarket, my country hotel. All the animals, all the little bits had vanished. She'd sent the lot to a charity shop. I screamed. Threw things at her. Bottles. Remote controls. Shoes. But she shut the door on me, refused to talk about it.'

Jim blew out a breath as Tink scurried over to him and begged for a pick up. Dogs always know. 'That's sad, Rhiannon.'

'Seren had managed to save some of them of them for me before they went – Richard E. Grunt, a few rabbits, couple of the little books and the bathroom set. We sneaked out and buried them in the garden one night when Mum was asleep. The Man in the Moon was our only witness.'

'Rhiannon, you don't have to explain—'

'That's when I started saving up. Every bit of spare money I got, I'd spend on buying every last Sylvanian back. Piece by piece. I saved up all my pocket money, got a newspaper round, washed cars, mowed lawns. That's the only thing I like about being a grown up. I can fight the battles I lost as a kid.'

'I do understand,' he said, stroking Tink's silky apple head. 'Our Craig used to say about your brain injury and how you liked things just so. I'll have a word with Elaine, don't worry.'

'I miss Seren,' I said, only then realising I had said it out loud. Jim seemed to be waiting for me to say more but I didn't.

'Of course you do. She's your big sister.'

'She's half who I am,' I said. 'She taught me lots of stuff. *Good* stuff. French plaits and tying shoelaces and how to wrap

presents so the corners were all tucked in. She's practical like that. She's a good mum.'

'I expect she looked after you too when you were younger?'

'Sometimes,' I said, the night of Pete McMahon's death flashing into my mind. His body on top of hers. Her drunken mumblings. The knife cutting through his ribs like a spoon through jelly. 'Sometimes I looked after her.'

A silence fell between us. Without a word, we both got up and continued our walk. Tink trotted along between us. I placed my feet in footprints other people had left behind. It's funny how you can't walk in someone else's footsteps, isn't it? It doesn't work. You end up taking too-long strides or placing your feet unnaturally to where you'd choose to put them.

We'd gone about ten minutes before Jim stopped and pulled a piece of paper from his back pocket. 'This came today.'

I knew what it was from the postmark – a letter from Craig. I'd been expecting it after Elaine intercepted the last one and set fire to it on the hob.

Jim rubbed his mouth. 'Can't ignore him forever. This is the fourth one.'

I scanned it through. His writing had got better. I'd only ever seen his scrawls on builder's invoices or scrappily-written shopping lists. Clearly he'd taken some sort of calligraphy class while he'd been on remand. 'I can't see the point of visiting. It would only be more lies.'

He shook his head. 'I know the evidence speaks for itself but it doesn't answer everything. It doesn't explain that on the night that woman's body was dumped in the quarry, he was nowhere near. He's on CCTV at Wembley, clear as day.'

'What about the others?' I said. 'The man in the park? The

semen all over that woman's body? The… severed penis in his van?'

I refrained from saying 'cock au van'. This wasn't the time for that joke. It was never the time for that joke but it was still a good joke.

'He's still saying he's being framed,' said Jim. 'That Lana sort he was seeing. He's still my son, Rhiannon. I can't give up on him.'

'He's Elaine's son too. She's given up on him.'

'She'll come round. We're not going to leave him in there to rot, not when there's a chance someone else is to blame.'

Tink nuzzled into the crook of Jim's arm. Jim turned to look at me, his eyes filling with water. 'I was the first person in this world to hold him. Before the doctors. Before Elaine. I won't leave him when he needs me the most.'

Jim had brought back boxes of our stuff from the flat; his clothes, vinyl, the dehumidifier, all his old football programmes. The remnants of sawdust on his jeans. I cried when I opened the boxes. I found a bottle of his aftershave – Valentino Intense. I'd stitched the guy up like a quilt and now I'm crying about it. Pregnancy screws you right up, I'm telling you.

'I'll go with you,' I said. 'To see him. I'll go. Not yet, but I'll go.'

Jim put his arm around me, eyes all glassy. We watched Tink run after a Jack Russell, chasing it round in circles like a furry whirlwind. And we laughed. It *was* funny. But both laughs were too forced.

Friday, 20th July – 10 weeks, 5 days

1. *Seagulls – this town is building-shaped croutons in a seagull-shit soup.*
2. *Man in the mobility scooter who tutted that I was taking up too much of his greeting cards aisle at the garden centre.*
3. *Sandra Huggins.*

One of the side effects of being pregnant is vivid dreams. I often wake up in a cold sweat, my heart racing, having spent most of the night before screaming at my mother or watching my sister Seren get attacked by birds or wolves or some strange man in a hood – those dreams seem to be on a loop in my head. Last night there was a new showing – the fortune teller from the hen weekend. It was an almost exact re-run of what actually happened.

Me walking into her shop on the seafront. The red-haired woman with smoker's mouth-creases and bad eyebrows. The crystal ball on its claw-footed stand. The Tarot cards spread out – The Hanged Man, Judgement, The Hermit, The Ace of Swords, The Devil himself.

You don't work well with others, she said. *You need to have no one.*

Staring into the ball, her drawn-on eyebrows furrowing in the middle. Pulling her hand away from the ball. Her breaths getting faster.

I won't be on my own, will I? I ask her. I'll have the baby?

No, she says, tidying the cards.

Does my baby die? I ask her.

I saw a baby covered in blood.

I smash her face in with the crystal ball and she crouches behind the table, cowering, her hands over her head. Even when she's unconscious I keep going. There's no stopping me. *I couldn't kill a baby. I'm not capable. There is good in me somewhere.*

But it's buried so deep, she says. It's the last thing she says.

*

This morning, once Jim's morning farts had cleared from the big bathroom, I treated myself to a bubble bath and a hair wash with two shampoos and the posh antenatal conditioner Elaine bought. Thing is though, my hair is STILL greasy. What happens in a preggo's body that makes her hair greasy? Why is my body giving my foetus all my shine and bounce?

Also – dry hands and feet – the fuh? I'm taking on water like the Titanic but every extremity is as dry as a nun's gusset. This kid is leaching all my moisture and redirecting it to my scalp. I looked at myself in Elaine's mirror and I cried. I cry at nothing nowadays. I cry at burnt toast and RSPCA adverts and when I got my dressing gown cord stuck in the front door and the UPS guy saw my foof. I suppose that's down to Heil Foetus as well.

You wanted *him to see it.*

I thought Marnie would have called this weekend about going

maternity clothes shopping but I guess she was full of it like everyone else in my life. Bullshit City, that's where I hang my hat.

Instead I have been dragged outside the house today to 'get a bit of fresh air in my lungs' even though I'm perfectly happy with my existing lungal air. Elaine reckons I'm depressed but I'm not. I've just got the morbs. Even serial killers get the blues you know.

We're currently sweltering our giblets out in motorway traffic en route to the garden centre.

'Do you want another Murray Mint, Rhiannon?'

'No thanks. Still working on the last one.'

I'm sitting in the back of the car, strapped in like a child. We used to go on seaside trips when we were kids – me and Seren in the back listening to music through shared earphones, Mum in the front, Dad driving. Mum feeding him wine gums. Dad turning up Spice Girls so we could all sing loudly. My Sylvanians would be buckled in beside me and on cold days, me and Seren would snuggle under the big green picnic blanket.

Jim and Elaine have the radio tuned to Coma FM. Usually I can't stand it because there's too much chatting and this lunch-time quiz where the callers are a sack of dicks, but they've just played 'Father Figure' and now I'm crying. It had been playing on a paint-splattered radio in a pet shop Craig and Dad were refitting as a tattooist's the first time we met. The week before he was arrested, Craig said it should be our first dance at our wedding. I wanted to do a routine to 'Opposites Attract' but he said it depended how pissed he got.

Yes, he used to annoy me. Yes, he cheated. Yes, he used to talk through movies and stub out his blunts on my Hygena

sideboard. But once upon a time he was mine. And I miss it. This is not the family I was meant to have.

*

We're looking at the potted trees – well, Jim and Elaine are. I'm updating AJ's Facebook page – he's 'in Moscow now, where water's more expensive than vodka'. Found a pic of the Kremlin and some random guy wrapped in winter knits that obscured his face to accompany the post.

I heard them talking about me when they thought I was in the loo.

'I wonder why she's not buying anything for the baby. Spends all her money on those toys. It's worrying.'

'If it makes her happy I don't see the harm, E, leave her be.'

'I'm not saying it's *harmful*. Just odd. She should be nesting. She doesn't read those books I got her, she doesn't talk about it, ever.'

'I know, I know.'

'We need to find out what her plans are.'

This exchange bugs me all the way round but I swallow it. At a quarter to midday, we headed into the café as Elaine wanted to 'beat the queues'. We ordered scampi and Jim told me to get the table near the play area.

I watched some toddlers on their springy ride-on things. A mum was stood behind one of the little girls, her hand on the child's back. Another was consoling a boy who'd banged his knee. She rocked him and kissed his forehead. There was an older lady – mid sixties – pushing two girls on the swings. They shouted 'Higher, Granny!' and she laughed. And they laughed.

The sun bounced off the metal swing post into my eyes. I got my bottle of Gaviscon out of my bag and swigged it.

Jim appeared with our tray of cutlery and condiments, gibbering away like an angry badger, and plonked it down on the table.

'What's wrong?'

'I don't believe it,' he huffed, setting out the cutlery. 'Bloody woman.'

'Who, Elaine?'

'No,' he said on an angry breath. 'Over there, third table on the right.'

I swigged my Gaviscon again and counted along the tables. Two women were eating croissants. The penny didn't drop immediately.

'Sandra Huggins,' he said.

The world around me stopped. A bomb could have gone off and I wouldn't have noticed. Those two words were enough for me to forget everything. My heartburn merged into something else – for the first time in weeks I felt my own heart beating again, faster and faster the more I took in her face. It was like I'd been dead and she'd brought me back to life.

I've never seen anyone I wanted to kill more.

'I don't know her,' I lied, barely able to sit still.

'You know her face, don't you? She's dyed her hair but it's her all right,' said Jim. 'I expect she's been given a new name, new home, all on the taxpayer's ticket. I bet those kiddies never got as much.'

'What kiddies?'

He leant across the table. 'Don't you remember? She was the one taking pictures of these kiddies at that nursery. Sending

them to these horrible men. Little boys. Babies. I think they're still in jail. Pity she isn't, rotting. I hope Elaine doesn't notice she's back round here.'

'Oh god, that's awful,' I said, watching Huggins's three chins as her mouth worked on her Danish. That one word circled my head like an eel: babies. Babies. Babies. She'd done it to *babies*.

Huggins was still as pig-dog ugly as the selfie they'd printed in the paper months ago. Not one of her teeth was aligned and she had the most disgusting forearm tattoos (names in Arabic writing, the obligatory Harry Potter quote, etc). There was a green coat on the empty chair next to her and a red leather handbag, gaping open like a saggy mouth.

'Vile woman,' said Jim. 'No, she's not a woman, she's a *creature*. I've got half a mind to go over there—'

'Don't Jim, think of your palpitations.' Hypocritical of me I know, seeing as I was pretty tachycardic myself at the time, only for a whole other reason.

He started his deep breathing exercises. 'I'm all right, I'm all right. Just can't believe *that* is allowed to walk around free. Should have thrown the key away. I don't know if I want this scampi now.'

'Come on, try to relax. It's all right.' The refrain of 'Spice Up Your Life' popped into my head and began reeling through it like ribbons.

'If Elaine sees her she'll go spare. One of the women at WOMBAT, her granddaughter used to go to that nursery. That Huggins creature had four kids of her own you know, all got put into care. Nasty.'

It always amazes me how such a warthog manages to get laid so much. Then you'll catch a glimpse of what's been banging

it – some eight-stone diarrhoea streak with three teeth and sovereigns on every finger. You know the type. There was no sign of a man today though – just a mousey woman in a paisley dress and questionable ankle boots.

Sandra was so close I could smell her cigarette smoke.

You need to nip this one in the bud, you cannot kill her. And stop sniffing that smoke. It's not good for me.

Mind you, I'd need an elephant gun to take her down.

As Elaine was bringing over our scampi, Sandra moved her chair back, as did the Mousey Ankle Boots. Sandra scuffed towards the trolley parked next to ours at the café entrance and wheeled it away.

'Sorry, need the loo again,' I said, getting to my feet.

I followed Huggins and Friend through the bedding plants towards an area of terracotta pots set out in towers on wooden pallets. The women were heading towards the herbs. The mousey one was clearly some kind of social worker – she had a lanyard around her neck and the tag read 'NewLeaf' – a quick Google confirmed my suspicions. NewLeaf was a rehab centre for ex-offenders. The closest branch was Plymouth. Obviously Sandra's case worker.

Mummy, what are you doing?

Mousey Woman's handbag was on her shoulder, but Sandra's red leather one was in the trolley, next to two geraniums and a bag of compost. She was picking out her herbs. I ducked down. I had to wait an age before they moved away from the trolley and went to compare lavender plants around the corner. Because I only had seconds, I decided to live within my means – I took the first thing my hand fell upon inside the bag – a small

brown envelope – then walked away slowly, blending into the celebration roses.

Inside the envelope was more than I could have hoped for – a wage slip from Mel & Colly's Farm Shop. Their logo was crossed carrots on a potato. The name on the payslip was Jane Richie – her new moniker perhaps. I knew where that shop was – out towards the motorway. I had her full new name, her National Insurance number, the total hours she'd worked that month.

I even had her address.

Monday, 23rd July – 11 weeks, 1 day

Jim asked if there have been any Airbnb bookings for the Well House.

'No, not yet,' I said. 'But I'm sure there will be, any day now.' Of course there won't be. Not now I've buried AJ in one of the flower beds up there.

I can't stop thinking about that old sow Huggins. You'd think that dismembering a body in a bathtub would leave me sated for murder for a long time but it hasn't. What if the 'serial killer cycle' is shorter when you're preggers? What if the feeling of balance and completion doesn't last so long when you're killing for two? There's nothing in the pregnancy books on it, of course, and Google is next to useless on the subject. Though my in utero Jiminy Cricket is putting the kybosh on all those sort of shenanigans via tiredness, heartburn and nausea, I want it so bad. I want *her* so damn bad.

Plymouth Star guy is back on the doorstep but he hasn't knocked. He's just sitting there, looking all handsome and fed up. I wonder if he wants my body? The state it's in right now, he can have it.

I went downstairs and peeked through the net curtains – there was a bunch of flowers next to him on the step. I opened the door.

'What's this?' I said, startling him into standing up.

'Hi,' he said, picking up the flowers – yellow and white roses – and handing them to me. 'To apologise for hassling you.'

'You're apologising for hassling me by hassling me. Are they bugged?'

He laughed, biting his lip.

'They are, aren't they?'

'No no, they're not bugged I assure you.'

'Be a waste of time if they were bugged anyway. We don't talk about the case at home.'

'Oh? Why's that?'

I pretended to zip my mouth. 'You're not getting in that way either, Sneak. I know your game.' I smelled the roses. They didn't carry any scent at all – mass-cultivated supermarket crap. Ugh. I handed them back to him.

'You're going to have to try harder than that.'

'What do you like then?' he said as I was closing the door. 'Tell me and I'll get it for you. Anything.'

'Not bribing me, are you?'

'No, but—'

'Cos if you are, maybe try doughnuts. Krispy Kreme for preference.'

*

That evening, Elaine dragged me along to her monthly WOMBAT meeting. They're a Christian women's group who go on outings, raise money for various different charities, eat cake and pray. Tonight's meeting featured their new 'Kindness Circle'.

Yes, it's just as dull as it sounds.

WOMBAT stands for the Women of Monks Bay and

61

Temperley and Elaine says it's 'full of characters'. There's Big-Headed Edna, Morbid Marge, Poll Potts, who dresses like a sister-wife, Pincushion-Face Grace, Erica the Overfriendly Troll, Bea Moore the Colossal Bore, Wheelchair Pat, Wheelchair Mary, Rita Who Sits By the Heater, Elephant Vadge Madge, Jean Coker the Strokey Smoker, whose palsy makes her look like she's constantly trying to eat her own neck, Black Nancy and White Nancy. Black Nancy calls me 'Bab' and is covered in dog hairs. She's knitting a cardigan for the baby, whether I want her to or not. I've only exchanged brief 'Hellos' with White Nancy but as far as I can tell she's a twat.

This is what I do now. This is what I have become. I meet up once a month with a group of women I don't want to know. We gossip, we pray and we eat cake. My life will return to normal when the baby's out in the open, of that I am sure, but while he's gestating, I'm stagnating. I'm a freak on a leash.

It feels odd. Not wrong exactly, just nothing seems to fit. Everything's too small. Too mundane. I'm a square peg and every damn hole is round. Yeah sure Baby Bear might be contented but Momma's getting grizzly.

Erica the WOMBAT secretary had the idea to incorporate Kindness Circle into the meetings and tonight's is the first one. Spurred on by ISIS and our world leaders basically all being megalomaniacal shits, she thought people needed to 'make time to be kind'. Everyone breaks off into groups like they're in the damn Brownies and partakes of kind activities – organising collections for the food bank, creating cross-stitch patterns for underprivileged traffic wardens or sitting around talking about how lovely everything is.

I heard the word 'lovely' precisely 126 times this evening. I want to hurt the word 'lovely'. I want to beat lovely to within an inch of its life, tie lovely in a sack and fucking drown it.

Erica, I should mention, is also responsible for the 'lovely' rhymes in the church hall kitchenette:

Wash, wash, wash your plates
Gently down the drain
Rinse rinse, rinse them clean
Then dry them up again

And on the fridge door there's

Welcome welcome, one and all,
To our communal milk and tea,
But if you use the last of them,
A refill's nice to see!

And don't get me started on *If you're happy and you know it wash your hands*...

They're so goddamn twee they make me want to gnaw concrete. Erica was all abuzz this evening having announced that the 'church hall fund has agreed to splash out on hanging baskets for the smokers' area'. You know, so people can admire the pansies while their tumours metastasize.

So I'm sitting there at Clit-Lickers Monthly and we have to go around the circle and say happy things. I'm with Erica, Tight Bun Doreen, Debbie Does Donkeys, One Armed Joyce and Rita Who Sits By the Heater. Erica's rattling through a long list of

contentments, which surprises me as she has a face that would make a blind child cry. Then it's my turn.

'Uh, I have nothing,' I said.

'Come on,' said Debbie Does Donkeys. 'There must be something.'

'It's a bit hard to think of anything right now. There's a lot of bad happening in the world.'

'Yes but we choose love,' said Rita. 'We might have to look a bit harder to find it but it is always there. Happy thoughts, you must have some.'

'No, I don't,' I say. 'I don't have any. I'm not a happy-go-lucky person.'

Tight Bun Doreen pipes up. 'Well perhaps if you *were* you'd find it easier to come up with something?'

'Perhaps,' I said, heartburn biting. Inside my head she is flat on her back beneath a hydraulic drill press. My finger's on the button.

Doreen's lips pursed. 'Maybe you need to change your world view?'

'Maybe I do,' I said.

'So? Do you have a happy thought now?' she asked.

'What, because you tell me I have to have one? Yes, all right then, I do.'

Doreen frowned and waited. 'Well? What is it?'

I continued to stare at her, smiling. 'Can't say else it won't come true.'

Later, Debbie Does Donkeys read the lesson – a passage from Luke about Jesus anointing a sinful woman – the lesson being that one who has sinned deserves a second chance because 'she has faith in the Lord'.

You can tell an evening has been a washout when the best part is being given a Bible. I was given my own *Good News Bible*.

I don't think they like me at WOMBAT. I heard a few whisperings about Elaine's 'beast of a son' and there were some sly looks, mostly from Edna and Doreen. Irritating people is the nearest I can get to fun these days so I'm going to go to next month's meeting. In fact, I'm going to read my Bible too.

Let's see what God has to say about the kind of sinful woman I am.

Wednesday, 25th July
– 11 weeks, 3 days

1. *Sandra Huggins.*
2. *People who use the hashtag #familyiseverything.*
3. *People who brag about stealing stuff from Buckingham Palace – what do you want, a medal? Though you're probably in the right place if you did.*
4. *Helen at Pudding Club who wants to ban fireworks, the works of Charles Dickens and clown gifs on Twitter. Apparently they're all 'triggering'.*
5. *Peter Andre.*

I'm bed-bound and teetering on the lip of insanity. I've watched back to back eps of *Ramsay's Kitchen Nightmares* even though I've seen them all before. I get up only to drink, piss, or puke and even then I'm dizzy. I'm lying here, falling down endless internet rabbit holes. I *could* read one of the preg books Elaine got from the library – *What to Expect When You're Gestating* or *Mummy to Be: A Day to Day Guide to the Most Magical Time in your Life* but I don't like library books in my bed. You never know what's been done to them. Or *in* them.

So I stick to online stuff, mostly Buzzfeed, Bustle and Jezebel. And you know how you look up one thing and it links you to

another and before you know it you're reading whole articles about Jeffrey Dahmer or water polo or coping with psoriasis, even though you don't have it? I somehow got on to watching the *Murder Made Me Famous* docu on YouTube.

The Miracle of Priory Gardens.

I watch it every time I want to see my dad. He and my mum are interviewed throughout, sitting on the wicker sofa in the conservatory at our old house, clutching each other's hands like they're about to take a death leap.

All the parents relived the moment they were told their son or daughter was dead. Then Dad relived the moment he was told I was the only survivor. Mum grips his hand tighter. Dad looks down, his hand wipes his eyes.

I couldn't take it in. I was sure she was dead. She's our miracle.

My big tough boxer dad, crying his eyes red.

Someone up there helped us out that day, that's for sure.

My mum says little in the docu – she just echoes Dad, maintaining her rabbit-in-the-headlights stare. There's footage of her giving me a hug outside the hospital when I was released. I missed her hugs as I got older.

There was some home movie footage of the kids who died – two-year-old Jack blowing out his candles. Kimmy in her dad's arms in the maternity unit. Ashlea in red boots in the snow. The twins eating ice cream. Their mum did *Britain's Got Talent* last year but a sob story only takes you so far if you can't sing for shit.

There's old news footage from before the presenters went grey – footage of people laying flowers outside Number 12. The sounds of wailing parents as they fight to get through the

police cordon. The glistening doormat. Three little stretchers. And then the money shot – me all limp, wrapped inside the blood-stained Peter Rabbit blanket.

Then there are the photo-calls of me coming out of hospital in my wheelchair, weeks later, bandage wrapped tightly around my bald head.

Me in my beanie hat being given the huge teddy bear on *This Morning*.

My first day at school, Dad wheeling me into the front office and us stopping so the press could take our photos.

Giving the thumbs up on my first day of secondary school.

Thumbs up again after my GCSE results.

The 'Hasn't She Done Well?' front page of the *Daily Mirror*, with me starting my A Levels and talking about wanting to be a writer.

There was an interview with the shrink – Dr Philip Morrison – who had treated the murderer, Antony Blackstone, for his psychotic rages.

You had one job, Phil.

'*He was a ticking bomb,*' said Phil. '*Allison's family knew the marriage was not a happy one – there were signs that he was controlling and abusive. He'd call her incessantly. Track her movements. Even monitored what she was eating so she didn't put on weight. Her sister had begged her to leave him and one day Allison found the courage. It appeared – at first – to be a mutual arrangement which Blackstone accepted. But it lit the spark in the powder keg.*'

Phil was the one who diagnosed me with PTSD after Priory Gardens, even though Mum swore it was 'growing pains' and, as I got older, 'hormones'. He always gave me a Scooby Doo

sticker after a session. It's one of the more depressing parts of growing up – we don't get stickers anymore.

There's a playground where the house used to stand now and a plaque on a sundial beside the slide bearing the names of all the kids. Mrs Kingwell's name too. My name isn't there of course, being the lucky one.

When Dad talks about it, I can feel his sadness. Otherwise, I don't feel anything. I can't even hate Blackstone, cos he's dead.

The closing footage on the documentary is me and Seren playing with the Sylvanians in the rehab centre. The boxes are dotted all around, wrapped in big bows. I'm lying in my bed and watching her, moving the figures about on my tummy and Seren is telling me some story about mice. It strikes me hard how she's the only person I have left in this world – the only person who knows the real me. Even though she despises me these days, I do miss her.

Priory Gardens was the spark in my powder keg. The reason Mum got sick. The reason Dad gave up. The reason I have little emotional reaction to anything except Death. I can't feel unless I'm killing. Then I feel everything.

We've had another note. This time I caught sight of the person who posted it as he was loping off up the seafront – a big guy in blue jeans, hoody. No other wording – just the same again. 'To my Sweet Messy House'. And a number.

'I don't want to fucking talk to you!' I screamed through the letterbox, screwing up the note and scuffing back into the lounge. Gordon Ramsay had started on one of the high channels – he was counselling a crying chef who'd lost all his microwaves.

*

Jim's been in – the estate agent says two couples are interested in Craig's flat. The forensics have finished, so he's released it for sale to start paying the lawyers. One of the couples is expecting. I imagine them walking around, hand in hand, looking in our wardrobes, talking about the 'nice views from the balcony'. Looking inside the cupboards that I watched Craig build, that autumn we first met. We got Tink from the RSPCA that autumn, a little warm ball of toffee ice cream who licked my cheek and stopped shaking the moment I held her. It's all I can do to prise her away from Jim these days.

Saturday, 28th July
– 11 weeks, 6 days

1. *Cafés that pre-butter toast or toasted tea cakes.*
2. *The guy that keeps posting illegible notes through our front door.*
3. *Weathermen who stand in hurricanes strong enough to blow cataracts from their eyes and 'can't believe how strong the wind is'.*

My Bible doesn't seem to be able to offer me any guidance on feeling less tilted than I do at the moment, aside from 'Offer yourself up to the Lord' or 'God's mighty hand will lift you up if you just believe.' Not a bad read though. That Delilah was a bit of a head case.

Marnie texted – Fancy a trip to the Mall to find your maternity clothes? I can chauffeur – Marn x

I was still annoyed by the fact it had taken her so long to ask but she was offering to drive, so gift horses and all that.

The traffic was bad on the way up but Marnie was in a good mood and when you've got stuff to chat about, it doesn't feel like you've been stuck in a car for hours. We talked about our respective families and how dead they all are, how I barely speak

to Seren in Seattle and how she barely speaks to her brother Sandro who lives in Italy and runs residential art classes.

'How come you don't speak to him?' I asked.

'Oh you know how it is, you grow apart as you get older, don't you?' she said and left it at that. 'Isn't that what it's like with you and Seren?'

'No, Seren says I'm a psychopath like our dad.'

Marnie glanced away from the traffic. 'Are you?'

I shrugged. 'Bit.'

She laughed. Probably thought I was joking, I don't know. We played the number plate game and she had cola bottles and sour cherries in her glovebox and Beyoncé on the Bluetooth so I was happy.

'Tim doesn't like me eating sweets at home,' she said, then bit down on her lip like she shouldn't have said it. 'He's got me into blueberries so I eat those instead. They're *incredibly* good for you.'

'Yeah I've had the blueberry lecture from Elaine. She makes these vile blueberry granola bars for me to peck at if I'm hungry. They taste like old teabags and feet. Why doesn't Tim let you have sweets?'

'He worries about diabetes and things.'

'Halo' came on and much to my intense delight, Marnie turned it up to full vol. 'This is my favourite.'

'Mine too,' I lied. Mine was actually '6 Inch' from the *Lemonade* album but I didn't want to break the moment.

Before too long we were singing. Unashamedly. Not even holding back on the big notes. It was so easy, so immediate. Like we'd been friends for years. All thanks to Queen Bey herself. We made it to the end of the song—

Then her phone rang.

It rang twice, both times Tim, first asking where she was and who she was with (I had to say 'Hello') and the second time to ask if they had any ant powder. Marnie did most of the talking and I noticed she kept asking if things were all right. 'Chicken Kievs for tea if that's all right?' and 'Back about six if that's all right?' His voice reminded me of Grandad's.

'My grandad never let my nanny have any freedom either,' I said when she had ended the call.

'No, it's not like that,' she said, for once without a little smile or a giggle at the end of her sentence. 'He just worries about me, especially now.'

'My nan blamed me for my grandad's death. She said I'd killed him.'

Marnie glanced over, briefly, as she indicated to come off the motorway. We came to a halt at the traffic lights. 'Why did she say that?'

'Cos I was there when it happened. He had a heart attack while he was swimming. He liked wild swimming. I was on the bank, watching him and I didn't do anything. He drowned.'

'Oh my god,' she said, as the lights went green. 'How old were you?'

'Eleven.'

'Well of course you couldn't have done anything, you were only a child. That's a terrible thing for an adult to put on such a young person.'

'Yeah, I guess. She'd taken me to meet Mr Blobby that summer too. Proper sadist, my nanny.'

She didn't laugh but patted my knee. I was going to tell her. The words were locked and loaded and ready to come out – I was going to tell her how I'd watched my grandad hit Seren that

morning for not bringing in the eggs and how much I wanted to kill him. To push him down the stairs or into the slurry or to drive an axe right down deep into the back of his neck while he was stacking the logs. But I didn't say a word. I didn't tell her that watching my grandad drown had been an exquisite pleasure. I kept that to myself because Marnie had patted my knee and seemed to care that I was the innocent one. And I liked the feeling. I wanted to hold onto it.

The Mall was heaving with people and though Marnie was more than happy to mooch about trying things on, I couldn't find a single atom of my body that cared about maternity clothes. She didn't buy a thing, even stuff she said she loved. Dresses she'd point out as 'stunning' or 'exquisite' she would hold up against herself then return them to the peg. When I called her on it she said, 'Oh I'll probably never wear it again anyway. It's a waste of money.'

'Bet he gives you an allowance every week, doesn't he?'

'No,' she said. 'This is my money.'

'My nanny used to get an allowance and she'd never spend it either. She used to squirrel it away. I never found out why.'

We hit the John Lewis café for lunch. I got a lemon and vanilla ice cream crepe, Marnie got a salad.

'Get some carbs down you for god's sake,' I said as we stood in the line waiting for the assistant to scoop my vanilla. 'You're drooling over mine.'

'I shouldn't,' she said, biting her lip.

'Why not?'

'Slippery slope, isn't it?'

Marnie's phone was out next to her plate the moment we sat down.

'So tell me more about Tim then,' I said. 'What's he like?'

Again, her manner changed, her voice lowered. 'He's Area Manager for that plastic shelving place on the ring road. Quite long hours but he loves it.'

'What did you do before you went on maternity?'

'Admin, council refuse department. Only for the last seven months though. Before that I was a dancer.'

'What kind of dancer?'

'Ballet and tap. I taught classes.'

'Why did you stop?'

'Well, we moved down here for Tim's job and then I got pregnant.'

'But you could go back to it someday?'

'Doubt it. The money's better at the council anyway. I did love it though.'

Her phone rang. 'Sorry, hang on... Hiya... Yep... that'll be nice... sounds good... Yeah, Rhiannon's still with me. Need me to pick anything up?... Okay... Love you.' She put the phone down.

'Tim?' I said, chewing my crepe.

'Yeah,' she smiled, theatrically rolling her eyes. 'He's booking the hotel for next weekend. Our sixth anniversary. Bit of a babymoon.'

'Six years,' I said. 'That's wood, isn't it?'

'I don't know,' she said.

'A wooden garden ornament or something?'

'He's not into ornaments. I inherited a load of china ones from my mum but I'm not allowed to display them.'

'Not *allowed*?'

'Well, it's only a few ballerinas with their buns broken off. I

used to play with them as a kid. My mum bought me one each time I passed an exam.'

I pride myself on a few things: my ability to defend the defenceless, to maintain The Act that I am a normal human being in polite society, and to trace vulnerability in people. I can sniff it out as easily as curry plant in a garden full of roses. And it was coming off Marnie in waves.

'Are you sure it wasn't Tim who made you give up dancing?'

She frown-laughed. 'No, my choice. He was right though; the pay *was* crap.' She stroked her bump. 'No regrets. I have everything I want. A great house and steady job and a healthy baby boy coming soon—'

Grandad used to fill Honey Cottage with his stuffed animals. Weasels and stoats and tiny birds that he'd shot out of trees with a pellet gun. Nanny never liked them. She said they looked like they were in eternal pain. Nanny liked Capo di Monte teapots and cherubs and porcelain roses, but she kept them in bubble wrap in boxes because 'they keep getting smashed'.

'I think you should put the ballerinas on display,' I told Marnie, mopping up my vanilla puddle with my crepe.

'It's no big deal,' she said, tucking into her salad again.

I was going to ask what she meant but she jumped into another conversation as she stabbed her lettuce. 'So will you stay on with your in-laws when the baby comes?'

Before I'd even opened my mouth, her phone rang again.

'Hiya, Hun... uh yeah I can pick some up... okay... yeah, still with Rhiannon. Oh great. Yep, I will. Thanks, love, see you later. Love you... Bye.'

My eyebrows rose.

'We need potatoes. Where were we?'

'We were talking then the guy you live with called twice about nothing.'

She carried on crunching her lettuce. We sat in silence, watching mums struggling with pushchairs, kids skipping along beside them, old friends meeting and hugging. On the next table a dad was talking his two-year-old daughter through the menu choices, like he was teaching her to read. Their meals arrived – he cut up her chips and taught her to blow on them. The child wanted him to feed her instead of doing it for herself so he was eating his meal with one hand, feeding her with the other.

A while later, our conversation restarted and we were back being easy together – I was telling her about WOMBAT and begging her to come along to the next meeting to save me from certain kindness brainwashing. I told her all about the little names I'd given them all—

When her phone rang *again*. I saw the screen – Tim calling.

She gurned apologetically. 'This is the last time, I promise... Hi, love... yeah, I think so... oh, that's good, well done... yeah that sounds—'

I grabbed the phone out of her hand and hit the End Call button.

Marnie shot up, grabbing at her phone. 'Why did you do that?!'

'Well for one because it's rude when you're talking to some-one—'

'He's on his lunch break! It's the only time he can call!'

'—and two, your husband's being an endless little bitch.'

She called him back and spent the next ten minutes apologising and eating shit like an absolute pro while I finished my

crepe and sipped my tea. When she came back to the table she breathed out long and slow.

'He's fine. He's fine.'

'Thank god,' I said, still chewing. 'I was so worried.'

'Why did you do that, Rhiannon?'

'Cos you're sleeping with the enemy. I staged an intervention.'

'Please don't ever do that again.'

A silence fell.

'Allison, the childminder at Priory Gardens, she was a battered wife.'

'I'M NOT A BATTERED WIFE!' she shouted.

Faces looked. Marnie sank down in her seat.

'I never said you were.'

'You don't understand him, I'm okay with it.'

'Make me understand it. I dare you.'

Marnie frowned. 'It's actually none of your business actually.'

'Two actuallys.'

'I don't care.'

'Show me your phone.'

'What?'

'Show me your phone.'

'No.'

I grabbed it out of her hand again and she tried to snatch it back.

'Give it to me. Rhiannon! Now, I want it, give it!'

'Uh, pregnant woman being accosted here!' I shouted, garnering glances as I fought her off me, but nobody in the café paid much mind. Typical. Pregnant women are pretty much invisible to the human eye.

There was a selfie of Marnie and Tim together on her screen

saver. She was smiling and he was hugging her from behind – like a chokehold. Hmm, attractive in an Aryan kind of way but a bit too much pulse for my liking.

I checked her call log and messages and once my suspicions were confirmed, I handed the phone back. She was hot in both cheeks, grabbing her jacket off her chair and flinging it on.

'Fifty-seven calls. In two days. And you *live* with the guy.'

She wouldn't look at me. She threw her handbag strap over her shoulder and shuffled out of the banquette.

'One hundred and seventy-six messages in a week,' I called after her as she waddled back through café, as fast as she could.

She snapped her head around. 'So what? He's protective. I told you.'

We got to the top of the escalators. 'Just cos you're married, doesn't mean he owns you. That kind of thinking went out with McBusted.'

'He's not your grandad, okay? He's not that Priory Gardens guy either. He's ex-army so he likes things just so and he fusses a bit, that's all. I get him. I get why he's like it and it's okay. I love him. End of.'

'No not "end of". Did he make you stop dancing?' She didn't answer. 'Does he hurt you?'

I tried to think of something women's refugey and supportive to say, but nothing came. All I saw was her eyes not daring to water and the only way I could think of helping was to go straight round to that plastics factory and anally violate the gutless little piss-tray with some sort of pointy thing.

She started down the escalator.

'Uh, what am I supposed to do, get the bus home?' I called out.

She waited at the bottom. I went down and stood beside her in silence.

'He doesn't hurt me. I promise. He needs me. But I don't want to talk about this anymore, okay? I'm asking you, please.' Her voice dropped to a whisper. 'Just be a friend today.'

For some reason that word 'friend' changed my outlook. I didn't want her to leave and I didn't want her anger. I wanted to stay being her friend.

'Let's go somewhere else, yeah? How about the museum?'

'Why the museum?'

'I used to go there all the time when I was a kid with my friend. Shall we do that?' She checked her phone. 'Oh sorry. What time does Goebbels want you back in the Stalag?'

She laughed at that. I didn't think she would. 'Six.'

'Bags of time,' I said. 'Come on. It's not far.'

We drove across town without another word about He Who Must Not Be Named and I gave Marnie a potted tour of Bristol and the harbour side. We took a slow walk up Park Street, tried on hats in a hat shop, shoes in a shoe shop and finally we went to my favourite place: the museum. I showed her all the best bits first – the gift shop, the Egyptian mummies, the rocks and gemstones, the amethyst the size of my head and the stalactite that looked like a willy. Then the stuffed animals gathering dust in their enormous glass cases – The Dead Zoo, as me and Joe called it. I could smell the Dead Zoo before we got to it – musty and pungent with age – and I was drawn to it like a moth. We found Alfred the gorilla, arguably Bristol's most famous son.

'Me and Joe used to imagine we were in the jungle and these were all our animals,' I told her. 'We lived in the gypsy caravan and at night, the mummies would come alive and we had to

hide in case they got us. Alfred would roar and beat his chest and all the mummies would run away. This is Alfred. You have to say Hi when you come here. It's like a Bristol law.'

'Hello Alfred,' she said, waving at him. 'Who's Joe?'

'Joe Leech. He was my best friend when I was a kid. I only knew him for a couple of summers. He was killed. Got knocked down.'

'Oh that's awful. I'm sorry.'

'Apparently when he was in the zoo, Alfred used to throw poo at people and piss on them as they passed underneath his cage. And he hated men with beards. I don't like men with beards either. Don't trust them.'

Marnie laughed.

'Does Tim have a beard at the moment?'

She thinned her eyes. 'No he doesn't.'

'Just checking. We used to spend hours up here, me and Joe.'

'Smells a bit strange. Some of them look so sad.'

'Yeah but look at the ones who are grinning. They look *insane*.'

'True.'

'Don't you find it fascinating? I find death fascinating.'

'No,' she said. 'I find it quite creepy actually.' She moved around the glass cases with caution as though any moment the ocelot or Sumatran tiger or glassy-eyed rhino might crash through the glass and flatten her.

'There's a dodo somewhere,' I said. 'That was Joe's favourite.'

'You look genuinely happy to be here,' she remarked.

'Yeah, I think I am. I was happy as a kid. Before Priory Gardens. And when I was with Joe. And Craig. Not so much since.'

This remark seemed to trouble Marnie all afternoon. She brought it up several times as we were wandering round but put it down to the whole Craig-being-in-prison and not-having-a-baby-daddy-around thing.

After the gift shop – where Marnie again noted several things she liked but wouldn't buy – we went over the road to Rocotillos where me and Joe Leech ate short stack pancakes and shakes for breakfast, and dared each other to blow cold cherries at the waiters. We sat on stools overlooking the street outside. Marnie said she wasn't hungry but I ordered her chocolate brownie freak shake with whipped cream and salted caramel sauce, same as me, and she ate every bite. The sky darkened and rain began spattering the window.

She sucked her straw in ecstasy. 'Mmm, I'd forgotten what chocolate tastes like. It's not good for you, too many sweets.'

'Is Tim afraid you'll get fat?'

She nodded, seemingly forgetting herself as she chewed the tip of her straw. 'He's worried about diabetes, that's all. He doesn't think it's good for me to gain too much fat.'

'No, I suppose it absorbs the punches too well.'

Marnie rolled her eyes like she'd known me for years and this was something 'typically Rhee'. 'Things change after you have a baby. Men can… stray. That's what I'm most afraid of I guess. I couldn't handle that. My dad cheated on my mum and it broke her heart *and* mine.'

'So if he cheated on you, you might find the strength to leave him?' A little thought owl flew into my mind.

'Don't even think about it,' she said firmly. 'I'd never forgive you.'

My thought owl flew out again. 'I'd like to meet Tim.'

'Why?'

I spooned some cream from my shake. 'Just to be sociable.'

'You're not sociable though,' she chuckled.

'I'm out with you, aren't I? What more do you want?'

She looked out of the window but I knew she didn't want to look at me. 'He'll be coming to Pin's cheese and wine. And she's planning a big fireworks party in November for her birthday as well. No expense spared.'

'Oh Christ,' I groaned. 'She's not going to invite me to those, is she?'

'Of course she is,' said Marnie. 'You're one of the gang now.'

'Ugh. I need that like a hole in the womb.'

'Pin's house is amazing. They're millionaires.'

'Whoopee shit.' I blew a cold cherry at a passing waitress. It missed.

Outside it was raining hard. People rushed past the window with briefcases on their heads and newspapers folded over like makeshift hats. 'What do you want to talk about then?' I asked. 'You choose. Ask me anything. Any question you've always wanted the answer to. Priory Gardens, Craig, you name it. Open season.'

Marnie stared at the window and took two bites before answering. 'If you counted every raindrop as it fell, how many raindrops would there be?'

'Huh?'

She laughed. 'I like those kinds of unfathomable questions, don't you? Makes me feel so small in the world. Like, how long would it take for you to count every single grain of sand on Monks Bay beach?'

'You must be the only person in the country at a private

audience with me who doesn't want to ask me questions about Craig.'

'It's none of my business, is it?'

'No, it's not.'

'I've got another one,' she said, the light flicking on behind her eyes. 'How do you know you're a real person and not in someone else's dream?'

'Isn't that a Take That lyric?'

Below the bench we were both swinging our legs beneath the counter, like we were children again. I wished we were.

I don't know how long we sat there – enough to share a cherry Bakewell freak shake between us and two slices of blueberry pie – and our questions kept on coming.

'Why is the sea salty?'

'Who picks up a blind person's guide dog poo?'

'Can you remember when you stopped being a child?'

'What was the first word ever said?'

'Do you ever hear your baby talk to you?'

Of course I said 'No' to that one. It wasn't time to play the 'mad' card.

'What's the best advice you could pass onto your child?' Marnie asked.

'I dunno,' I said. 'Mind's gone blank.'

'I like "Find your bliss",' said Marnie. 'I heard someone say that once and it stuck with me. What's your bliss?'

'Don't know. Haven't found it yet.'

'You said in the museum you weren't as happy now as you were when you were a kid. Maybe it's having kids? Maybe that will make you happy?'

'Mmm. Life's full of maybes, isn't it? You never know for sure.'

'Maybes and babies,' she smiled.

'I still feel like a kid myself.'

'You'll be okay, Rhiannon. It'll all fall into place. It'll click, all of a sudden. And then you'll know who you are for sure.'

I smiled like my face meant it. Would have been much easier if it did.

Tuesday, 31st July
– 12 weeks, 2 days

1. *Grown adults who are afraid of dogs. Strap on a pair, FFS.*
2. *Pop up advertisers. In fact anything that 'pops' at all.*
3. *Woody Allen.*

'I can't understand it,' said Jim, crunching through his All Bran. 'No bookings at all?'

'Sorry.' I packed my face with as much humility as it could muster.

'No it's not your fault, love. If you ask me the tourism board has a lot to answer for. This isn't a destination area anymore. Nothing for the kiddies. The funicular hasn't had a lick of paint for decades. Council keep putting up the rates so the little independent shops can't afford to stay put, and that new leisure centre's *still* not finished. Six years they've been promising that.'

Note: I don't get an iota of blame. Note: he doesn't check Airbnb himself. Trust, you see. Complete and total trust. I can't help finding Jim almost unbearably sexy sometimes.

Another dizzy spell on my way back upstairs – it's altitude that seems to affect it. I had one yesterday on my way up to

the Well House. I lay on AJ's grave for a full half-hour until it passed. Something to do with my blood pressure. I'm going to have to start carrying around emergency chocolate with me like a St Bernard.

I checked out Tim Prendergast's social media to get the measure of the man. His avatar is a pic of himself in one of those seaside cut-outs – a fat man in a stripy bathing suit wearing a Kiss-Me-Quick hat.

What a wit.

His eyes are blue with ice splinters in them. I don't even have to meet him to know he's a fungus-addled prick of the highest proportions. And for a self-confessed 'outdoorsman' who loves hill walking, he doesn't half spend a lot of time tweet-stalking celebrities. You know the type of thing – RTing how good their books/films/TV shows are. Incessantly @ing them in, saying *Good job on The One Show tonight…* or *Loved your movie – what a talent you are*! *We're lucky to have you,* and asking them for shout outs and free tickets. The worst part about it is he gets replies. He trades on that tried and tested logic – people will believe anything if it's a compliment. And it works.

I honestly don't know what Marnie sees in him.

Talking of her, I haven't heard anything since Saturday. Two texts so far have gone unanswered. I wonder if he's throttled her. I wonder if I should go round there. I know where she lives – in one of the new houses in Michaelmas Court. She mentioned it at Pudding Club as the number was the same as their anniversary – the fifteenth.

The *Plymouth Star* guy was back on the doorstep today, along with several others from the tabloids. He is such a snack, honestly, and it thrills me to wind him up – to play the part of

forbidden fruit now I know he wants to eat my ass so badly. I felt quite sorry for him, jostling to be the first to hound me as I sashayed down the front path in my heels and swishy top, like I was at Paris Fashion Week.

'You brought my doughnuts yet?' I called out to him.

'You were serious about that?'

'Of course,' I smiled, gliding through the garden gate. Oh boy was I working it today. On the other side I turned back to him and he smiled like we were sharing a secret.

Gusset dryness = history.

Wednesday, 1st August
– 12 weeks, 3 days

Drove myself back to the flat to pick up the last of my stuff – only had to stop once on the motorway to vom at the roadside. Otherwise, uneventful.

The flat is all but empty – most of Craig's stuff has gone into storage. AJ's blood dot remains – barely visible to the human eye, but to the psychopath's eye, there's no mistaking it. Looks more brown than red now.

Mrs Whittaker's moved out – gone to live in Margate with her sister Betty. She 'can't be trusted to live on her own anymore', so Leafblower Ron informed me in the lift, as he coiled his extension lead around his elbow.

'Has anyone else moved in there then?' I asked.

'Not yet,' he said. 'But the cleaners went in yesterday so I suppose the agent's found someone.'

'It's probably for the best,' I said, trying not to think about the night I cut him up in that bathtub. The foetus doesn't like it.

I like thinking about my daddy being alive, not cut into six pieces on an old woman's lino.

Afterwards, I bought some Rice Krispie cakes and a bunch of pink gerberas and roses and went round to Lana's flat. I took

a chance that she still lived in the one above the charity shop in the precinct and lo and behold, when I rang the bell at the side entrance, she came to the door. She nearly slammed it in my face but I put my hand out at the last moment.

'Please, Lana, please let me in. I've come to apologise.'

She pulled the door back slightly so that I saw for the first time the extent of my handiwork. She was purple from her forehead to her chin – I almost laughed but stopped myself in time.

'I can't believe you didn't press charges,' I said. 'You should have.'

'Yeah, well,' she said. 'I figured I owed you that at least.'

'Thank you. I truly am desperately sorry. I brought cakes.'

She opened the door wider and I followed her up the narrow staircase – think Anne Frank's house with junk mail and stair rods.

I passed her bedroom – the door was ajar, the duvet unmade, clumps of clothes dotted around the floor – knickers, socks, some hideous pyjama bottoms covered in Minions, a dressing gown draped across the bed. The bed where she'd moaned in my boyfriend's hot ear and bitten his lobe as her vagina gripped his penis and he slid into her so many times…

'I'll put the kettle on,' she said, ushering me through to the lounge. Each of the worktops in the poky beige kitchen was covered in debris – side plates with hardened puddles of butter, smudged glasses, sticky cutlery, greasy frying pans, and saucepans ingrained with old scrambled egg.

'How are things at the *Gazette*?' I asked when she brought a mug of tea in. There was a purple fleece throw on the sofa, all rumpled into a nest where she'd been sitting watching *Bargain Hunt*. I sat in the armchair.

'They've put me on gardening leave,' she said, sitting down and wrapping herself in the blanket. 'Got someone in to replace me already.'

'I know the feeling,' I said.

'Katie Drucker?' she said. 'Yeah she's, well, malleable. You know Linus is back after his eye operation? Daren't be off sick for any length of time in that place. Someone will jump in your grave. Do you think you'll go back?'

'No, don't think so. I feel quite free actually.'

'I miss it,' she said.

'So shall we talk about the elephant in the room or shall we let it quietly shit itself in the corner?'

Lana took a breath and put her mug down on the table. 'I can't believe Craig's capable of doing those things.'

'I don't know anymore,' I said, putting my mug down too. 'I don't want to believe it but the evidence, Lana.'

'But on New Year's Eve at least, he was definitely with me.'

'All night?'

'Well no, but—'

'Where were you, here?'

'Yes.'

'And what time did he leave?'

'After the bongs, about twelve-fifteen?'

'The police said Daniel Wells was killed between midnight and four. I didn't hear him come in.'

'What about the other two?'

'He said he was out with the boys on February twelfth. Gavin White was killed in the park around ten p.m. The boys said he nipped outside for a fag around that time. It's possible is all I'm saying.'

'Oh god. But that woman in the quarry. That *wasn't* him, was it?'

'I don't know. They found evidence all over the scene.'

'But he was in London, he couldn't have killed *her*.'

'I'm as stumped as you are,' I said, catching sight of my lying face in her glass cabinet. 'All I know is that I'm afraid. I'm afraid if they let him out, he will come after me for not giving him an alibi. He went a tiny bit *Scarface* because I said I wouldn't lie for him.'

'He's asked me too.'

'There you go,' I said.

'But I *was* with him on New Year's. For a bit.'

'You've got to let your conscience be your guide, Lana. I've got the baby to think about. What if he's released and he hurts us?'

'Don't say that.'

'If you know what's good for you, you'll stay well away from him.'

'I haven't seen him for weeks. I wouldn't, not now.'

'But you're going to give him an alibi for New Year's Eve?'

'It's not an alibi, it's the *truth*.'

'You were with him right up until he killed that man and severed his penis. What are the police going to make of that?'

She wringed her hands. 'I can't lie to the police.'

'I'm not saying you should lie. You should think carefully before claiming he was with you all night. Because if he's going down, he will bring you down too. That's the kind of guy he is. I know it's shocking but we have to protect ourselves. Craig's capable of anything.'

*

I nipped into town after Lana's to pick up some pregnancy vitamins and Gaviscon from Boots. Saw Claudia at the perfume counter. She didn't see me.

My auntie Claudia!

I don't miss the *Gazette* at all. Why would I? Why would I miss Claudia's patronising orders and Ron's letching, and downing tools every hour to make coffee for people too educationally far above me to make their own? Why would I miss the Cuntasaurus Rex Linus Sixgill and his excruciating attempts to be funny? And, for the record, I don't give a shit that he wears an eye patch now – cancer doesn't suddenly make an arsehole clean.

I miss the gonk from the top of my computer screen. That's all I miss.

My daddy gave you that.

I also saw one of the PICSOs, Anni, pushing a buggy out of Debenhams. Anni and Pidge turned out to be quite good friends in the end – both of them went to the police separately to air their suspicions that Craig had been abusive – they'd seen bruises on me, told them of my evasive behaviour when asked about him. But of course, I had The Act to keep up – poor, manipulated, brainwashed girlfriend. Innocent victim. Deny, deny, deny. Pretty soon even they washed their hands of me. People I Can't Scrape Off were officially – Scraped.

Anyway I managed to avoid both Anni *and* Claudia and I was so busy avoiding people I knew that I ran straight into someone I didn't *want* to know.

Heather – aka the woman with the yellow scarf who I'd mistakenly rescued the night I killed two rapists in a quarry. Today the scarf was mauve. She caught up with me near the floral gardens.

'Rhiannon?' she said, eyes wide. Breathless. Hopeful? 'Oh my gosh!'

'No,' I said feebly, switching direction from where I intended to go – the Cookie Cart – to the car park at the back of the big church and the relative safety of my car. She blocked my escape.

'I've been hoping every day I might bump into you. Can we talk?'

I switched to the river path. She followed me, kept trying to converse.

'I've been coming to the *Gazette* offices for weeks, hoping to catch you—'

'I don't work there anymore.'

'I want to talk. Please, give me five minutes.'

'No. I bloody knew I couldn't trust you. Bugger off.'

She didn't get the hint. Her foamy soles stalked me like the opening chords of 'Billie Jean'. 'Hear me out. I promise it won't take long.'

I had visions of her mounting my bonnet, such was the fervour in her voice, so eventually we sat on a bench in the floral gardens, looking for all the world like two colleagues having a dainty, cross-footed lunch on a summer's day. Rather than what we were – rape victim and her heroic serial killer liberator, reminiscing about the night one lost her shit and killed two men to protect the other's sorry ass.

'I've been thinking about you constantly since that night.'

'You make it sound like we had an affair.' I looked around to see if anyone was listening in. The water cascaded over the little weir. Two pigeons were pecking at a discarded sausage roll under the opposite bench.

'My husband thought I had.'

I afforded her a raise of eyebrow.

'I was all fidgety and checking my phone for news updates in the days after. I was terrified someone had seen my car or seen us walking back from the quarry.'

'Keep. Your. Voice. Down.'

'I was in chaos, Rhiannon. I'd have these night terrors and relive the whole thing, waking up in a cold sweat. It affected my work, it was awful. Anyway Ben – my husband – confronted me about it and I told him.'

'Oh great—'

'No no, he was so grateful. He's not going near the police, I promise. Why would he? He doesn't owe those men justice. As far as he's concerned, they got it. Police think those men are responsible for seven rapes along that same road where they took me. That night could have ended differently for me if you hadn't been there. What I don't understand is why you were there at all. Why your car was parked up. And how even in the pitch dark you knew your way across those fields.'

'I grew up around there.'

'Were you waiting for them?'

'Yes,' I said, without the slightest intonation. 'You got in the way.'

The chestnut tree in the centre of the park had been hacked away by the council. I used to sit underneath it eating my lunch sometimes. It would shelter you from a sudden downpour or the hot sun. Now it looked like a huge hand reaching up to the sky with all its fingers sliced back to stumps.

Heather eyeballed me. 'You enjoyed it, didn't you? Killing them?'

I stared at the pulse in her neck, thumping away.

Her voice dropped to a whisper. 'Did you kill the others as well? The ones your boyfriend—'

'I don't have to listen to this,' I said, standing up.

'No *please* don't go,' she said, standing up as well. 'I'm sorry. Those others – from what I read they were bad people.'

It was my turn to eyeball her. She was wearing a mauve BodyCon dress and while she wasn't fat, it was still far too tight for her. I could see her belly button. I could see the mole *in* her belly button. That's just ridic.

'What do you want? Money? Tough shit.'

'I don't want anything.'

'You want to threaten me?'

'Rhiannon I've represented rape victims for twenty years. I've seen the full impact rape has on a human being, both women *and* men. And their families. It's worse still when they have to relive it in court. That could have been me and it wasn't, thanks to you.'

'What do you mean, "represented" them?'

'I'm a solicitor. Ben is too. We practice—'

'Yeah yeah, I don't want your life story, thanks.'

'I wanted to give you this and to say again, thank you. Even if you didn't mean to, even if you enjoyed it – thank you.' She handed me a business card with W&A embossed on one side, and a phone number and a tiny etching of a golden gondola on the other.

'Wherryman and Armfield,' I said.

'Armfield passed away some years back so it's just us Wherrymans now. We're based in Bristol and Ben and I live locally with our boys. Sorry, I know you don't want my life story. Call me, if you need anything. Anything at all. If I can't help I can probably find someone who can.'

She got up and started walking away from me without another glance. Then without warning she stopped and turned around to face me. 'I knew you'd done this before. I knew it that night.'

She looked like she was about to say something else but her mouth kept closing like a fish's – scared to bring the words forth. And then they came.

'Patrick Edward Fenton.'

'Who?' I said.

She started walking away, her scarf fluttering up on the breeze. 'Last I heard, he was working in Sportz Madness in Torquay.'

'Why would I care about this?'

'He's my one that got away.'

When she'd gone, I stared at the card. Keeping it was a link – to her, to that night, to the two dead men. I was about to post it into the bin at the side of the bench when a thought struck. Gift horses and all that.

Saturday, 4th August
– 12 weeks, 6 days

1. *The person who tries to draw a swastika on the fence outside the hospital but keeps getting the prongs the wrong way up.*
2. *Quorn manufacturers. Stop kidding yourself. It tastes nothing like it.*
3. *Sandra Huggins.*

Had one of my dreams again – this time about the baby. I'm in a garden and in the centre is a deep pit and the baby's at the bottom, naked and kicking and crying. I climb down inside but when I get to the bottom it's gone, though I can still hear it crying. And I look up and standing at the edge of the pit is a woman holding a bundle. I can't get out. And the shaft of light above me gets smaller and smaller. And I can't scream because my mouth won't open. What in the name of cock does *that* mean?

Jim and Elaine were out early at the hospital for Jim's check-up, leaving me to feed Tink, a loud sing-a-long to Nicki Minaj in the shower, and a damn good wank. There being no decent dicks on the horizon, this is about as good as my sex life gets these days. There are three remote possibilities – a bin man who

bears a passing resemblance to Ryan Reynolds, the blond guy in the dry cleaners who wears *Iron Man* socks, and what Elaine calls 'The Element', who sits on the war memorial in piss-stained joggers, drinking Diamond White and telling passers-by how Frank Sinatra stole his medals.

But for now, to the Masturbation Chamber it is.

It's so much better when the olds are out. You try fudding yourself off with a silent vibe when your bedroom wall is cracker-thin and your mother-in-law's practising her descant for 'All Things Bright and Beautiful' in the next room. Now that my sickness seems to have subsided, my other symptoms have come screaming into view. Horniness is one of them. Another is mood swings. Yeah, I know, I'm a psychopath, mood swings come with the territory, but these are more frequent – like Quasimodo on a bell rope.

Any given day I'll start off Angry (e.g. gameshows), then veer into Sad (e.g. woman on TV with kid born without eyes) then I'm awash with Guilt (e.g. shouting at old man crossing the road/anxiety dream about AJ) then euphorically Happy (e.g. being in the garden or watching documentaries with Tink and Jim). This rotation sometimes only takes about twenty minutes.

Hungry for some junk, I took a little trip to the mini mart and then walked with Tink up to the Well House.

A tranquil, former fisherman's cottage built in the 1700s and burnt down in the 1750s, it's newly-thatched and white-washed, a little gravel path winds through the trees to the front door – painted blue with a brass knocker shaped like a knot of rope. Through the back garden gate there's a patio right in the sun spot, with two chairs and a glass-topped table. The walls are

thick granite and the ceilings are low and uneven. The floors are all worn flagstone downstairs and hardwood above and in the living room is an inglenook hearth with wood burner and a log basket. You can burn allsorts in there.

I'd like to burn all the furnishings Elaine chose for the place – burn them and shoot the ashes into space. It's where Cath Kidston goes to masturbate. It's all brand new chintz, but still chintz. I wince at chintz.

Jim bought the Well House three years ago. It had been on the market for over a year, and the agent had had no luck, owing to the amount of money needing to be spent on it, and the gaping hole. This was why it was called the Well House – it has an authentic medieval well in the kitchen floor which serves no real purpose. It's just a deep hole. Only it's a *listed* hole, so Jim's not allowed to fill it in. There's a strong Perspex tile over it, bolted at the four edges. Without it you'd take three steps inside the back door and fall straight in. Jim's installed lights halfway down it so you can marvel at the abyss below you. I like to stare down into it. Predictably, it stares back.

Craig had done some of the work on the house himself. He'd laid the patio slabs one weekend and me and Tink had gone with him. I sat on the edge of one of the raised beds and watched him work.

'I can't get enough of you,' I said. 'I like watching your muscles as you lift those heavy stones.' He kept coming over for kisses. We couldn't keep our hands off each other. He lay me back gently on the soft earth and eased his hand under my skirt. His fingers moved my knickers to one side and slipped inside me. I came with my eyes to the sky, my feet either side of his neck and the scent of honeysuckle in my nostrils. I was in

love that summer. I don't think I realised what love was until Lana Rowntree took it away from me.

For a good hour today, I was content to just sit in the garden playing with Tink and stuffing my face with all the things Elaine doesn't let me eat at home – crisps, bread, Dairy Milk, Dairy Milk melted on hot waffles with squirty cream and four scoops of salted caramel ice cream. Then more bread, more Dairy Milk, Dairy Milk spread on toast. Neither she nor Jim ever go up to the Well House – Jim because his angina bites when he walks uphill – so I'm left to my own devices. It's become my sanctuary.

I watered the raised beds – the scent of tea roses is so strong in the hot sun. I mowed the lawn and then me and Tink lay on the warm soil of AJ's grave watching the butterflies in the buddleia and listening to the cries of distant gulls. A strange sense of calm came over me as I lay on that warm soft earth. I don't know if it was the heat of the day or the mildness of the sea breeze or the thought of the rotting pieces of my former lover buried a few feet beneath me, but I felt happy.

Blissful.

Maybe this is enough. Maybe I don't need dark alleyways and stalking missions anymore, waiting hours outside some random's house having read about him in the courts roundup. Randoms like the Blue Van Rapists. Like Gavin White. Like Derek Scudd, the paedophile I'd stifled to death in his living room, bringing me to such ecstasy I'd creamed my knickers. Maybe I'll devote my life to the #MeToo and #BalanceTonPorc campaigns instead.

Maybe I won't.

I went to the kitchen and pulled open the cutlery drawer. I took out a bread knife and a smaller fruit knife. I put them on the side – underneath the spoons and spatulas, there was one

more – a stainless steel twelve-inch carving knife with a riveted handle. Needed sharpening but 'Dishwasher Safe'.

Don't.

'Just Huggins,' I said, pressing the blade to my cheek. 'Just to see if it's still as good.'

No.

'It'll be all right. I won't get caught.'

Of course you will. She's in a bail hostel. That place has CCTV, twenty-four hour wardens. Use your brain, not mine.

I had a sort of panic attack – I got all breathless and the nausea reared its head again. My brain swam and I had to pull up a stool and sit down. I put the carving knife back in the drawer where it swiftly disappeared amongst the other utensils.

'You don't want me to kill, do you?' I said. 'It's you doing that.'

It's not safe, Mummy. And if it's not safe for you, it's not safe for me.

*

As I walked back down towards the town, I spied that detective woman, DI Géricault, sitting on a seafront bench. She wasn't doing anything in particular – looking out to sea; khaki raincoat tight around her, hair scraped back in a mother of pearl clip, brown leather handbag perched on her knees, feet pointed and together, not blinking, even in the wind.

She had seen me – there was no point pretending otherwise.

'Nice to see you again.'

'Hello, Rhiannon.' She turned languidly to face me, as though waking up from a pleasant dream.

'Sorry, I didn't wake, you did I?'

'No, I was waiting for you as a matter of fact.' She unclasped her bag and retrieved a small notepad and a pen. 'I've got some more questions about Craig. Where is it best to talk?'

'Not at the house,' I said. 'Elaine can't cope with it. We can go over to Bay Bites.' I pointed towards the café.

Over a cappuccino (for her) and a hot chocolate with cream and extra sprinkles (for me), she asked me every question about Craig she hadn't previously asked – about his mates, men he'd previously worked with at the quarry, men he'd recently done jobs with on building projects. And my dad.

'Craig and Tommy were close.'

It seemed rhetorical but I answered anyway. 'They were, yes. Dad thought a lot of him.'

'And they worked together.' She put her pencil to her lips but didn't chew it.

'For a while, yeah. He took over Dad's building work when he got sick.'

'Get to know Tommy's friends as well, did he?'

'What do you mean?'

Géricault left her question hanging in the warm café air between us. I knew exactly what she meant – and she knew I knew it too.

'If you're asking if Craig was a vigilante like my dad then no he wasn't.'

'Is it possible that Tommy and Craig shared some mutual acquaintances? Maybe Tommy introduced Craig to a guy down the pub one night after work perhaps. Someone he'd done a job with?'

'I don't know.' I slurped my hot chocolate even though it

was fiery-hot, and tried my best to effect a meek visage. 'You'd have to ask Craig.'

'We have.'

'What did he say?'

'Not much. Who is Craig particularly close to nowadays?'

'Eddie, Gary and Nigel are his oldest mates. He went to school with Eddie and he met Gary and Nigel when he was at technical college.'

'Do you get on with them?'

'I tolerate them, as much as anything. They all seem to share a brain. I don't know who's using it at the moment.' She didn't laugh. 'Why?'

The woman in the kitchen fishwifing it about her son's wedding and scraping endless plates into the recycling caddy was getting on my last tit.

'Why didn't you tell us that you and Craig had got engaged a few days before he went to Holland?'

'I didn't think it was important.'

'You've recently sold your parents' house.'

'Yes.'

'Presumably when you and Craig were married, your share of your parents' house – over three hundred grand – would be half his?'

'I guess so, yeah.'

She checked her notes. 'And the other half of the house sale went to your sister who lives in… Seattle? Seren Gibson?'

'She's moving to Vermont soon but yes. It was an even split after the solicitor's fees and whatnot. What's this got to do with Craig?'

'You're not even slightly concerned by the fact that he asked

you to marry him just a few days before he was arrested for multiple murder?'

'I tend to only see the best in people,' I said. I don't know how I didn't smile. 'Craig's not after my money. He's not like that. Honestly.'

She sat back, stirring her coffee. 'You love him. I can see it, right there.' She pointed two fingers towards me. 'You'd do anything for him.'

'What are you getting at?'

'Rhiannon – I don't have to tell you that aiding and abetting a felon is almost as serious as committing the crime yourself, do I?'

'No you don't have to tell me that. And I wouldn't anyway. I had no suspicions about Craig at all. I didn't even know he was sleeping with my own colleague, let alone catfishing guys and… all that other stuff you say he's done. You want answers about Craig, I suggest you talk to Lana Rowntree. I've told you everything I know.'

'Your father Tommy was a convicted murderer, Rhiannon – a murderer of sex offenders, who consorted with similar men who targeted guess what – sex offenders. Now two men and one woman are murdered in cold blood – at least one of them being a *sex offender*, and *your* fiancé's DNA was found all over them. I'd say I'm talking to exactly the right person, wouldn't you?'

*

After dinner, Jim, Elaine and I were sitting in the living room not watching *Britain's Got Talent* – Jim had pulled up an occasional table and was planting seeds in a little germination tray, Elaine was doing her Kindness cross-stitch for WOMBAT. I was

glugging Gaviscon, courtesy of my lunchtime inquisition with Géricault. I Googled Patrick Edward Fenton.

I wish I hadn't.

The guy was fairly recognisable – Liam Gallagher hair, beer gut, tatt sleeves and ear spacers. Inordinately large nostrils too – I could probably slide a Sharpie up each one without him even noticing. There was one picture with his spacers taken out and his ears looked like they were melting.

Anyway I digress. Initially I found the story of how the snub-nosed maggot had downloaded thousands of child porn pictures. 65,000 in all.

> **Fenton, 50, was arrested after police searched his home in Winterbourne, Gloucestershire and seized two laptops and a phone.**

My acid reflux started to bite.

> **Police analysis revealed the devices contained over 65,000 indecent images of children aged two to twelve, comprising 966 Category A images – the most serious – 6,722 Category B and the rest at category C.**
>
> **Fenton pleaded guilty to all charges. His defence barrister claimed that since his arrest Fenton has completed a self-improvement course with the Bristol branch of NewLeaf, a clinic specialising in treating sex offenders and is genuinely apologetic and ashamed of his actions.**
>
> **He was handed a suspended jail sentence at Bristol Crown Court.**

The prosecution barrister was Heather Wherryman – my damsel in distress.

But that wasn't the only article I found relating to Fenton. This case was ten years ago. There were three more recent stories. Clearly not *that* ashamed of his actions then.

A twelve-month sentence followed attacking a child in a playground in Mannamead, Plymouth. And last year, he was caught masturbating in the children's book corner of a library in Minehead and charged with public indecency. But it was the last story that caused me to dry heave.

The RSPCA had been called to his home in the Weston-super-Mare area. A neighbour reported sounds of animals in distress. Inspectors found cats, matted and half-starved. Dead snakes in dirty tanks. Sickly rabbits covered in shit. And a dog that looked like Tink, shut inside a bathroom and left to starve. Scratches up the wallpaper. Chunks bitten out of the skirting board. A slow, agonising death.

That was the one that got me. Right in the murderous feels.

Take it easy, Mummy. All this acid is not good for me.

I swigged my Gaviscon.

So Patrick Edward Fenton is still out on licence, receiving 'treatment' for his addictions, walking the streets, past playgrounds where children play, probably still has a library card too. All right he's not allowed to keep animals again but who's going to check on that? And what'll he get if he *does* keep animals again? A fine? A community service order?

Why is he free? If it's *his* human right to freedom cos of his 'mental condition' then it's *my* human right cos of *my* 'mental condition' to kill him.

Don't you dare.

'You'd rather this guy was out there, waiting for you?' I angled the laptop screen at my stomach. 'Look at him. Look what he did to those animals. God I'd give the world and a handful of planets to see that guy suffer. You think he should be allowed to walk around, as free as a bird?'

Technically if he was a bird, he'd be flying.

'Yeah and I'd be pointing up at him with a shotgun.'

I'm scared, Mummy. You'll get in trouble.

'No I won't. Torquay's not far from here, just along the coast—'

It's not the right time. You'll get caught. Forget about him.

'I could go to that kebab shop, follow him, pretend to chat him up, drug him with some of Elaine's Tramadol—'

I SAID NO.

Heil Foetus has spoken. Better keep old Patrick on ice for a bit.

Tuesday, 7ᵗʰ August
– 13 weeks, 2 days

1. *Sandra Huggins.*
2. *Patrick Edward Fenton.*
3. *Men who still aren't getting the memo that women don't like to be felt up on public transport – grab me by the pussy, you'll take your dick home in a bag.*

The Bible pretty much says that if I repent my sins and love the Lord, I can do what I like. But this is true of anyone, isn't it? Like, if the Blue Van Rapists repented their sins at Heaven's Gate, would they be let in too? And Derek Scudd, despoiler of ten-year olds? And Gavin White? And Pete McMahon – the man who would have raped my sister had I not been there? We are not the same. You can't wash that shit away with a few Hail Marys. Everything is fake and wrong and I hate the world.

I threw the book across the room and did some baby research instead. Apparently, the foetus is now the size of a peach – and a hairy peach at that. It's covered in a 'fine downy hair called lanugo which regulates the baby's temperature and which will disperse before birth'. Allrighty then.

So today I've read things, I've taken my vits, I've walked Tink, I've lied my ass off to Jim about a cancelled August booking

for the Well House ('so near, so far'), watched some Gordon Ramsay and put together my Sylvanians Post Office. I'm a bit disappointed, to be honest. The eBay seller said it was used but I didn't expect there to be hairs stuck in jam on the shelves or a used plaster in the cash register. And some of the stamps had been licked. Ugh.

I've also been up to the Well House to tend the garden – well, I deadhead and water and mow the lawn but for the most part I like being with AJ again. I can't take Tink up there with me anymore though – she won't stop trying to dig him out. Dogs always know.

And now I'm bored. I keep getting Sandra Huggins's payslip out and looking at it. Flat 17b The Esplanade, Monks Bay. I know which building that is. It's wardened and has key card entry. There's no way of pretending I'm her carer like I did with Derek Scudd—

You're not killing her, I mean it. I'll be so cross if you do. It's too risky.

'I'm not stupid. I *know* it's too risky. But how else do I get to her?'

You don't. At least not while I'm in here. You have to protect me, above all else. I don't want you to kill.

'Just her. Or Fenton. Her or Fenton and then I'll stop. Please.'

I. Said. NO.

See? This is what I get. Stymied at every turn by a hairy peach who monitors my every move. Fucks ache. I need a hobby. I need to go fishing.

Catfishing.

*

I've spent the entire day by the cybernetic riverbank, seeing what's swimming. It's quite fun once you select the right kind of fish. No point baiting the confident, good-looking types. And once you've weeded out the gimps, wimps, fuckboys, flakes, prison inmates and dick pics, you can concentrate your efforts on a select few morons. Currently my keepnet comprises:

- *Indian Prince aka The Lovestruck One*
- *White and Nerdy – aka The Panty Sniffer*
- *Lord Byron – aka The Wordy One*

I met them all via a dating site called Slave4U.com. This site specifically pairs up weirdos who want to be belittled, beaten up, trampled, dominated or 'sissified', with those who wish to belittle, beat up, trample, dominate and sissify. So, as you can imagine, it's a real playground for someone like me.

Indian Prince can't spell or if he can, he does a good job of hiding it.

I can feel my election rise in my boxers, he says.

Oh god not another election. I haven't got over the last one.

Do you liek [sic] *having your prissy locked?*

Can't remember the last time my prissy was locked. He's invited me out for dinner several times – he'll pay – but I told him I want to get to know him better before we advance to Rohypnol and chips.

White and Nerdy spent three hours one night saying how much he wanted to kill himself. I said he should so I could get back to sleep. But his pain is entertaining. He's having problems at work or something. He keeps telling me I have gorgeous eyes and that he wants to 'tie me up and do me all day and night'.

Bear in mind I can barely sit through *EastEnders* without falling asleep at the moment, I'd like to see him try. White and Nerdy adores Sweetpea though. He'd do anything for her.

Like tell her he thinks he loves her after just few hours' texting.

Or carve a flower into his skin.

Wednesday, 8th August
– 13 weeks, 3 days

Chronic horn has properly kicked in. I've exhausted PornHub for every category of video it has to offer and there's only so many packs of Duracell a woman can buy before it starts to look like she's creating an incendiary device. I could do with a serious cockular implant right about now. There's a new weather boy on *Up at the Crack* of a morning who certainly fits the bill. There's no Donkey Dick Tompkinson to leer at anymore since they fired his ass for sleeping with the intern but now there's Nick, a thirty-something stud meteorologist. You can see his pec muscles tighten under his shirt when he's pointing to East Anglia. That's what I call a warm front.

You allow anything human up here and I'll bite it off.

Le sigh. I either need to screw someone or kill someone soon. And at this moment in time, I don't give a shit which.

One of the catfish perhaps. Indian Prince is my current favourite. He's unintentionally hilarious. He messaged me this morning:

IndianPrince: Sweetpea why you not message again last night? I wait but yoo do not come. I make love to you

and tell that you have captured my soul and are the pure duplicate of an angel but you gone. What did I do? I look forward to read from you.

Sweetpea: Soz. Fell asleep. Did you do as I asked?

IndianPrince: Yes! I did! I send you the picture! I drew it on my leg. I love that we came together last night!

Well, *he* came. I was watching *Cat on a Hot Tin Roof* and doing quizzes on BuzzFeed. Turns out I only know twelve out of fifty capital cities, am fifty-six per cent more Kurt than Goldie and my Patronus is a hedgehog. There's a line in *Cat on a Hot Tin Roof* that really chimed with me actually. It's something the alcoholic says – I wish I'd written it down now. Something to do with him drinking to hear the click in his mind – the click that turns the hot light off. That's what I have – a hot light. It's on all the time, nothing cools it. Killing cools it. At least it used to. Who'da thought Paul Newman had the answer? Elaine's banned me from his creamy Caesar dressing though, aka the only thing that makes her salads bearable. Endless witch.

Later on, Indian Prince sent through a picture of his home-made leg tattoo – a pathetic marker-drawn flower on his upper right thigh.

IndianPrince: You see? My angle I did that for you to show you my love.

Sweetpea: You don't love me enough to do it properly.

IndianPrince: I do my love! I love your lovely hair, your shining eyes, your lady parts. I want so badly mate you.

Sweetpea: *[stops laughing]* Then do the flower properly. Or else you don't love me at all. Other men have done it,

why haven't you?

IndianPrince: My religion doesn't allow tattoos

Sweetpea: I don't want you to get a tattoo. Do it yourself. With a knife. You would do it if you loved me.

IndianPrince: Will I be able to spend another night with you?

Sweetpea: If you do this for me, you can have me Every. Single. Night.

IndianPrince: I can???? And you won't talk to any other mens?

Sweetpea: No. My body will only be for your eyes. You can watch me tease myself while I talk to you on Skype if you like.

IndianPrince: I can??? You promise me my lady?

Sweetpea: Of course. I'll keep myself pure for you. But you have to do the flower. It needn't be a big one.

IndianPrince: I will do it for you my love, my precious angel of love.

Sweetpea: Do it. I want to see your blood.

Two hours later, a video message *plink*ed into my inbox. It was him, leg up on the bathtub, shaking hand carving the flower shape into his thigh, crying like an endless little bitch. It's a small flower, as expected. A pussy like him can't take pain for too long. Then he messaged again.

IndianPrince: My love, I done it for you. It hurt so much. Have I pleased you? I am in so much pain but this means that you are mine now, yes? We can finally be together my angel?

BLOCK.
Haha.

Thursday, 9th August
– 13 weeks, 4 days

1. *People who pick the raisins out of food. STOP ORDERING THINGS WITH RAISINS IN!*
2. *People who constantly ask me how 'far along' I am and when I tell them inform me that 'it must be twins' because I'm so big.*
3. *Scientists who STILL haven't invented an easier way to do pregnancy.*

The vivid dreams show no sign of abating. I'm dreaming about everything from the the *Gazette* to the childminder at Priory Gardens to breaking the necks of live chickens at the dinner table. I have dreams about AJ too. He is always alive when I see him – alive and smiling, rather than in eight separate wrapped pieces under the warm earth at the Well House. The baby doesn't like me dreaming about AJ. I get woken up in a full sweat, this terrible screaming in my ears— *NO! NO! NO!! I WANT MY DADDY BACK. I WANT MY DADDY BACK!* — over and over again.

Woke up at 3 a.m. in such a sweat and couldn't get back to sleep. Scrolled social media and the news channels for updates on Craig. Four mentions of me out of twenty-four – in each

story I was simply 'The Gripper's Pregnant Girlfriend' and it went on to talk about Priory Gardens. I was not a person in my own right – I was either the child survivor of *that* guy or the girlfriend of *that other guy*. They were the headliners. I was just a bit part.

I switched to my apps to see if there were any fishies swimming around. White and Nerdy took the bait first:

White and Nerdy: Hey baby girl. What u doin up so late? X

Sweetpea: Bad dream ☹

White and Nerdy: Wish I was there to cuddle u in bed X

Sweetpea: Me too. How are your thighs now?

White and Nerdy: Still stinging. Worth it though. Can't stop thinkin bout you

Sweetpea: Aww. That's nice.

White and Nerdy: Thinkin bout U + me gettin sweaty in my bed soon X

Sweetpea: Ooh Daddy, that sounds hot.

White and Nerdy: What are you doing today, baby girl? X

Sweetpea: School as usual. Got an A in my maths test.

White and Nerdy: That's cool baby. U gonna be wearing a skirt today? X

Sweetpea: Yeh. Do you like me in my school skirt? I'll send u a new pic...

White and Nerdy: Yeh. You get me hard. I love lil girls, smoller the better ☺

Sweetpea: I am very small Daddy

White and Nerdy: You wanna do this for real? You wanna meet? X

Sweetpea: I've never met anyone before from online. U sure it'll be OK?

White and Nerdy: It'll be fine baby. You rly wanna give me ur *cherry emoji*?

Sweetpea: Yeah Daddy. Let's meat.

Later that day, I met Marnie at the boating lake in the park – Jim was putting his latest model boat on the water for the first time – a smaller version of the HMS *Victory* with cannons and ropes and sails and even a tiny eyeless and armless Nelson in the crow's nest. There were a few people around with tiny motorized yachts and steamers but most had hired life-sized rowing boats for the afternoon. We both watched from the bank as Jim proudly put down the *Victory* on the water and watched as it floated away.

Marnie seemed fascinated with it. She seemed fascinated by everything. 'Is it motorised, Jim?'

'No, *Victory* wasn't motorised,' Jim laughed, folding his arms all dad-like and proud. 'She was a sailing ship.'

'But how will you get her back out of the pond?'

Jim looked at me and Marnie in turn. We all looked back to the boat. It had already floated off into the middle of the lake. 'I hadn't thought about that. I just wanted to see if she would stay upright.'

We left him talking to the park keeper about retrieving his half-Nelson, which was by this point sailing off back towards Portsmouth, while Marnie and I took a stroll around the park. It was crowded for a Thursday, mainly joggers and dog walkers

and families feeding the ducks or playing mini golf. We stopped at the sweet shack and bought a pound of pick and mix, which we scoffed in the shade of a weeping willow.

'Your bump looks better than mine,' I told her, my tongue navigating a sherbet lemon that was fizzier than I'd been expecting. 'It's rounder. Mine looks like a duvet's been rammed up there.'

Marnie laughed, gnawing at a liquorice cable. 'Hey I thought of a new question – why doesn't Winnie the Pooh ever get stung?'

'I have no idea. He does poke about in a lot of beehives doesn't he?'

'He's *always* in beehives. And he never ever gets stung.'

'Maybe bears don't *get* stung. Maybe the bees know better?'

'Do dentists go to see other dentists or do they do it to themselves?'

'Nice. How about who was the fat lady and when does she sing?'

'I know this!' said Marnie, sitting up. 'No I don't. It's something to do with baseball and an opera singer at the end of the game. Think that's it.'

'Makes sense.'

We rarely talked about our pregnancies or gossiped about boys or people we both disliked. We seem to have bypassed that whole thing and gone right back to childhood questions we'd always had but never asked. We seemed to like it better that way.

Sometimes the real world would crash in though – like a scrap of newspaper in a flower bed in the park that read **Gripper Killer Vigilante Theory**. Marnie pretended not to see it.

'You can ask me about it if you like,' I said.

'It's none of my business.'

'You must be curious.'

'Well yeah, but—'

'So ask me. Ask me what it's like living with a suspected serial killer. Ask me if I met any of the victims or if Craig fashioned soup bowls from their skulls. Anything, I don't mind.'

'Was he abused?' she asked. 'Is that why he only kills sex offenders?'

'He wasn't abused,' I replied. 'And I don't think they were all sex offenders. It's a coincidence. Paper talk. Fake news.'

'Oh,' she said. 'The papers say he's part of some gang of vigilantes. Like your dad was.'

'As far as I knew he worked alone,' I said.

'Oh.' We walked towards a willow tree and sat down in its shade. 'Do you still love him?'

I didn't think. The word flew out of me. 'Yes.'

Our morning was largely uneventful, aside from Jim's *Victory* debacle. It wouldn't really be worth recording but for one tiny incident. We were sitting beneath the weeping willow, people-watching and swatting away flies, and a dandelion clock seed landed in Marnie's hair. I reached across to flick it away and she winced – like I was going to hit her.

I pulled the clock from her hair and showed it to her.

'Oh,' she laughed. 'I wondered what you were doing.'

'You thought I was going to hit you.'

'Of course not. It was just unexpected, that's all.'

'My nanny used to do that,' I said. 'Wince at sudden movements.'

'It was a one off, don't start.'

'Nanny was conditioned to expect it. And so are you.'

'I'm not, Rhiannon.' She angled back on her hands and crossed her feet over. 'Can we change the subject?'

'Okay,' I said. I lay down on the grass and closed my eyes. In seconds I smelled the coconut scent of her hair and felt her lie down next to me. 'Why do people fly kites? I mean seriously, what's the point?'

'I have no idea. I guess because it looks nice? Is it a skill?'

'The wind does all the work though.'

'True,' she yawned. 'You could say the same about Jim and his boat. Or the people paying to row about for half an hour. What's the point?'

'"Believe me my young friend, there is nothing – absolutely nothing – half so worth doing as simply messing about in boats."'

She squinted my way. 'Huh?'

'*The Wind in the Willows*,' I said. 'My favourite book.'

'Mine too!' she said with a broad grin full of teeth. 'That's so funny!'

'It's not so funny, it's a good book.'

'I always like that bit where Mole's lost in the Wild Wood and Ratty comes and saves him and they go to Badger's hollow and get toasty warm in front of the fire. What's your best bit?'

'When Toad dresses up in drag and steals a train. It's the last bit I remember her reading to us.'

'Who?'

'Allison. At Priory Gardens. We were meant to come back to it later after juice and biscuits. Then he came in.'

The silence enveloped us. Marnie lay her head back and closed her eyes.

'If you swallow an apple pip, will a tree grow inside you?'

'I doubt it. I've swallowed millions.'

'What if it gets planted somewhere? Like in your spleen or something?'

'Dunno. Why doesn't glue stick to the inside of the bottle?'

'Good one.'

We carried on like this for an hour or more, asking imponderable questions and listening to the creak of oars and the splashing of the rowing boats and seagulls calling out in the sunshine. I didn't realise we had fallen asleep until someone's pit bull puppy was licking the soles of my feet. The sky was darkening and the park was half-empty.

'What time is it?' Marnie croaked.

'Half five.'

'HALF FIVE?' she shrieked, levering herself up as quickly as she could. She fumbled for her phone inside her cardigan pocket. 'Seventeen missed calls. Oh my god.' She showed me the screen. 'I've had it on silent. Oh god!'

'Oh well, never mind.'

'Did you put it on silent?'

'Nope.'

'God, he's probably been out searching.' She went over onto all fours and slowly got to her feet, gathering up her bag and cardigan.

'Jesus, is your ankle tag beeping? I'll come with you and explain.'

'No, don't come. He already thinks we're having an affair.'

'With *me*?' I said.

'He gets paranoid.'

'Well I like you Marnie, but I ain't ever going down to Pastrami Town, just so you know.'

She laughed, losing her anxiety for a moment. 'Don't, this is serious.'

'No it's not. Look, you spent the afternoon with me talking about boring baby shit and watching model boats, that's all. You haven't done anything illegal. Tell him to strap on a pair.'

She laughed the laugh of easier-said-than-done. 'I'll need to do a lot of sweet-talking. I'll see you soon, okay?'

'What you going to sweeten him up with, Netflix and chill?'

'We don't have Netflix. Tim says it's a waste of money.'

'Ugh. The sooner you ditch that guy the better.'

Friday, 10th August
– 13 weeks, 5 days

1. *Elaine – so far this week I've had lectures on Why I must not have pain relief in labour because I 'won't be able to bond with my baby', Names I mustn't call said baby and repeat choruses of Foods You Mustn't Eat.*
2. *Tourists (again).*
3. *God.*

So I fancied a day trip today. Me and no one else; a casual, breezy little jaunt along the coast to Torquay. Nothing to write home about. Had a nice wander about the shops and the seafront. Browsed the postcards. Played in the arcades. Bought some fancy shoes. Took the fancy shoes back cos they rubbed my heels. Ate a fuckful of fat ice cream in an ice cream parlour. Watched the entrance of Sportz Madness opposite like the proverbial hawk, that kind of thing.

I don't condone this, by the way.

It only dawned on me when I was halfway through my second full fat clotted cream ice cream cornet with raspberry sauce that it might not be one of Patrick's work days. That I might be wasting my time and setting myself up for chronic disappointment, acid indigestion and heartburn. But the gods were clearly smiling

down on me today, as was the sun. He rocked up for work at five minutes to midday. And I got my game face on.

You can't expect to get away with this one. In broad daylight? In a town you don't know? It's a suicide run.

'No it's not. Trust me, will you?'

All afternoon it took. I couldn't be too eager but at the same time I couldn't afford to be too vague. I had to strike that happy balance between *I'm not crazy* and *I want to fuck you until it falls off*.

No mean feat, lemme tell you.

So I wandered around the shop for a good long while, unzipping sports bags I had no intention of buying, trying on vile luminous sports gear that was never going to fit me and attempting to spin basketballs on one finger. My path kept on crossing with Fenton's and I attempted conversations about the basketball spin (he couldn't do it either), which colour grip to buy for my tennis racket and the pros and cons of Memory Sole trainers. He was standoffish at first – barely said a word – and I had to buy two pairs of Skechers before he'd even crack a smile.

But he *did* smile and so did I, wide and all encompassing – Venus's mouth awaiting the curious fly.

Saturday, 11ᵗʰ August
– 13 weeks, 6 days

1. *Waitress in Nando's at the services whose eyebrows rose when I ordered an extra side of spicy rice AND chips for lunch. Even though SHE wears elasticated jeans and has stretch marks on her neck.*
2. *Women who go on coach trips and sit next to me and allow Murray Mints to clatter off their teeth the whole damn journey.*
3. *Women who go on coach trips, sit next to me and insist on making chit-chat about Alfie Boe.*

Managed to get out of Pin's cheese and wine party with a legitimate excuse – Elaine has wangled me a place on the WOMBAT coach trip to York. Hmm – frying pan or fire? I'll take the frying pan. I'd actually rather go back to Sports Madness and play with Patrick again but Elaine has spoken so yippety fuckity doo, I'm coming too. She says a 'change of scenery will do me good'. So far the only scenery has been the M5 – it's gridlocked. The air conditioning's patchy and the coach reeks of Chanel. Can't stand Chanel. Mum used to wear it.

Every woman here is a ginormous waffle goblin and they've taken it in turns to comment on my bump and inform me of their

own birthing horror stories. I've had stillborns, torn vaginas, a 'breast is best' lecture, two shitting-myself-in-the-birthing-pool anecdotes, several husband-goes-off-sex-cos-your-sex-hole's-a-mess warnings and Debbie Does Donkeys regaling me with how she pissed herself in Smiths and Tony Hadley walked past.

I have no idea who Tony Hadley is but Debbie still seems mortified about the whole incident, thirty years on.

We've just had an impromptu Kindness Circle. We all had to wax lyrical on 'paying it forward,' 'it' being kindness of course. I mentioned Kevin Spacey was in the movie but that he was better in *The Usual Suspects* and they all went quiet and changed the subject to Alfie Boe on *The One Show* last night. I'd forgotten the eleventh commandment of Kindness Circle you see – Thou Must Not Mention Ye Olde Sex Pests. It reminds them there's a real world outside.

There is one glimmer of potential awesome on the horizon...

I'm going to kill again. Tonight. And the baby seems okay with it.

*I don't think you'll go through with it, that's all *folds tiny arms**

As soon as Elaine mentioned York last night, I realised my little catfish White and Nerdy didn't live that far away in Nottingham. I said I would 'kill to meet you today.' I know – a bit on the nose but Sweetpea needs her fun. *Devil horns emoji* He's going to leave work early. He wants me so bad.

A message came through when the coach stopped at the services. I went in and bought a packet of mints, a cheese and pickle sandwich and a Tear and Share bag of cheese and onion. I don't plan to tear *or* share:

White and Nerdy: Hey babe. Am on train. Can't wait to see you later X

Sweetpea: I'm still scared about meeting u

White and Nerdy: Nuthin to be scared of babe. You know me by now. X

Sweetpea: Will it hurt me?

White and Nerdy: Only at first cos ur so small but after that you'll enjoy it

Sweetpea: You know I'm only 13 tho, right?

White and Nerdy: Yeh baby. If it doesn't bother u it doesn't bother me X

Sweetpea: Hotel has vacancies, I checked

White and Nerdy: Good girl X I'm a bit older than I said, does that matter? X

Sweetpea: How old?

White and Nerdy: 27 babe. That ok? X

Sweetpea: That's ok. Can you tell me ur real name now?

White and Nerdy: Kameron

Sweetpea: Cool! I luv that name.

White and Nerdy: Thanks baby. Hbu?

Sweetpea: My name is Lia

White and Nerdy: *heart eyes emoji*

Sweetpea: You'll make sure my virginity's gone forevs by tonight, won't you?

White and Nerdy: Oh yeh babe. Don't u worry about that X

I've tried hard to convince White and Nerdy that I am indeed the unworldly school girl I say I am. I guess paedos have to be careful these days, what with all the vigilante outfits lurking on

the dark web. You have to be quite persistent when questing after perverts who believe children should be seen and felt up. It's not as though you can ride around in a van marked FREE KIDS and hope they'll just hop in the back.

I snagged my 'Lia' pictures from the Facebook of Pin's eldest, Cordelia; a selfie-obsessed pouting numbskull with tits bigger than her head and weak privacy settings. I figured she'd be just the sort to converse with a 'Justin Bieber lookalike' like Kameron. He does look a bit like Justin Bieber.

Well, Justin Bieber if I tried to *draw* Justin Bieber. With my left hand.

In the dark.

While having a stroke.

*

I'm in some tea room called Betty's eating a cream tea surrounded by a zillion chattering women, most of whom I wish would just start bleeding from the eyes. My face aches from fake smiling. I've suffered an endless mooch around a Viking exhibition, been force-fed fudge and an interminable lecture on buttresses at York Minster by an old battle-axe called Glenda with a lump the size of a small apple on her leg. My own legs ache from traipsing. The only thing that's keeping me going is the thought of later. He's messaged again:

White and Nerdy: Train delayed ☹ Hard thinking about
2nite, babe X
Sweetpea: I know, Kam. I can't wait to see you too. ☺
White and Nerdy: See you at 6pm x
Sweetpea: Will you bring me some flowers?

White and Nerdy: Of course baby. Anything for my girl X

*

This city is CCTV mad – like pigeons, they're on every roof-top – but this hotel isn't for some reason. I checked it out on Google maps before I said I'd meet him here. Google maps is a good friend to someone like me. The hotel's your bog-standard Premier Inn on the outskirts of the city – three storeys high, car park peppered with wind-blown litter and backing onto a care home. There's a leafy walkway through to the care home. Nicely dark, nicely quiet.

I have exactly one hour until our coach leaves the pub one mile away. Operation: White and Nerdy has begun.

Please don't do it, Mummy.

*

My new Big-Ben-synced wristwatch tells me it's precisely 6.25 p.m. White and Nerdy is twenty-five minutes late. He may have pussied out.

*

6.39 p.m. Still no sign of him. I'm not giving up yet. This is too good an opportunity and I've come too damn far.

*

It's 6.43 p.m. I'm now hiding with my shopping bags behind a sign advertising 'Sunday lunches' and 'Kids eat free.' Someone has daubed an S in front of 'kids', hilariously. My steak knife vibrates in my pocket. What a waste of time and effort. Bloody paedophiles are so unreliable.

It's not safe. Go back to WOMBAT. The coach will be leaving soon.

*

6:46 p.m. – I hate this guy. The old feeling is back in the centre of my chest – acid reflux and pure unfettered rage are a bad combination. And I've left my Gaviscon in the magazine pocket on the coach.

Stop, Mummy, go back to the coach park, this isn't safe.

*

6:48 p.m. – Some loud people have just walked past the hotel entrance and gone into the Hungry Horse. They've spooked him perhaps. Or if, as I initially thought, he was bullshitting me about being on the train and hasn't even left the comfort of his laptop in his parents' spare bedroom.

I was going to go easy on him. Now I want to eviscerate the bastard.

Please don't do it. You don't know the area. Anyone could see you. It's too risky. GO BACK TO THE COACH.

*

6:51 p.m. – A man's appeared on the leafy path. He's wearing a red hoody and jeans, scuffing his trainers. He has no arse in his jeans – classic paedo sign – and he's got a rucksack on. I wonder if it contains the alcohol I requested. He's checking his phone. Can't see his face. I have to make sure it's him.

Don't get your phone out. Don't switch it on. The police can triangulate it. They'll know you were here.

But at that second, the man turns around. He's carrying flowers.

Sweet peas.

Bingo.

Please don't do it, Mummy. Please. Please.

'I wouldn't put us in danger unless I was sure.'

My heart starts to thump. I can't catch my breath.

PLEASE! What about me? I might get hurt.

'Pipe down. Momma's got work to do.'

No, I won't let you. Go back to the coach, now! GO BACK! GO BACK! DON'T DO THIS!

*

The coach was late leaving anyway, thanks to a burst colostomy bag and an accident on the bypass which meant the driver had to recalibrate his satnav. Now we're pootling along in heavy traffic – my heart's still thumping, my face still sweating. The chatterings include choruses of '*Oh, Wasn't York Minster Lovely?*' and an encore of '*None Of Our Husbands Understand Us*'.

I, Rhiannon Lewis, walked away from a certain kill tonight. From certain happiness. I've never done that before. Reserves of unused adrenalin have flooded me and I feel so sick. My heartburn has ignited but I'm out of Gaviscon. The air conditioning has completely broken.

And there's this pain in my stomach.

Sunday, 12th August
– 14 weeks exactly

We had to stop twice on the motorway for me to vom. I would be embarrassed but I'm too angry. And my stomach still hurts.

I thought it would have eased by the time I got into bed last night but it got worse. In the toilet at the services I saw blood on my pad. Only a tiny bit but it was unmistakeable. I couldn't put it down to the light in the toilets or my tired eyes – it was red.

It's pitch dark and raining outside my bedroom window – the rain's pattering on the leaves of the horse chestnut. I need the loo again but I daren't. Last time I went there was more blood.

'Please stop hurting me,' I said.

I don't like it when you kill people, Mummy. You have to stop.

'I didn't kill him. I stopped.'

You're going to lose me like you lost Daddy. You'll have to wrap me in a bedsheet too when I bleed out of you.

'Stop hurting me. Stop that pain.'

No. You have to learn. This isn't good for me. Your adrenalin rushes, your blood pressure rises and I get scared. You have to keep me safe.

Radiating pain racked my lower body so deeply I could feel

it in my knees. I took two paracetamol and felt a throbbing sensation in my knickers. I clamped my thighs shut tighter.

I put bath towels on the bed and lay as still as I could. 'Am I losing you?'

You will lose me if you kill people. I don't want to do that. I don't like it.

'You TOLD me to cut your father into pieces not so long ago. Did you grow a conscience when you formed eyelids or something?'

That was to get you out of a situation. You'd already killed him. I couldn't stop that. But I can stop you now. You get caught, I get caught and that can't happen.

'I won't get caught. You need to trust me. You know how I get when I don't kill. I suffer, you suffer. Stop that pain, please.'

I held my breath for as long as I could before letting go. I kept doing it until I couldn't hear the voice. Within an hour, the pain had dissolved to an ache, then a wisp of discomfort, before disappearing altogether.

'Thank you.'

He didn't answer.

When I woke up this morning, I had to wee but I didn't look in the toilet. I knew a lot of liquid had come out. Heavy liquid. I flushed. I caught a brief glimpse of my pad – redder.

'Talk to me. Say anything. I need to know you're still there.'

Nothing.

I think it's gone. I think I flushed it away.

Monday, 13th August
– 14 weeks, 1 day

My appointment was twenty minutes ago but they're running late. I'm not as annoyed as I could be. I can wait a bit longer to be told I've lost my baby. For a person who has few actual feelings, I'm feeling a hell of a lot right now.

Guilt. Anger. Acid reflux, of course. Adrenalin. Fear. Emptiness. So much emptiness.

I don't want this to be the end. Okay, so I hadn't planned this baby, nor was I enjoying pregnancy but I liked it being there. I liked lying in bed watching my belly, knowing I wasn't alone. Now faced with being told I'm empty, I ache. I know I don't deserve it. I know if anyone deserves to sacrifice their kid for their sins it's me, but I'd rather be dying myself right now than lose it. I've brought my Bible with me to the hospital. I thought it might help. I haven't been able to focus on it for long – my mind keeps wandering to What's Coming Next – but I figure just holding it could help. There's a Qur'an on the bookshelf. And a Torah. Might try them as well in a minute.

'Rhiannon Lewis?' the woman said, appearing as if from nowhere rather than the door I'd been staring at for the past half hour. A water balloon burst in my chest. I didn't notice

anyone looking over but I heard the whispers *'Is that her from the news?'* *'Priory Gardens.'* *'Boyfriend's in prison…'*

I was ushered into the same dim little room with the gurney where I'd had my twelve-week scan two weeks ago. The sonographer was pretty nondescript – brown bob, chunky heels, chin wart, wedding ring. How do people with chin warts get husbands? Beats me. She sat down beside the gurney.

'Right if you'd like to hop up on the bed and get comfy. Can I pop your t-shirt up and tuck your trousers over? That's it.'

'Pop' and 'tuck'. Such sweet words – such an abominable prelude. By this point, my heart was doing somersaults.

'Are you all right? Feeling a bit weepy? Okay, let's get this done, shall we?' She tucked some scratchy tissue paper under my bra and waistband, squirted the gel on my tummy then pressed the probe around.

I looked up at the ceiling. I didn't want to see that black screen.

Chin Wart pressed over my abdomen and I'm lying back, counting the ceiling tiles, tears trickling into my ears. The screen reflected in her glasses.

'Don't you want to see it?' she asked.

'What happens now? What do I do?'

'What do you mean?'

'Where does it go?'

There was this noise. Thumping.

'Is that my heartbeat?'

'No, it's your *baby's* heartbeat.'

Chin Wart showed me the screen. It was there. It was *still* there. It had a head, a skull, a spine. Long legs, little stubby arms. And a heartbeat.

'It's still there?' I gasped. 'I didn't piss it out?' I was crying freely by now.

'No,' she frown-laughed. 'You thought you'd miscarried?' I nodded – it was all I could do. 'It's right there, look.'

The image warped and went all underwatery, like we were going into a different world, but there it was – this little alien thing. With long legs like AJ's. I've been wondering if it will look like AJ when it comes out. *If* it comes out. If it doesn't dissolve in my acidic juices in the meantime.

'I can't believe he's still in there,' I said, and Chin Wart laughed too as though *Duh? Where else would he be?*

'Ah love,' she said, handing me a tissue. 'It's all right. It's all good.'

Bloody feelings again. Bloody *this* feeling again. This horrible ache. This horrible surging ache. 'I can't believe it.'

I noticed the little throbbing in the middle of the alien. It wasn't just a blob – a Grain of Rice, a Fig, a Lime. It was a tiny human who'd survived all the shit I'd put it through. I couldn't take my eyes off it. Millions of scans are done all over the world, every day, and to every woman when they see their baby it's the most fascinating thing. The only difference here was that this was *my* baby. How was *this* murdering body nurturing *this* living thing?

'How big is it now?' I asked, wiping my eyes on my sleeve, 'I've been sort of measuring it in fruit and veg.'

'Oh fruit-wise I think we're talking about a lemon now.'

We've come a long way from the poppy seed. I could see arms, legs, eye sockets, brain, bones. I'm doing something right amidst all the wrong.

'You're sure it's okay?'

'I'm as sure as I can be,' she said. I told her about the bleeding. 'Speak to your doctor about that. All looks fine here as far as I can see.'

I've never been good with trusting people but I guess I have to. Chin Wart's the one with the qualifications and I thought I'd thrown out my own baby with the piss water. She said the pains last night could have been 'practice' contractions.

'If all goes well, there's nothing to suggest you won't carry to full term.'

There's a troubling phrase – *if all goes well*. Nothing certain in this game.

'Is there anything I can do to keep it happy?'

'Keep taking your Pregnacare vitamins. Eat the right foods. Take it easy. Don't do anything too strenuous, nothing that'll raise your blood pressure.'

Catfishing paedos and baiting rapists definitely off the agenda then.

'I'll be a good girl, I promise.'

The Lemon was going ballistic on the screen, bouncing around like he was on a little trampoline. It made me laugh.

I strode out of the hospital like I was in a Beyoncé video. I stopped at the Tesco Metro to buy some health shit – chia seeds, curly kale, all that Pinterest crap The Thinspirators swear by. I stopped by the hardware store and bought the smoothie maker in the window. I walked up to the Well House, feeling as springy as when I'd killed that taxi driver, that rapist in the park, that guy in the canal. What if Marnie was right – maybe *being a mum* is my bliss? Maybe giving life is better than taking life after all?

As I was walking the Cliff Road, I heard a voice…
I'm back.

'You sneak… where did you go?'

Just giving you a scare, that's all.

'Unbelievable.'

Yeah I know. But you had to be taught a lesson, didn't you?

'You were right. It's all about me and you now. I'm going to be good.'

Sure?

'Yeah. I feel fantastic. I haven't felt this good in ages. Now I know I've still got you, I don't need to kill anymore. You're all I need to get by.'

Are you sure I'm going to be enough for you, Mummy?

'Yes.'

What about Sandra Huggins?

'I don't need her.'

What about Patrick Edward Fenton?

'I don't need anyone.'

I stood outside the front gate, stopping to take in the breath of sea air on the clifftop. I breathed in the scent of the wisteria on the back wall. I kicked off my shoes and climbed up onto the raised bed where I'd buried AJ, scrunching my toes so the soft earth ran through them like sand. It felt like coming home.

I think this is all I need. This is enough. This is my bliss.

Ten weeks later

Thursday, 27th September – 20 weeks, 4 days

1. *Jim and Elaine and their utter inability to watch any news bulletin, TV programme or film without providing a joint commentary on it.*
2. *People (Jim) who scroll through TV channels too fast.*
3. *Jim and Elaine's neighbour Malcolm who is converting his attic and banging wood from dawn to dusk – I hope you fall off your scaffolding and break your fucking neck.*

So I guess it turns out that being good means being BORING.

Nothing has happened. Seriously. It's all been pretty pass-the-noose. I have spared you updates on my bowel movements, trips to the garden centre with Jim and Elaine and TV marathons of *Call the Midwife* and some war saga Jim likes. I have become a dried up husk version of my former self.

On the plus side, the baby is still okay. Also - I'm hairier; yet another side effect nature has thrust upon me without warning. I've given up shaving. There's no point going to bed dolphin-smooth just to wake up looking like Hagrid. For a while, it was easy. My focus had shifted. Now, it's shifted back again.

Physically, I'm feeling better. No more sickness or chronic

thirst, energy levels are up. I'm getting the odd headache and spate of constipation and my breasts feel like two tenderised beefsteaks but my moods are, on the whole, as level as they can be. I've been doing a preggo yoga DVD with Marnie in the front room (which usually turns into a game of The Floor is Lava or we collapse into hysterics from all the farting), I'm practising my breathing with the help of YouTube tutorials (well, I've watched ten minutes of one video) and I've been trying my best to avoid situations likely to make me angry (i.e. people).

In short, I have kept to my word and been a good girl. Ish.

Until today. Today has pushed me to the edge and dangled me over it.

First thing this morning, Elaine walked in on me having a wank. They said they were going to Sainsburys and both called out 'Goodbye' and I could have sworn I heard the front door close behind them. As it turned out, Jim had only gone out to put the bags for life in the boot. Elaine then took it upon herself to come back upstairs for her Nectarcard and then 'popped my head round to say goodbye' only to see me, legs akimbo.

It's not as though I could pretend I was doing anything else because I was butt-naked and the vibe was going at top speed. I didn't even hear the door open – she just apparated at the bottom of my bed. And though I threw my vibe across the room, it was still switched on and juddering across the carpet like a maniacal worm – I had it on the 'Tongue' setting.

Damn woman.

When they came back from shopping it was slightly awks for a bit but, my hormones had settled down and I joined them out in the garden – Jim was picking lettuces, Elaine drinking her coffee and doing her Sudoku, and Tink was chewing her

squeaky duck. I sat cross-legged under the Japanese maple listening to them chit-chat while I read my pregnancy book. We were a family again.

Until after lunch – roast lamb for them and onion and feta tartlet for me, followed by rhubarb crumble. We then sat down for a cup of tea and the afternoon movie – *Forever Young,* starring Mel Gibson.

Now I might be packing more manic than your average street preacher but I think even the mildest person would get irritated watching a film with Jim and Elaine. I was also bone-tired after a massive pastry-heavy meal – the kind of tired where you feel you're constantly dragging around a dead bear whenever you move – and I kept falling asleep only for these sodding World War II fighter planes on the surround sound to keep waking me up.

But if there's one thing an irritable pregnant psychopath who's had her daily wank interrupted doesn't need it's to spend the afternoon explaining the plot of a movie to a pair of half-wits, one of whom was knitting and the other whose eyes were on twenty-two down ending in LY.

It all started when Mel Gibson came out of his suspended animation chamber at the army barracks.

'So where is he now then?' asks Elaine as she *clickety-clack*ed.

'He's in nineteen ninety-two,' I said, fully awake.

'What happened to Norm from *Cheers*?'

'You'll find out, don't worry.'

'He died, did he?' said Jim.

'Who?'

'Mel Gibson?'

'No, he's there look, in the box thing. He's just cold.'

'Why's he cold?'

'Because he's been frozen for fifty years.'

'That wouldn't happen.' *Clickety-clack, clickety-clack.*

'Shall we watch something else?'

Elaine: 'No no, keep this on. I like Mel Gibson.'

By this point I am mentally yanking out all her veins and arteries and wrapping them around her irritating scrag of a neck.

Jim pipes up. 'Is that little lad his son?'

'No, he's a random kid who found the box in the army camp.' *Clickety-clack.* 'Who's that other boy?'

'His friend.'

'Is that Harry Potter?'

'No, it's Elijah Wood. He was Frodo in *Lord of the Rings*.'

Clickety-clack go the needles. *Tappity tap* goes the pen. And then…

Jim: 'Is Jamie Lee Curtis his wife out of the coma?'

'Jamie Lee Curtis is a woman in nineteen ninety-two. She has nothing to do with Mel Gibson, okay? Her son just found the box he was frozen in, that's all.'

'So she's staying with Mel Gibson now?'

'No, *he's* staying with *her* at her house until he can figure out what's happened.'

'And what *has* happened?' *Clickety-clack.*

I sighed and waited for the plot to explain itself. It didn't.

Jim pipes up. 'What's wrong with him now then?'

'He's ageing.'

'Why's that?'

'Because he's been in suspended animation for fifty years and that's what happens to a person's body when they're woken up after all that time.'

'Is that his wife?'

'No, that's Norm from *Cheers*'s daughter in the present day. She's just told Mel Gibson that Norm is dead.'

'Ahh. Why's he in pain?'

'Because he's AGEING. It hurts him because it's happening too quickly.'

'Oh his wife didn't die in the coma then, she's still alive?'

'Yes.'

'Well their little boy would have aged, surely.'

'ELIJAH WOOD IS NOT THEIR SON.'

Clickety-clack. Clickety-clack. Tappity-fucking-tap.

'She'd be an old woman now, his wife, wouldn't she? Was she frozen as well?' *Clickety-clack.*

'No, he thought she died in the coma.'

'When?'

'Back in nineteen fifty-two. Just... watch.'

So the film ends with the great romantic scene at Mel Gibson's not-dead-wife's house where she's old and he's old and finally they're together again. And Jim pipes up...

'Has she got the same disease as Mel Gibson?'

'OH FOR FUCK'S FUCKING COCKING WANKING SAKE!' I screamed, slamming the lounge door behind me – my expletives still rattling the crystal.

I got up to my bedroom, flopped down on the bed and screamed into my pillow until I felt my voice break. I've been here ever since.

Friday, 28th September
– 20 weeks, 5 days

Jim and Elaine made it through the night – I should get a medal for that alone. Elaine's talking to me over breakfast like nothing happened. She even said 'Why don't we make a start on the nursery this weekend? You'd like that wouldn't you?'

I didn't know if she was talking to me or to Tink – she'd been feeding her scrambled egg from a teaspoon at the time.

Apart from shouting at them yesterday, the only bad thing I've done in the past ten weeks is eat a tuna and mayo sandwich – mayo is one of the foods I'm 'specifically not allowed' – on the WOMBAT outing to Warwick Castle last month. Hope I haven't stunted a thumb or something.

Marnie had her baby earlier this month – a boy, 7lb 11oz. No complications, Tim held her hand throughout. They've called him Raphael.

'Oh like the ninja turtle?' I said when she called and told me.

'No, as in a tribute to my dead dad.'

Turns out her dad was Italian before he died, and lo and behold he was called Raphael too. I like the name anyway, though I always fancied the Michelangelo turtle as a kid. He

was stacked and brought the laughs. Is that weird? Fancying a turtle? Add it to the list, I guess.

Had my anomaly scan today – no anomalies as far as could be made out. My sonographer was called Mishti and she had the softest hands I've known so far. She had another bit of news for me too.

'Do you want to know the sex? We can tell today, quite clearly.'

'Yeah, well I already know but you could confirm it for me I guess.'

'Oh, did they tell you at the last scan?'

'No. A mother knows, doesn't she?'

'Sometimes.'

'It is a boy, isn't it?'

Mishti bit her lip. 'Do you want to know for sure?'

'You can tell me for sure?'

'Yes, I can tell you for sure.'

'OK then tell me for sure.'

She pointed at a section of the screen. 'It's a girl.'

'A girl?! That's ridiculous,' I said. 'He sounds like Ray Winstone.'

'Ray Winstone?'

'Yeah, Ray Winstone.'

Mishti didn't seem to know what to say to that. 'I'm not sure I know what you mean.'

'I can hear *him*. Talk to me. From beyond.' Nope, still frowning; still the look of *Imma call security right now if this bitch doesn't start making sense*. 'Sorry, that sounds mad, doesn't it? I… had a dream where Ray Winstone was in… my womb.' I'd managed the impossible – I'd made it sound worse.

She laughed. 'Well it's lovely that you have such an early bond. Lots of mothers and fathers are disappointed when they get the news they're not having the baby they tried for.'

'No, it's not that. I'm just surprised, that's all. I was so sure it was a boy. But it's not. It's a girl. I'm having *a girl*'.

When I got out of there, I was bursting to tell someone. I wanted to tell my mum. But the nearest thing I had to Mum was Seren. So I called her.

It was 6.31 a.m. in Seattle. She answered croakily on the twelfth ring.

'Rhiannon? What do you want? You woke us up.'

'Seren, I wanted to tell you something.'

Mumble mumble *sigh sigh* 'What is it?'

'It's a girl.'

'What's a girl?'

'The baby,' I sobbed. '*My* baby. My baby is a girl. And everything's fine, I didn't lose her! I'm going to order a Doppler from Amazon – all the forums say they're tricky to use and you can get the baby's heartbeat muddled up with your own but I think it'll be fine if I read the instructions. Did you have one? I just want to be able to hear her heartbeat whenever I want, you know?'

'Rhiannon, I didn't even know you were pregnant.'

Saturday, 29th September
– 20 weeks, 6 days

1. *People who wear high-heeled trainers.*
2. *People who spit on pavements.*
3. *Unnecessary film remakes –* Point Break, Mary Poppins, *anything that came after the first* Ghostbusters *or* Jaws, *etc.*

So I may have told you a pie of the porky kind and I'm not proud of it. If there's one place I can be honest it is here so I'll just say it; my good girl act has slipped slightly in the past two months. I've been paying visits, that's all, to Patrick Edward Fenton. I've been driving down to Torquay and monitoring him. Window-shopping you might call it. Once Heather had told me where he worked, where he *still* works, it was a cake walk to find out where he lived and what his preoccupations are. Buying video games. Selling sports equipment. Watching children.

Today I'm back in Torquay. Back in Sportz Madness. Watching him.

Old Foetus Face doesn't seem to mind. No aches and pains as yet. No beyond-the-womb diatribes about how I shouldn't be here, how I shouldn't be doing this, how I should leave Patrick

Edward Fenton alone to live the rest of his life in perfect peace and paedophilia.

Not on my watch.

I hovered over him as he measured a young blond boy's feet for new football boots, clocking every single movement of his fingers on that boy's feet. Watching him chat, as nice as nine pence to the boy's mother, lacing up the boots, chucking in some boot cleaner for free because 'we like our customers to go away happy'.

Ugh. Fake – thy name is Fenton.

When the blond boy had got his boots and gone to the cash register with his mum and her Mastercard, I made my move.

'Hi there, how are you?'

He looked up at me from a sea of boxes and discarded football boots. He smiled – tongue stud, yellow teeth, three fillings.

'You measured me up for some trainers the other week.'

'Oh yeah, they all right? Not too tight?'

'No, they're fine. I'm wearing them now, look.' I showed them off. He nodded. 'Listen, I know this is insane and I promise you I'm not some total weirdo but I'm new in town and I don't know anyone down here. I've seen you in here a few times and you seem lovely. I wondered if you'd like to go for a drink with me?'

'A drink?' he said, wiping his greasy forehead on his wrist.

'Yeah.' I gave it my best smile-and-hair-flick combo and tried to adjust my head so my eyes twinkled kindly in the harsh lighting. 'Just hang out, my treat. I think you're so attractive. I bought two pairs of shoes from you – didn't you guess?'

'No, not at all.' He laughed in that awkward way guys do when you tell them you fancy them. Not that I did, of course. In fact, I found him obscene. And skinny too – an elongated

bag of white bones wrapped in badly drawn tattoos and tied up with manky festival wristbands. And his breath stank of egg. He had nothing going for him – no social etiquette, no banter, no hygiene. Hence the partiality to romancing kindergartners I suppose.

Are you going to tell him about me? Or am I just expected to come along for the ride?

'Yeah, all right,' he grunted. 'I don't finish 'til six though.'

'That's okay. I've got my car down here. I'll pick you up. I'll see you later then. Oh by the way, my name's Lia.'

'Paddy,' he said. 'Well, Patrick.'

'Lovely to meet you, Patrick.'

*

I'm parked up outside The Leprechaun gastro pub. It's the only one in town without CCTV in the car park, as far as I could tell from Google maps. It took three lagers for the pills to kick in. He's snoring on the back seat. I'm sticking to my promise to run him home now. I didn't say *which* home though so technically, anything that happens to him now is his own fault.

Tuesday, 2nd October
– 21 weeks, 2 days

1. *People who can't spell my name, e.g. everyone.*
2. *People who assume it's OK to shorten my name even though that conversation hasn't actually been had, e.g. everyone.*
3. *People who touch my bump without being invited (woman in supermarket, woman at doctor's surgery, child at bus stop).*

Read this article on Mental Floss this morning, all about bad mothers of the animal kingdom. Harp seals are brilliant mums for the first two weeks then once they stop feeding, they abandon their kids and go out on the pull. Cuckoos lay their eggs in other birds' nests cos they can't be bothered to raise them. And pandas are notoriously shite at child-rearing. They eat the wrong food, sleep for about twenty-three hours a day and don't shag nearly enough to conceive.

I am a human panda, it would seem.

And did you know that infanticide is quite common in the animal kingdom? Well I didn't. Lions do it, meerkats do it, and over forty species of monkey do it, according to the nature programme me and Jim watched last night. It's one of the

ways they ensure the survival of the fittest. See it's all well and good encouraging kindness and humanity but what if we are programmed to be brutal? What if it's instinctive?

I'm still having vivid dreams – clearer than I've ever had before. Last night, I dreamt I kept the baby in the freezer and I got her out, placed her on a chopping board and sliced her up thinly between two slices of multiseed bread. I have no idea what this means, other than the fact I will probably be a useless mother, but I always knew that anyway.

Went up to the Well House to make myself feel better. I sat on the edge of the well and ate a bag of Pick and Mix. The screaming started the moment I sat down.

'I'VE BROKEN MY FUCKING FOOT! GET ME OUT YOU BITCH!'

I shone my torch down inside and was met by a flash of brown hair and a dirty, streaked face. He baulked.

'Hi Patrick.' I waved, chewing my cola bottles.

'WHAT THE HELL… ARE YOU DOING? I'M HURT!'

'I know.'

'GET ME OUT!'

'How?'

'I DON'T KNOW, GET HELP. I'M IN SO MUCH PAIN.'

'You hungry?'

'OF COURSE I AM! I'VE BEEN DOWN HERE THREE FUCKING DAYS!'

'Good. Stay hungry.'

I left soon after that exchange. I refuse to be being spoken to like that in my own fake house.

*

I'm not doing any of that nesting stuff I should be doing yet. Nowhere near ready. I haven't even picked out a cot. That's one of the useful things I've learned from the preggo books though – *every* woman thinks she's a useless mother at some point. Nobody feels ready or sane or comfortable in the weeks leading up to the birth. Most women feel vile and uncomfortable and greasy and ugly throughout.

Most women except Leslee Mytesky, that is.

In the spirit of being a good mother, I've started reading mummy blogs to see what kind of things they're doing so I can emulate them. One such blog is the Baby Frog Blog, written by this uber-fit personal trainer called Leslee Mytesky who's based in LA and the worst kind of human to engage with if you're feeling self-conscious.

For a start, she's married to some millionaire who invented this tracing paper that scientists use, meaning Leslee doesn't work – she spends all her time pumping out babies and keeping fit – her 'one true passion'. She posts pictures of her yoga and pole dancing poses and daily smoothies made with chia seeds and flax and spirulina in a bid to shame breeders like me who've surrendered to the lard. She shares inspirational mantras such as 'A negative mind won't allow for a positive life' and 'The body is a temple – keep it clean and pure for your soul to reside in.'

My knife would like to reside in her skull.

She's the kind of woman who would stop halfway through a food sex session to track calories. Leslee's on her sixth kid and the blog chronicles her daily fitness regime – the aforementioned yoga, kettle ball training and jogging.

I've done some deep dives on her Instagram – every other

picture is of her washboard stomach, her uber-cute LA-smile kids, a video of one of them saying 'Good job, Mommie' after tasting a particularly vomitous smoothie at their massive cobalt kitchen table.

She has more followers than I do on Instagram. Mind you, there's an account called Maggie Thatcher's Beef Curtain that has more followers than me on Instagram.

Leslee's husband Chad finds her 'so sexy when she's pregnant' and apparently, they 'can't get enough of each other in the bedroom. Hee! Hee!'

Hoe. Hoe. I wanna slice her self-righteous ears off. I want to hack at her buns of steel and fry them in front of her. I want to puncture her LA air head.

I am *not* a Leslee. There's nothing to rejoice about pregnancy. Everything hurts too much. My head aches and I need to poo except I can't summon the arse muscles to deal with it. It's been baking for three days. The baby could come out first at this rate. Christ if I can't even push out a poo, what hope is there for me squeezing out a kid?

Everything's swelling too. I feel like a Weeble. I smashed all my Weebles as a kid. I made them fall over. And stay over.

There's another blog which features this British model called Claudette Billington-Price who's documenting every step of her pregnancy like it's the most fascinating thing on God's earth. She's had her first kid and has 'snapped back into shape with the help of Pilates'. I guess it helps that she only weighed about four stone wet through to begin with, and has bugger all else to do but exercise. She says 'there's no excuse to pig out'.

Ooh cash me ousside, Bitch.

I'm going to eat what I want when I fucking want, you

sanctimonious sun-kissed, plastic-nosed, pert-breasted, peachy-butted streak of perfect piss.

Vital nutrients my ASS. After spending so long watching what I eat and trying to lose weight (granted I didn't watch it for long or succeed in losing any) my body is now choosing to get as fat as it bloody well likes. And the vital nutrient it needs right now is pastry.

So fuck you, Leslee Mytesky. Fuck you, Claudette Rillington-Place. Fuck you, Elaine.

Fuck.

Fucking.

You.

Good job, Mommie.

Thursday, 4ᵗʰ October
– 21 weeks, 4 days

1. *Doctors' receptionists who have conversations with their colleague about argan oil while you're booking an appointment for a vadge prod.*
2. *Doctors' receptionists who double check your prescriptions in a room full of people so everyone knows you're waiting for VAGILEVE and ANUSOL. ANYONE AT THE BACK NOT QUITE HEAR THAT?*
3. *People who say 'Quite fresh this morning, isn't it?' or 'Isn't it close out today?' e.g. Elaine.*

Went to visit Lana today. Took her some homemade cakes and hung out with her for the morning. I took Tink along too cos I knew she liked dogs. Her washing was drying on an airer in the lounge and Tink peed on her Minion pyjama bottoms. I didn't say anything.

Her fridge was empty so I popped to the corner shop for her and bought her some essentials – milk, eggs, pizza. She's cut herself again – there are ten lines on her right forearm now, where before there had been only three.

'Dear oh dear,' I said. 'You have been in the wars, haven't you? Where's your First Aid kit?'

I am such a good friend. Even when I'm faking it, I'm better than most.

I'm still horny all the time though. I can get turned on at a hog roast or from watching Jim change the bin liner in the Brabantia. Anything long being shoved into anything narrow seems to do it for me. Even a slightly engorged carrot. It's getting ridic. We were had watching *Embarrassing Bodies* the other night and the sight of bollocks the size of gala melons had me fizzing. Then Elaine got all twitchy and switched over to Diamonique on QVC. I could have punctured her eyeballs with her own knitting needles.

I've even found myself flirting with Jim. I'm laughing at his crap jokes, purposely going downstairs in my see-through t-shirt and no bra. It's a major highlight of the day watching him squirm and not look. I wonder if he's the same size as Craig.

We were watching this nature documentary about the animals of the Serengeti last night, me and Jim. We watch a lot of programmes together when Elaine's dropped a Tram cos neither of us sleep well. Mostly gardening programmes or news bulletins with the sound down. He cares so much about stuff. World events especially. I watch his face as he's making his little outraged comments about ISIS and tax hikes and 'those poor, poor people in that bus crash'. I don't get how to make the tears come when I'm watching stuff like that.

Sometimes I get angry, especially if it's a piece on child exploitation or animal cruelty but anger is all there is. That's all there ever is.

Anyway, we were watching this lioness rolling in the sand, inviting the male lion to mate her. I sat down next to him on the sofa with a view to cuddling in. I'd changed into my PJs

and my tits were unbra'd. In the ad break, he got up to make himself a cup of tea and there was definite tenting action south of the border. When he returned he sat in the opposite chair.

The narrator on the documentary talked about the dangers of lions when they're hungry or horny. Not just lions, my friend. Not just lions.

Apparently, The Horn is normal for preggos, so says one of the books, *You and Your Antenatal Vagina*:

You might experience an increase in libido. This is due to increased blood flow in your pelvic regions and raised hormone levels. Your breasts will feel more sensitive and your vagina will be more lubricated so grab your man and prepare for the best sex ever!

I miss having someone who can take care of that for me. Despite being a psychopath, I like cuddling. I miss that after sex. Craig was a cuddler. AJ not so much – he'd give the big spoon a go but more often than not he'd get hard again as his cock poked my butt crack. I wonder if that *Plymouth Star* guy might be up for some one-on-one. I could cuddle the shit out of him.

Leslee Mytesky's husband Chad seems to be practically perfect in every preppy way, of course. This morning she was extolling his virtues yet again in between smoothie recipes. 'Chad likes my body any shape but it's so swell that I can still fit into my skinny jeans a week after giving birth.'

Yeah, put on three stone and see how much Chad loves you then, you self-righteous sow. Chad clearly prefers his women with tits and hips optional – why else is she working so hard? Who puts their own body through that kind of shit for them-selves?

In today's Instagram post, Chad is making a heart shape on

her bump. I want to boil Chad in a vat of her 'super healthy superfoods soup'.

*

It's 3.12 a.m. I've had a full-blown, sweaty-backed, screaming-out-loud nightmare about AJ. We were in the woods, having sex, and then all of a sudden he disappeared and I was alone. It was raining hard. I heard noises and I started running and then I looked behind me and he was chasing after me, screaming. And every step he took, more of his limbs were falling off.

Help me, Rhiannon. Help me. Don't take my baby away.

And his feet fell off and he was running on stumps. And his hands fell off and the blood gushed out. And his arms fell off and one of his legs and he stumbled to the ground and started crawling and I could only stand there and watch as his body slithered towards me like a snake. His head was the last thing to go and it fell into my hands. I was staring at his face and he was saying it over and over again.

'*Don't take my baby away. Don't take my baby away.*'

Now I can't get my heart rate back down and there's something odd happening in my bump – bubbles popping. I'm either gearing up to break wind or the baby's in distress. I've unpacked the Doppler. It's quite neat – a little white electronic box with a small stick attached, like a chunky white crayon on a string. I squeezed the gel on my tummy then ran the crayon over it. For a good ten minutes, I couldn't hear anything. I tried it with earphones in to amplify the sound and eventually got it – the sound of everything being all right.

Thump thump thump. 146 BPM. 152 BPM. 140 BPM.

I was still restless though. The dream was so damn real. What

did it mean, *don't take my baby away*? Take it where? I kept being drawn back towards Elaine telling me we were going to decorate the nursery this weekend – the room she had in mind was the one adjoining mine, what is currently my 'dressing room'. It's got all my Sylvanians in it. Where are my Sylvanians meant to go if the baby has their room? I can't kick them out.

While I waited for the Doppler to reveal its noises, I messed about with my phone – my memory was full so I had to delete some files, mostly Tink on the beach or Jim's garden. I found a video file of AJ that I'd forgotten I had – taken in the woods one lunchtime. Where we'd gone to have sex. On top of where Dad and Dad's friend had buried Pete McMahon. And I had stood there under the Man in the Moon, holding the torch.

In the video, he's got his top off and the sun is glinting off his chest through the trees. He's dancing as I film him from the ground, then he comes over to me, bends down and looks right into the camera singing 'Can't Get You Out Of My Head'. There's thirty-two seconds of it.

And as I played it, the beats came through on the Doppler.

I turned the video off and gradually, the beats returned to normal. I played it again – up they went. Unmistakeable. So hard. I played that song twenty times. I looked on AJ's Facebook to see if there were any more videos of him and found one of him playing a guitar and singing – 'Never Tear Us Apart'. His audition tape for *Australia's Got Talent*.

The Doppler beats grew louder again. It was unmistakeable. And as AJ sang, my tears rushed at me, all at once, before I could hold them back.

'You love your daddy, don't you?' I said into the darkness of my bedroom.

No voice came back. It didn't need to. I played the singing again and again and listened to the beats multiply each time. 'I'm glad you loved him. It means you're not like me.'

Friday, 5th October
– 21 weeks, 5 days

1. Detective Inspector Nnedi Géricault.

I've pooed! It was humungous and painful and looked a bit like Harvey Weinstein but it's out now, running wild and free. I feel like I've achieved something this morning. I almost announced it when I came downstairs, I was so proud of myself, but I was stopped in my tracks by the sound of Jim's serious voice talking to someone in the lounge.

I pushed the door open and at once my heartburn ignited.

'Rhiannon, this is DI… '

'Géricault,' I said. 'We've met. Hello again.' Tink had been on her lap and on opening the door she scampered over to me. Tink, not DI Géricault.

Looks like she's got Tink onside then…

The woman stood and offered her hand. I shook it. She was halfway through a cup of tea and a ginger nut.

'Where's Elaine?' I asked Jim, knowing her struggles with the police.

'She's having a lie down, love,' he said. Translation: she's upstairs necking Tramadol like Smarties and listening at the bedroom door. 'DI Géricault wanted a quick word.'

He didn't say who he wanted a quick word *with* exactly, but judging by the way Géricault was staring at me, I guessed.

'If that's all right?' she added.

'Yes of course,' I said. I looked at Jim, hoping he would get the hint to take Tink out and leave us to it, but Jim being Jim wouldn't get a hint if I stapled one to his ball sack, so I had to ask him. I took his warm place on the sofa, facing her. 'Sorry about the pyjamas. I didn't realise how late it was. Can't seem to get enough sleep at the moment.'

'That's fine,' she said, flicking over the pages of her pocket book. 'How is everything with the baby?'

I puffed out and held both sides of my belly for maximum fed-up effect. 'Oh you know, getting there. I'm half way at least but, yeah, so tired all the time.' I almost told her about the poo but I guessed it wasn't the time. Or the person. Or the subject. Who *can* you tell something like that? Who'd be interested? A doctor? It was rather enormous.

I had expected Géricault to enter into a conversation about how *she* felt when *she* was pregnant but she didn't. She didn't mention having kids at all. She smiled a smile that didn't reach her eyes and flicked her notepad over. 'So I was telling Mr Wilkins that there's been a new development. We have, as of yesterday morning, charged Craig with two more murders.'

My mouth dropped and my hand immediately went to it as though to catch whatever was going to fall out. 'Oh my god. Are you serious?'

She reached across to an iPad on her armrest, flicked it on and swiped. Then she turned it around to face me. Pictures of two men – mugshots – one gaunt and unshaven, the other black with gold stud earrings and pockmarks on his forehead. I

recognised them – Red Gloves and Balaclava Boy, aka The Blue Van Men, who'd tried to kidnap and rape Heather Wherryman.

'Who are they?' I asked, Confusion Face plastered on like mud pack.

'Kevin Fraser and Martin Horton-Wicks. Burglars, petty criminals and, we believe, multiple rapists. On April tenth they were—'

'Oh god I remember,' I butted in. 'I was working at the *Gazette* at the time. Their van went over the quarry.'

'Yes that's right.'

'And you think Craig did it?'

'We're fairly sure it's linked to this case, yes. We need to know from you where Craig was that night.'

'April tenth,' I said, searching in my mind. 'He was probably at home.'

'Probably?'

'April tenth, April tenth,' I said again. 'Can I check my phone? It'll be in there, whatever we were doing.'

'Sure.'

I got my phone out of my dressing gown pocket and hit Calendar. *Pidge's Birthday Sleepover*, I'd written. 'I was at my friend's house. Pidge – Alice Peale. It was her birthday sleepover.'

'You were having a sleepover?' she smiled.

'Yes. Well, Netflix and Ben and Jerry's. Makeovers, girly stuff, you know.'

'And Craig was there too?'

'He would have been back at the flat I guess.'

'So he definitely wasn't with you?'

'No. Have you asked Lana Rowntree? If he knew I was going to be out for the whole night... '

Géricault sipped her tea. 'We've already spoken to Miss Rowntree. She says she wasn't with Craig.'

Oh deary, deary me.

'Looks like he doesn't have an alibi then,' I said, before realising that sounded too chipper. I brought out the big guns – the middle-distance stare and tears, silent and pure. 'Shit. Five people. He killed *five* people?'

'In fact, Miss Rowntree has reneged on both her alibis for him.'

I concentrated on frowning. 'She wasn't with him on New Year's?'

'Apparently not.' Her stare was unwavering. 'Are you in touch with Lana Rowntree at all, Rhiannon?'

'No, why would I be? Can't stand the woman.'

'You haven't spoken to her at all recently?'

'Not since I went into the office a few weeks after Craig was arrested. Suffice to say I haven't been back since.' She was waiting for more. 'There was an incident. I hit her. Quite hard. A few times.'

Géricault's eyes went all catlike and thin. 'She didn't report it?'

'She didn't press charges, no. Oh, come to think of it I did drop some flowers round a couple of weeks ago as an apology. Sorry, baby brain.'

The lounge door creaked open and Tink scurried in. She jumped up on Géricault's lap and started licking her cheek manically. She was bloody *warning* her about me, I know she was. *Don't.* Lick. *Trust.* Lick. *Her.* Lick. *She.* Lick. *Kills.* Lick. *People.* Géricault didn't lose her cool once – she just plonked her back down on the carpet.

'She likes you,' I giggled.

The detective scribbled a note in her book.

'I guess you think I'm pretty stupid, huh?' I said, wiping my cheek. 'Missing all this. Not seeing what he was like.'

She flicked her head up. 'Let's keep an open mind for now. Tell me about Julia Kidner.'

Cue White Guy blinking gif. 'I'm sorry?'

'The woman found in the quarry. You were at the same school together.'

Busted.

'She went to the same school as *me* but I wouldn't say I knew her, no. We weren't friends.'

'Why didn't you tell us this information earlier? When her body had been identified? When you knew Craig had been linked to her death?'

'I didn't think it was important. She was only at my school for a year. It was a big school. Our paths barely crossed. What are you getting at?'

'Rather a coincidence that your boyfriend is accused of murdering one of *your* school friends, isn't it?'

'No. She wasn't my friend'.

'Craig's DNA all over the scene, all over her body. And yet Craig, we know for a fact, was nowhere near that quarry on the night she died.'

'And?'

'He was at a football match in London.'

'So?'

'It points to him having an accomplice. Or maybe, he didn't kill Julia Kidner at all – someone else is making it *look* like he did.'

I was aware of the muscles around my mouth. 'Framing him, you mean?'

'We're looking at all possibilities.'

Hmm. Did she smell my porky pies? Was she waiting for a confession?

'I don't know what to tell you.' I stared down at her hand of missing fingers. She saw me looking. 'How did you lose them?'

She didn't wait a second. 'Where were you on the night Julia was murdered, Rhiannon?'

I sat back, doing my best impression of shocked and appalled. 'Am *I* under suspicion now too? Do I need a lawyer?'

'No, we just need to get everything straight. Where everyone was. Where everyone *says* they were. You didn't go to Wembley with Craig?'

'I hate football. I was at home for most of the evening.'

'You know that for sure?'

'Yes.'

'Most of the evening?'

I sighed. 'I took the bins out, walked Tink and went down to see my neighbour, Mrs Whittaker. She lives in one of the flats downstairs. At least she used to, she's moved now. I used to go round and watch *Midsomer Murders* with her sometimes, to keep her company. She can vouch for that.'

'We've already spoken to all your neighbours,' she said, all soft-voiced like she was ordering cocktails. She scrolled back through her notes. 'Mrs Whittaker didn't mention you popping over that night.'

'She has Alzheimer's. She forgets things easily.'

Géricault looked at me for the longest time. I could not read her at all. She had no smell about her, no emotional giveaways.

She was like a book with a blank cover and no writing in. The human equivalent of a closed door. I've never met anyone so emotionally closed off. Apart from myself, I suppose.

'Where does Lana say she was that night then? Have you asked her?'

'She was at her flat. Alone,' said Géricault with a sniff.

'There you are then.'

'Yes. There I am then.'

I wondered if she had something else on me or if she was boxing clever. The only thing linking me to Julia that night is Henry Cripps' car, which I'd used to transport her body in. But how would Géricault know that? She wouldn't. She doesn't know anything for sure but that's what they teach you in the police isn't it – Assume Nothing, Believe Nobody, Challenge Everything.

Don't say another word.

So I didn't. For several minutes. She scribbled in the pad. I got up and stared out of the bay window.

Finally, the detective started packing away her iPad and notebook and stood up. 'I think that's all for today.' My heart was thumping and my body washed over with relief. 'Thanks for your time.' We shook hands again. 'Will you thank your father-in-law for the tea?'

'He's not my father-in-law. Craig and I aren't married.'

'Oh sorry, of course you're not,' she said, scratching her temple with one of the few fingers she had on her left hand. 'It's good of them to put you up though, isn't it? Let you into their lives like they have.'

'I don't have anyone else,' I said, guiding her out to the front door and turning the latch. 'They're good people. And I *am* carrying their grandchild.'

'Yes,' she said, stepping outside, before turning to me on the doorstep. 'Oh, we tried to get you on your mobile. The one starting oh-seven-one-eight.'

'Shit, sorry, yeah I had to get a new one.'

'Could we have it for our records?'

'Sure.' She gave me her number and I sent her a blank text to test it.

'Great, thanks for your help. I'll be in touch. Bye now.'

I closed the door behind her and put my forehead on the hallway wall to cool it down. I was shaking. 'What the hell was that?'

She's onto you.

'No she's not.'

Why else would she ask for your new number?

'For reference.'

It's only a matter of time before she starts questioning why you're carrying around a burner phone when your old one was on contract.

'You're being paranoid.'

What if she checked the triangulation of your phone and Craig's phone on the night of the Victory Park murder? I've seen them do that on Line of Duty.

'I always turn my phone off when I'm about to... why would she be checking *my* phone anyway? *Craig's* the suspect.'

Police check everything. She could be looking into forensic anomalies.

'What anomalies?'

A long hair at a crime scene? The odd clothing fibre? You on CCTV in Birmingham killing that taxi driver?

'They're still investigating that. Anyway, didn't ISIS claim that one?'

No.

'Either way, *I* haven't been troubled.'

Doesn't mean you're in the clear. And now she knows you and Julia went to the same school. What if she finds some witness who saw her bully you? You're in trouble, Mummy.

'Play it cool. She knows nothing. There's too much evidence against Craig already to suspect me.'

But Craig wasn't there the night Julia died. They know someone else did her.

'Look at the facts. Lana's in our pocket, Craig's in the slammer, and they have no motive, no opportunity, no witnesses and no weapon to say otherwise. Everything's rosy in the garden.'

Yeah. For now.

Saturday, 6th October
– 21 weeks, 6 days

1. *People who drag chairs into tables on hardwood floors.*
2. *People – someone dies on Twitter – 'Oh such sad news. Thoughts with friends and family' and 30 seconds later, they're throwing out party emojis to celebrate a Harry Styles single (e.g. Scarlett from Pudding Club).*
3. *People who answer their phone while talking to me, e.g. Marnie.*

Who needs Géricault when you've got God on your side? I was reading Romans and I came across chapter 13: 4: '… if thou do that which is evil, be afraid; for he beareth not the sword in vain: for he is the minister of God, a revenger to execute wrath upon him that doeth evil.'

How bout dat? Turns out, I am doing God's work. Sort of. In a way. Who could wish for a better wingman?

Another note from the Phantom Bad Handwriter this morning – 'To My Sweet Messy House'. That's the fourth one we've had. The photographers were back out in force on the doorstep too, and there was a new buzz about them, like a swarm of worker bees. Only one bee had got the memo that I

like doughnuts though. I was presented with an open box of Krispy Kremes.

'Hey Rhiannon,' said *Plymouth Star* holding them out to me as though they were an ermine-lined cushion and crown. 'Fancy a Strawberry Gloss today? Or a Lemon Cheesecake? Chocolate Dreamcake? I got Blueberry Glaze too cos I know pregnant women are supposed to eat blueberries.'

'A plain one please. Why gild the lily?'

He looked inside the box. 'Oh. Think someone had that one already.' He glared behind him at his cameraman who was already clicking at me despite the stained PJs and zit cream on my chin. For once I didn't care. I think I've actually reached that point in pregnancy where your dignity goes out the window and you're immune to how your appearance might offend people.

I ignored the hubbub of the other journalists and beckoned *Plymouth Star* guy forwards. 'What are you after this morning then?' I asked, removing the Chocolate Custard and stuffing half of it in my face. The net curtains in the lounge twitched. Elaine was watching me from behind the bay window.

'I wanted to get your take on the latest two charges. Any chance?'

'I'm shocked and appalled, obviously.'

'Yeah?' he said, all buoyant and eyes-alive. 'Craig's something of a hero this morning. Have you seen The *Mirror*?'

'I try not to look in a mirror these days if I can help it.'

'No no,' he said, getting out his phone. He held it out to show me. Top story of The *Mirror* newspaper: **GRIPPER KILLER TARGETED SEX OFFENDERS: New vigilante theory about Sicko Wilkins.**

'Oh right,' I said, mouth still working on the doughnut.

'It's changed the mood of the nation towards him somewhat this morning. He's becoming a bit of a hero. At least three of the people he's charged with killing were alleged sex offenders. He's all over social media.'

He clicked open his Twitter feed. The top five trends were all about Craig:

#Vigilante

#TheGripper

#BlueVan

#WilkinsIsOurSaviour

#Dexter

'They've forgotten about the woman in the quarry then,' I said.

'Well the *Mail* are reporting that it's not looking likely that she was one of his now, since she doesn't fit the pattern, see?'

'Not their pattern I suppose.'

'Public seem to believe it.'

'Interesting.'

'So could we get your view on it?' He flashed me the most brilliant smile I'd ever seen. Better than the last one.

I flashed him one back. I've never said no to a man who brings me doughnuts. He was hot and horny and though I might have been mistaking 'I want you' signals for 'I want to exploit you' ones, nor did I care.

'Want some?' I held out the last chunk of doughnut. He hesitated, only for a sec, then leaned forward and wrapped his mouth around it, slowly, his lips grazing my fingertips. It was the most sexual moment I'd had in months. Something throbbed south of the border. I'd forgotten I had one.

He laughed. 'Great. All right if we come in then?'

'No, not here. My mother-in-law can't deal. I'll meet you at

the café on the beach – Bay Bites. Say one p.m? Give me time to wash my carcass.'

He nod-grinned and closed the doughnut box, holding my stare. 'I'll bring the rest of these with me. My name's Freddie, by the way.'

'See you later, Freddie-by-the-way.' I held his stare as I sashayed back into the house, more Rhianna than Rhiannon.

I closed the door behind me. I wasn't misreading those signals but I didn't quite understand them. Maybe he had a preggo fetish, I thought. Or he was a feeder – one of those guys who keeps a thirty-stone woman and pours melted ice cream down her neck through a funnel. I could be one of *them*. That'd solve the man drought *and* the serial killing in one fell swoop. I'd be too fat to kill *and* I'd get regular cunnilingus. Mmm, that'll do Babe, that'll do.

'Who was that?' said Elaine, wringing her hands the moment my slippers hit the kitchen lino.

'Local press. Nothing major.'

'Did you say anything to them?'

'No, of course not.'

'You're lying, Rhiannon. You talk to that one every day, I've seen you.'

'I feel sorry for him. He's only a junior reporter, looking for a break.'

'You've arranged to meet with him. What are you going to say?'

'Nothing. He brought doughnuts again. I panicked.'

'Don't go, please. I beg you. Nothing good can come of talking to those vultures. They'll twist everything you say, I know they will. Please Rhiannon.'

I floundered. There I was, torn between another possible sexual moment with Freddie-by-the-way at the café, where we could lick toast crumbs from each other's palms or something, and Elaine's pitiful pleading.

'Of course I won't talk to them,' I sighed, enveloping her in a hug.

She cried in my arms. 'Don't let them take you as well.'

*

Patrick's no fun anymore. He doesn't scream as much now. I sit there on the edge of the well, pouring water on him or chucking down the odd Go Ahead biscuit that Elaine keeps buying me but which I do not like. He just sits down there, dry-sobbing, saying his leg's gone green.

Once people reach that end-of-life stage it all gets quite dull. I should probably do something about him soon. Didn't think that bit through. Bit of a hairy moment today when Jim was talking about going up there.

'No need,' I said. 'It's fine. I've been going up to check on it for you.'

'Yes I know, but I could take my tools up and see if anything needs doing before half term. Might get a few bookings then if we're lucky, do you think?'

'Yeah, might do. But there's no need to, Jim, honestly. The place is quite tidy and I've been keeping the lawn down and watering the plants for you.'

'Ah, you are a good girl. I don't know what I'd do without you, Rhiannon. You've been such a tonic the last few months.'

'Well it keeps me out of mischief, doesn't it?'

He put his arm around me and gave me a squeeze.

Pudding Club this afternoon was as noisy and intimidating as before only this time with added sunburn and itching thrown in thanks to the climate change induced Autumn heatwave– we met on the beach for a picnic. We all had news – Nev was getting over 'the worst cold ever', Helen's Fair Trade coffee morning had been, and I quote 'a riotous success'. Scarlett's mother-in-law had been diagnosed with Parkinson's. The details of how the family were told were so drawn out.

I switched off and imagined the seagulls pecking at chips on the esplanade behind her were actually plucking out the scant remains of her brain.

I hadn't seen Marnie in a week and though we'd kept in touch via WhatsApp, I'd missed her. She looked haggard – her eyes were all sunken in and her hair was unkempt. Her jumper was on backwards and there was a small white stain on her leggings knee. I didn't say anything.

Pin brought along more food than any of us could possibly get through – mostly puddings of course – homemade vegan brownies, gluten free date and walnut cake, lemon meringue pie, frangipane tartlets, and orange and ginger cupcakes. This seemed to entitle her to hold court for two hours about her husband's promotion and pay rise. Marnie and I rolled our eyes until they quite ached. I'd only brought along Nutella sandwiches and shop bought jam tarts. Marnie had forgotten to bring anything at all.

'Maybe if we lie down and pretend we're asleep, she'll stop talking,' she whispered and lay her towel out behind her on the sand. I copied.

'I wouldn't mind so much if the other three were better company.'

Marnie chuckled. 'I know. Helen's such a know all.'

'Scarlett's thicker than a thigh pie.'

She giggled. 'Nev's tits scare me.'

'Me too!'

Scarlett steered the subject onto a movie she'd watched the night before starring Ruby Rose.

'Oh I dig her so much!' said Nev, pouring out a cup of elderflower pressé. She looked ready to pop with her twins. 'She's my spirit animal.'

'You can't say that,' said Helen, a glob of lemon curd dripping from her chin to her placenta-coloured sun dress.

'Say what?'

'That something is your "spirit animal". It's cultural appropriation.'

'You say that about KFC. I'm only chatting informally.'

'It's dehumanising, Neveah.'

'To who?'

'Well, to Native Americans for one thing.'

'Oh are you Native American then, Helen?'

'You don't have to be Native American to be offended by that.'

'God, you can't say anything without someone folding their tits over it.'

'I'm only schooling you so you don't get shut down by somebody else.'

'I don't need *schooling*, Darlin'. I think you'll find lots of people say it.'

'Doesn't make it right. Do you know, we commit hundreds

of racist micro-aggressions every single day…' She then started listing them all.

Pin fell asleep, Scarlett reapplied sun cream, and me and Marnie ventured up to the sand dunes with Raph in the papoose leaving Nev to get the lecture full throttle.

'When did this become life?' I sighed as we sat down.

Marnie laughed. 'She sent us all a glossary of terms we shouldn't say a while back. All "dehumanising" phrases that have leaked into common parlance. I literally don't know what's safe to say anymore.' A grizzle floated up from the papoose. 'Oh god, Raph, don't wake up yet, not yet, not yet please.'

'So… childbirth then,' I said. 'Tell me.'

She stared out towards the horizon. 'You don't want to know.'

'Nightmare?'

'The worst.'

'Did Adolf mop brow and play his Wagner tape for you to relax to?'

I got the side-eye. 'My husband was there throughout, yes. He cried when he cut Raph's cord.'

'When's he going to cut yours?'

She sighed, rubbing Raph's back. He kicked his legs so she got him out and cuddled him into her neck, rocking him side to side. She closed her eyes. 'I could honestly fall asleep right now.'

'Do it,' I said. 'I can watch Raph for you.'

'Mmm,' she murmured, handing him over to me as she lay back on the sand. 'Thanks. Just ten minutes.'

A family had appeared along the beach: old codger Grandad showing off his footie skills, pregnant Mum being the ball boy, Granny misfiring kicks like a remedial and Daddy recording the memory on his phone for when they're all dead. A little kid

squealed and ran after the ball. They were all smiling. It was a memory they'd all clutch onto for dear life one day.

I held Marnie's baby into my neck and stroked his head. He was softer than petals and his eyelashes fluttered on my skin. I rocked him like she had, rubbed his back like she had, imagined he was my baby. Imagined this was normal. That this was what I was born to do. And although I would have certainly protected him from any attack as though my life depended on it, I did not want to hold him infinitely. I did not feel the need to hold him again.

I sometimes forget that one of these is in me, cooking away. That it's not just some lump of dough AJ's squirted in my oven that I'm trying not to burn. Some days it's merely a protrusion. I don't stroke it all the time like Marnie used to. Like I see other 'mums' do. Maybe that would help. Raph started grizzling and Marnie instantly woke up.

'I'm here,' she said, levering herself up and forcing her eyes open.

'He's fine,' I said. 'I've got him.'

'Oh thanks,' she said, lying back down. 'He hasn't pooed, has he?'

I sniffed. 'Nope. He fancied a bit of Auntie Rhee time, I think.'

She smiled. 'You're good with him.'

'Mmm, what if I'm shit with my own though?'

'You won't be,' she said. 'You'll love her to death.'

'That's what I'm afraid of,' I mumbled.

'Huh?'

'Nothing.'

She turned over onto her side, propping her head up with

her bundled coat. 'Have you got your nursery sorted out yet? Cots and bedding?'

'No.'

'We could go shopping again, pick out some bits.'

'I'll probably do most of it online. Or pay someone to do it for me.'

'But it's the fun part, shopping for baby things. You haven't got to the nesting stage yet but you will.'

'What's the point of nesting when I don't have a nest?'

'You've got your own storey at Jim and Elaine's,' she chuckled. 'Two grandparents on tap. You've got so much support, Rhiannon.'

'They're not the grandparents.'

'What?'

'Craig's not the dad.'

'Oh. Right.'

'A guy from work. He's gone travelling for a year.'

'Does he know?'

'Yeah. He doesn't want to be involved.'

Ugh. I don't know how you can bear to look yourself in the mirror, Mummy.

'Are you going to tell Jim and Elaine the truth?'

'Where would I go if I did? I don't have anyone else. In an ideal world they *would* be the grandparents. In an ideal world this *would* be Craig's baby. And he wouldn't have strayed and I wouldn't have needed to... '

'To what?'

'Move in with them,' I said. 'I don't know. I watch other mums, I watch you, doing the mum thing, cleaning up puke and kissing his forehead and you do it so randomly.'

185

'It's instinct. You love them so you can't help but show it.'

'What if I *don't* love it though?'

'You will. I told you, it's instinctive.'

'But I don't *have* the same instincts as other people.'

'You do. You just don't *think* you do.'

'Me and Jim watched this documentary the other night, all about the science of being born. It said that babies are susceptible to their mothers' fears or anxieties. They inherit them.'

'I guess that makes sense,' said Marnie, eyes drifting towards the boats on the water.

'Well what if a mother *has* no fear? Does that mean the child won't have fear as well? How will it know how to stay away from things that will hurt it?'

'Like what?'

'Hot stoves. Tall trees. Paedophiles. There's millions of threats to a baby in the world. How the hell am I supposed to keep her safe?'

'You'll be okay, Rhiannon. I know you will.'

'How do you know? You haven't known me for long. You don't know what I'm like. They had these lab rats on the documentary and the mother rat was biting and attacking the scientists trying to take her babies away. At one point she actually *ate* one of her babies because she thought it was the safer option. She'd rather *kill* her own baby than let anyone else kill it.'

'You're being irrational,' said Marnie. 'You're going to be a fantastic mother. You're already worried about how you're going to protect her; doesn't that tell you something?'

'No.'

'You might not think you feel love but you do. It comes naturally.'

186

'But I read this article about mothers who can't bond—'

'Then stop reading the articles,' she said. 'You *will* be fine. If I can do it, any idiot can. And if you need help, I'll be here.'

Something shiny happened in my chest. The funicular railway clanked to a halt behind us. 'Seriously?'

'Of course.' She checked her watch when she said it, which irked me.

'Why don't we take a trip on that?' I suggested. 'See the bay from the top of the cliffs?'

She turned and looked at it and laughed. 'You must be joking.'

'Go on. It's been going since Victorian times. It's never broken down.'

'No, I can't, Rhiannon. I can barely look at the thing. I fell off a flying fox when I was nine. Been scared stiff of heights ever since.'

'That means Raph's going to have a morbid fear of heights too then. He'll be the only one of his mates who'll wimp out at Alton Towers. He'll never get in a plane, go travelling—'

'That won't happen, I won't let it.'

'You won't be able to do anything about it. He'll see you're afraid of heights and he'll be afraid of them too. You'll pass it on.'

'I won't.'

'You will. Don't think, do it. Don't let it control you – you control *it*. Kill the fear stone dead.'

'What are you afraid of, Rhiannon?'

'Nothing,' I lied.

She smiled. 'I'd love not to be afraid of anything. I'm such a wuss.'

'Then don't be.'

'Maybe,' she said, looking at the railway again as it began its slow ascent. She turned back and closed her eyes. 'Not today though, okay?'

'Fair enough.'

'Hey, I have a new question for you,' she said, looking past me along the beach. 'Why is that woman watching us?'

There, on a bench overlooking the bay, about 200 yards away from us, sat DI Géricault, face turned in our direction. Not reading, not waving, just looking my way. And something heavy replaced the shiny in my chest, almost as though it had never been there.

Thursday, 11ᵗʰ October
– 22 weeks, 4 days

Jim drove us up to Bristol today to visit Craig. We had to be there half an hour before the visit time, and we were shown to a separate building to check our credentials and have our bags searched. Some paunchy little barnacle in a uniform gave me evils as he pawed through my rucksack, which I had to leave in a locker. And I had to have my photo and fingerprints taken and my passport checked. Literally. I mean, the fuck?!

Anyway, rigmarole over we made our way over to the main prison. Got another pat down and a metal detector thing swiped over me and then we had to go through an airport security doorway and all our accessories – phones, wallets, bags, coats – were sent through a conveyor belt camera thing. The doors were all biometric and solid metal. No escaping that bad boy.

And there was nothing natural around at all. No flowers, nothing green. The corridors smelled like sweat and cigarettes. And tar – hot tar.

Claustrophobia was on me like a cape as we sat at a table in the boiled cabbage-stinking main hall, waiting for the prisoners. In one corner of the room by the tuck shop was a kids' play area with tiny plastic chairs, buckets of Lego and a large square play

rug bearing the motif of a busy town. Six kids headed straight for it and started tipping out blocks and toy cars.

Craig looked awful. He'd lost about two stone, his skin was the grey colour of the walls and he was wearing a cheap standard-issue grey tracksuit with no strings, and Velcro trainers, all of which looked too big for him.

It was hella awkward. We didn't hug and he wouldn't even look at me for the first five minutes. He could have been a stranger, not the guy I'd lived with for the past four years. He occasionally glanced down at my stomach when Jim was doing the talking, but I might as well have not been there. Jim tried to get a conversation going about Elaine's church rota, then the new town bypass. The Well House. What a whizz I was at computers.

He still didn't look at me.

'I spoke to your brief,' Jim said. 'It's looking like June for the trial.'

Craig shook his head, mouth all thin. 'I'm not staying in here 'til then. I'll top myself.'

'Don't you dare say that, Son,' said Jim. 'You've got responsibilities now.' Jim pointed at my stomach. 'Don't you forget that or her for a second.'

Craig glared at me. 'They showed me photos in the last interview. Photos of what I'd "done". That Julia woman… her fingers were cut off. Hair missing. Her neck was cut to the bone.'

I feigned morning sickness and said I needed to get up and move around a bit. Jim pulled my chair out for me and I went to the tuck shop. As I waited in the queue, I turned to look back at our table. Craig was looking at me for the first time over his dad's shoulder. His eyes were all watery.

He was pleading with his dad, voice lowered, leaning in. Jim

kept shaking his head and looking away and doing these deep sighs.

When I got back to the table, an officer approached and Jim stood up. 'I'm going to the loo, love. I'll take my time. He wants to talk to you privately.'

'All right,' I said, putting his uneaten KitKat and tea down between us.

The officer led Jim back through the door we'd come through. Craig didn't say anything for the longest time. His head was tilted and he was fiddling with the hem of his hoody against the table.

'Did your dad show you the baby scan? It's as big as a pear now. I don't know what type of pear. One of those little yellow ones I suppose.'

'Police have charged me with two more,' he said.

'I know,' I said.

'Them blokes in the quarry. Matched my boot print on a patch of mud. And they found blood on my black hoody.' His leg went into jiggle overdrive under the table. He was like an engine running. Breathing heavy. Eyes down.

'I know,' I said again.

And then he looked up at me. 'They've got mobile phone records that say my tablet was at the scene, even though I know *I* wasn't. I was home that night. You said you were at your mate's for a sleepover.'

'I was.'

'Bullshit!'

'Keep your voice down, darling… '

'Don't "darling" me. *My* footprints. *My* DNA. That… thing hidden in *my* van. There are only three people on this earth who could have done this: you, me or Lana.'

I afforded him a double eyebrow raise. I thought he deserved it.

'And Lana *was* with me the night that van went into the quarry. Know how I know? Because I was fucking her in *our* bed. So that leaves you.'

I blinked. I breathed. I blinked again. And I shrugged.

'Is that all you've got?' he shouted, fast blinking. He looked possessed.

Two officers made for our table in a pincer movement. Craig held up his hands in a mock surrender and after a warning, they moved away.

'Say something, Rhiannon.' He said it through gritted teeth. His eye-water juddered. He looked like he was ready to pounce. Like every sinew in his body wanted to strangle me. 'Four years I've lived with you. We were going to get married. We had a future.'

The play area was getting rowdy – two little boys were arguing over a box of bricks. One had a Mohican and brand new Nikes, the other was wearing a Buzz Lightyear onesie and baby Dr Martens. They started screaming at each other and Buzz wrenched the bucket from The Last of the Mohicans' hands and he fell to his arse with an earth-shattering shriek. Adults appeared and pulled them apart, then they started crying and kicking out and the adults were swearing and Buzz's mum smacked his arse for embarrassing her.

'Say. Something. To. Me. Rhiannon.'

'You been raped yet?'

He looked winded.

'I guess being the alleged killer of sex offenders makes you a bit of a hero in this place, doesn't it? Admit it – it's been easier since they started calling you a vigilante rather than a perv.'

He stared at me.

'Lana's reneged on her alibis, so that's a problem, isn't it? But let's say for argument's sake she's framed you. Be easier, wouldn't it? Lana planted that guy's penis in your van. And *she* killed that man in the park and put your semen on his coat. And Julia Kidner – she raped her post mortem with a dildo covered in your semen. And why? Because you dumped her. That's all. Crime of passion. She already has more cuckoo than Switzerland so it's an easy assumption to make, isn't it?'

He wouldn't take his big eyes off me. His mouth opened to speak and though I waited, no sound emerged.

'In fact, I'm pretty sure that if I go over to her flat right now, I'll find jam jars of your semen in one of her cupboards. Let's say a kitchen cupboard, under the sink. She borrowed your hoody. And wore your boots. And framed you for all of it. Because she's obsessed with you, see?'

He shook his head, eyes on mine.

'And you almost *destroyed* her when you dumped her for me and the baby. She's had multiple bad relationships and she thought you were The One. Everyone at work used to say she was a car crash. She's tried to take her own life a few times. She has all those old scars on her arms. I mean if anyone was going to do something like this, it would be Lana, wouldn't it?'

A single tear trickled down his left cheek. 'Why?'

'Anger, I suppose. It's so destructive. You can only control an urge for so long. And then one day, something'll happen – a bereavement, a redundancy, finding out your beloved is eating some other girl like ass-pie – and the urge comes rushing back. Like fucking Backstreet.'

'Jesus...' He seemed to be hyperventilating.

'So, here it is: this was all Lana; that broken woman with the

scars up her arms and strange little jars in her flat. She flipped. Once she's in the frame, all you have to do is bide your time. Let your defence team switch their investigation from "I didn't do it, Sarge, honest!" to "I didn't do it but I know the woman who did." And hey presto. Some compelling new evidence comes to light and you're off the hook. Free to look through windows without bars again. Free to dance on grass barefoot. Free to watch your child grow up.'

'I can't do that to her.'

'Yes you can. And you will.'

'No.'

'Yes.'

'Oh my god. Why are you doing all this? I slept with her, that's all. Most women would cut up my clothes or stab me and get over it.'

'Well in case you hadn't noticed, I'm not most women.'

'I won't let you do this. You're a psycho. A fucking—bunny-boiler.'

I gasped. 'How *dare* you. I would *never* boil a bunny. But if that's the way you want to play it then fine. Your. Loss.'

'What do you mean?'

'It means, Craig – I'm living with *your* parents.'

He swallowed.

'And I'm carrying *your* baby.'

A tear rolled down his other cheek and his head dipped completely. The defiant stare had vanished, replaced with a grey wash of nothingness. He sat back in his chair, unable to catch his breath. The last time I'd seen his face that shade of grey Hodor had snuffed it on *Game of Thrones*.

I looked down at my stomach for extra effect. 'I'm capable of everything, Craig. You should have realised that by now.'

Another tear fell. He looked back up at me. 'You must want me dead.'

I shook my head. 'No, I don't. Sometimes it's more fun to watch them squirm.'

Jim was coming back over.

'Lana—' Craig mewed.

'Yes?' I cupped my ear for extra effect.

'—killed them.'

Jim reached the table and frowned when he saw Craig's face. Craig was looking at him, as though pleading with his dad to read his mind.

'He got a bit upset, about the baby,' I told him. 'But I told him everything was fine on the last scan. Ten tiny fingers, ten tiny toes.'

Two tears now, four tears, quick succession.

'He'll be out in no time,' I said. 'Won't he, Jim?'

Jim sighed. 'The police aren't looking for anyone else, Son.'

'They will,' I said. 'We have to hope.' I looked at Craig who looked to be on the verge of another bitch fit. I stroked my belly. 'You need to get your defence team onto it, Craig. For your child's sake, if not yours.' I leant across the table and kissed his cheek. 'Lana's your Obi Wan.'

It seemed to take a while for him to get his shit together but eventually, and miraculously, he did. And he said the words 'Lana did it.'

Excellent. Cue *Mr Burns hands*.

Tuesday, 16th October
– 23 weeks, 2 days

1. *Woman who barged past me in Marks & Spencer in a too-tight blouse.*
2. *People who pick up their dog's shit in a bag – then leave the bag.*
3. *My own appetite – I'm so starving all the time, Elaine has begun leaving ready-chopped fruit out overnight, wrapped in cling film, so I can attack them first thing in the morning like some kind of ravenous Santa.*

I had another nightmare – this one set exclusively in the bath tub at Mrs Whittaker's flat. I woke up, sweat running off me in rivers. This time, it wasn't AJ I was cutting up – it was the baby. I was chopping up the baby.

It was on my mind all morning. Jim got me to help him 'bed down the garden for winter' and though it took my mind off it for snatches of a while, it was my background music throughout. We cleared the gutters – Jim did all the ladder work while I held the bucket – scrubbed out the water, packed away the garden furniture, raked the leaves, and Jim had me going around collecting the seed heads of the poppies, agapanthus and teasels – he

said we can sow them again next year or spray them gold for Christmas decorations.

You've no idea how much I wanted to look forward to that. But I couldn't. All I could think was that by Christmas, I'd be two months away from being a mother. And life would never be the same again.

At lunchtime, a new distraction reared its head – Freddie-by-the-way was on the doorstep and he looked incredibly pissed off with me. I could tell because he said 'Rhiannon – I'm so pissed off with you.'

'Why?'

'Three appointments you've made with me,' he said, face darkening, 'you haven't showed at any of them. I waited for two hours at The Porthole Café yesterday and yet again, no show. Now I'm a big boy, Rhiannon. Tell me to go away if you want, but don't keep making empty promises.'

'I'm sorry,' I said.

'Are you just flaky or what? I don't get it.'

'I'm playing with you. I like to play, it's fun. Don't you like to play?'

'What, make appointments and not turn up? How is that fun?'

'It's fun for me.'

He shook his head, raking his hand through his hair, and clapped his hands by his sides. I sensed this denoted frustration and/or Look at my sleek hair and super-toned thighs. I appreciated both.

'Well I'm done, officially,' he said. 'I won't be doorstepping you again, don't worry. I don't want your story that badly. You win. I'm out.' He started back along the path towards the gate.

'Lana Rowntree,' I said. He turned back. 'There's your story.'

'Who's Lana Rowntree?'

'You want to get the #CraigWilkinsIsOverParty trending on Twitter – Lana's your gal. Craig's been seeing her for the past year. Police say he couldn't have done at least one of the murders. She has no alibi.'

His eyes searched around for a second. 'Are you dicking with me again?'

I shook my head. 'I can give you her address. You show up there with a camera and ask her yourself. Craig's defence team are switching their case to focus on her now – so there's your exclusive. If he's innocent, Lana's the next suspect. The least you'll get is a wasted journey if she's not in.'

'And if she is in?'

'You'll come face to face with a suspected murderer.'

Friday, 19th October
– 23 weeks, 5 days

We've been getting funny phone calls over the past couple of weeks – three so far. Each time they hang up. Withheld number. The latest was this morning.

'It's probably a journalist,' Jim says. 'Don't you answer it, Rhiannon. You leave them to me.'

Lana called the house today, too, out of the blue. She didn't hang up – she actually asked me if I'd go down and see her. She sounded, as far as I could make out, quite distressed. I wondered if Freddie had paid her a visit. I hadn't seen him since his proclamation of my dickery in the front garden.

To be fair, I *was* a dick.

I took her some homemade cakes and fresh flowers – sweet peas, of course. She was already crying when she opened the door and looked even more horrendous than she did last time. Baggy pyjama bottoms half a foot up from her ankles, greasy hair, socks like spaniels' ears – she was the full *Get the Look* centre spread for manic depression. It was a hot day and I didn't have a coat on and she was getting the bump in all its glory. The purple storm clouds on her face had vanished completely – no evidence of me on her at all.

'I'm sorry, I'm sorry, I can't stop crying.' I rubbed her back.

'You're crushing the cakes. Come on, it's all right. Tell me all about it.'

It was about Freddie. He'd gone straight there on Tuesday when I'd given him the nod. He'd stayed all afternoon and had pitched up again the following morning. Lana had given him way more than she should have, namely about the affair. Things they'd done. Things they'd said. How Craig dumped her when he found out about the baby.

'What did you tell him about all that for?'

'I couldn't help it. He was so charming and friendly but now he won't leave me alone.'

I checked through her lounge window. 'Well he's not here today.'

'The story goes to print today. He says the nationals will be down here tomorrow. What the hell am I going to do?' Along came the tears.

I took the cling film off my cakes and offered her the plate. She took one and started eating. Something in her had mewed and shrivelled, just as something in me had woken and begun to roar.

'You've been busy,' I remarked, faced with a seating area so deluged in paper and washing baskets full of clothes I couldn't decipher clean from dirty. Stacks of envelopes were piled up on every available flat space. The whole place stank of a vanilla PlugIn. 'What's with the letters?'

She made her way over to a Lana-shaped space on the carpet and sat down cross-legged. She then proceeded to fold letters and stick down pre-addressed envelopes. 'Sorry, I've got to get all this lot in the post by four.'

'Your face has healed nicely,' I said, pulling my handbag strap back up onto my shoulder from where it had slid down. The jars were getting heavy.

'Yeah.' She cut her tongue on an envelope as she licked it and I ran to the kitchen to get her a glass of water to wash down the blood. I secreted the jam jars in the under sink cupboard while I was there. Safe and sound.

'I keep thinking about what I told the police,' she said, taking the glass. 'I'm so worried, Rhee.'

'Why? You've told the truth – there *were* pockets of time unaccounted for when he *could* have slipped out and committed the murders. That's all.'

'No but they've twisted it. He's going to hate me. What if he gets out and he comes looking for me?'

'Well if he's not a murderer you've got nothing to worry about.'

'I acted so childishly when he told me you were pregnant,' she said. 'I cut my arm in front of him. I said I'd kill myself if he didn't stay with me. All that's going to go against me.' She sobbed. 'I'm so sorry for what I did to you.'

'I told you before, that's over now. This is bigger than that. That DI Géricault, she interviewed you before, yeah?'

'Endless bitch.'

'She's only doing her job, be fair.'

'No, I won't. It's got nothing to do with me, why won't she leave me alone? Why won't everybody leave me ALONE?'

'Géricault told me that on the night Julia Kidner was murdered, Craig was in London. Watching a football match. They have him on CCTV.'

'So what are you saying, he *didn't* kill her?'

201

'Or he *did* but he didn't dump her body. They think he had help.'

'Oh my god.'

'Now I know where *I* was on that night. Where were you?'

'Here.'

'On your own?'

'Yes.'

'Any neighbours corroborate that?'

'I don't have any neighbours. The ones in the flat next door were kicked out in April for squatting. It's just me.'

'What about CCTV outside?'

'Only in the direction of Morrison's car park... '

'So if you went out, you wouldn't be picked up on CCTV?'

'No, but I didn't. I rarely go out at night anyway.'

'Except if you're meeting Craig?'

'Yes.'

I sat back and sighed. She reached for the cakes, picked one up, sniffed it, then put it back.

'Have you gone off them?' I said.

'No, I'm not hungry right now.'

'I'm sorry to bring all this to your door, Lana, but I'm only preparing you for what's coming. You and me are innocent. We have to stick together.'

I went to the window, looking up both sides of the street. 'You've got to be strong and stick to the new story – he *did* have time. It's perfectly possible. You knew nothing about it.' I pressed my nose to the window again.

'What are you looking for?' She got to her feet.

'Spies.'

'Spies?!'

'Yeah, Craig's defence team. Do you know who owns that red Audi?'

'What red Audi?' She barged me out of the way and peeked out.

'I saw a guy sitting in it when I arrived. He's still there.'

'I don't know. I don't know that car.'

'You should keep an eye. Craig's solicitor's ruthless, a real pit bull.'

'Why would he be watching me?' She looked out, eyes fixed on the car.

'To try and undermine your testimony. If he can prove you're lying—'

'Oh god, why is this happening to me? First the *Plymouth Star* guy won't leave me alone, then Géricault, now them!'

'They'll watch you twenty-four-seven if they have to, just to get a bit of dirt,' I said, my breath fogging up the pane.

She barged me aside, looking through the window herself. As she did, she knocked a pile of envelopes off the dining table. I picked them up – it was received post. Junk mail mostly, *To the Occupier* envelopes, leaflets, flyers for carpet shampooing. And a plain white envelope with a prison postmark.

'Sorry, can I use your loo?' I said.

'There's no paper,' she said, distracted by the Audi. 'Use kitchen roll.'

I sneaked the letter under my jumper on my way to the toilet. He must have written it the second after I'd left.

NUMBER: MM2651
NAME: Wilkins
WING: G554

Dear Lana,

I want you to know first of all that I'm sorry for the way I treated you. I literally don't know how else to say that cos I did what I thought was right for R and my baby. But I feel so guilty for how I left things with you. I still love you.

Everything inside me quenched up.

I didn't do <u>anything</u>, you have to believe me. I know we haven't known each other for long but you know me well enough. I'm not gay and I couldn't do any of those things, especially not to that woman. I wouldn't harm a fly!

'He's a demon with a fly swat, so that's a lie for a start,' I said. 'And he hates wasps.'

I'm sorry the police are hassling you – I know Rhiannon has got to you about changing alibis. That's not your fault. I don't blame you. I can see how bad all this looks but I swear I am totally innocent and I know you are too. I swear on my baby's life—

Interesting.

—If I'm guilty of anything, it's falling in love with you...

Oh you absolute lying little skank-licking pig dog pus-boil from Hell's filthiest armpit.

> But listen to me – Rhiannon is dangerous. Stay away from her. I don't know how I didn't see this before – I guess I wasn't looking. I can't say any more now because, to be honest, if she finds out I'm contacting you, I don't know what she's capable of. Or I do know what she's capable of and that's why I'm afraid. Please stay away from her. She's toxic.
> Just know this – I do love you, Lana. With all my heart.
>
> Craig xxxx

Four kisses. One for each of the years he and I were together.

Told you. It was Daddy who loved you, not him. He's a waste of space, Mummy.

I folded up the letter and posted it inside my jeans pocket, my throat burning. I pulled the flush and stepped out.

And there goes the alarm ringing in my head.

'I don't want to be here anymore,' said Lana, back in her space beneath the window. 'I've been thinking about ending it all.'

'Oh.'

'And I know what you're going to say but I can't cope. I don't have anyone.' She was halfway through a Rice Krispie cake, tears falling into the empty cupcake case. 'What would you do if you were me, Rhiannon?'

I breathed out, sitting down on the arm of the sofa next to

her. I stroked her hair. 'I don't think I'd want to live either if I were you. And I have a support network in place – Craig's parents, good friends at my antenatal group. My Christian townswomen's guild. I have plenty to fill my time. And not to mention Craig's baby on the way. I have something to focus on.'

She took another cake. 'I want to do it. I want to do it before they come and find me.'

'Seems like I can't talk you out of it.'

She shook her head.

'How will you do it?'

'I don't know.'

'There's the multi storey car park in town?'

'I don't like heights.'

'Well you'll only have to go up there once, won't you?'

'I don't think I can. You need courage to take you own life.'

'You *are* courageous, Lana. You're so strong. It's not going to get any better, is it? And then there's the trial. How are you going to get through that?'

'I'm not.'

'There you are then.'

'Will you help me?'

'Help you how?'

'Be there for me. Call the ambulance and stuff.'

'You don't want an ambulance, do you?'

'No, I suppose not.'

'I mean, this isn't a cry for help, is it? It's a statement of intent.'

'Yes.'

'Okay so what are you going to do? Keep talking about it? Keep slicing up your arms and crying in this poky flat with no proper job, no purpose, no one to support you?'

'My mum and dad—'

'They'll understand eventually, don't worry about them. You can write them a little note if you want.'

'I could do it with pills. There's some paracetamol in the bathroom cabinet. I think I could do pills.'

'I have some more in my bag if you want them.'

'I can't believe I'm doing this. I can't believe this is how it ends.'

'It'll be so easy, Lana. You'll just fall asleep and then all of this will be over and done with forever. No more worry, no more sleepless nights. Gordon Ramsay clap done.'

'What?'

'Nothing.'

'Will you stay though? Make sure I don't wake up.'

'Of course I will. It's the least I can do.'

Monday, 22nd October
– 24 weeks, 1 day

1. *The elf who tangles up my earphones, my hair in the morning and Jim's garden hose before I water the flowers – it's getting personal.*

Went back to our flat today – the new couple were moving in. I watched the removal guys unloading their furniture. All IKEA shit and one white goods delivery from John Lewis. He carried her over the threshold. She was one of those preggos who has only put weight on at the bump so the rest of her was basically the same – a pencil with the rubber in the middle. Leafblower Ron stopped to chat with them. He didn't see me.

Drove round to Claudia Gulper's house after. I knew she'd be at work so the place was deserted and I still had AJ's key. Technically not *breaking* and entering – just entering.

It was a family home with no family – just remnants of one bitter, twisted old shrew; a shopping list on the fridge, cork board loaded with To Do lists, yoga class times and neatly-written recipes, instead of term dates or letters about parents' evening. Accents of copper and a pervading smell of proper coffee and fresh flowers. Fruit basket. Large manicured back garden. Huge lounge with cream carpets and marshmallow

sofas. Next door to AJ's empty room was a box room, bare but for a yellow bees and flowers border – the beginnings of a nursery for the sundry babies she never got to keep.

We're quite similar in a way, me and Claudia. She never got what she wanted either. Her passive aggression is my aggression. I'm aggressive enough for the both of us.

Went into town afterwards to get some maternity trousers – I can't deny it anymore. I've popped out of every single normal pair I own. I've also gone up two cup sizes in my bras, so I have to wear these hammocky things now. I am officially one of the whale family – the youngest member of the pod.

How can this be when it's only the size of a bloody grape-fruit?

I'm not a grapefruit anymore – I'm an ear of corn. If you were any kind of mother you'd know that.

Continuing the *Home Alone* theme that has dominated my life of late, I then continued my journey to my little hideaway on the clifftop to eat junk and watch rubbish – no one came out and stopped me.

I Googled Lana Rowntree. No news has broken yet. They haven't found her. Surely she'd smell by now.

I lay on AJ's remains in the flower bed and fell asleep – comforted by my new non-pinchy trousers and the distant swelling of the sea beneath the cliffs. The weather is still pretty balmy so the soil was warm beneath my back. The baby's heart rate didn't go up like I thought it would. Mine did though.

*

At the Where's Your Womb At? meeting tonight it was Bake Night and I'd forgotten to bake anything. Being good kind

Christians though, the others had brought along 'plenty to share'. Scones, Victoria sponges, macaroons, Battenberg, trays of baklava, iced fancies, cupcakes with little emoji wafers on top. They'd gone all out. Not that I partook in any of it, of course. I don't trust other people's homemade offerings if I haven't first inspected their kitchens. Come on, you've seen what I keep in mine. Next meeting is a creative writing class as several Wombats are producing their own novels. Erica has titled the session 'Tightening Your Opening'. I'll just leave that one there.

One of the younger WOMBATs – Amey Plainface – brought her baby twins in to show everyone. Now I like children, but these kids were butt-ugly. One was chubby and boggle-eyed and the other had this massive blood blister on its cheek which you can't ignore on a baby because it's so damn big. It was a quarter the size of its head. It was a blood blister on legs.

I hope mine doesn't have one of those. Can you have plastic surgery on a newborn? I have enough trouble loving humans as it is without them having squashed tomatoes on their faces.

Amey was full of it though – all smiley and proudly showing off old Boggle Eyes and Blood Blister and all the WOMBATs crowded round the double buggy to gaze at them like they were a Banksy. They were all *Awww, aren't they adorable?* And *Bless their little cotton socks*. I dropped in a few *Ahhhs* but my heart wasn't in it.

'It'll be you next, Rhiannon.' Amey grinned, rocking the buggy.

'Yeah,' I smiled my most convincing smile.

'Do you know if you'll go natural or C-section?'

'Uh, dunno.'

'You haven't thought about it?'

'No.'

'I went natural. It is best for them, there's no doubt. I'm stitched from John O'Groats to Land's End, mind. Are you creaming your stretch marks?'

'Every day, yeah.'

'You stretch everywhere don't you? Least I did. Still, they're worth it.'

'Are they?' I said, looking down at old Boggle Eyes Billy and Squashed Tomato Features. 'Well that's all right then.'

I watched her doing the mum thing. Burping and snuggling and all that. I tried to imagine me doing it but the images wouldn't come.

'I can pass on some of my old maternity wear if you like. I won't be needing them now. *Definitely* not having any more.'

'Oh right. That would be brilliant. Thanks.'

I couldn't bear the thought of stepping into someone else's clothes. Her old skid-marked jeggings and vanilla-sick tunics? No thank *you*.

'And they're growing out of all their old romper suits too. I'll get a nice bin bag up together for you.'

'Thanks. Again.'

It was only when everyone else started on the tea and fruit cake that one of the babies started crying and Amey settled on a chair in the corner of the hall and heaved her tit out of its sling.

'I'll let you get on,' I said, creeping off like Burglar Bill.

'You can stay and watch if you like, Rhiannon,' she smiled, draping a muslin over her shoulder. 'Might pick up some tips?'

'Oh great.'

'I've got the hang of it now but it was agony at first. I never thought I'd get it right.' There was a dried patch of puke on her bare arm. I dry heaved.

'No need to look so alarmed. It's quite natural.'

'Yeah, yeah of course.' She stuffed her burger nip into the mewling thing's gob and it latched on like an alien. 'Fucking hell!' I blurted. My remark echoed around the hall thanks to the acoustics and then I had everyone judging me – the Jesus Christ figurines, the stacks of Bibles, the tea ladies through the kitchen hatch, even the emoji sugar craft on the cupcakes. 'Sorry. That looked so painful.'

Amey didn't take offence. 'No, it's all right. It was uncomfortable at first but you get used to it. I've got nipples like World War One helmets now!'

'What happens when they both want feeding?'

'I do them both at the same time,' she said, indicating a pillow folded over in the buggy's undercarriage. 'Or I bottle feed, whatever's easiest. I'm their mum so I do what needs to be done. It's instinctive.'

There was that word again – instinct. I knew the kind of instincts *I* had and not one of them was maternal. That instinct wants to argue, to slap, to kick, to chide, to slit throats open wide, to stab, to stake, to flay, to knock people down and laugh as the wheels bump over them. And it doesn't matter how much I starve that instinct, it still won't die.

I wondered if somehow my maternal instincts would samurai through all those other ones when I give birth. I wondered if I wanted them to.

Every atom in my body wanted to stop watching the sight in front of me but I had to at least pretend to be interested, so

I started talking to her about what kind of pram I should buy, trying my best to look everywhere but at her giant throbbing bagpipe and the chugging haggis on the end of it.

'So, twins,' I said, swallowing down a heave. 'So your vadge is pretty much toast then?'

Thursday, 25th October
– 24 weeks, 4 days

1. *Journalists who use pictures of preggos and say they're*
   'flaunting' their bumps. Can't exactly hide them,
   Dickhead. You try smuggling a dinghy up your jumper
   and let's see how good you are at hiding it.

Patrick's stopped talking altogether now. I can only see the top of his head when I shine the torch down – he's slumped against the side of the well. He's scratched up the walls and there's a hell of a stink rising. I've chucked a couple of Magic Trees down there and put the lid back. I'll deal with him later.

We had another funny phone call this morning. Elaine wants to change their number and go ex-directory. Jim says they'll give up soon. This is the tenth phone call we've had.

'If I answer they might speak?' I suggested.

Jim's having none of it. 'I'm not having you bothered by it. They'll go away eventually. Let me handle it 'til they do'.

My body has become an eyesore. My tits have overinflated and gone as veiny as Stilton. My nips should be in between Brioche buns. One of the mummy bloggers bangs on and on about the beauty of a pregnant woman's body. 'You're creating

life, being the incredible wonderful woman nature always wanted you to be. Embrace life, both yours and your baby's!'

I would imagine that kind of thing is much easier to say and mean when you're a millionaire living in Martha's Vineyard with an oil tycoon husband, seven maids and all the chia seeds your gullet can cope with. Unfortunately for the rest of us, it just sucks.

I read this article on Aeon about the biological warfare of being pregnant. Apparently there's this species of spider that allows her young to suckle blood from her legs until she weakens. Then the babies eat her alive. In mammals, it says 'the foetus can also release its own hormones into the mother's bloodstream, and thus manipulate her.'

Interesting.

I'm not manipulating you. You're manipulating yourself. You're crazy, Mummy.

'You sure you want to pull on that thread, Foetus Face?'

Texted Marnie this morning – no response. Haven't heard from her since the Pudding Club picnic. God friends are weird.

Elaine decided I needed to get out of the house so she took me for 'a bit of retail therapy'. A coach crash on the motorway meant the roads were clogged around the retail parks so we had to sit in boiling hot traffic for an hour to make a two-mile journey. She wanted to go to Baby World, this massive aircraft hangar type place crammed to the rafters with every single thing you could possibly need to prepare for a new baby. She said it was time I started nesting. So she's forcing me to nest. So there I was, sitting in the car, trying to get nesty to no avail. I kept wondering about the coach crash and how many were dead. I imagined them hanging out the windows.

The minute she parked up she put the steering lock on – as she usually did whenever she or Jim went anywhere. Even that little action annoyed me. She was so bloody afraid of leaving anything anywhere, of going on holiday to anywhere other than that same crappy little hotel in the Lake District on the same date every October with Jim. Same room, same view, same cutlery. Ugh. I hated everything about her today. And I did not want to be thinking about what the baby needs right now. I wanted to think about what *I* need right now.

Which was Sandra Huggins. On the end of my knife.

The sheer amount of stuff inside Baby World was mind boggling. The only thing it didn't sell was actual babies. I didn't have a clue where to begin. Luckily Elaine had made an A4 list.

'Right, first thing's first, we need to order the cot… '

It was sweltering inside the store – air conditioning on the blink – and every aisle was rammed with young mothers pushing too-big buggies and families walking five abreast so nobody else could get by. Beside a bank of car seats, a woman was admonishing her child – a girl of about eight. She repeatedly yanked her wrist in time with what she was saying.

'Why. Do. I. Have. To. Keep. Telling. You? Are. You. Stu. Pid?'

The little girl was smiling and picking her nose. The woman let go of her, and the girl went straight back to what she'd been doing before she was so rudely interrupted – pulling a stash of squeaky giraffes from a low shelf. Immediately, the woman yanked the girl's wrist towards her and repeatedly smashed her backside with the flat of her hand.

'You. Won't. Be. Told. Will. You? Stu. Pid. Little. Girl.'

The kid was bored. Christ on a crunchy-assed cracker was she bored. I knew it. Why didn't her mum?

You know when you're so bored you want to crawl on your back and rub your head into the carpet? *That* bored. I get that. Whenever I was bored as a kid I'd want to set fire to something, usually Seren's clothes. Squeaky giraffes all over the floor was them getting off lightly.

The woman smacked the girl again and the girl whined and then the whines turned into cries. I heard someone breathing too close to me and I snapped my head around, only to realise it was me. My breaths. I was raging.

What are you going to do?

'I'm going to wring that bloody woman's neck.'

Leave it. It's nothing to do with you.

'Who stands up for her, eh?'

Not you. Don't get involved.

The smacks rained down.

LEAVE IT.

And then a thunderous *punch* boomed in my stomach. Like an explosion. A little bomb going off.

'AAARGH the hell was that?!' The entire shop swivelled its head 360°. I sat down on a toadstool, part of some small dining set.

'Sorry,' I said to no one and everyone. 'Think it kicked.'

'Oh god, what's the matter?' cried Elaine, careering round a corner with a stack of fragrance free wet wipes and a heap of pink bibs.

'She's kicking me. Ow! Shit, she did it again!'

'The book doesn't say to expect kicks this early,' said Elaine, dropping the bibs and wipes and yanking *Pregnancy 101* out of her handbag.

'Well I'm not imagining it,' I said, holding the front of

my belly for fear of it splitting open and spilling out over the floor.

Hurts, doesn't it?

'Do you want me to call an ambulance?'

'No, I'll be fine,' I said. 'Just need to sit down for a bit.'

She left me alone for a few moments on my toadstool like some kind of murderous elf, before there magically appeared a glass of tepid tap water. Holding it was a dark-haired boy cashier. He ticked all the symmetrical boxes and I think was legal enough to have sexual intercourse, so I developed a crush. I tried flirt-laughing when he started up a convo but Elaine salted my game with all her concern.

The kicking continued and I continued to 'Ow' and Hot Cashier Boy got bored and went to flirt-laugh with some preggo Ariana Grande lookalike in the nipple pads aisle. I'm starting to get the feeling I may never see cock again. And my vadge will be toast by the time the kid comes out. Sex will be like 'chucking a plum down Wookey Hole' according to Nev.

Glad to see you've got your priorities straight, Mummy.

I downed the water – I hadn't realised how thirsty I was – and managed to shake off Elaine, saying I needed some air. I walked around the grass verge of the car park until the kicking stopped.

'What's the matter with you?' I said. 'Why are you kicking so hard?'

I don't like it when you kill people in public, Mummy. It makes me sad. I don't want you to get caught.

'I wasn't going to kill her.'

Your stomach acids were bubbling. It makes me uncomfortable. You've got to calm down.

'What's with you anyway?' I said as I crossed the threshold of Halfords. A man wheeled out a brand new mountain bike with a receipt flapping on the handlebars and gave me The Look all people give me when they catch me self-conversationing. 'Yeah I'm talking to myself, get over it.'

Your behaviour is becoming increasingly erratic.

'Out of interest, this Foetus Code of Practice you operate under – what's the deal with Patrick? How come I had no side effects when I waited all day for him outside that sports store? When I drugged him? When I pushed him down the well? Hmm? Where were you then?'

That was at home. It's too risky in public. Too many people. Too many cameras. You WILL get caught.

'I won't.'

You will. You're not thinking straight. You're getting tired again, slowing down.

'I don't need you to tell me how to fertilise eggs, all right? You have to let me make my own decisions. I know what I'm doing.' I sat down on a bench. Another joy of late pregnancy I've discovered – I can't stand up for any length of time anymore.

You want to kill all the time. I've seen your dreams. I've seen you studying Sandra Huggins's payslip. I've been there when you're waited for her in that car park where she works. You're being too obvious. You love killing more than you love me.

'Then how come I walked away from White and Nerdy? How come I *haven't* killed Huggins yet? How come I haven't stabbed anyone for months?'

Because you do love me. Just not enough.

I watched a couple going inside Baby Town – her with the big bump and slight waddle, him with Craig's haircut. They were

holding hands and stood aside as Elaine came out to corral me back inside.

'Come on,' she said. 'Changing table. They can deliver in ten days.'

Elaine took charge. I followed her lead, trying to look interested. We filled the trolley:

- *sleep suits (six newborn, six 3–6 months, six 9 months 'cos we don't know how big she'll be when she's born, do we?'*
- *vests, bibs, cardigans (three), hats (four), socks (two packets of six), muslins ('for dribble and sick')*
- *four packs of nappies (newborn)*
- *a changing bag with little clowns on it*
- *environmentally-friendly wet wipes*
- *a breast pump (ugh)*
- *two boxes of humungous breast pads (ugh ugh)*
- *pregnancy pillow ('Sleeping on your back decreases the flow of blood to the baby so it's best to lie on your side')*
- *two nursing bras (Sizes – Humungous)*
- *two bottles with various sized teats*
- *two bottles of sterilising fluid plus bottle brushes*
- *Baby Mozart CD (because 'she can hear everything now and we can train her to be clever')*
- *Infant Milk Starter Pack x 6 bottles*
- *a Moses basket ('so she can sleep right next to you')*
- *cot sheets and cellular blankets*
- *newborn papoose*

- *a nasal aspirator – which SUCKS BOGIES OUT OF A KID'S NOSE*
- *a pram with pram blankets*
- *a small plastic bath*
- *baby oil (had no idea that had a use for actual babies)*
- *a rear-facing car seat*

All the stuff! Bits and pieces and packets and boxes and bags. All totally overpriced but if I didn't have it all, the baby wasn't going to survive. I NEEDED all of it. I had to KNOW what to do with every item when the baby needed it. That was my job now. But it was too much. Elaine could have removed every item from that trolley and replaced it with bags of crisps and I wouldn't have cared. I couldn't find it in me. It wasn't there.

'I don't want to do this,' I mewed, entering my pin in to the machine.

You'd rather I died?

'No. I just don't want all this. All this responsibility. All this change. It's all about you now. What about me?'

Those days are over, Mummy. You've got to roll with the punches.

'Do I?'

Monday, 29ᵗʰ October
– 25 weeks, 1 day

1. *People who call into the 10 Minute Takeover on Radio 1 and request the same damn songs we hear 24/7.*
2. *The man who reads the news on local TV – clear your goddamn throat.*
3. *People who ask you how your weekend was – nobody truly gives a shit.*

Jim was acting strangely before he and Elaine left for the Lake District. He was hovering in the kitchen. Wiping surfaces that didn't need wiping. Rearranging fridge magnets. Shaking crumbs out of the toaster. I got the impression he wanted to talk.

I wondered if it was because of this morning – his dressing gown had come undone as he was making the porridge. I'd got an inadvertent flash of cock and balls and my eye had stayed too long. That happens sometimes – I lock on to a target and won't lock off. Visible cock bulge is one such target.

'Rhiannon – I wondered how you might feel about us taking Tink with us? I know she's your dog and you're her primary carer—'

'Go for it,' I said.

His face brightened. 'You know we'd look after her, don't you?'

'Of course. She loves you, Jim. And she likes new places, new sniffs.'

'I wanted to do something different this year. We always go to the same hotel, same room, same hiking group, same pub-lunch every day. If Tink's with us, we might be inspired to try different things.'

'I thought you liked the sameness?'

His voice lowered, though Elaine wasn't even in the house. 'I suggested Jamaica, Hawaii, Barbados, cruises. She's always wanted to go up to Edinburgh and see the castle. I suggested the sleeper and a hire car and then we could work our way along the west coast for a couple of weeks. Not book anything, just… be a bit free.' He shook his head. 'I suppose it's best to keep things simple this year, I don't know.'

We both watched Tink outside, dragging a two-foot dried bull's cock up the lawn. 'It'll still be a nice rest. A change of scenery for you both.'

'You're sure you don't mind us taking her? It's two whole weeks, love.'

'She'll have a ball. And sometimes you've got to do what's best for someone else, haven't you? Never mind how it makes you feel.'

As soon as the words left my mouth I knew I wasn't talking about Tink anymore. And I knew what I had to do.

*

I was sitting in the silent lounge waiting for an important call when my phone finally *ding!*ed in my pocket. Only it wasn't

223

the message I was expecting. It was from Lord Byron, one of my fish. Rich guy. Lives in a house so large it has eaves – proper Tudor eaves and gold-framed portraits. I've seen them in the background of some of his photos.

LordByron61: I'm wearing my big boy nappy to my conference like you told me to. It is such a thrill!

Sweetpea: I'm so happy for you.

LordByron61: Oh Sweetpea you are so wonderful my darling. I can't tell you what it means that you don't think I'm too strange for you. My conference is in Weymouth. You once told me you live along the coast, yes?

Sweetpea: Yes.

LordByron61: So could I see you? Could we play together at your house?

Sweetpea: Have you carved the flower yet?

LordByron61: I will do it for you today, I promise. And then you'll tell me where you live?

Sweetpea: I'll tell you where I live, I'll be here for you and I'll do anything you ask of me. *If* you carve the flower into your skin…

LordByron61: Oh my darling that would be fantastic!

I received a picture message about two hours later when I was in the garden, pruning the hedges – a grey-haired, pink thigh, scratched up and scabby at the edge of a perfectly carved flower. Not a sweet pea – he'd gone rogue and done some kind of tulip. Not a bad effort. His conference was clearly over for the day – in the photo I spied hotel toiletries by the sink.

Sweetpea: You're such a good boy. Sweetpea is going to have fun with you.

LordByron61: It hurt so much but will be worth it when I get to see you. I love that you have a kinky side too ☺ Will you feed me later? I would love to suckle your teats.

Sweetpea: I thought you wanted a playmate, not a mother?

LordByron61: I want both. I have two outfits you can wear – nurse and a romper suit like mine but pink. I'll bring them both.

Sweetpea: Whatever floats your buffalo, I guess.

LordByron61: I'll bring my sippy cup and all my toys. What's your address?

*

There's one thing worse than hearing Cubicle Fart in a Ladies' restroom and that's going in straight after another woman and getting their arse-warmed seat. Ugh. I'd take my own toilet seat with me everywhere if I could.

Claudia had taken the day off work especially to meet me. She sensed on the phone that I 'needed a friend'. Not that she *was* a friend, mind you.

We met in The Roast House – an independent coffee shop in Periwinkle Lane near the *Gazette* offices. I can handle the smell of roasting coffee beans now, but I still can't drink it. Me and AJ had met there once for sausage sandwiches – no, that's not a euphemism. I got the impression that the baby wanted to feel close to her dad in some way other than lying on the soft earth above his decaying remains. She's weird like that.

She started kicking the moment Claudia walked in.

'Oh my god!' I said, my bump radiating pain. I was sucking in breath so quickly my teeth went cold.

'What's wrong? What's the matter?' said Claudia, face loaded with alarm.

I clutched my bump, blowing out like a windsock as the jolts hit me – heels and fists, heels and fists. 'It's fine. Baby *loves* kicking me.'

She smiled, sliding into the booth. She'd put on weight – the sleeves of her jacket strained at the shoulder. 'Such a wonderful feeling I imagine. How are you getting on, Sweetpea? You look fantastic – absolutely blooming!'

'Yeah I'm okay,' I squirmed as frogs continued to jump in my lower portions. 'I'm piling on the timber like a log truck though. And I never thought I'd have to sleep in a bra. It's been a real game changer.'

'I bet,' she smiled.

Tell her.

Apart from weight gain and a switch to a plum lipstick, Claudia hadn't changed – still the three neck moles, still the veiny feet in too-high stilettos, still the coffee breath and split-endy hair and permanent Resting Bitch Face.

'How's life at the Gutsache?'

'Good,' she laughed, fiddling with the serviette under her mineral water. 'We all miss you.' Hmmmm. 'We've lost a few members of staff recently. Gina the receptionist left… '

As predicted.

'… and did you hear Daisy's gone as well?'

'Daisy Chan?'

'Yeah, she got a job at the *Manchester Evening News* and moved up north. Ron was fuming after investing so much in her.'

I smiled. 'So she lasted less than a year then? What a waste.'

'You should have had that job, Rhiannon.'

'Yeah, I know I should.'

'I should have done more for you.'

'Yeah, you should.'

We ordered – she a tabbouleh salad and a mineral water with ice; me a medley of breads (the love affair with the carb continues) and an apple juice 'absolutely without ice'.

We talked about the weather. We talked about Brexit. She asked about my non-existent antenatal classes and I made up a boatload of lies about how well pregnancy is going.

'Do you feel bonded to it yet?' she asked with a sparkle in her eyes like Christmas morning.

'Oh for sure.' I smiled. 'It's everything I've ever wanted.'

Liar.

We talked about Linus's eye cancer and how the old sphincter bruise is getting on with an eye patch. I dropped in the odd 'Aah' and 'Poor guy' in all the right places. I wouldn't wish cancer on anyone *but* Linus.

'It looks like he's beaten it at least, which is such a relief,' she said.

'You don't "beat" cancer,' I replied. 'Trust me. You're its plaything for a while until it gets bored and leaves you alone but it always comes back.'

'Well, he's on the right medication.'

'It'll come back, Claudia. He *will* die of it.'

She cleared her throat and started complaining about the stickiness of the table top, which I'd noticed but was happy to ignore. Claudia rifled in her Poppins-esque Moschino bag and pulled out a pack of antibacterial wet wipes. She had everything

in there – hairbrushes, water, phone charger neatly coiled up, notepad and pen, pack-a-mac. Organised. Prepared.

And then we talked about the killings.

'They had a vigil in town.' She sniffed. 'One night in July. *Gazette* organised it, galvanised some local sponsorship. Did you read about it?'

'No, I'm a bit out of the loop with the goings on around here.'

'Hundreds turned out. There was a piper and a minute's silence. We did a ten-page spread featuring the victims a few months ago.' I could hear the next question rumbling along the tracks. 'Do you think he did it, Rhiannon?'

He didn't do it Auntie Claudia, she did. SHE DID!

I did my starey-eyed middle distance thing. 'I didn't want to believe it at first. It still seems unthinkable.' Time for a bit more bullshit, methinks. 'I keep getting this thought that Lana knows more than she's letting on.'

'Lana Rowntree?' said Claudia, choking on her water. 'Seriously?'

'Yeah, something doesn't add up about her. I mean we've always known she was a car crash but one of the murders – Julia Kidner – Craig definitely didn't do. He wasn't even in town, he was at Wembley. And yet his semen was found on and in her body. Lana has no alibi for that night.'

Claudia stared me down in her unavoidably contemptible way. 'I don't blame you for attacking her in the office. I could feel your pain.'

'Could you?'

'Definitely. When I found out my husband was having an affair, I made the same noise you did when you launched at her.' She patted my hand – why does everyone feel the need to touch

me, all the time? 'But you look great, Rhiannon. You're clearly the one who's come out of this smelling of roses.'

'Well, not quite roses,' I said. 'Sweet peas, at least.'

'Mmm, I love sweet peas.'

'Lana's not doing too good, I hear.'

She shook her head. 'Haven't seen her for weeks. Have you?'

'I popped over to her flat a few months back to apologise for hitting her. Took some flowers. She didn't look great. Her arms were all scabbed up too.'

'Rhiannon – don't spend any time worrying about Lana, for god's sake. After what she did to you, she doesn't deserve an ounce of your sympathy.'

'I guess.'

Tell her now.

'Have you heard from AJ at all lately?' I asked.

'No but he's updating his Facebook and he's sent me a few DMs saying his WiFi's patchy. Seems to be having a wonderful time though. He's in love with Tibet. Staying with this nice family. Have you heard from him?'

'No,' I said.

'You *were* seeing each other before he left, weren't you?'

'Briefly.'

Before you threw boiling water in his face and stabbed him twenty-eight times in the chest.

She sniffed. 'I knew it.'

'It was nice to have someone who cared about me. Craig had checked out of our relationship – I think trying for a baby took it out of him. I felt bad for cheating but then I found out Craig had been cheating on me.'

'I completely understand,' she said. 'Same thing happened

with my husband. Trying for a baby became everything and he felt shut out.'

'Still' I said, at least Craig had his "hobbies" to keep him happy.' I laughed – too soon, I realised.

Claudia sipped her water. 'AJ talked about you all the time.'

'I know.' The baby started kicking again. 'You told me once.'

Bloody bloody bloody TELL HER!

Claudia took a deep breath. 'I was only looking out for him. I wanted him to focus on his job – he only wanted to focus on you. He said I was obsessed with the idea that he might find love when I couldn't. Had quite the argument about it. I take it it's over between you two?'

As over as it can be when he's three feet under in six sections I suppose.

Our meals arrived. 'He hasn't messaged in months so I guess so, yeah. I think you're quite glad about that, aren't you?'

Claudia unfolded her serviette and lay it down on her lap. 'I'm sorry?'

'I know you've never liked me, Claudia.'

'No, that's not true. I was just looking out for him.'

'I overheard you and Lynette from Accounts once, talking about me in the Ladies' at the *Gazette*.'

Her mouth stopped chewing lettuce to form a perfect O.

'I heard you say that you'd never felt comfortable around me, that I didn't stand a chance of getting the Junior Editor job anyway, even though I kept applying, year on year. Oh, and you called me a freak.'

Her mouth then formed a perfect I, a green thing visible between her lateral incisors. It was putting me off my medley of breads.

'It's all right, it's one of those things,' I said. 'I *am* a freak – I'm a *super* freak. I'm super freaky. In my defence though I *am* brain damaged.'

'Rhiannon. I didn't mean anyth—'

'It's fine, honestly. Just save me the bullshit, Claudia. Don't tell me I should have got the job and that you should have done more and that you've always liked me because those are lies and I'm all stocked up on lies.'

She put her fork down next to her salad. 'God I feel awful now.'

'You're bound to because I've caught you out.'

'Still. That was unprofessional to talk out of turn like that. I am sorry.'

'You've been through a lot. I understand. Three failed IVFs, isn't it?'

She frowned. 'Yes. A few years ago now.'

For crying out loud…

'And two failed adoptions, was it? Or three? Five miscarriages – one stillborn. You're bound to be bitter.'

She pushed her plate away, deliberately avoiding eye contact. The restaurant had got busier now and the clang and clank of cutlery and smell of rich coffee beans had amplified.

'I get why you are the way *you* are,' I said. 'You get that I'm the way *I* am. We've both been through stuff. Jesus Christ I'm so bitter I could spit into a hole in the ground and grow a thousand lemon trees. You asked life for a baby and life's given you everything but.'

Her face had gone hard. 'Why did you call me, Rhiannon? I thought you wanted to catch up on old times or ask about having your job back.'

'No, I didn't.'

'So did you just want to rub my nose in something? What is it?'

The kicking intensified. Somewhere in the restaurant, another baby was squawking for attention. I rubbed my bump and breathed out so deeply the serviettes fluttered off the table top.

'AJ's the baby's father, Claudia.'

Her eyes flashed, her coffee cup clashing with her saucer. 'What?'

The kicking stopped.

'He's the daddy. I can't prove it right now but it is his.'

She sat up, forcing her tired eyes wider. 'Oh my god. Does Craig know? Do his parents know?'

I let my eyebrows do the talking and sipped my elderflower pressé.

'Gosh. So that's my grandniece or nephew in there?'

'Niece. It's a girl.'

She stared at my bump like it was glowing.

'Do you want to be in her life, Claudia?' The moment I said the words aloud it was like a great heavy rucksack had been taken off my back.

Her face was blank. 'Do I? You want me to?'

'I don't trust myself to do the right things for her. I need back up. All these pregnancy books talk about having back up, lots of back up. I don't have anyone. The baby's related to you so—'

'Oh my god.' Claudia scrabbled around in her handbag for a tissue and blew her nose. The waiter came over to ask if the food was all right – neither of us answered and he moved away.

She looked down until he had gone again. 'Do you mean this?' she said, eyes going all glassy.

'Yeah. I'm not that religious but we could have a christening or something and do it officially. You can be her godmother.'

Claudia clutched her blouse as her tears came harder. She seemed to straighten up and blew out a few times. 'Sorry, this is so unexpected.'

'Unexpected in a good way?'

She laughed and a bubble of snot blew out of her nostril which she quickly wiped away. 'A wonderful way!' Then she did what I had feared – she came out of the booth and made a beeline towards me, embracing me, then the obligatory bump rub because my stomach is public property now.

'That baby is going to be the most spoiled baby ever,' she chuckled.

I should bloody think so. She has a pool, doesn't she? And that downstairs office would make an awesome playroom. Wendy House in the bay window. Little kitchenette. And one of those motorised kid cars.

Her face relaxed to the extent that she didn't look like Claudia anymore. She wasn't in business mode – she wasn't that tight-suited pointy-nosed queaf who'd order me about, delegating all the shit jobs, refusing my pay rise, calling me Sweetpea. She was just Claudia – 'Claudie' as Ron called her.

'I like the idea of her being spoiled,' I said.

'Oh she will be. I promise I'll do whatever I can for her, anything. Oh Rhiannon, I can't stop smiling! Do you need somewhere to live, both of you? Craig's parents aren't going to want you living with them once they find out.'

'We're okay for the time being. Thanks.'

'What about AJ? Does he know?'

'Yes, he knows. And he doesn't want anything to do with us. Probably why he's staying away.'

LIAR.

Claudia frowned. 'That doesn't sound like the AJ I know.'

I shrugged. 'He didn't want me telling you cos he knew you'd contact him and get him to come back. Please – follow my lead on this one. Leave him out of it. And I don't want his mum and stepdad knowing either.'

'But they have rights. Let me call them, they can get through to him—'

'No, I don't want that.'

'But—'

'Do you want to be her godmother or not? Because if you're going to start interfering with my wishes—'

'I won't say a word, I won't interfere at all, I promise you. This is your baby and whatever you say goes.'

'I've got to know I can trust you, Claudia. And if I can, you can see her as often as you want. She can be a part of your life.'

She nodded sharply. 'I hear you, Rhiannon. You call the shots.'

'Yes, I do.'

Wednesday, 31ˢᵗ October
– 25 weeks, 3 days

1. *'Warren' in ASDA who said 'Need a bag, Madam?' while eye-browsing my tits. Don't you eyebrows ME, Pig Features, I'll check YOU out.*
2. *People who use the word 'lovely' as a term of endearment. 'Hello lovely. Hope you're okay, lovely.' When did that become a thing? I'm going to start calling people by adjectives. 'Thanks, Sleeveless. Well done, Hideous. Watch out, Agreeable, that piano looks unsafe...'*
3. *Those smug California tourist board adverts.*

So there's a cauliflower in my womb and a bee in my bonnet.

It's my mum's anniversary today. I can see the date coming at me when October begins every year – like an oil slick in the road, and every October thirtieth I have to relive the last time I spoke to her, the last time she spoke to me, the sound of her death rattle as I filled my cup at the cooler.

Pregnancy hormones aren't helping either. Nor is my ever keen sense of loneliness. It's like all of these things are rolled up together in one hideously spiky little ball and it keeps bouncing around inside my head. Wall to wall, floor to ceiling. *Bounce, bounce, bounce* it goes. Never letting up.

Today it doesn't feel so good to be in an empty house where there's no noise at all, not even Tink's bell as she scuttles around sniffing out crumbs and squeaking her toys. There's no Jim fiddling with a model boat on the kitchen table. No Elaine chopping me up fruit for snacks or telling me endless facts about what different cravings mean or asking if I've got haemorrhoids yet. There's no sound at all except the sea outside whipping up into a storm.

Monks Bay is particularly anxious about storms. There was one a few years ago that took out the power and claimed some clifftop caravans. Storm Alice, it was called. Killed three people. It's a strange fact actually that storms named after women claim more lives because nobody takes them seriously. Some boffin in America did some research and apparently you're scientifically more prone to being killed by a Hurricane Rhiannon than you are by a Hurricane Craig. From an early age girls are told to stay away from strange men. Nobody warns boys about women like me.

Gender bias once again working in my favour.

I woke up thinking about Mum. That final day at the hospice was the nearest I've come to an out-of-body experience. Even though our relationship had soured over the eight years since Priory Gardens, to lose your mother is to be partially unanchored to the Earth. Like there had always been these ropes fixing me in place – Mum and Dad. When Mum went, one of the ropes snapped. When Dad went, I didn't feel like I was anchored anywhere. Except perhaps to Craig.

I walked into that hospice knowing what I was going to see but still not prepared for it. I saw the other women through the windows of the communal lounge, seated in big armchairs

having their chemo. Silk scarves and pale yellow faces; rows of wilting tulips. Mum's room stank of lavender and hand gel. Dad was mopping her dry lips with a wet cotton bud. Her face was so dry and small I could have taken it in my fist and ground her to dust.

'What does dying feel like, Mum?'

'Go away, Rhiannon.'

'Tell me how it feels. Are you in pain?'

'Leave me.'

'Take me with you.'

'No. You stay. Suffer with them.'

Seren said I brought Mum's cancer on. She said my violent temper and behaviour at school made her life a misery – teachers said I was acting out and that I needed time to adjust. Then came the lying, and the stealing, and the setting fire to things. Cutting her hair. Stabbing her leg with the kitchen scissors. Dad was the only one who understood me.

'You talk about Dad like he's some kind of god and he's not – he's a psychopath. Like you.'

I'd hate me too if I was Seren. I called her anyway.

It was the decent thing to do on such a day, and though my mask has slipped of late I do sometimes still try to be a decent person.

'Hello?'

'It's me.'

There was a delay on the line, as usual. 'Rhiannon? Are you okay?'

'I'm fine. How are you?'

Another delay, about ten seconds. 'Yes, I'm fine. What's wrong?'

'Nothing. I wanted to say Hi. It being The Day and all.'

'Yeah, I saw it on the calendar. I would have called you.'

'Liar.'

'Rhiannon? Is everything all right?'

I nodded, even though she couldn't see me.

'Rhiannon.'

'Everything's fine,' I said. 'I'm extra hormonal today, that's all.'

'How are things with the baby?'

'My ribs ache. And I've got this beach ball in my stomach. And my tits are sore and I can't lie on my front anymore.'

'But the baby's all right?'

'Yes, the baby's all right.'

The longest delay yet. She hadn't heard me. Or maybe that message hadn't reached her.

'Have you done any antenatal classes? I found them very useful when I was having Mabli.'

'Yes.'

'You know they say blueberries are great for pregnant women too. I ate a bunch of them when I was expecting Ash.'

Oh good the blueberry lecture again. I so enjoyed it the first eight times.

'How's Craig?'

The question fell on me like a shout. Did she know?

'He's fine.'

'Cody might have some building work for him when we move into the new place. He could use someone with Craig's expertise. Is he around to have a quick word about it?'

'Not at the moment, no. When do you move to Vermont?'

'Less than a week now. But the new place needs quite a bit

done to it. We were going to ask you both over for Thanksgiving. We'll be settled in by then. Cody and Craig can do the boring man stuff and we can spend some time together. We'd pay for your flights of course.'

'I'll be in my third trimester by then. I won't be able to fly.'

'Of course,' she said, her voice an octave higher.

Shit, I thought. She was trying to build bridges. She wanted to see me, see *us*, and she knew nothing about Craig's arrest or the forthcoming trial, none of it. I can guarantee if she had the slightest inkling that Craig was in jail, she would know beyond a shadow that I was the one who put him there.

She should know. I want her to know.

Don't you dare...

'Listen I have to go,' I said. 'I'll get Craig to give Cody a call soon though yeah? Sounds like a great opportunity for him.'

'Yeah, is everything okay between you two?'

'Yep, everything's cool. I've got to go, I've got a pot boiling over, sorry. Speak soon.'

'Bye Rhi—'

I hung up. Shit, that was shabby. I hadn't prepared for that. That's one of my rules – Be prepared – but stupid baby brain had made me forget all about that possibility. Seren never asks about Craig and I didn't dream she'd ask us over there for Thanksgiving. What's *that* about? And why now?

Why do you always have to suspect the worst? Why can't it just be a nice invitation to see your sister on Thanksgiving and mend a few tears?

'Yeah, all right, *Look Who's Talking*, I was actually being rhetorical.'

Perhaps she's feeling lonely because she's leaving for the other

side of the country where she's spent all her adult life? Perhaps she just wants to see her sister?

'Perhaps you should carry on foetusing and button your gills, hmmm?'

I turned off my phone and put it back on my nightstand. She'd made her feelings about me quite clear when we were younger. I was a psychopath. A cancer. You can't erase that with turkey and cranberry sauce. Not that I'd eat it anyway.

All the worry you caused them, Rhiannon. You're a vicious little bitch. I wish you were dead, not Mum.

Yeah I went off the rails for a while but can you blame me? Most teenagers go off the rails at some point and few of them are beaten about the head with a lump hammer.

Jesus, World War One was *started* by a teenager. I'm a frickin' delight compared to *that* guy.

My own mother could barely look at me in the weeks leading up to her death. *Why did you do that to your sister? What's the matter with you? Stop this, Rhiannon. Stop reading funeral catalogues in front of me, can't you see how insensitive you're being? You don't even cry anymore.*

It's one messed up world that lets someone like me even think about having a baby.

*

Marnie couldn't meet me today – she and Tim are 'taking Raph out for a day in the countryside, feeding the ducks, pub lunch, etc'. The kid is two months old but yeah, feed the ducks, I'm sure he'll get a lot out of it. I haven't seen her now for a week. He's told her to stay away from me, that's what it is. She's disappeared from WhatsApp too, I've noticed.

Or have I been blocked? Ooh, I have tasted my own medicine and it tastes BITTER!

Lord Byron was the only person on the planet who seemed to care whether I was dead or alive today. I was in the kitchen at the Well House eating the greasiest chips in the world and trying to ignore the stink from Ground Zero that had permeated its way up through the whole house, despite drilling the Perspex tile back in place over the hole.

Byron's *ding!* came through on my phone.

LordByron61: I can't wait to see you tonight my angel. Could you give me your postcode now for my satnav?

Sweetpea: Don't drive. There's a train from Weymouth at 6pm.

LordByron61: Why my darling?

Sweetpea: Because I said so. Do as I ask you please or I won't play.

LordByron61: Will you pull down my nappy and smack my bum?

Sweetpea: Yes I will do that the moment you arrive. I'll make it all red.

LordByron61: My winky is getting all stiff thinking about that.

Sweetpea: Oh dear. I didn't tell Winky to do that, did I? I will have to smack you twice as hard now.

LordByron61: Oh yes, Sweetpea, yes! I can't wait to see you.

I had it all planned out. No one would know where he was going. No CCTV of him getting on or off a train. A little extra in his drink on arrival. And *bam*, mine all mine.

I didn't hear the cauliflower's voice until I was digging out my Sabatiers in the raised bed next to AJ's.

No, stop this right now. This is wrong. I won't let you bring that man here.

'It's sex. Nothing more.'

You're going to kill him. That's why you're digging up the knives. No, Mummy, you can't you can't you can't.

'He's not some innocent, he is a pervert. A sixty-one-year-old man who dresses up as a baby. He likes to be fondled and played with. He likes to breastfeed. He wears adult nappies and drinks from a bespoke sippy cup with his name on it. Don't you find that all a tad disgusting?'

He's not hurting anyone. Plenty of people have weird kicks. You've got the weirdest one of all, remember?

'I'm going to *have* my fun.' I ran the dirty blades under the kitchen tap to wash them clean. I lay them out on a dry tea towel on the counter and smoothed away the droplets the steel. 'If you wannabe my lover, you gotta get with my friends,' I sang happily, holding the largest knife against my cheek like a cool caress.

You're not doing this.

'You can't stop me.' I rooted in the drawers for a coil of rope I'd spotted.

You want me to bleed out of you? Do you want to lose me?

She started kicking me, proper big frogs this time. I sat down on the kitchen stool. 'You're bigger now, it's safer. Your heart is stronger every night. And this isn't going to be in public – he

will come here. Safe, silent. I can take all night with him if I want to and no one is going to stop me.'

You don't want to do this. You don't want to risk my life again.

I banged in the drawer. 'You SAID I could do it if it wasn't in public.'

You're scared.

'You wouldn't let me kill the guy in York because you were scared someone would see. You won't let me go and kill Sandra Huggins, even though I know all her movements now *and* I've thought of a way to get her back here.'

You're really scared.

'And even though I've gone to great lengths to procure *this* guy *and* arrange for him to not tell anyone where he's going, STILL you won't let me.'

You're scared about giving me to Claudia. You're scared about how much you're going to love me.

'NO I AM NOT, I'M NOT SCARED OF ANYTHING!'

You are. You don't want anyone to have me. You'd rather kill me than let me out into this dark dark world.

And then I blew.

Anything not nailed down went flying. Plates, glasses, pots, jars, bags, fruit bowl, fruit, sieves, spoons, spatulas, Sylvanians, and the chips I'd just bought. I sat back down on the stool and breathed deeply in and out, watching the grease stains on the cupboard doors shimmer in the light, the broken china still tinkling down the sink.

But I wasn't done.

I picked up the knives. I went in the lounge and stabbed everything soft in my vision – carpets, curtains, the backs of the chairs. *In in in in in in in in in in in in in in in,* over and over

and over and over and over until I sat down in the middle of
the carpet, breathless, surrounded by feathers and white stuffing
like a kid in the snow.

The bump had tightened all over.

Feel better now?

'FUCK OFF.'

My phone *ding!*ed again.

LordByron61: Let me know your address my angel. I'm
going to finish my conference early, pack my toys and
come on over. I can't wait to see you, you're all I can think
about!

*I'm going to tie my cord around my neck if you don't put him
off. This is your final warning.*

Sweetpea: Sorry guy. Voices in my head say I have to
leave you alone. Enjoy your weird life masturbating into
adult nappies. Oh and if you want a last piece of advice,
buy the chunkiest rope you can find and string yourself
up on one of your rich bitch eaves you pathetic piece of
human shit.

BLOCKED.

I threw my phone at the sofa.

*Good. See, you're a hero now, Mummy. You just saved a
man's life.*

'LEAVE ME ALONE.'

You don't mean that.

'I *do* mean that. Life was better before you. Before you stopped me doing EVERYTHING I like. You're changing my body in ways I never thought imaginable – you've ruined my tits, turned my vagina blue, my hair greasy, split my arsehole. I've pissed and vomited out half my body weight, every day I grow out of some other clothes that normally fit like a glove and I have feet only fit for Crocs. I hate AJ for putting you in there. I hate him.'

You don't hate my daddy.

'I *do*, I hate him. I'm glad I tore his head off his shoulders. You understand me now you little shit? I hate that you're inside me and I can't even cut you out!'

It was only the sight of myself holding the knife reflected in the TV screen that stopped me. I had it pointed directly over my stomach. I threw it away from me and it disappeared into the drifts of upholstery stuffing. I tried to stand up, getting a head rush and having to sit back down again.

'I can't take much fucking more of this.'

All right all right, keep your mucus plug in.

'STOP. TALKING. TO. ME!'

It was then I noticed the blood. I'd cut myself. I didn't know where the blood was coming from but it was all over my hands. I went out to the hallway and looked in the mirror.

The bump. It was coming from the bump.

I'd nicked it, only slightly at the top, but the knife was so sharp and so long and it had penetrated both my T-shirt and my skin. I watched as a single trickle snaked its way down over the mound in a perfect red arc.

'You don't work well with others. You need to have… no one.'

'*But I won't be on my own. Will I? I'll have the baby.*'

'*No.*'

'*What are you saying? Is my baby safe? What happens to it? You said I was going to be on my own. Please, I need to know.*'

'*... I saw a baby... covered in blood.*'

'Please say this was all she saw in that crystal ball before I stove her head in with it. Please tell me this is it. This is as far as it goes.'

I don't know how long I'd been standing there in the hallway mirror, dabbing my stomach nick with tissues, when there came a loud knock at the front door behind me. I froze, sinking down to the carpet, heart thumping.

'Not the police, not the police, not the police... '

KNOCK KNOCK KNOCK. 'Hello?' A man's voice.

I waited. Two more knocks. A clearing of a throat. The throat clearer eventually moved around to the back garden. I heard footsteps on the path. The creak of the gate.

Did I lock the back door? Did I cover up the hole when I got the knives out? I couldn't be sure. I couldn't breathe.

Another throat clear and a tap at the back window. And then my name. And then I stopped breathing altogether.

'Rhiannon? Are you there?'

Friday, 2nd November
– 25 weeks, 5 days

1. *Chocolate and cake makers at this time of year – why can't I buy anything that doesn't have green slime oozing out of it or a fucking ghost motif on top?*
2. *People who tell me I'm blooming when I feel like I've been dragged through a sewer pipe with my mouth open.*
3. *That modelling family The Hadids.*

Managed to survive Halloween with just a handful of Trick or Treaters. Elaine had thoughtfully bought a bucket of lollies for me to hand out even though she didn't 'agree with it as a festival.' A Dracula kid with psoriasis grazed my wrist as I gave him the bucket. Haven't felt clean since.

One of the mummy bloggers this morning – 'Baby Bliss' – was eulogizing about her experience of Lotus birth and what an enriching experience it was. She buried her placenta underneath a tree in the garden *voms*. Her best friend – called Calendula, yeah – threw a party where she served her placenta up to guests in a frigging stroganoff. Another woman – can't remember her name but there was a picture of her in a hairy cardigan and she clearly doesn't use shampoo – still breastfeeds her ten-year-old.

I know I'm one to talk but do some women really lose their shit when they become mothers or what? I can't have that much more shit to lose.

I'm getting daily texts from Claudia – how am I? Do I need her to come down and help with anything yet? Am I eating enough blueberries?

I'm going to look like Violet Beauregard if I eat any more blueberries.

Craig appeared at Bristol Crown Court today – pleading Not Guilty to five counts of murder. I followed the updates on the *Evening Post* website. Photographers swarmed the Reliance van when it swung through the black gates, climbing over each other to get the blurry money shot of Craig through the tiny window. It came on the main news at lunch too.

I took off his ring today – my eighteen-carat white-gold solitaire with 'Forever' engraved inside. My fingers have swelled and it was hurting. Saw The Element outside the arcades still mumbling on about Frank Sinatra and swigging his Diamond White. We ate our lunch together. His Eau de Urine cologne doesn't bother me as much as it used to. I gave the ring to him – I said he could pawn it.

We'd only just scrunched up our Greggs bags when Marnie walked past on the seafront with her pram. She was wearing a long black trench coat and aviator sunglasses and had a takeaway Costa in the cup holder. I crossed the road and stood right in front of her, blocking her path.

'Hello stranger,' I said.

'Oh, hi.' Her smile disappeared after one second.

'Haven't seen you in a while,' I said, walking beside her. She didn't slow down so I was constantly running to catch up.

'No, we've been so busy, honestly. October is crazy for some reason.'

'It's November now.'

She stopped and looked at me, then carried on walking.

'The baby's taking up all of my time. I can't even think straight at the moment, I'm sorry I haven't been in touch. How are you getting on? Have you started your antenatal classes?'

'No. So what's the real reason you haven't been in touch? Never mind the bullshit. Oh lemme guess—'

'If you call Tim a Nazi again I swear I will carry on walking and I won't say another word to you, EVER again.'

We were both stopped now, face to face. 'I wasn't going to say anything at all. Your words there, Marn.'

'Stop it.' She pushed her sunglasses up to rest them on her hair. Dark circles. 'Stop needling me.'

'Needling you? All I said was hello and I haven't seen you in a while. You're the one with a pine cone up your arse.'

'I'm tired. And that's not bullshit. Raphy had a bad night and I don't know my own mind this morning. I needed some air. A new perspective rather than my bedroom wall or the lounge or the kitchen.'

We both looked up at that moment to see the funicular railway coming to a halt at the bottom of the hill. 'Well if it's a different perspective you're after, you can't get more different than that. Fancy a ride?'

She puffed. 'No. I don't do heights.'

'Raph will be scared of heights if you are. Saw my mum jump onto a chair from a spider when I was four. I've hated them ever since.'

She rubbed her forehead. 'I don't want to pass it onto him.'

'Well come on then. Rouse, rouse.'

*

We paid our money and Marnie almost turned back when we realised the pram wouldn't go through the turnstile. Fortunately, the man in the ticket office said we could leave the pram with him until we came back down.

'Sorted,' I said.

'Is it safe in the rain?' she asked, as I helped her with the papoose.

'Oh quite safe,' said the man. 'The Victorians went up in all weathers.'

She smiled weakly as we took our seats on opposing benches inside our green car. The wood was scrawled all over with graffiti – nothing particularly original, the usual hearts and cocks and *I Love Minge* daubings. Underneath my seat there was a flattened Capri Sun and a brown apple core that was stinking out the whole compartment despite the open window.

For the longest time, Marnie refused to look outside. She sat biting her lip, knee jiggling, stroking Raph's head, silent.

The bell rang and she noticeably tensed, squeezing the baby tighter. He started wailing and she pushed her smallest knuckle into his gob. The cart cranked and moved, lifting us gently up the incline.

'Oh god oh god oh god.'

'So what's going on then?' I asked, feet up on her seat. She shook her head, eyes closed, both hands clutching the walls of the car. 'You're not answering texts, you're ignoring my calls—'

'I'm not ignoring you.'

The smell of damp rock and rain rushed through the window and I inhaled it deeply. 'Then why aren't you answering me?'

She stood up, then sat straight back down again when the car juddered. 'Why did I let you talk me into this? I shouldn't be here. They have to stop it.'

'Are you not coming to Cardiff on Saturday then?'

'What?' She opened her eyes.

'The coach trip with WOMBAT. Remember? Shopping and a show? Overnight stay?'

'Oh, no no no, no I can't.' The car jolted and she shrieked, still holding the sides. 'Is it nearly over?'

'No, it's only just begun.'

'I don't like this. I need to get out.'

'Why didn't you let me know about Cardiff? Why leave me hanging?'

'Don't talk about hanging, please,' she breathed. 'I told you, I've been busy, I haven't had time. And my phone's been playing up—'

'Oh and a bit more bullshit left in the tank, is there? And there's me thinking we were all out.'

She looked directly at me, heaving for breath. A sheen of sweat had popped out over her forehead. Raph was still wailing and she wedged her knuckle in again. 'Okay, I'll tell you the truth. When I'm out with you, I'm too happy. And Happy is not good for me.'

'That makes zero sense,' I said. 'Less than zero in fact.'

She sat down, still concentrating on her breaths. 'I just feel like if I'm happy too much I won't be the right person anymore.' She was staring so intently at me. It was the same expression Julia had on her face when I cut her throat. Must be fear.

'You'd rather be the person you are now?' I said. 'Scared? Controlled? Every movement monitored? Humiliated in front of your friends?'

'He doesn't humiliate me.'

'You told me Tim announced to the Pudding Club that you'd wet yourself in Costa after you found out you were pregnant. And he told them how much weight you gained.'

'It slipped out. He didn't mean to.'

I sighed, over-theatrically. 'You displayed those ballerinas yet?'

'No.'

'Look I'm not going to launch into the full Wilson Phillips medley here, Marn, but why are you so afraid to be happy? Why can't you loosen up?'

'I don't want to be alone again. I don't function. Before I met Tim, I was off the rails. I was a lost soul. Tim made me feel safe and got me out of Leeds and away from all my bad influences – my friends, family – and he brought me here. I was a wreck after my mum died. I hit the bottle, hit the clubs. I was addicted to sex and freedom. The euphoria of it, you know?'

'Yeah, I know that feeling.'

'But it was drowning me. When you and me are together, it takes me back to that feeling of being free. And it scares me. It's a great feeling but I don't want to lose myself again. I don't want to go back.'

'*I'm* alone.'

'Yeah but you're stronger than me. I'm too scared, Rhee.'

'But you want to leave, don't you?'

'No, I don't. I can't let go.'

'You have to. You could be anything, Marnie. You could

go anywhere. Isn't there some place in the world where you'd love to go?'

'Alassio,' she replied, eventually 'In Italy. It's where my family comes from. I'd go and live somewhere near my brother.'

'Then go.'

'I can't. My brother hates Tim.'

'I wasn't suggesting you take Tim.'

'I'm not like you, Rhiannon. I can't throw caution to the wind like that and up sticks. I have a family.'

'Ooh, way harsh Ty.'

'You know what I mean.'

'You don't have to be like me. Just don't be like *this*,' I told her. 'Don't be scared all the time. He's the one making you scared. Let go of the walls.'

'No.'

I held her wrists and gently prised them off the walls of the cart.

'Stand up.'

'I can't.'

'I'm standing up too. Stand with me. Come on, you can do it. You don't have to open your eyes. Stand up, Marnie.'

Inch by inch, she did. The cart jolted and she yelped. Raph grizzled.

'I'm still holding you, Marn.'

Tears trickled down both her cheeks. 'I don't like this. I don't feel safe. What if I fall?'

'You can't fall, I'm holding you.'

'I can't do this.'

'Come to Cardiff on Saturday with me.'

'It's too risky.'

'It's a Christian women's day trip. The riskiest part will be deciding which hymns to sing on the coach. Or a slightly stale Dundee cake.'

She opened her eyes. 'You don't know what I'm like when I'm off the leash, Rhiannon.'

'Take a risk once in a while, Marnie. I dare you.'

'Don't start that again.'

'You might enjoy it a tiny bit.'

'I'm afraid.'

'Afraid of what? Tim?'

'Of myself.'

'You're stronger than you think, Marn. You've done this. You've conquered your fear of heights today alone.'

'Huh?' she said, looking around. The cart had stopped. We were back at the bottom. And she hadn't even noticed.

Saturday, 10th November
– 26 weeks, 6 days

Marnie *did* come to Cardiff. I don't know what she said to persuade Tim to let her but she was waiting for me at the coach when I rocked up with my overnight bag. I squealed and she squealed and it was like the last twenty years and the babies and Craig hadn't happened and we were just two besties meeting up for a school trip.

The first half of the journey was fine apart from a bit of coach-seat backache – we ate our pick and mix, sharing earphones to listen to our tunes. She loves Queen Bey almost as much as me but doesn't know as many words, obvs. We watched a movie – *The Passion of the Christ* – until Elephant Vadge Madge was sick and it was switched off. I'd initially thought Marnie had left Tim at home for the day but of course, he was never far away.

Six texts. Two calls. One FaceTime. And we'd only been on the road two hours. So yeah, that pissed me off.

We stopped at the services to use the toilets and here t'was that I made one of my world-famous boo-boos. I spotted a pub called The Stagecoach and I bought Marnie a drink.

'So you can loosen up,' I said, holding up a glass of White Zinfandel as she returned from the toilets.

'No I can't. I'm breastfeeding.'

'This is your day off, remember?'

'I'm not good with drink, Rhee. One glass and I'll be out for the count.'

'Go on, it's only a few sips. Stingy bastards charge five quid for that and it's no more than a tooth-full. It'll take the edge off.'

'Edge off what?'

'Your anxiety.'

'I'm not anxious.' She fiddled with the glass stem. 'I love Zinfandel.'

'I remember you saying you missed it when you were pregnant. Go on, neck it. Be less Marnie today, be more Rhiannon.'

She swilled that thought around for a moment before necking the Zinfandel in three gulps. Then she ordered another.

'I didn't know how much I wanted that,' she said, wiping her mouth with the back of her hand. 'It'll be out of my system by tomorrow, won't it?'

'Yeah of course.'

I went to the loo for the second time and when I got back to the coach, Marnie motioned me to join her around the back where she produced a pack of cigarettes.

'You don't smoke.'

'I used to,' she said. 'Tim got me to quit. I've had these in my bag for months'

She lit one up and threw her head back. 'Fuck me gently, that's good.'

It was around this point that I fully got what she had meant

when she said she was afraid of herself. Because when Marnie drank, Marnie changed.

'You're cashing in all your bad girl chips today, aren't you?' I said, full of pointy-toe goodliness – Nanny McPhee to her sudden onset Chris Brown.

'That wine's done me the power of good. I feel so relaxed.' She laughed, almost maniacally, like laughter was a new thing for her. 'I do need to loosen up, you're right. I was way more Rhiannon, once upon a time.'

'Yeah?'

'Oh yeah,' she said, reaching into her bag and pulling out a little bottle of the Zinfandel she'd been drinking in the pub. 'Here's to loosening up.'

'Where did you get that?'

'I bought it when you went to the loo.' She giggled like an imp, stubbing out her cigarette on the coach and lighting up another. Her head lolled back so hard I thought it might fall off. 'Jesus Christ almighty. That's like an orgasm for the mouth.'

Big Headed Edna was wandering past the bus with her carpet bag. 'I hope that wasn't the Lord's name I heard then.'

'Yeah he was here, Edna,' Marnie called out, quick as lightning. 'He was going into Burger King. I waved but he didn't recognise me.'

Edna did her best bulldog-chewing-a-wasp impression and shuffled back onto the coach.

A group of lads, clearly on a stag weekend, sauntered loudly across the car park towards a pimped-up green hatchback, clutching McDonald's bags.

'Oi oi!' they shouted across at us. No, not us. *Marnie.* I

forgot I have The Bump now – the finest Cock Repellent on the market today.

Marnie lifted her top to reveal her pendulous lactating tits.

A chorus of cheers and *Wahey!*s followed as one of the lads – a good ten years younger, tanned orange and stacked like a champion boxer – laughed hysterically and made a beeline towards her. You know the type – fake tan, Peaky Blinders haircut, crisp black jeans, tight V-shaped torso and permanently hard pecs. I stood back in the shade, not quite believing what I'd seen as a zephyr of scattered detritus whipped up around me.

Some hideous Ibiza remix of Prince's 'Get Off' blared out, as their engine purred and honked at their chief fuckboy. I suddenly felt about a hundred years old so I shuffled back onto the coach with all the other crones.

Marnie was last on board, around twenty minutes later, so giddy she could barely sit still. 'They're on a stag weekend. Troy – the one I was talking to – says we can join them in Cardiff tonight if we like. He's lovely.'

'He's about eight.'

'Twenty-two actually,' she said, with a firm eye roll.

'And why am I caring about this exactly?'

'They've asked us out for drinks.' She was laughing like a Wimbledon audience – at absolutely nothing.

'Us?'

'Yeah, you and me.'

'Why me?'

'I said I wouldn't come out without you. They all seem lovely though.'

'Well they would, wouldn't they? You showed them your tits.'

The horn honked a shave-and-a-haircut and sped towards the M5.

A Malteser rolled out from under the seat in front of us and Marnie scrabbled around and ate it straight off the floor, fluff and all. 'It's a bit of fun. They've booked a special package at this club in the city centre – Meetz – queue jump, private lounge, waitress service *and* mixers. One of them's getting married next weekend. Go on, what do you say?'

I did the double take at my abdominal mound and waited for her to get the hint. She didn't. 'Uh, I can't drink? And we're supposed to be on a Christians Are Us coach trip, in case you've forgotten?'

'Yeah I know, but go on, it'll be fun. Come with me, please?'

'What about Heil Husband? Don't you have to clock in at the Eagle's Nest this evening? He'll tell if you're drunk. He'll smell it down the phone.'

'You're the one who told me to ditch the guy. You're the one who said Tim was a controlling little bitch and that I needed to take off my ankle tag. So I am. I said I will call him later and I will. I don't want to think about tomorrow, Rhiannon. Today is what matters.'

*

I know I know, I'll be old one day, and Check my privilege and all that, but Jeeeeeesus Christ old women move slowly. Cardiff Castle was fun and all but only because Marnie was there. And her being pissed out of her mind did make it funner – she was so easy to trip up. They had a trebuchet in the grounds and we spent an inordinate amount of time talking about the different screams each WOMBAT would emit as we fired them over the

ramparts. We laughed at codpieces, pretended to steal antiques and swore unabashedly. The other WOMBATs made it clear they were NOT amused, particularly Edna who had 'gone to great lengths to organise this trip' and didn't appreciate our behaviour.

I don't think I stopped laughing all day. Marnie started it. She said Rita had an 'arse that looked like two bin bags full of water', and I chimed in with 'At least she doesn't have headstone teeth like Debbie Does Donkeys.' Unfortunately we were in a stone corridor with good acoustics and both women heard every word. White Nancy ranted about the 'language being tossed about like confetti' as well. So we're not in their Good Books right now. I don't think we're even in the library.

If wombats had feathers, they'd be a-ruffled right about now.

Had to check in early to our hotel so Marnie could sleep off her wine binge, and then I hit the shops alone. I ate lunch in a swanky Italian eatery in Cardiff Bay called Acqua in Bocca where the waiter looked like Salt Bae and persuaded me to go for the pine nut and ricotta ravioli, even though pine nuts always get stuck in my teeth, I don't like ricotta and I'm not that keen on ravioli. Wasn't so bad though. Everyone else around me seemed to be having turkey Milanese or steak, the sight of which doesn't repulse me as much as it did. I may have turned the corner on meat.

Why did you take that man's steak knife, Mummy?

I got back to the Radisson late afternoon, walking like a puppet, my feet throbbing, my face sweating and my baby kicking the shit out of me because I'd had a glass of Prosecco at lunch. I crashed out on the bed and I've been here since. Got to start getting ready in a minute. We're meeting the Fuckboyz at 7 p.m. Sometimes having a friend is totally overrated.

That Prosecco's gone up my umbilical cord and into my brain. It's brain damaging me. I hope you're happy.

*

Marnie was pissed to begin with. There is no doubt whatever about that. She'd thrown up all the Zinfandel but our feet had barely touched the threshold of Meetz when she was downing double vodkas. Then she reached a new pinnacle of pissed-ness – the Say Anything to Anyone Phase. She offered the doorman a blowjob and called a passing cyclist a Bike Wanker.

Superb gentlemen on the coat check – he checked my coat but didn't bother to *check* my coat. I made a mental note to tip him extra.

The 'Fuckboyz on Tor' – from Glastonbury, hence the excellent pun – had all turned up as promised. No road accidents had taken them out in the meantime. All dressed up in crisp short sleeves, shiny pointy shoes and trousers so tight you could read their sort codes, Fuckboy Troy had texted Marnie and told her to meet them all on Level 6 on the top floor.

'Marn, are you sure you want to do this?' I said as she grabbed my wrist and led me towards the lifts.

'Yes,' she said, sharp as a sword. 'Yes I do.'

Meetz was your bog-standard city centre venue with six levels of club rooms – the ground floor, which was all decked out in a jungle theme with wicker chairs and glow-in-the-dark cocktails – was dead. Level six – our level – seemed to bear an electro theme. The lights were blinding, the music was repetitive and the barmen all wore epilepsy-inducing waistcoats.

Get me out of here now.

I should have gone back to our hotel after the first drink

but something stopped me – Marnie. I sat there for hours on the end of a booth upholstered in mermaid's skin, feeling like a nun in a brothel, watching her dancing, drinking and flirting with every member of the group. She wasn't the only one of course. They were all at it and the room was packed out with people flirting, Gangnamming, shuffling, whip nay-naying, slut-dropping, fingering and twerking, a pot-bellied guy pouring lager over himself and a gangly woman in glasses throwing up in her handbag. I even watched some gelled-up douchebag drugging his date's Budweiser but I didn't warn her – it was the redhead who'd barged past me in the queue outside.

As I downed virgin cocktail #3 I lost the will and ordered a Prosecco.

You do realise I'm getting more brain damaged by the minute here? I'm gonna be on posters.

Four Fuckboyz hooked up with four random Ladiez and disappeared, and Marnie and Troy were necking in the corner of the booth. I held out a vague hope that at least one of the Boyz would be able to hold a conversation – there's usually one in any group like this who can – but on this occasion I was completely wrong and they were all cunts. I soon summarised they were only interested in women willing to put out there and then – conversation optional. I let one of them – Bradley, nineteen – feel my tits but warned him if he touched my bump I'd snap his fingers back. He laughed. Brain-wise he was pretty atticky. I don't know what Marnie saw in Troy either. Why are herpes-ridden fuckboys with half haircuts so appealing? I don't get it.

'So what do you do then, Rhiannon?' Bradley slurred in my ear.

'I'm pregnant.' I swigged my Prosecco. It felt thick in my mouth.

'Yeah I know but before that.'

'Oh I don't know. I worked in a bank or something.'

He laughed for no reason. 'Which one?'

'Uh, NatWest.'

He laughed for no reason again. 'Do you like it?'

'No.'

'Fancy another drink?'

'Just ask, *Do you want to have sex with me round the back of the bins – yes or no?*'

He laughed for a third time and my fist began to twitch. 'Well, do you?'

'You're really not picky are you?'

'Nope.'

'Any hole's a goal?'

'Yep.'

'Pink or stink?'

'How 'bout both?' He swigged his lager and laughed another fucking time. All he did was laugh and swig lager. I wanted to flay the skin from his acne-ridden face and reupholster the booth with it.

Troy and Marnie slid out of their banquette, her holding onto him like he was her walking frame – a walking frame with a boner like a hockey stick in its shorts. 'We're heading out to lounge, all right? Catch yous laters.'

'Where's the lounge?' I asked Bradley when they'd gone.

He was talking to the size six brunette ensconced between him and the next guy. 'Our private room next door. We've got

it, like, all night. It's more, like, private, so they can have a bit more privacy, kind of thing, like.'

Out in the corridor, the doors on the five lounges were closed but there was a glass porthole in each. The rooms were lit with different light bulbs – the Green and Yellow booths had people shagging inside them, in the Blue lounge three men were asleep and the White one was empty. I found Marnie and Troy heavy petting in the one that looked like the Pink Panther had just exploded in there.

I didn't knock.

'Marn? I'm going back to the hotel. Will you be OK on your own?'

Troy pulled slowly away from her neck. Marnie had her eyes closed and her head all lolled forward. 'I'll see she gets back, no worries.'

I looked at her. I looked at him. 'Preferably unraped?' I suggested.

'Eh?'

I afforded him a bored eyebrow. 'You might want to rein your cock in a bit seeing as she can't even hold her head up right now.'

'Oh piss off, Buzzkill.'

Marnie was asleep on his shoulder. He continued licking her neck.

'Marn, are you coming back to the hotel? Marnie?' I flicked her ear.

'Bug-off,' she slurred. 'Fun here.'

'See?' said Troy. 'She's having fun. Off you fuck then, Buzzkill.'

His piercing blue eyes lasered me. The point of my knife through each pupil – what a sight that would be.

I left them to it and stormed out slamming the door – well,

as much as I *could* slam the door when it got caught on the high pink furry shag pile.

I was in the packed corridor, inhaling vodka vomit and getting brain ache from the house music, looking for the lifts to anywhere when I heard the voice.

Don't leave her with him.

'I'm not staying here a second longer. I hate clubs.'

She doesn't know what she's doing. She's been drinking all day.

'My feet are killing me, I've got a headache, it stinks in here and all I can think about are those two Scottish shortbread biscuits in the mini bar.'

She needs you. She's the Mole out in the snowstorm and you are the Rat. You have to find her.

'Why should I?'

Because she's your friend. Remember when Joe Leech died? How bad you felt because you weren't with him?

'What am I meant to do exactly?'

You've still got the steak knife from the restaurant.

'Woah, you've changed your tune.'

Look, they're leaving.

I hid myself behind a group of women wearing little more than bras, pants and red feather boas, and watched as Troy led Marnie out of the Pink Panther room, along the corridor and back through the club, holding onto her waist. She was giggling and stumbling, her dress caught in her knickers. I lost sight of them at the cloakrooms where I picked up her coat.

Outside, the dark doorsteps of every pub and club clustered with smokers and little evil faces guffawing and *hee-hee*ing over nothing. I put on my coat and watched as Marnie and

Troy headed into the night. A woman in a silver lamé dress was slumped against a lamppost, throwing up. Her friend stood behind her shouting abuse at a taxi driver for being late.

A group of guys in dresses wearing silk 'Chaz's Stag' sashes smoked in the entrance of Lloyds Bank. Another group of students were lined up along the windows of a Polish supermarket, shagging like they were in a time trial.

Nobody noticed me. I was a creature of the night, picking my way through clumps of wind-blown litter and shining black puddles, not taking my eyes from my friend and her date. I pulled up the hood.

A guy lying on the pavement with his trousers round his ankles was crying into an empty burger box. A homeless guy and his Staffy were sitting in the doorway of Monsoon, eating a burger. I opened Marnie's purse and gave the homeless guy the three remaining £10 notes. It was starting to rain.

'You sure about this? You're not going to press your eject button?'

She's in trouble. You're all she's got.

I walked past people sprawled on the pavements, rolling in the middle of the road, shouting, fighting, a guy in a rugby the there shirt surfing on a pile of stuffed bin bags, a hen crying because she'd lost her balloon. Two police cars raced by, sirens blaring. Hi-vis jackets milled among the crowds, 'having a word' with two women in yellow 'getting lippy'.

I walked on, as though through a forest of trees rather than the open world, restricting my view of it as best I could within the hood's frame. I could smell Marnie's perfume all around me.

Keeping my eyes on Marnie and Troy as they shambled along the street, laughing and feeling each other up, I waited

far enough back so as not to be seen. He took her away from the melee, down a quiet side street called Wharton Place, in the other direction of where the police had been. Troy looked around – looking up – no CCTV. I ducked into a hairdresser's doorway and heard him – 'Come on, we're nearly back at your hotel, look.'

We were nowhere near our hotel. Our hotel was in the other direction.

There was a road off the side street – Baker's Row – comprised of back entrances and bins. Troy manoeuvred Marnie into a cobbled alley just off it.

I took the steak knife out of my bag and poked it up inside my sleeve. I hung my bag on an outside tap.

'Are we going to do this?' I whispered, barely catching my breath.

You've got no choice.

I heard Marnie murmuring. 'Sick.' And then an urge and then a splash.

'Ahh, shit – you've got it on my kicks, man.'

'Ohhh… all better,' she lazy-laughed, hair in her face, eyes, mouth.

Do it. Do it now!

'Come here now. Stand up. No, you're not going anywhere, love.'

He's going to rape her – you have to, Mummy, go!

I moved closer, ducking down behind a wheelie bin.

More murmuring. 'No,' she said. 'Can't.'

'Let's get these knickers off.'

What are you waiting for? KILL HIM!

I moved two more steps closer. Troy had her pinned to the

concrete wall by his chest, his face on her bare breast, sucking it hard. Biting it. Big tanned hands grabbing at the sides of her thighs, yanking down her knickers. Her eyes were closed. 'No. I can't, I can't.' Batting his hands away.

I couldn't catch my breath. The rain beat down. 'What if I miss?'

You never miss. Get him in the neck before he knows what's hit him. Otherwise he could hit you. And if he hits you he'll hit me. Protect her, protect me. KILL HIM NOW.

Marnie's knickers were around her feet – one of her shoes was off. Troy unzipped his fly. He pushed her against the wall, forcing her legs around him.

Shank him. Hard.

I came up behind him, stealthy as a lioness raised the knife and stabbed down into the right of his neck – carotid artery – the bit that pulses. His knees buckled. He grabbed out. Marnie sank down, groaning.

'What?' she murmured.

The blade was lodged deep in Troy's windpipe – I figured once the vocal cords had been severed there'd be no noise. At least, no screaming.

HARDER.

There was breathing in my ears – mine. Deep. So deep. Like the air was raking me clean from top to toe. Cleansing breaths.

He grabbed at the knife handle, his fingers bloody and slippery and pulled it out, and went down like a hot rock, onto his knees.

'Ahh fuck man fuck… '

Finish him.

He was pumping out and the blood was trickling to the

ground, meandering through the cracks in the cobblestones. I straddled his abdomen – feeling his writhing body between my thighs was like coming home. I wrenched the knife out of his grasp and stabbed it down into his stomach, again and again – I kept going. *In. In. In. In. In. In. In.*

He gasped. I gasped.

Okay enough now.

In. In. In. In. In until I felt bone beneath blade and his breaths grew fewer, his muscles weakened where blood wasn't pumping to them.

He felt so good, squirming beneath me. Body to body. Life to death. I felt myself cum in my leggings – thank god I double-gusset now. A full body shiver with the rain on my face and my hands on the knife.

ENOUGH NOW!

I pulled out the knife and wiped the blade clean on his shirt. He lay there gargling – eyes wide, looking straight at me. The urge to hold him as he lay dying was horrendous but I controlled myself admirably. I rinsed my hands under the tap. Then came back to him to witness his dying breaths.

I bent over, his blood cough spraying my face. 'Sorry to kill your buzz, babe.'

It was as I stood up that I felt the nausea rise. I swallowed it down.

Troy gargled, a sink draining of water. The vocal chords should have been severed – stupid Google – I hadn't gone deep enough. He obviously worked out so he was fit and could fight it.

You need to get out of here.

He sat up, but I pushed him back down, held the clean knife point directly above his windpipe and pushed down.

Eyes still searching, mouth gaping, blood flicking out in spurts. AJ's face on his. AJ's head falling away from his neck.

Nausea rising, I stood up and threw myself at the wheelie bin where my stomach turned out everything it had digested that day.

LEAVE. NOW.

'Is that you? Is that you making me sick?'

Marnie stirred beside the bin. I wrang out her rain-soaked knickers and put them in my pocket, easing her to her feet.

'Wha—?'

'It's all right, it's me. We're going home now. It's okay. It's all okay.'

Sunday, 11th November
– 27 weeks exactly

1. *Hotel bathroom signs that bang on about re-using*
   towels to save the environment – I don't give a rat's ass
   about the environment. I'll leave lights on, taps on. If
   I'm paying £100 a night to sleep, I'll shit the bed to get
   my money's worth.

The elation went as quickly as it arrived. I know it's not me – I know it's Her – the Swede. I can't enjoy killing when I'm pregnant, that's a fact now. It's become like eating meat – abhorrent. I should feel like dancing. Adrenalized in every limb, reeling with pleasure. But I'm empty.

You killed my daddy that way. Remember his face in the bath as you cut off his arms?

I threw up again in the bush outside the hotel. We had looks from the receptionist when I stumbled through the lobby with Marnie after midnight, both soaked and dragging ourselves along like we'd just spent a heavy night on the lash – the very image I was trying to cultivate.

Daddy's blood dripping down the bathtub. Pooling in the sink. Bones cracking under your hammer blows.

I changed Marnie out of her wet clothes and hung them on

the towel rail in the bathroom. I wrapped her in a hotel dressing gown and tucked her into her bed, making sure to prop a pillow against her back to keep her on her side in case she puked.

Which she did around three o'clock, in the bin, before slumping back into bed. I slept for about an hour in all, and had a succession of terrible dreams. AJ in his bath of blood. A baby roasting on a spit in a castle kitchen. Wild dogs tearing a child to pieces. I had a shower at four when I couldn't stand Marnie's snoring any longer.

All seemed to be well in the Land of the Uterus, amazingly – no pains, no bleeding and the Doppler gave me a strong heartbeat when I checked. There was nothing to worry about, but there was still background nausea all the time. And the strong feeling of knowing what I had done last night was wrong.

I haven't even started on the paranoia. I'd gone too public with this one. Worse than Birmingham. What if there was CCTV? What about clothing fibres? My vomit in that wheelie bin? Maybe the rain would wash any trace of myself from his body. Rain was my friend. It was still raining as I dried my hair, looking down from the hotel window on to the empty streets below.

Marnie was quiet first thing. Apart from my 'Do you want to use my conditioner?' and 'Black coffee?' questions, both of which were answered with a shake of her head, she barely said two words. I went down to breakfast on my own – none of the other WOMBATs appeared to be speaking to me. Big Headed Edna threw me a look which I couldn't decipher – it either meant *I'm angry you snubbed* Chicago or *There's no room at our table*.

Either way I sat at a table on my own.

Tight Bun Doreen eventually came over and spoke to me

when I was halfway through my fruit salad. The second she opened her mouth I wanted to punch it.

'Rhiannon, some WOMBATs have complained about yours and your friend's behaviour yesterday.' She blinked rapidly and her wattles quivered as she spoke. 'And with you not coming to *Chicago*, I'm not sure it's wise to come on any more outings.'

'Figures,' I said, spooning in some melon and flicking over the pages of a *Sunday Telegraph* left by the previous table occupant.

'I'm sorry?'

'Well, none of you have been comfortable with me or Elaine being in your group from the start, have you?'

Edna scuttled over to stand by Doreen. 'That's not true, Rhiannon.'

'It *is* true. Elaine's only a member because she sits in sack cloth and ashes while you lot pile on the guilt. I won't do that and that frustrates you.'

'Well honestly, I ask you!' Edna gasped.

'I've seen the sly looks, heard you all talking in corners, the whispers about Elaine's "beast of a son" and "the beast's pregnant girlfriend". I guess forgiveness only applies if you're over sixty.'

'Now that's not fair,' said Doreen. 'You and Elaine have been welcome at WOMBAT from the start.' Wheelchair Mary zoomed across to join in.

'Tolerated, I'd say. Especially by you two.' Some people just have that face don't they? A face that draws fists. It's probably not their fault on some level, but on some other level, it entirely is.

'Murder is a sin,' Mary chimed in. 'I *don't* think you should

be allowed in this group, *either* of you. The man is a monster. It's bad enough that his parents have to live in the town without you infiltrating us as well.'

Doreen tried to quell the situation, as did Black Nancy who came over with a plate of fruit and yoghurt from the buffet.

Edna took no notice. 'If you're a family that supports murder, regardless of who did it, then shame on you.'

'God murdered people,' I said, to an audible gasp from all three of them. 'Loads of 'em. Old Testament's full of murder. God was killing people left, right, centre and back. You all seem to sanction *that*.'

'That's blasphemous!' Wheelchair Mary chided. 'Totally blasphemous.'

'No it's not, it's a fact. I underlined some passages in my Bible, look,' I said, fumbling for it in my bag. 'Sodom and Gomorrah – thousands dead… shedloads of Israelites, all the first borns of Judah – ordered BY GOD.'

Doreen crossed herself. Edna's wattles flapped in the breeze.

'Kings,' I said. 'The Lord sends two she-bears out of the woods to tear forty-two small boys to pieces because they *laughed* at a *bald guy*… Samuel Six verses nineteen to twenty – the Lord strikes some men of Bethshemesh because they *looked* at the Ark. Then there's Lot's wife, and don't get me started on Exodus.'

'You're underlining passages about murder?' said Doreen.

'Yeah. It interests me. Ezekiel. "I will fill your mountains with the dead. Your hills and your valleys and your streams filled with people slaughtered by the sword. I will make you desolate forever. Then you will know I am God." And you're having a go at Craig because he offed five sex offenders?' I shook my head. 'God works in hella mysterious ways.'

Marnie properly woke up when we were halfway home on the train, and while her sickness had gone, her guilt had returned.

'I can't believe it,' she said, over and over again. 'Why are we on a train?'

Up until that point she'd been going through the motions unquestioning. 'Oh yeah we've been kicked out of WOMBAT. I forgot to say.'

'But we paid for those coach tickets.'

I grabbed her hand, opened it, and placed a crisp £20 on her palm. 'Courtesy of Big Headed Edna. I got you a cereal bar and a black coffee from the trolley guy.' I pushed them across the table towards her.

'All because we didn't go to *Chicago*?'

I rifled through my handbag for some Polos or gum or something – the hotel breakfast was sticking to my tongue. 'Not just because of that, no. Our behaviour at the castle yesterday. Our language. What I said at breakfast. What I did at breakfast. Mint?'

She shook her head. 'What did you do at breakfast?'

'Poured yoghurt over White Nancy. Pushed Wheelchair Mary into the pyramid of jams. Called Edna a name.'

'What name?'

'A bad name.'

She exhaled long and slow. 'What the hell is Tim going to say? I can't lie to him. He'll find out that we didn't go to the show.'

'How? He doesn't know anyone at WOMBAT, does he?'

'He'll know if I'm lying. What am I going to say to him?'

'You'll say "Heil Honey, I'm home. Here's your

rainbow-coloured pencil from Cardiff Castle. We had a lovely lunch yesterday, saw a terrific performance of *Chicago* – that *X Factor* reject isn't auto tuned after all – and a great night's sleep at the hotel." *That*'s what you'll say.'

'I can't say all that. I'll forget.'

I shoved the mints back in my bag. 'So you're going to tell him about Fuckboy Troy and the half a haircut then, are you?'

'I was drunk most of the day, I didn't know what I was doing. See this is why I was so afraid of letting go. I don't know when to stop.'

'Birds born in cages think flying is an illness.'

'What?'

'It's a quote I saw online. I was looking for information on battered wives and Google threw that up.'

'I am NOT a battered wife.'

'That's what you did last night, Marnie. You flew.'

She frowned but it wasn't at me – she was looking at my handbag as I was doing it up. The tip of the steak knife had caught in the zip.

'What's that?'

'Fruit knife.'

'It's big for a fruit knife.'

'I like big fruits.' I pushed it in, zipped up the bag and posted it under our table. 'So anyway, back to the matter at hand and your obvious disgrace.'

'Oh god what else did I do last night, Rhee, please tell me?'

'What do you remember?'

'The club. Lots of pink everywhere. Being sick. My foot was cold – I lost my shoe. The music. My head was banging. I stubbed my toe on a door. And you and me in a lift. You were

laughing. And I remember waking up. And all my money's gone. I didn't spend it all, did I?'

'You drank the place dry.'

'Oh god.' She leant towards the table, head in hands.

I zipped my bag tight and put it back underneath. 'You don't remember anything else?'

'I was wet. And you pulled off my dress. I woke up in a bath towel.'

'It was raining. I wrapped you in that to keep you warm.'

'You looked after me. Thank you.'

'Totes welcs.'

'Did I fall over? I remember a wet floor. Cobbled stones.'

'That was in the hotel bathroom, Marnie.'

'No, I was outside. I saw you and a guy.'

'I pulled him off you.'

'Rhee, tell me everything, please. I need to understand this.'

'You were going to have sex with him.'

'Oh no—'

'But you didn't. I took you back to the hotel and put you to bed.'

'You're sure he didn't touch me?'

'No. I wouldn't let him. Now wipe it from your mind, okay? Nothing happened. We had a boring time, saw a boring show and communed with boring old women. It's over.'

'You're such a good friend.'

'You better believe it.'

Wednesday, 14ᵗʰ November
– 27 weeks, 3 days

1. *The two wiry, over-animated drug addicts waiting for methadone at the pharmacy – insectile creatures without socks, sniffing like their nostrils are forever trying to catch the merest fleck of heroin on the air.*
2. *Jittery woman with the huge nostrils in the shoe shop – she spent as little time serving me as possible before retreating to the safety of the jauntily-angled slippers in the window, rearranging ones which didn't look quite jaunty enough.*
3. *Sandra Huggins.*

Jim and Elaine spent the morning showing me their photographs from the Lake District – all 308 of them. Tink was in every shot – perched on a rock, walking in the woods, sitting next to Jim in a country pub. Cuddles with Elaine on the boat on Lake Windermere. She was 'as good as gold' apparently.

Got a new midwife – she's about nineteen, has green hair and is covered in tatts. She's called Whitney or Tiffany or something, and had just passed her exams so obviously she's been assigned to me. Far too jolly for my liking. She gave me a blood test today – I'm a bit anaemic but 'nothing to worry

about.' She said I should be eating more foods with iron in, more Vitamin C, eggs, pulses, leafy green veg.

'Anaemia,' I repeated after her. 'That's quite a nice name isn't it?'

'For a baby?' said Bitch Midwife. 'I'd say that was tantamount to abuse!'

'What are your kids called?'

She included props with her answer – a pendant opened to reveal a picture of two toothless darlings. 'That's Chantelle and this one's Braydon.'

'Mmm,' I said. 'Lovely.'

'Have you got any names in mind?'

'Mmm, I'm going to have four girls and I'm going to call them Violence, Anarchy, Mayhem and Pandemonium.'

She laughed. 'So which one's this then?'

'Have to wait and see, won't you?'

Oh and my Cardiff kill has hit the newspapers. Cop a load of this …

THE FAMILY of a man who died in Cardiff city centre at the weekend have paid tribute to him.

The body of 22-year-old Troy Shearer was found by a passer-by in the alleyway off Baker's Row in the early hours of Sunday, 11th November. A Home Office Post Mortem has confirmed that Troy died from multiple stab wounds to the chest and neck.

Troy's mother, Melanie Samways, paid tribute, saying: 'Troy was a much loved son. His whole family is completely devastated. He was a real character and if you met him, you would always remember it.'

Detective Chief Inspector Lauren Merton said: 'This was a

*tragic way for Troy's life to come to an end after just going out
for a good time with his friends. His death has left his family
understandably distraught and our condolences of course go to
them during this tremendously difficult time.*

  *'The investigation continues at pace and we still want people
to come forward with any information they believe may assist our
inquiries.'*

What a saint, eh? I imagine Troy worked with homeless people in
his spare time or volunteered for the Make a Wish Foundation.
Only the good guys ever seem to die.

  Nipped into Tesco on the way home. Bought a box of frozen
eclairs. Didn't even wait for them to thaw.

Friday, 16th November
– 27 weeks, 5 days

1. *People who touch me unannounced.*
2. *Middle class white people who have barbecues and
    invite me to them.*

I didn't want to go to Pin's party. My in-utero Jiminy Cricket
had sent a new batch of sluggishness, so while the spirit was at
least half-willing, the flesh was fucked. Slept most of the day,
washed, dressed, and around 4 p.m. made my way over on the
water taxi to Temperley – the richest area of town.

The climb to her house almost killed me – Pin and her family
lived in a mansion set back amongst the trees like it was in
hiding. It was more glass than house – huge wide windows
allowed a view of everything inside, so there was no excuse for
anyone missing just how rich they were. Huge art sculptures
on the landing, plush cream sitting rooms and a hallway the
size of Jim and Elaine's whole house. This was a money family
and no mistake.

A young girl with inbreeder's teeth and ears greeted me at
the front door with 'You can't come in unless you've brought
presents.' She talked in spit with her nose in the air, like most
posh kids do.

'Hi Rhiannon, do come in,' said Pin, lugging her bump along the hallway in a hideous oversized paisley playsuit and gold sandals. 'Mulberry – can you ask Daddy to bring up some more Pinot Noir, there's a good girl.'

Mulberry merrily skipped off like all rich kids do when they know they're never going to have to do a day's work in their over-privileged lives.

I crossed the threshold, handing her the bottle of value lemonade I'd brought along. 'Happy Birthday.'

'Thank you, darling,' she said, holding me in a headlock and sticking a hairy-faced Clinique kiss on both cheeks. She scoped my burgeoning bump and held it at the sides. 'You're looking swell, Dolly!'

'You can talk,' I said, scoping her abdomen which looked like the wolf's in that kids' book where he ate the big rocks. And then she did something horrific – she pushed her bump against mine **so they were touching.**

Nausea ambushed all my senses.

What the hell is she doing, Mummy!? Get it off! Get it off!

'Um, what are you doing?' I awk-laughed, trying to breathe it out.

'Clive?' she called out. 'Take a picture, darling. Rhiannon's here.'

Clive, a small bald man in head-to-toe Blue Harbour and wicker shoes scurried around the corner with his phone held out like he was detecting something – in this case, a random humiliation opportunity for me.

'Do the thumbs up, Rhiannon,' Pin giggled, posing for the camera.

Oh Christ, not the thumbs up as well as the bump-to-bump. *Click.*

'Aw, that's great,' Clive chuckled. 'Rhiannon hi, sorry, we're trying to get as many double bump shots as possible. We're doing a collage.'

'How wonderful!' I pain-grinned, nausea abating.

'Everyone's outside, Rhee,' said Pin. 'We've done a barbecue as it's still so warm this evening and we'll be having a few fireworks a bit later on, hope you're okay with that? Some people feel rather triggered by them.' She rolled her eyes. I knew she was talking about Helen.

'I don't trigger easily, don't worry.'

'Do go out and mingle. I'm keeping an eye on my brioche.'

I knew the moment I stepped out onto the patio that I didn't belong.

Lit by tea lights and fairy lights in the evening gloom, the garden was a cacophony of chatter and childish squeals. Mostly straight, white people stood around in groups or sat on lines of chairs like lazy, middle class firing squads, laughing *Fwaar Fwaar* and quaffing from fizzy glasses. There was an essence of horse about every face. A curly red-head with Bugs Bunny teeth struck up a convo about the thickness of the barbecue smoke as we were both coughing.

'Did you see that bastard in China who fried the dog in a wok?' I said.

'Uh no, no I didn't.'

'It was disgusting,' I said. 'Do you know they do that in China? And Korea. They fry animals alive cos they think the meat's tenderer.'

At some point during my continued rant about dogs in hot woks, she moved away. I was about to head over to the bouncy castle in the middle of the lawn where all the kids were playing,

when I was collared by the Pudding Club, having some debate about immunisations.

'I'm so worried about it,' Scarlett said, stroking her bump. 'Lodi wants the baby to, like, have his jabs because his uncle, like, didn't and he's got, like, autism. What do I do?'

Nev swigged her champagne. 'We chose not to immunize Jadis *or* Alannah, and it never did them any harm. Doctors get paid for immunizing so that's why you get scare stories. Kids are kids, they're gonna get sick.'

Helen was on it like a Scotch bonnet. 'But you forget these vaccines are *proven* to do their jobs. There's so many benefits.'

'Like what?' asked Nev.

'It helps them fight disease, particularly measles. I remember one lad when I was a nipper got measles and he had to have all his limbs cut off.'

'There's no 'arm in it,' I said, looking at them in turn – three witches stirring their cauldron.

'Well quite,' said Helen, all earnest-face, turning to Scarlett. 'Get the immunizations done ASAP. It's your duty as a mother.'

'Are you going to, like, get it done then, Rhiannon?' Scarlett asked.

I grabbed an elderflower pressé from a passing tray. 'Um, no.'

'You must!' said Helen. 'Why wouldn't you?'

'Cos I don't care.' I'm lying, by the way. Of course I care. But the thrill of watching Helen's growing outrage was too tempting. I take my giggles where I can these days, since my little joy sponge took up residence in Wombville.

'You MUST Rhiannon. This is your baby's life we're talking about.'

'Then I'll let the baby decide for themselves later on, I guess.'

Helen flushed. 'No, you have to *prevent* it. It's too late by the time they come down with anything. I've worked with hundreds of children over twenty years and I've never met one that's been damaged from immunizations. I have met a few who were very ill due to *not* getting immunized though.'

'Right,' I said, quaffing my pressé. 'Mmm, that's refreshing. What time do the fireworks start?'

'So you'll have the shots done then?' said Helen. It was not a request.

'SIR YES SIR!' I saluted, snapping my heels together, which garnered a few looks from other straight white folk and a sly smile from Nev.

Helen's husband Jasper – a human streak of undercooked pastry if ever I've seen one – came scuffing over to say he'd left his 'cardie' in the Land Rover and could he have the keys cos it was 'getting a bit chilly'.

The buffet wasn't your Iceland Sliders or Kentucky bucket affair – it was all homemade blinis and dim sum and brioche buns of barbecued Wagyu beef, bone china dishes of the most middle class crisps money could buy – Chorizo and Opera House, Camembert and Yacht Club, Foie Gras and Golf Trouser, complete with flag labels. I hit it harder than a fat girl on prom night – sans any meat-based delicacies, obvs. Jiminy Cricket still no likey.

None of the conversations around the buffet table were particularly engrossing.

'We tried goat's milk but it made Giles ill so we went back to yak.'

'Plum came first in the gymkhana on Rollo... such a scream!'

'We bought a beach hut at Bude, only a hundred and fifty

K, give or take. Bring the family once the Aston Martin's out of dry dock.'

'We use cocoa bean husks in our flower borders now. The whole garden smells like warm brownies in high summer, it's DIVINE!'

'Oh isn't it awful in Syria? More Verve Clicquot anybods?'

If Craig had been there, we'd have found a quiet corner and kept to ourselves and made our own fun – play drinking games or taking the piss – but being on your own leaves you open to the elements on these things. A Davy lamp and a pickaxe couldn't get me into any of these conversations so I headed along the stepping stone footpath to the lawns where the kids hung out.

I poked my head through the window of the Wendy house to find four girls playing with fake food and plastic cutlery.

'Mind if I join you guys?' I said. 'I'm bored.'

'Do you want to play Homes?' piped up one kid with purple ribbons threaded through her corn rows. She was cooking at the plastic stove – a delicacy called Stone Soup.

'Yeah go on then,' I said, squeezing through the door which they all found hilarious. I sat down on a pink bean bag big enough for one buttock.

'Have you got babies in your tummy like our mum has?' piped up a little girl wearing glasses who was grilling mud pies.

'Yeah, I have. You must be Nev's daughters.'

Glasses nodded. 'How did your baby get inside your tummy?'

Corn Rows smacked her sister's arm. 'You mustn't ask that, Alannah, cos it's rude. It's cos the daddy and the mummy have a special cuddle and the seed is what squirts out. *That* makes the baby.'

286

Alannah stared at me open mouthed.

'I'm Jadis,' said Corn Rows. 'And she's Alannah.' She pointed to two other girls dressing transformers in Barbie clothes in the corner. 'That's Calpurnia and Maude, and outside is Ted.'

Ted, dressed in a Thor outfit, complete with hammer in his belt loop, seemed to be sucking a garden snail from its shell.

Jadis handed me a cup of air and a plate of plastic chicken with weeds. I said I was veggie and she swapped the chicken for a ping pong ball.

'That's unicorn poo,' she said proudly.

So we played Homes – and I did a roaring trade in hair plaiting and first year curse words and then following a quick make-up sesh, where they all ended up looking like replica JonBenéts, they put on an impromptu catwalk show up and down the footpath. We then went on a bug hunt in the orchard. I haven't enjoyed a party so much in years.

But there was an incident.

So, during our bug hunt, I noticed Alannah had disappeared. Ted the Snail Sucker had seen Pin's little shit of a daughter Mulberry put a worm in her hair and told me she was crying in the Wendy house.

I poked my head through the window. 'What are you doing in here?'

She sniffed, brushing her Bratz doll's hair.

'Wanna talk about it?'

She shook her head and carried on brushing.

'Okay… so wanna do something about it?' She scratched her little green face. 'I think Mulberry needs to be taught a lesson, don't you?' She held out her forearm – felt tip pen scribbled all over it. 'Did she do that?'

She held up her ankle. More scribbles and the words –

Your ugLy

'Right, that little bitch ain't taking any more of your sunshine. She puts a worm in your hair, you put a snake down her knickers.'

Alannah giggled behind her hand. 'She draws on your ankle, you tattoo her face.' She giggled again. 'She hurts you, you kick her in the face and yell "Not today, Satan." Okay? No. Bloody. More. Repeat after me.'

'No buddy more.'

I heard my name being called from beyond the Wendy house and looked up to find Marnie, walking hand in hand across the lawn with old Wifey McBeaty. He was as I had imagined – tall, stocky, blond Hitler-youth buzz cut and no neck. He was pushing the pram and wearing the same as all the other men – crisp pastel Polo shirt, cargo shorts and deck shoes. He didn't look like a wife-beater. He looked like an estate agent. For the Third Reich.

'I have to go cos my friend's here. Go back and join the bug hunt. Put the bugs back when you're done, okay? Don't let Ted eat them.'

Me and Alannah fist bumped and she scuttled off as Marnie and Tim reached the Wendy house. Marnie looked good – no signs of Cardiff remaining. A mask of fresh make-up, clean hair and new dress. She had clearly taken my advice and wiped last Saturday from her mind.

'Hey Rhee,' said Marnie, leaning in for a hug and an air kiss. 'This is Tim. Tim, this is my friend Rhiannon.'

I got a small but definite squiggle of excitement in my stomach when Marnie called me her friend – she'd done it three times now.

'Nice to meet you,' we both said, shaking hands.

So this is the man who stopped you dancing and calls you every five minutes and won't let you do anything ever, I thought.

His handshake was as stiff as a shark's fin. He clutched a bottle of masculinity in the other hand. 'What's she been saying about me then?' he asked. Mancunian accent. Damn, I like Mancunians as a rule.

'Oh, she never stops talking about you,' I said, bending over the pram to look at Raph, sleeping soundly.

He nuzzled Marnie's ear. 'That's nice, babe. How's your pregnancy?'

'Laugh a minute,' I smiled, quaffing my pressé.

We talked about all things baby at length – Tim seemed fascinated by it, whereas I was bored. He also seemed obsessed with divulging all of Marnie's secrets when it came to embarrassing episodes during her pregnancy.

'Did she tell you about the time she wet herself in the queue in Marks & Spencer's? God that was funny, wasn't it, love?'

Marnie blushed. 'Not at the time, no.'

'But she had terrible constipation in the later stages, didn't you? Do you get any of that?'

'Not at all,' I lied, sensing he was trying to embarrass me. 'Most days I could shit through the eye of a needle.'

That wiped the smug smile off his face.

'I'm going to pop in and see if Pin wants a hand with anything,' said Marnie, blush burning holes in her cheeks.

Don't you hate that? When people introduce you to perfect

strangers and then disappear, leaving you squirming for conversation? This has happened so many times now that I resolutely refuse to make the effort.

Turns out I didn't need to.

'Read about your bloke in the paper,' said Tim. 'Christ what a weirdo.'

'Yeah, isn't he just?' I said, as we gravitated back over to the buffet.

'And Priory Gardens. Saw you on the news. I remembered your face.'

'Yep, sole survivor of a massacre *and* a murderer. Want an autograph?'

He laughed, swigging his bottle with one hand and rocking the pram with the other. Whatta man.

'So you lived with him for four years? And you didn't have a clue about any of it? The gay stuff and what he was doing and that?'

'Uh no, no I didn't,' I said, reaching past him for the halloumi bites.

'You going to testify when it comes to trial?'

'Looks like I'll have to, yes.'

'And with the baby too – how are you going to cope on your own?'

'I'll manage,' I sighed. 'I'm like a lioness. Did you see that documentary? Fascinating.'

'Was that true what your friends said, him beating you up and that?'

His breath carried notes of garlic and it was making my stomach or my baby – I couldn't work out which – do flips. Luckily, Marnie returned with two empty buffet plates and

handed one to Tim. 'You getting to know one another?' she asked, the way parents do when they want stepsiblings to get along.

'Yeah,' I said. 'He was asking me all about Craig's dirty little secrets.'

'Oh Tim, you didn't! I said not to mention it.'

'I just asked about how she's going to cope if he's banged up for life.'

Tim looked at me as Marnie leaned over the buffet for a samosa. His eyes were on my feet, my legs, travelling up to my bump and finally my face. It was quite unabashed. Actual eye-fucking me.

Not every guy who looks at you wants you. FFS.

'Did you tell Tim all about Cardiff, Marn?'

She stuffed a samosa in her mouth and chewed slowly. 'Yeah, it was good, wasn't it? We should take the baby when he's older.'

'Did you enjoy the show?' said Tim as Raph grizzled in the pram.

'Yeah, a real toe-tapper, wasn't it, Marn?' She chewed and nodded.

'She doesn't think she wants to join WOMBAT full time,' said Tim, loading his plate with crisps.

'Oh? Why ever not, Marn? Didn't you enjoy yourself?'

Marnie eye-pleaded me not to carry on talking. 'Yeah, of course I had a great time. I missed Tim and Raph, that's all.'

'Of course you did,' I said, crunching down.

Raph started crying. A waft of crap rose up from the pram opening.

'He's shat,' said Tim, pulling a bag from the under-carriage.

'Oh, I'll do it,' said Marnie, going to take Raph from him.

'I'm all right, I'll go and do it in the car, spare everyone else the stink.'

With Tim gone, Marnie found herself stuck facing her latest fear – me.

'Are you all right?' I whispered.

'Don't touch me,' she said, moving away and walking up the garden.

I followed her. 'What's the matter with you?'

She was tensed up like a jagged stone was stuck in her neck. 'I've spent all week acting my arse off, pretending nothing's wrong. Trying to scrub it from my skin. I'm good at pretending. But I can't pretend around you.'

'Pretend what?'

'Pretend it's okay. Because it's not. I can't even look at you.'

'Uh I've clearly missed an instalment here, Marnie, care to fill me in?'

She pulled her phone from her jacket pocket and handed it to me. The screen was open on a news article – last Tuesday's date.

A YOUNG man has been found stabbed to death in a Cardiff street.

The victim, in his twenties, was found at 3.30 a.m. in the morning, a spokesperson from South Wales Police said. The body was inside an alleyway in Bakers Row, off Wharton Street in the city centre. He was pronounced dead at the scene.

A police cordon is in place at the junction with Wharton Street. Detectives are carrying out a number of inquiries this morning including looking at CCTV footage and a forensic examination of the scene.

Anyone who has information which may assist detectives

investigating this matter is asked to contact South Wales Police on 101 or anonymously via Crimestoppers on 0800 555111, quoting case reference number 66721/44.

'Gosh,' I said. 'That's so sad. Poor individual.'

Marnie snatched the phone back. 'It's him, isn't it?'

'Him? Him who?'

'Don't lie to me, Rhiannon. It's Troy. You did that?'

'*Moi?*'

She shook her head as the tears came. 'Oh my god. You stabbed him?'

'You'd rather have been raped? It was Hobson's Choice.'

'What?'

'You don't remember anything, do you? The club? Walking along the main street? Him in the alley? You falling onto the cobbles.'

'I knew I was on the ground. I said I remembered that.'

'Yeah well I saved you from him. He was going to rape you. So I did what I had to do. I protected you. You're welcome.'

It took her a few moments to get the words out. 'You had a knife. No, I saw it in your handbag on the train. You said it was a fruit knife. I knew it wasn't.'

'You need to calm down, right now. Go and knock back some of Pin's punch or something before Mein Fuhrer reappears.'

'You don't care. You don't care at all, do you?' She shook off my arm.

'Okay okay, here I am not touching you, Elle Sensititivo.'

She shook her head. 'Did you kill the others? The ones... did you frame your boyfriend... oh, Jesus.'

'It's not as black and white as all that, I can explain.'

293

'No, you don't have to. Stay away from me, Rhiannon, okay? Please.'

'Fine. But we're still friends, aren't we?'

She shook her head and her cheeks puffed out like she was going to be sick. 'I don't know what you are.'

That cut me. Somewhere deep inside my chest a fissure opened up and it wouldn't close. I tried to tell myself it didn't matter, that I'd lost friends before, that *she* didn't mean anything to me.

The only trouble was – she did.

Tim had left Marnie alone for all of five minutes before he was back, wanting to know what we were talking about. I could feel my sword hand beginning to sing so I exited stage left to find the loo. And it was while I was sitting on the toilet, still trying to work out how saving someone from certain rape had lost me my only friend, when there came a blood-freezing scream from outside.

Nobody knew what was going on until Pin came sprinting up the garden with Mulberry, face red all over. I thought she'd gone a bit heavy-handed with the face paints. But I soon realised it wasn't paint but blood.

'What's happened?' asked Nev, leading the herd behind Pin.

'She's been kicked in the face,' Pin heaved, sitting Mulberry on the breakfast bar.

I stayed in the hallway, watching the dramatic events unfold.

'Is she all right?' asked Nev.

'No, she's not. *Your* daughter kicked her in the face.'

Mulberry snorted bubbles of blood. 'She called me a mudder fudder.'

'Sssh, baby, sssh now, don't repeat that word,' cooed Pin,

cradling one side of her face and applying wads of damp tissue to her nose.

Nev baulked away. 'Jadis did *this*? No, she can't have.'

'No! Not Jadis! *Alannah*!'

'Alannah?' Nev laughed. 'Don't be silly. Alannah wouldn't hurt a—'

'She did! She did!' Mulberry screamed. 'And *she* told her to.'

Mulberry pointed at me. I walked back into the kitchen. Outside, faces looking at me. Inside, faces looking at me. Parents held children away from me. It was a *Home Alone* moment – *Look whatcha did, you little jerk.*

Except I didn't feel embarrassed. I felt rather excited. The attention was invigorating. Champagne corks popped in my tummy.

'Everything bleeds more from the head,' I said. 'Looks worse than it is.'

Pin turned to me. '*You* told Alannah to kick my daughter in the face? Did you teach her that word, too? WHY WOULD YOU DO THAT?'

Jadis appeared by Nev's side and cuddled against her thigh. 'Mulberry's always picking on Alannah, Mummy.'

'I told Alannah to fight back. And it looks like she has.'

Alannah was outside, sobbing against the shoulder of her other mummy, Deb. Mulberry was still ambulancing it at the breakfast bar.

A low muttering from the patio – *So irresponsible. Who tells a child to do that? Has she not heard of the naughty step?* These were echoed by Pin.

'I feel sorry for that baby of yours, Rhiannon, if this is your parenting style. And thanks to you there are *two* children crying

their eyes out on what was supposed to be a happy occasion. Thank you *very* much.'

Silence. More stares of disapproval. A clearing of throats. A scraping of plates. *Rhiannon, you're such a disease.* Some of the children went back outside, all on fire to get back to it.

'I take it the party's over then,' I said, setting down my glass and looking around. 'I was looking forward to the fireworks.'

I could see their lips moving – Tim was conversing with one of the dads, cuddling baby Raph. I looked over at Marnie for some back up. She looked away.

Wednesday, 21ˢᵗ November
– 28 weeks, 3 days

I'm still pissed off about the barbecue.

I feel sorry for that baby of yours, Rhiannon, if this is your parenting style.

I'm not pissed off because of what she said or how she said it but because I didn't have a rebarbative bon mot at the ready. I can normally take someone down like a lumberjack but on this occasion, she hit a nerve.

Because Pin's right. I *do* have a terrible parenting style already and my kid's not even born yet. I teach children swear words. I teach them to kick other kids in the face. I baulk when babies cry. I am going to be a terrible mother. I was always going to be. I'm a taker of life, not a nurturer of it.

Ordered the replacement stuff for the Well House today – exact replica crockery, cushions, sofa and one armchair. Cost me an arm and two legs because most of it was only available on eBay but what's done is done and cannot be undone. It's all being delivered there. I've just got to find the impetus to go up and clear the mess before it arrives. Soon.

Marnie's not answering texts. Or my WhatsApps. Or my

tweets. Is she going to tell the police on me? Who knows? Maybe she should.

Elaine has left WOMBAT. Doreen and Edna had a 'quiet word' (ambushed her) at Monday night's meeting. She sulked in her room most of yesterday and this morning. Hasn't said two words to me or Jim since.

She did say one thing to me this morning at breakfast. 'I read an article about pregnant women and the bugs they can pick up in soil, Rhiannon. Probably better if you stay out of the garden altogether.'

Yet another barricade in the road. No high-altitude sports, scuba diving or sheep worrying for me either. I hate being pregnant. Did I mention that?

I can still read my Bible though, that particular avenue of pleasure is still open to me. I'm not giving it back to WOMBAT, even if they ask for it. I read it all the time, usually before bed. Probably why I'm not sleeping at the moment. Me and the Bible see eye to eye on a few things. Murder, yes. But with regards to revenge it gets a little cloudy.

Like, in Peter 1 verses 3–9 it says 'Do not repay evil with evil. The face of the Lord is against those who do evil.' But in Thessalonians 15 it says 'Always seek to do good to one another and to everyone.'

So how can removing something which has caused such pain to humans, like a paedophile or a rapist, not be doing good to mankind? You've got to be cruel to be kind, haven't you?

And in Romans – 'Vengeance is mine, I will repay' says the Lord. But even the Lord needs a day off doesn't he? I'm just easing his workload. A bit like when I worked at the *Gazette*, though instead of making the coffee, opening post and doing the

flower show write-ups nobody else wants to do, I'm killing those people God doesn't have time to. I don't get why it's so wrong.

I want to kill again, in my head. But my body is betraying me on that score. Killing Troy was not satisfying. While this baby is baking inside me, I know killing won't fulfil me like it used to. Maybe it never will again, I don't know. I never expected to feel this way. Tilted. Off-kilter. Wrong.

I don't get why Marnie isn't talking to me. I don't get why she blanked me in town this morning when I went over to her. She's supposed to be my friend, my *best* friend. Maybe she is and that's why the police haven't been over here already. She's keeping my secret like a true friend would.

I feel grim. My Saturday night high has faded and in its place sits this gelatinous murky splat – a great big Jabba the Hutt-sized lump of poison in my chest. I want my friend back. I want to hear my baby again and not just through the Doppler. I keep tapping the bump—

Tap tap tap. Knock knock. Who's there? Foetus. Foetus who?

But I get nothing back. Everybody leaves me. I have a friend in Jesus, I keep being told, but where's he when he's at home? Where is my sign that He is with me, watching over me, like the Man in the Moon? Do I just have to believe? I don't know if I can do that.

It's all bullshit, isn't it? Yet again. I'm drowning in it.

I walked up to the Well House to begin work on my mess – I couldn't leave it any longer. I stayed in the garden for a while and lay on AJ's grave. Everything's colder and the garden has died back to prepare for the winter frosts. It didn't make me feel any better. I let myself in through the back door preparing to face the onslaught—

—but it had all gone. Every last bit of it. Every broken shard of china or clump of stuffing from the sofa had vanished, like it was never there. And there was a new smell about the place too – like a dry cleaner's smell. I could still get the whiff of rotting human beneath it but someone had definitely cleaned up. Mary Poppins had magicked that shit away. The torn up sofa, the torn up curtains, the broken plates. All gone.

In the lounge, the only stick of furniture was the armchair.

And today someone was sitting in it. Alive and smiling.

And, unless I was mistaken, wearing the smug smile and raincoat combo synonymous with a police detective.

'Hello, Rhiannon,' he said. 'I wondered when you'd come back.'

*

I can't record what happened during the following thirty seconds because I blacked out. There must have been a rush of blood to my head as I saw him sitting there – big bulky guy, lying back all relaxed and triumphant like Diddy at the Met Gala – and I went down like a brick on the living room carpet.

When I came round, I was lying on the floor with my feet up on two cushions. He was sitting in the armchair.

'Hey, you're awake,' he said. North London accent.

'Who the hell are you?' I said, backing into the wall. My bump had tightened like a basketball and my head thumped. I couldn't get to the kitchen – couldn't get to my knives. One stride and he'd have me.

He stared, taking me in, a strange little smile forming.

'Who. Are. You?' I repeated. 'Are you with Géricault?'

'It's Kes, Rhiannon,' he said, grinning as though that were

300

the answer to all the questions swarming in my head. 'I ain't changed that much in two years, have I? Bit greyer about the gills, I s'pose. You got my notes, didn't you?'

My heart thundered. Flight or fight, fight or flight, fight or flight. Well I was in no fit state for either. He'd got me – a fish in a barrel, flapping violently.

'What notes?'

'I put at least five through your door. You're staying with your in-laws on the seafront, yeah? It's Kes, Rhiannon. KES.'

My brain wouldn't function. His face kept swimming in and out of my vision. There was nowhere I could run except thirty metres or so straight out the front door and over the clifftop. It was dead end time.

'DS Hoyle then? Keston Hoyle? Sorry, *ex* Detective Sergeant – I retired almost a year ago.' He rubbed at the grey patches to his temples which I thought was strange because he didn't look that old.

I got up, steadying myself on the wall. He didn't move from the armchair. It was then the confusion-fug and panic cleared. I recognised him.

'The notes? *To My Sweet Messy House*?'

He frown-laughed. 'My notes said "Tommy's Mate, Keston Hoyle" and my phone number. I tried calling – a man kept telling me to bugger off.'

'We thought it was the press. You could have pretended to be a friend from school or something.'

'Didn't think.'

'Your handwriting's terrible. We thought you were some nutter.'

He opened his hands out. 'My mistake. Should have gone all caps.'

I went to sit down but seeing no other seats, Keston got up from the armchair and offered me his. 'You used to spar with Dad down the gym.'

'Yeah, used to go down there quite a bit before my knee op.'

I laughed, out of relief I guess. It grew clearer the more I looked at him. The twinkly smile, eyes shining, large rough hands like maple leaves. Where before I'd just seen 'police' now I saw him the other side of a punch bag, smashing the crap out of it as Dad held it. Laughing with Dad in the café after his session. Sitting on a chair in our kitchen, Mum making tea, Dad standing against the counter. Helping Dad and me bury Pete McMahon that night in the woods. Warming my frozen hands between his. He was a good friend. *One of the best*, I could hear Dad saying.

A tile fell into place in my Keston Tetris. 'You came to the funeral. You and your wife brought a wreath – Arsenal colours. Asiatic lilies, red roses, chrysanths.'

'Sounds about right,' he smiled. 'Me and her ain't together no more.'

'She brought me and Seren round a big hamper the week Dad died. And you went to see Dad at the undertaker's. I was coming out as you went in.'

'I always do that for my mates, to see them off, like. Don't know why, always have. Always wished I hadn't with Tommy though. I keep remembering him like that and that wasn't Tom.'

Sometimes I can see people's feelings. In Keston's face then I could see what he saw in that coffin – the wisps of hair. The shrunken mouth. The yellow skin. That wasn't Dad, Kes was right. We both remembered him as he was. Muscles. Tatts. Goofy grin. The boundless energy of a young dog.

'There's a picture of me as a newborn and he's holding me on one hand and Seren's hanging from the other with her feet off the ground. "Atlas holding my world," he'd written on the back of it. He was so strong. But when he got ill, he started disappearing. First came the hair in the drain. Then wearing his wedding ring on this thumb. I saw his watch slide off his wrist.'

'He was a bloody titan,' said Keston. 'Came through for me in a big way.'

'Did he?'

'Oh yeah. Did time for us, didn't he?'

'For you?'

'All of us. All the boys. When he went down, they knew other people were involved but he never said a word. Never gave them one name. He'd have done longer if his cancer hadn't spread. I'd have got in more trouble than any of them. Lost my pension, banged up. You can guess how they treat coppers in chokey. And a *black* copper? You've got his eyes.'

'He said I could have them.'

His smile was wide and full. 'Chip off the old block, aren't you?'

A flash of pride shimmered in my chest. It was nice to meet someone who remembered Dad like I did; to hear someone talk about him like he existed. Like he wasn't some Hiroshima shadow only I had seen, or an imaginary friend conjured by my own rancid mind.

'Tom said you liked watching it. What we did to those men.'

I said nothing.

'Yeah. He said you had a fascination for it. I know it's you, Rhiannon. I know that bloke of yours is innocent. How many is it now?'

303

I knew better than to argue. So I just chewed my lip. A half shrug. 'You lost count?' Kes's voice had got louder. Scratchier. Smoker's gravel. He sat forwards, shaking his head. 'All bastards, yeah?'

'Yes, all bastards.' It was the first lie I'd told him.

'You reap what you sow, Rhiannon. Always.'

'You didn't.'

'No, cos I had people like Tommy looking out for me. And I promised him that if things got hairy, I'd look out for you. He was chuffed when you and Craig got together.' I stared him out. 'Does he truly deserve all this?'

'He slept around.'

Kes frowned. 'Hardly a fair exchange, is it? Five murders for a shag?'

'It wasn't a shag. He loves her.'

'Still doesn't compute.'

'I want him to suffer.'

'He's staring down the barrel of a life sentence, Rhiannon. I'd say you've more than won this round. His brains are on the canvas.'

'Why don't you make a citizen's arrest then? You must want to.'

'I suppose I could bring them down here and get tests done on that hole in the kitchen. I could get them to dig up those flower beds'n all. Tell them to look closer at your movements on the nights of the murders your boyfriend's supposed to have done. But you could do the same to me, couldn't you?'

'Could I?'

'Sure. You could tell them you saw me at the quarry that night Lyle Devaney went over. In the warehouse that day. In the woods.'

'I need a drink.' I appeared to be checking with him whether it was okay that I got up. He followed me out to the kitchen, keeping his distance. There were two un-smashed glasses in the cupboard. I got one out and filled it. I drank it all down, then refilled. I could not quench my thirst.

'Why should I trust you?'

'Do you remember that night you killed your sister's boyfriend? And you, me and your dad digging that pit in the woods behind the house? Only you and me know about that.'

'And the Man in the Moon.'

'What?'

'The Man in the Moon was there too. Peeking through the trees. Watching us.'

'Rhee, listen to me – my DNA's all over them bones.'

'He was my first one, Pete McMahon.'

'But you did it for the right reasons, didn't you? Because of Seren. Because of what he was doing to her.'

'She never forgave me for that.'

Kes stood on the edge of the well. He removed the torch from the top of the microwave and shone it down. I followed the beam. The hole was empty. 'Looks good, doesn't it?'

'Where is he?' I said.

'Still down there, in some form. Alkaline and potassium hydroxide – stripped him down to the skeleton. It's only the natural process that happens to a body once it starts to decompose. I just sped things up a bit.'

'But I can't see anything at all.'

'Well he's got a fresh layer of concrete over him now. I'd keep that Perspex off it 'til it dries out a bit more. Let the air get to it.'

'When did you do all this?'

305

Kes pulled the breakfast stool out for me. 'Soon as you left the other day. You ain't been back here since. Thought you could use a hand.'

'I don't need anyone to clear up after me.'

His eyebrows jumped into his hairline. 'Well clearly you do. When were you going to start on that?' I shrugged. 'Who was he anyway, Hole Man?'

'Patrick Edward Fenton.'

Kes plucked his phone from his back pocket and did a quick Google. 'Yeah fair enough, fair enough.'

'Thanks for… that,' I said, gesturing vaguely at the entire house.

'Want me to sort anything else while I'm here?'

'How do you mean?'

'You mentioned Géricault. She's onto you, is she?'

'Do you know her?'

'I know *of* her. Jesus, Rhiannon, that's a bloodhound on your scent there. Not much personality but she's increased the force's hit rate by twenty per cent since her promotion. Takes no shit. Works all hours. You don't care, do you?'

'I like killing,' I said. 'I know who I am when I kill. I kept it at bay for a while when I was with Craig but it soon started leaking out of me again. I can't stop. I can't find a reason *to* stop.'

He looked at my bump. 'There's a big reason right in front of you.'

'I don't think that's going to be enough.'

Keston pursed his lips. 'Géricault *will* work this out and when she does – not *if*, *when* – she'll throw the book right through you. There's serial murderers in prisons who've spent decades in one room. Could you handle that?'

'No.'

'All day every day with one hour outside in a cold concrete exercise yard? Killers so dangerous they're not allowed near other people? Constant abuse? Shit in your food. Sharing landings with junkies who scream their cells down all night long? Or worse still, they'll chuck you in Broadmoor.'

'Yeah thanks for mansplaining the prison system in such technicolour.'

'I'm on your side here, Rhiannon.'

'I need it, Kes. I need to kill. I need Sandra Huggins.'

'Who dat?'

I pulled out my phone and brought up the bookmark with her news story on. I handed him the page featuring her mugshot.

'She's tagged. You can't go near her, certainly not in your condition.'

'My condition, my condition,' I scoffed.

'Rhee, look at the size of her.'

'She's a danger to my baby,' I said. 'To *all* babies.'

'Yeah, she's one of many. Jesus, do you know how many sex offenders walk among us every single day?'

'No.'

'There ain't enough prisons. There ain't enough *landmass* to build the prisons for all those fuckers. It's not like Pokémon – you can't catch them all.'

'You and Dad did.'

'No, we caught a chosen few who kept beating the system. Ones we knew were off the radar and vulnerable. And a couple of their lawyers, that was it. You have to stop all this. Right now.'

The kitchen felt tiny and stifling, like I was Alice growing bigger until my arms and legs were going to come shooting

through the windows. I could smell the PlugIns that Kes had installed – disgusting synthetic lavender.

'I need to get out of here.'

I ran, through the back gate and along towards the coastal path and fields beyond. The sea beneath the clifftop was choppy, the swell smashing the rocks. All the air in the world wasn't enough.

'You can't keep doing this and thinking you're immune,' came his voice behind me. 'You're following breadcrumbs into a prison cell and once that cell door closes behind you, it'll never open again. And what about your kid?'

'What about her?'

'Have you thought about what's going to happen to her?'

'Of course I have.'

'That's your future in there. That's the one good thing you have, believe me. Nothing's more important. You'll realise that when she's born. Maybe being a mum will be enough for you and you can leave all this behind.'

We both stared out to the horizon, the calm sea beyond the waves.

'I can try and rub out some of your footprints, Rhiannon, but it'll only keep Géricault at bay for so long. I think we've got to get you out of here.'

'Out of where?'

'The country. I know an old lag. Big Fat Duncan. He's into dodgy passports.'

'An old lag? You mean he went down for it?'

'No, he went down for burglary. He's one of us though, don't worry. And he's a specialist at the passports. You'll have a whole new identity.'

'So what happens to Rhiannon Lewis?'

We watched the waves below breaking and exploding against the cliff below. He didn't answer and I didn't ask again.

'I have money.'

'Good. You'll need it.'

'Where will I go?'

'Ideally somewhere with no extradition treaties. Argentina, China, Bahrain, Russia.' He got out his phone.

'Have you done this before?'

He punched in a number. 'Not for a while.'

'So is this lag like *Better Call Saul*?'

'Not quite. He can get you good documents, but that's about it. It's going to take time though and we'll need to get some new photos done as well. We can do that up there.' He nodded back towards the Well House. 'The rest is up to you.'

Friday, 23rd November
– 28 weeks, 5 days

1. *People who don't put the separator down for you at the supermarket.*
2. *Old guy with half-moon glasses who sneezed all over the Pick 'n' Mix – where you gonna hang your specs when I cut your fucking ears off, old timer?*
3. *People who preach, rant or vent via the Twitter thread. It's like one morning I woke up and everyone's Martin Luther King.*

Helen from Pudding Club's texted – Nev's twins were born at 5.38 a.m. this morning. Then she put a load of bollocks about their weights and heights and how they're both on the tit already. All pretty yawn. She signed off with a request – £30 for some flowers 'from us all'. So I'm still on the round robin for freebies even if I can no longer attend their parties?

Ugh, BLOCK.

My bump is in spasm – an inverted trampoline. This hasn't happened before and I don't know why it's happening now.

'Talk to me. Why are you doing that? What's wrong?'

Nothing. She hasn't spoken to me since the night of Fuckboy

Troy. I can't find her heartbeat on the Doppler. I'm going to the hospital.

*

The baby has hiccups. According to Bitch Midwife, this is normal and I had no need to worry. 'You're just being an over-protective mummy,' she said.

I'm so uncomfortable. There isn't a known sitting position that doesn't hurt me in some way – placing too much pressure on some part of my body. She gave me a diabetes test – I had to drink this thing and she took my blood. All good, she thinks. Bitch Midwife wasn't in the least bit interested in any other symptoms – the return of the sluggishness, the constipation, the itching on my bump, the insomnia. She just said 'That's pregnancy for you!' and laughed cartoonishly, like Porky Pig.

'But her heart's beating?'

'Yes, she's all good, don't worry. How's the new book coming along?'

'Great, yeah.' I forget some of the lies I tell. She thinks I'm a published novelist. Newsflash – that particular avenue of delights was cordoned off some time ago but she thought it was terribly glam and impressive when I said I wrote books so I left her to dream a little dream of me.

'Are you still doing your yoga and swimming classes?'

'Oh yeah, I'm up to twenty lengths a day now.'

'Ooh well done you. That'll pay dividends. Made lots of mum chums?'

'Yes,' I shuddered. Mum Chums. Ugh. I could absolutely piss on her until her dying breath.

Tried calling Keston but his phone's switched off. Marnie's

still not talking to me either. I WhatsApped her and she doesn't have an avatar anymore and all I get is one grey tick on my sent messages. That means you're Blocked, right? It'll be him that's done that – Heinrich Timmler.

I tapped the bump. Still the silent treatment. Even the Sylvanians aren't doing it for me today. I'm so bored.

*

I awoke with a knock on my bedroom door. Jim.

'You've got a visitor, Rhiannon. DI Géricault wants to have a word.'

She sat cross-footed on the edge of Jim's armchair – brown leather handbag on the floor, black raincoat, silk blouse and a skirt with little pink flowers all over it. Monsoon, maybe Next. Everything ironed. Even her hair, scraped back in a clip. Gold ear studs. Orderly. Pursed. That was Géricault.

Jim made his excuses and left us to it. She motioned me to sit down opposite, on the sofa. I tried to sit with some grace but that didn't happen.

'I thought I should let you know there's been a development in the investigation – Lana Rowntree has died. Apparent suicide.'

I tried to find my shocked face.

'You don't seem shocked.' That didn't work then.

'I knew she was depressed. She's tried it before.'

'It appears she's been dead for at least two weeks. You saw a bit of Lana during the months up to her death, didn't you? Became good friends?'

'I wouldn't say "friends", no. I felt sorry for her. And I felt bad that I hit her in front of everyone in the office. But no, we weren't friends per se.'

'When was the last time you saw her?'

'Few weeks ago I guess. Why?'

She stared at me. Picked up her half-empty cup of tea – Jim had brought out the best china for Géricault. Everyone else had to make do with mugs. She sipped then put the down the cup carefully, no clink. 'We have you on CCTV heading in the direction of Lana's flat on October seventeenth.'

'And? You think I killed her? You've got Craig locked up and now you're coming after me too? What's the matter with you people?'

'We want to know if you saw Lana on the day of her death. It may help her family understand why she took her own life.'

I yawned twice – she didn't. Twice. If I didn't know better, I'd say she was a psychopath too. Maybe it takes one to catch one.

'Sometimes people break,' I said. 'Life gets too hard.'

'What tipped her over the edge, Rhiannon? Seeing your bump?'

'Yeah, that's it, I think you've cracked it. I, Rhiannon Lewis, am solely responsible for what goes on in other people's heads now. Cuff me then, Detective Inspector. I am guilty as charged.'

She sighed silently. 'I'm not accusing you, I'm asking for your help.'

'Lana was complaining about the press when I saw her last. This journalist guy was hounding her. Craig's defence team were too. She was getting it from both sides.' A rotisserie of male attention – thought Lana would have liked that.

Will you concentrate on looking shocked and appalled before we both end up sewing mailbags?

'Which newspaper?' asked the detective.

'*Plymouth Star*, I think.'

'How did they know she was involved in the Gripper case? That information hasn't been made public until now.'

'You'd have to ask them.'

'There were traces of Tramadol in Lana's blood.'

'Oh?'

'A strong painkiller, not prescribed to her. In fact, we found no other traces of it in her flat at all.'

'How strange.'

'Her former colleagues at the *Gazette* have said she was a bubbly personality, particularly during the months she was seeing Craig. They said it was the happiest they'd ever seen her.'

I looked at her, as pointedly as I could. 'You're generally a happier person when you're getting sexed though, aren't you?'

Géricault fished around in her handbag and pulled out her iPad. She swiped the screen and handed it to me. I stared at it. I couldn't make out what it was at first but then it drew me in – a body on a sofa. A blonde. Reddish purple skin. Bloated face. Curled up in the armchair. Dried puke on the armrest. Dead sweet peas on the coffee table.

'As you can see putrefaction has begun—'

My initial reaction was of course nothing. I should have baulked. I should have dry-heaved or something, shown her how repulsed a normal person would be to such an image. But I couldn't. I wanted to show her who I was for a second. While it was only us in the room.

'Sweet peas,' I said, looking up. 'My favourites.'

She didn't answer. And for the first time I saw something in her eyes. She knew what I knew. And for a moment, we were on the same page.

Footsteps in the corridor outside. I shrieked, giving it the full

BAFTA and pushing the iPad away from me. 'Urgh! Why are you showing me that for god's sake?'

Jim came rushing in. 'What? What is it? What's happened?' He picked up the iPad from the carpet. 'What on earth is this? Dear God almighty!'

'It's Lana,' I said to Jim, clinging to his cashmere. 'She's killed herself.'

'The woman our Craig was – oh god.' I cuddled in to his jumper and sobbed, thankful to give my aching face muscles a brief rest.

'Were you there when Lana killed herself, Rhiannon?' asked Géricault.

'Jim – she's victimising me. She keeps following me and showing me things I don't want to see. She's crazy. She's showing me pictures of dead girls. This is police harassment, please get rid of her, PLEASE.' I pulled away from Jim and clutched my bump, sitting back down on the sofa and breathing like I was in some practice class.

'I think you had better go, DI Géricault.' Jim handed the iPad back to Géricault and I watched her cross the lounge floor, Jim guiding her through, standing in front of me like a human shield. I did my best to look afraid.

'Thanks for your time.'

Jim led her out to out to the front door, politely threatening legal action the whole way. I didn't hear Géricault say another word.

You need to call Keston. Right now.

Monday, 26th November
– 29 weeks, 1 day

1. *People who ask 'Is it the weekend yet?' on a Monday.*
2. *People who leave their car engines running outside for, like, HOURS.*
3. *People who email attachments – then forget the attachment.*

South Wales Police have one blurry CCTV image of a 'hooded woman walking through the Cardiff streets' but nothing fixed on my face. God bless the rain down in Cardiff. God bless Keston Hoyle. Maybe this means I can trust him. I want to trust him but I can't help thinking he's too good to be true. Has Dad sent me a friend when I need one the most? Is Keston an angel in disguise? *Send me another sign, Dad. A sign that I can trust him.*

The paps are back on the doorstep and this morning, one of them shoved his camera against my bump. I ripped it out of his hands and smashed it on the ground.

'Oops,' I said, waltzing past him along the footpath. 'I'm so sorry.'

'… sue you, bitch,' I heard. I heard something else about how expensive it was. Another guy started snapping away, though his camera was hanging on a strap around his neck so I couldn't

do the same to him. 'We only want your side of the story, ya miserable cow.'

I got up close to the guy who'd shouted, so close I had to whisper right in his ear. 'Well when you ask so nicely, how can I refuse?'

'You owe me a new camera.'

'Prove it,' said Freddie-by-the-way, my black-haired hero.

'You were there, you saw her do it.'

He looked at me, then back at the guy. 'I saw nothing, mate. Fake news. It's everywhere.'

He got right up into my face so that his pot belly smushed against my bump. The sides of my eyes had clouded with an angry smoke. 'You broke my camera and you're going to pay.'

'*You* broke your own camera when you shoved your hand up my slit. Whose story would *you* believe?'

He stepped back and knelt down to gather up the shattered sections of his former camera, still muttering the words 'bitch' and 'sue.'

Freddie guided me along the footpath towards the gate. 'He's had warnings about this before. Are you okay?'

'Yeah of course. Where did you spring from?'

His voice was wobbly. 'I came to see you. Have you time for a coffee?'

The coffee embargo still in place, Freddie and I walked along the seafront instead. He bought me a strawberry ice-cream with double flake. We did the small talk thing for a while – turns out we both eat KitKats the wrong way, both have Chihuahuas called Tink, and both prefer *Grease 2* to *Grease*.

'Where do you stand on *Sister Act*?' he asked.

'Oh *Back in the Habit* is far superior.'

'Snap again!' he laughed. 'Wow, what are the chances?' We then broke into an acapella version of 'If you wanna be somebody, If you wanna go somewhere… ' only stopping when we got looks from two surly dog walkers in Mountain Warehouse parkas.

'Well I don't know why we're talking about *Sister Act*.'

'No, me either actually,' he laughed. 'So, I've quit the *Plymouth Star*. Handed in my notice. I've said I'll stay on 'til the first week of January.'

'Why?'

He looked out to sea. 'You heard about Lana Rowntree, I suppose?'

'Yeah.'

'That was the last straw. "Get down there," my editor said. "Follow it up, no matter what it takes. Get the story." Two weeks later the woman was dead. That's on me, Rhiannon. That's *my* fault.'

'No it's not.'

'It is! She killed herself because *I* was harassing her. Day and night. Whenever she took the milk in or put the bins out, I tried to get a word with her. She kept telling me to go away. And I didn't.'

'Craig's defence team were onto her as well, it wasn't *just* you.'

'I can't stop feeling guilty about it. Anyway, it's done now. I just wanted to apologise to you. I won't see you again after today.'

A silent wind whipped up around us, blowing his hair and mine around our faces. When it had settled again, I said 'Fancy a shag before you go?'

His jaw dropped. 'Um. I'm actually gay?'

'You don't sound so sure about that.'

'No, I'm really gay.' He got his phone out and clicked it on – the screen saver was of him and another guy, cuddling in tuxedos. 'Couldn't be gayer. That's our wedding.' He scrolled along. Cutting the cake. First kiss. First dance under flashing disco lights. Their kids – Milo and Tilly.

'Sexy husband. Cute family. Lucky bastard.'

'I'm sorry if I gave you any false—'

'No, it's all right,' I sighed. 'Shoulda known. You're too nice to be straight.'

He laughed. 'You're nice too.'

'No I'm not.'

'Yeah you are.'

'I only started talking to you cos I thought you might shag me.'

'Doesn't make you a bad person.'

'Yeah it does. I'm horrible. The only thing I gave a shit about in *The Green Mile* was the mouse.'

'Me too.' We looked at each other and his face split into the most shit-eating grin I'd ever seen.

'Oh don't do that. I hate forbidden fruit.'

'Sorry. Look, why aren't you milking your fame more? A little birdy told me that you'd been offered loads of telly work and magazines.'

'It was all the same kind of thing, mostly agents offering crap money to do crap personal appearances and donkey work. One was a gig on that TV channel where the women answer phones with their tits out. Another guy mooted the possibility of a post-baby workout DVD. Bloody cheek.'

Freddie laughed and hopped up on the sea wall. 'Craig's story is interesting enough but you've got the whole Priory Gardens thing and a baby on the way. Personality. Looks. You've got star quality, Rhiannon. You're Delires van Cartier.'

'Haha, yeah right.'

'No, you are. "Let's get one thing straight, my dear. I am not, nor have I ever been, a Las Vegas showgirl. I am a headliner." That's you. You shouldn't be in the back row. You should be centre stage.'

'Doesn't seem right, Freddie,' I told him. 'People have died, remember?'

'Of course, of course,' he said, all his sparkle evaporating.

I was joking, naturellement. Craig's fame while he'd been in prison had bugged the hell out of me. I'd tried to avoid it, but it's impossible when you live in an online world most of the time like I do. Playing Best Supporting Actress to him was not something to enjoy but to endure. It was the only way.

'I was writing something about you,' he said, pulling a folded piece of paper from the back pocket of his jeans. 'You don't have to read it now—'

I snatched the paper out of his hands and started reading. It was an article, all about me. Me. Me. Me.

Rhiannon Lewis: A Born Survivor For The Age.

It's impossible to open a newspaper these days without reading some hideous doom and gloom tale for our times; stories of such evil or brutality that you wonder if the human race is worth saving. 'Look for the helpers' we are constantly reminded, for they are there in the worst of times.

But so too are the survivors; those who keep hitting the deck but who rise up again like a phoenix, shaking ash from its feathers. Sometimes it is good to be reminded that people like Rhiannon Lewis exist. People who have been dealt such cruel cards but who keep on keeping on.

Rhiannon was six when fate struck a devastating blow in a tragedy which shocked the nation. She and five of her friends were subjected to a frenzied attack at their child minder's house in Priory Gardens, Bradley Stoke, Bristol. The child-minder – Allison Kingwell – had begun divorce proceedings against her estranged husband, Antony Blackstone, and for him it was the final straw. He broke into the house one morning and murdered her young charges in cold blood – Rhiannon was the only one to survive. And somehow, she came back stronger with the help of physio and speech therapy. She walked again, talked again, attended school, passed all her exams and went on to university. This year she and her boyfriend had discovered they were to have a baby so they got engaged.

But Fate wasn't finished with Rhiannon yet.

A second earth-shattering card was dealt. Not long after learning of her pregnancy, Rhiannon's fiancé was arrested and charged with murder – multiple murder. Craig Wilkins – the West Country man charged with the brutal slayings of five people in what has been dubbed the 'Gay Ripper' Murders – is awaiting trial in Bristol Prison. He has been denied bail.

Clearly Rhiannon had thought her days of being a media fixation were over when I meet her on the doorstep of her parents-in-law's house one warm July morning.

'I just want to get on with my life,' she says...

I turn the page but it's blank. 'That's all?'

He shrugged. 'Yeah, well, you wouldn't speak to me about it.'

'I was enjoying that.'

'Good. I'm glad you liked it.'

'What will you do next?' I asked, handing the page back to him and finishing off my cornet.

'Dunno. My husband Jason's applying for ad agency work in London.'

'Freddie and Jason?' I sniggered. He afforded me a rather bored-looking eyebrow. 'Aww, that's so sweet you guys finally made up!'

He smirked. 'We've heard all the jokes.'

'You applying for jobs too?'

'Yeah, there are a couple of editorial assistant jobs I'm applying for. I'd like to be at one of the big newspapers. I still want to be in journalism – a magazine, maybe. Features and stuff. I'll make the tea and sweep the floor if I have to. Need to get my foot in the door.'

'And a big exclusive story might help you do that, I suppose?'

'God no, I wasn't insinuating anything, I promise!' he said, horrified. 'No, Rhiannon. We're done, I promise. I came by today to say I was sorry. That's it. And if I can make it up to you in any way, please let me know.'

'I suppose a shag's still out of the question?' I chanced. He laughed a lot. 'All right, all right I get the picture. So journalism is your bliss?'

'My what?'

'Your bliss. The thing you most love doing.'

'Yeah, I guess. Well, I like writing. I like researching stories.

And I like meeting people and finding out about their lives. I'm interested in others.'

'Wow,' I said. 'What's that like?'

He laughed, even though I was genuinely interested to find out the answer so I laughed along with him. We passed the snack shack. I bought a stick of Monks Bay rock with a picture of the funicular railway on the wrapper. 'Here. Something to remember me by.'

'Thanks,' he smiled, slipping me his business card in return. 'Freddie Litton-Cheney – Journalist'. The *Plymouth Star* newspaper address was crossed out in blue Biro.

I did the approximation of a smile and hope it reached him as intended. 'Good luck, Freddie. I hope you get your big break.'

*

I've been sitting here for an hour. Catfished a few more pervs – some kid called GeekBoy3000 in Florida is the latest to draw the flower. He sent me a ten-minute clip of him crying and saying how much he loved me.

BLOCK.

Some capuchin-faced dude with wispy grey hair calling himself The Impregnator flung me a few dick pics.

BLOCK.

Then I found some filtered messages from a guy I'd muted months ago, saying he was going to toss himself off his local viaduct if I didn't respond to his flower carving. So I did.

Sweetpea: Kill yourself. You're no good for anything else.

BLOCKITY BLOCK BLOCK BLOCK BLOCK BLOCK BLOCK. It's a block party all up in here today.

Then I updated AJ's Facebook page again – he's 'in Thailand now, meeting up with his friends'. For a dead guy, he sure as hell gets around.

'Ow!' I got kicked for that.

Anyway, I Photoshopped a picture of his head onto some other Australian gap year friend of one of the PICSOs and put him on a beach in Phuket, playing with a stray dog. It's not the most proficient Photoshop job ever but unless you're looking for anomalies, I don't think you'd see it.

Gordon Ramsay clap DONE.

This is what I do now. I update a dead man's Facebook page. I catfish perverts with no intention of ever meeting up with them. I sit in the car park at Mel & Colly's Farm Shop and wait for Sandra Huggins to clock on.

I come back at closing time to watch her leave. It's been the same rota for the past week. Being close to her is the nearest I get to happiness.

There's more to life than happiness.

Oh yeah, the Aubergine is talking to me again.

It won't make you feel good. You'll be sick again. I'll make it worse. If you make her bleed, I'll make you bleed.

*

The farm shop itself was a charming little place – a large shed with a corrugated roof, selling everything a middle-class person could possibly want – overpriced organic fruit and veg, camel's milk, jams, chutneys, locally-sourced rare breed pork and eggs, plus a range of artisan cheeses and gift ideas for people you

hate – floral notepads and candles and the like. Out the front there were signs for 'Eco logs – chop your own' and sacks of dry kindling and coal. They'd already trimmed up for Christmas – tinsel draped along shelves, fairy lights around the fridges and a full-size neon Santa by the entrance, offering a tray of mulled wine tasters and mince pies. 'Eat Drink and Be Merry' read the sign around his neck.

I spied the paedophile formerly known as Sandra Huggins – now 'Jane Richie' – stocking up the Christmas card rack. Jee-zuz. She was even uglier than I remember from the garden centre. Granted she'd lost some weight – prison food'll do that to you, I guess – but she was still greasy and jowly AF. I became aware of the positioning of the Sabatier in my rucksack.

'Hi there,' I said, as breezy as breezy gets.

'All right?' she replied, looking me up and down. This is a standard response I have found in my limited career as a Paedo Chaser. Both Fenton and Derek Scudd looked at me the same way. They're processing whether you're going to be nice or throw acid. Sadly, I had no acid to hand. Also, for a homespun farm shop, they were surprisingly tooled up when it came to CCTV.

I had no plan of what I was going to say or do – I was just looking at her and thinking about what she'd done to those babies in her care. The pictures she had sent to those men. Those children she had supplied. I powered down long enough to speak. 'Where are the gluten free pasties please?'

She huffed as she put down the stack of Christmas cards, walking over to the far end of the shop where there were two large chest freezers, full of frozen pastries and pies. She presented the sight with her thick, rough hand, like a pissed-off magician awaiting applause.

'Great, thanks,' I said, smiling sweetly. Inwardly I was baking her in an oversized pie and boiling her bones down to glue. I wanted her so badly I became quite aroused looking at her, as she waddled back to her Christmas cards – the way a lover looks. Except in my case, I didn't want to fuck her. I did want to stick something inside her though, right up to the hilt.

Again and again and again.

Mummy…

'I know, I know,' I said, pretending to look through the chest freezers, keeping one eye on Sandra Dee. I checked the time – the store would be closing soon. I was all out of options. I had to follow her home.

Mummy please don't do it…

So I waited back in my car in the car park. Around 5.05 p.m., Sandra Huggins left the store – red handbag on her shoulder, green fleece over her forearm. She locked up and walked over to one of the picnic tables out the front, leaning against it. Within five minutes, a green Vauxhall Cavalier with filthy mud flaps swooped into the car park and pulled up alongside her. She got in to the passenger seat and off they went. I started my engine—

I'm sending the pains now…

'Oh Jesus wept!' I cried out as my abdomen tightened in the middle, taking my breath away.

I told you it was too risky. I told you to walk away.

'You let me kill Troy. She deserves it!' I turned off the engine.

Go home.

'All right, I'm going. Please stop the pains, please!' I hurriedly Googled *What to do if you have pains pregnancy help ow*. The first result back was Braxton Hicks contractions. Dehydration was a cause.

I grabbed the bottle of water from my rucksack and necked it in one long series of gulps.

It's not dehydration. It's me. I don't like it when you kill people. How many more times do I have to say it?

'Stop them, please. Stop them, I'm begging you.'

Go home then, Mummy.

'I'm going, I'm going.'

Tuesday, 27th November
– 29 weeks, 2 days

Ugh.

Thursday, 29th November
– 29 weeks, 4 days

1. *The programmers of afternoon TV – how many times has* A View to a Kill *been on this year exactly?*
2. *People who have wide asses and block whole aisles in the supermarket so you can't get through and see which mayonnaise you want.*
3. *People who leave piss drips on toilet seats.*

Today I awoke with leaking breasts and constipation. So while my tits are running amok, in my backend it's gridlock. And then Elaine sat me down at the dining table and assaulted me in my dressing gown.

Well, not assaulted, per se. Assaulted my eyes with a chunk of tedious forms to fill out.

'What's this?' I said, still bleary-eyed from a crap night's sleep and yet another avalanche of vivid dreams about roasting my baby on a spit.

'This is your birth plan. What the midwife gave you at your last appointment. I thought we should fill it out. Come on.'

'This was in my rucksack.'

'Yes but you haven't looked at it. I think we should.'

'You went into my rucksack?'

'Yes, I didn't root about, don't worry. Now—'

If she *had* rooted about, she'd have found my diary. And my knife. And probably a small flashing sign that read *A serial killer owns this bag. Best not tell her you went through it uninvited.*

'Page One, where to give birth. Where would you like to—'

'Hospital.'

'Right, or there's the choice of home birth or water—'

'Hospital, bed, doctors, nurses, drugs.'

'Okay. How about birth partners.'

'None.'

'Are you sure, love? Me and Jim could—'

'No birth partners. Next question.'

'What about positions during labour?'

'Positions?' I said. 'The normal position – flat on my back with my legs in the air in screaming agony please.'

'Or it says you can squat or stand.'

'Can I cross that bridge when I need to, do you think?'

'Okay.' She ticked some box then flipped over the page. 'Pain relief.'

'Yes.'

'It says you can try breathing, massage, acupuncture… '

'Drugs.'

'Entonox, pethidine, epidural.'

'Yes.'

'Which ones?'

'Every ones.'

'Skin to skin contact – do you want to hold the baby after it's born?' I didn't know how to answer that. Luckily I didn't

have to; Elaine made up her own mind. 'Yes of course you do. Have you thought about what you want to do with the placenta? Some mothers choose to keep it attached and do what they call a lotus birth.'

'Ugh, no way. Burn the bloody thing.'

'Rhiannon, language, love.'

'I don't want to eat it, cook it or wear it as some bang on trend beret. I don't want to upcycle my umbilical cord as a bicycle pump or blend my amniotic fluid with chia seeds to make a tasty smoothie. And I am not wheeling around a buggy with a giant splat of pulsing raw meat inside it. Get rid of it. All of it.'

'Okay.' She ticked another box. 'Now episiotomies. That's when they have to cut your vagina—'

At this point, I left the room. She hasn't mentioned the forms since.

Later on, the cot she made me order from Baby World arrived and Jim started putting it together. They've made a start on the nursery – the room I was using as a dressing room. They're even talking of 'knocking through so the baby's only ever a couple of steps away from you'. So that'll be joyful.

*

Elaine doesn't want me in the house while they're painting – even though it's fumeless paint she 'can't take the risk ' – so I've been sent to walk Tink along the seafront.

I try and try but try as I might, I can't see the baby in that room. I can't imagine her ever coming out of me. I can't imagine me holding her skin-to-skin. I can't imagine her lying in that cot, kicking out, balling her fists into knots, sucking

her knuckles, looking around. I don't *want* her in the cot. I don't *want* her in that room. I don't want her to be outside of me where everyone can get to her. Where Sandra Huggins can get to her. Where men like Patrick Edward Fenton can get to her. In me, she's safe.

Am I though? It's pretty dicey in here, Mummy, I have to say.

My phone is going. It's Seren. Hmmm, what's this about? I wonder.

'Hey, Rhee.'

'Oh hi, how are you?'

'Good thanks. I called to say Happy Thanksgiving.'

Oh right. Thanksgiving. Her husband Cody makes her call me at least once a year on this day because 'deep down, you're glad you have a sister'. 'Same to you. How's things? How's your new place?'

She sounded upbeat for once. 'Can you believe I'm actually only five hours behind you now? We're so much happier here, I can't tell you.'

'It must be early there, Seren. It's eleven a.m. here.'

'Yeah, I've been up since three getting everything ready. Can't sleep at all! The kids took ages to get off last night too.'

'Nice,' I said, letting Tink off the lead as we ascended the beach steps. 'What do you have to get ready?'

'All the food. We've got three sets of friends coming over tonight, sleeping over, and they've all got kids so me and Cody are doing a bit of a banquet and the kids are going to have a sleepover in the den.'

It all sounds so Meg Ryany and nice doesn't it? I looked out across the sea, wondering how cold the water was.

'... you know the usual turkey and trimmings and I'm doing

332

a monkey bread stuffing and a sweet potato salad, pumpkin pie with cookie crust and the kids are doing a treasure hunt in the garden. They've made a ton of friends real quick at their school. We're all so much happier here.'

'Yeah, you said. Happy. Got it.'

'It's in no small part down to you, Rhiannon.'

'Me?'

'Yeah. I know I bit your ass a little about selling Mom and Dad's place but now that we have, we've been able to move here much quicker than we thought. It's our dream house.'

'I'm glad it's all fallen into place for you,' I said, lobbing Tink a stick she didn't run after. 'Whereabouts is it?'

'We're in Weston in Windsor County. There's not much to do here but the climate's better and it's so beautiful. The locals have been so welcoming.'

'I'm pleased for you.'

'Thanks. So, you okay?'

What do you care? 'Yeah I'm fine.'

'Are you on maternity leave now?'

'Yeah. Craig's decorating the baby's room today so he's sent me out of the house so I don't breathe in any fumes. He's paranoid, bless.'

'Aww that's so sweet. So he's okay? And the baby's all good?'

'Yeah, we're all fine. Couldn't be happier. Craig's so excited about becoming a daddy. And I've got a great antenatal group – we all meet up regularly for a cuppa and a natter, you know the kind of thing. A few of them are coming over later actually. We're having a girly night with ice cream and mud packs – some Meg Ryan DVDs I think.'

'You sure you're okay, Rhiannon?'

'Yes I'm fine.'

'You don't usually enjoy stuff like that. You know, fun. And friends.'

'Maybe motherhood's changing me.'

'Good,' she said. 'I'm so glad.'

I heard another voice in the background at her end. 'What was that?'

'Cody said he's looking forward to meeting you and Craig in the New Year. The kids want to as well. He's got some time off in February – we could come over when the baby's due and help out?'

'They want to meet *me*? Your "mentally deranged" sister?' I watched Tink sniffing in a clump of seaweed. 'Haven't they seen those Aileen Wournos documentaries on Netflix? Don't they know what I'm like?'

'Don't, Rhiannon, okay? I'm trying to mend our bridges here.'

'I never burned them, Seren.' It went all quiet at her end. Removing all traces of snark from my voice I said 'I'm just surprised, that's all. You've never wanted to introduce them to me before.'

'They ask about you all the time. You're the only aunt who actually remembers their birthdays.'

'You *do* get my cards then?' I looked out to sea. I wondered how deep the water was.

'Or you could come here when the baby's born and see our new place. You would absolutely love it here, it's like Honey Cottage but so much bigger. We've got six bedrooms. You and Craig can have your own bathroom too. You get so much more for your money out here.'

'How is it like Honey Cottage?' I asked.

'Well there's log fires, wooden eaves, vegetable garden, a pumpkin patch, chicken coops. Big but cosy. We love it here.'

'Yeah, you already said that.'

'So how come you and Craig are still in the flat? You could buy a house with your share of the money from Mom and Dad's place, couldn't you?'

'Yeah. But we like it here. And it means we don't have to work as hard. We can just – be together. Enjoy life.'

'Good for you.'

'Yeah. Do you ever think about Honey Cottage?'

'Sometimes,' she said. So many things here remind me of it. In one of the bedrooms it has the exact same wallpaper as Nanny's room. And the oak beams and the horse-riding trail going through the back field. I think about the bad stuff too.'

'Seeing those men pull Grandad out of the river?' I said.

'Yeah.'

'I remind you of the bad stuff, don't I?' I looked out to sea, wondering where my body would wash up if I drowned today.

'Don't. We're having a nice conversation here. Don't dredge up the past.'

'The past has a habit of dredging up all by itself.'

I stroked my bump. A swift kick batted my hand away. Even Tink had gone off into the dunes with some Jack Russell, the floozy. Seren was so in love with her rich bitch American Pie life she hadn't thought to check the British news recently. Craig's little spell at HMP Bristol had completely escaped her notice. I enjoyed my little bit of power over her.

It was on the tip of my tongue to tell her but I didn't. I just sucked on it like a particularly fizzy lemon sherbet.

Saturday, 1st December
– 29 weeks, 6 days

1. *The guy who presents* Diners, Drive-Ins and Dives.
    Lucky bastard.

I don't know why that phone call to Seren has depressed me
so much. I think it was hearing her talk about Cody and the
kids and their Thanksgiving dinner and all their friends coming
round. It made me realise that I could have had a life like that,
instead of this one. I can never have that. If I was torturing
Sandra Huggins right now, I wouldn't even think about it. In a
parallel universe, maybe I am like that. Maybe I can enjoy the
simple things like hosting dinner parties and making gorilla
soufflé or whatever the hell it is.

The new stuff's been arriving at the Well House – just the
new sofa to come. It's like nothing ever happened there. No
tantrum. No mess. No inadvertent stabbing of my pregnant
stomach. No Patrick. The chemical dry cleaner's smell lingers
but I don't think you would notice it was covering a worse
odour. It's clearly not the first time Kes has done this.

I was rearranging my Sylvanians canal boat this morning and
setting up the candy shop next door along the tow path when
Elaine came in 'to get some washing for a full load'.

'What's happened to this one?' she asked, pointing to the headless cat sister on the carpet.

'She died,' I said. 'I'm going to bury her next to her parents.'

'Do Sylvanians make graveyards?'

'No, but there's a wedding chapel for sale on eBay that I've been thinking of getting. It's got a little wedding car with ribbons on it and a bride and groom. I can make gravestones out of cardboard. I'll bin the bride and groom.'

She picked up the little cat head. I looked up at her. She was staring inside the house at the trashed living room – the knocked over Christmas tree, the broken window. 'Did Tink do this?'

'No,' I said, taking it from her and putting it back where it was. 'They had a burglary on Christmas Eve and the cat mum was murdered'.

'Oh right,' she said. I heard a crackling behind me – she'd found the Penguin wrappers under my pillow.

'It's not fair on the baby if you eat too many sweet things,' she said, scrunching them up and taking them and my pile of clothes out with her.

Fair? She wants to give me a lecture on what's fair? If this was a fair world we'd have a few more Bowies and a few less Kardashians. We'd still have Victoria Wood and Rik Mayall and Prince, and cancer would hit all terrorists right in the bollocks. Everyone on *Ex on the Beach* and *Love Island* would walk straight back into that fucking sea and never come out. *That* would be fair.

If this was a fair world, people like *me* wouldn't be able to have babies. I'd be as barren as the Gobi Desert. But I'm not, am I? Everything I do for this baby is wrong. I'm not exercising enough, I'm not eating properly, I'm not planning for its future

enough. I'm eating too many Penguins. According to Elaine, my kid should already have a nursery place, a full Jojo Maman Bebe wardrobe and an ISA.

I didn't say all this of course. I try not to say too much around Elaine anymore if I can help it. A) she doesn't listen and B) she bores the electrolytes out of me.

I'm now being sent Braxton Hicks even when I'm *thinking* about Sandra Huggins so, little by little, I'm learning to live with the fact I can't go near her, however much I want to.

Ow.

*

Did Tesco. Pretty uneventful except for the fact I couldn't stop farting. Something I've eaten despises me. I dropped one by the Lurpak, did a complete circuit, went back to get milk and it was *still* there in the air, lingering like a Dementor.

*

So Géricault turned up at the house this afternoon with my old mate DI Tubby Guy from *Grease*. Things escalated quickly.

'I'd like you to come with me and my colleague to the station. We need to clarify a few things.'

'What things?'

'Details about the ongoing investigation into Craig's alleged crimes.'

She hung on that word 'alleged' like it was a precipice. 'We need you to provide an official witness statement, that's all.'

'I can't do it here?'

'We'd like to get everything on tape, if that's all right with

you.' It wasn't a question. 'And we know how stressful our visits can be to Mrs Wilkins. Perhaps you'd like to spare her the anxiety today and come with us instead?'

Shit. Shit. Shit. Shit. Shit. Hang on, see what they've got first.

Elaine called out from the kitchen. 'Who is it, Rhiannon?'

'Jehovahs,' I called back, turning to Géricault and friend again. 'If I'm under arrest she will need to know. And I'll need a legal.'

'You're not, Rhiannon. And you won't.'

I span Elaine a yarn about a Pudding Club meeting I'd forgotten all about and left with the cops.

Three hours it took to get to Bristol in Saturday traffic. Neither of them spoke to me the entire journey. Tubby Guy offered me a mint but that was all. They didn't even have the radio on.

When we arrived, I was plonked in a grey interview room for another two hours where I had to go over all the same crap I'd told them before – names of Craig's closest friends, how long he had known my dad, what sort of relationship they had. How many times I had gone to see Lana. They played CCTV footage of me, clear as glass, walking through the town on my way to her flat – Tupperware box of Rice Krispie cakes under one arm, flowers in the other.

'What's in the box?' asked Tubbs, sucking on a mint.

'Cakes. I made her some cakes.'

'What sort of cakes?'

'Rice Krispie cakes. Lana's favourite.'

'Why would you do that?' asked Géricault, tearing the wrapper on a packet of Extra Strong Mints and posting one silently through her lips. She didn't offer me one.

'I was trying to be nice,' I said.

'What's in the cakes?' asked Tubbs.

'Rice Krispies and melted chocolate. They're fairly easy to make. I can write down the recipe if you need it.'

Tubbs leant forward as Géricault leant back. 'What else?'

'Nothing. Sometimes I put baby marshmallows in them or raisins, but most people only want the Rice Krispies and the chocolate. Why gild the lily?'

Géricault's mint clicked off her teeth. 'When I came to your house the other week, Rhiannon, I used the bathroom. These were in the cabinet.'

She slid a colour photocopy across the table. 'For the benefit of the tape I am showing Miss Lewis a photo of a bottle of Tramadol, prescribed to Mrs Elaine Wilkins of Yellow House, The Esplanade, Monks Bay. Jim Wilkins informed me that Elaine had been prescribed them for anxiety but she was on a low dose. We have spoken to two people who saw Lana between the dates you visited her—' she checked her notes '—first week of August, first week of October, again with cakes and flowers and again the eighteenth of October, when this CCTV footage is from.'

'Which people?'

'A hairdresser and the man who runs her corner shop. They both say her personality deteriorated over this time. She became jittery, confused and on one occasion, extremely paranoid with "pin-prick pupils". All are side effects of abuse of this drug, which she wasn't prescribed.'

'And?'

'Why did you go and see her for a third time?'

'She asked me to.'

'Why?'

'She was getting harassed by detectives and journalists and she wanted someone to talk to. She seemed sad.'

'And you were there to cheer her up?'

'Are we going to talk about the fact you were snooping around my house without a warrant?' They both looked at each other. 'You tell me I'm not under investigation and then you go rummaging about uninvited in bathroom cabinets? What's the police ombudsman's view on that?'

Géricault placed the colour copy of Lana's body next to the pill photo. Then a picture of the sweet peas I'd brought her. 'A post mortem on Lana Rowntree's body found traces of Tramadol in her stomach. Large traces.'

'And?'

'Other contents included paracetamol, whiskey, cereal and chocolate – potentially your Rice Krispie cakes.'

'She didn't eat the sweet peas then?' I said.

'You brought her those flowers. You brought her those cakes. Did you lace the cakes with Tramadol, Rhiannon?'

'No I did not.'

Tubbs leant forwards again. 'You wanted Lana out of the picture. You made her change her alibis so Craig would be left in the shit, and when she was at her lowest ebb, you encouraged her to kill herself.'

'Why would I get her to change her alibis and *then* make her kill herself as well?'

Gericault rubbed her chin with one of her finger stumps. 'You like the thrill of it?' Géricault suggested. 'You like playing with people's emotions? Perhaps because you don't have any yourself.'

I smiled, licking my dry lips. 'I made Lana some cakes to cheer her up. What she did after I left is nothing to do with me.'

'Where did she get the Tramadol from?'

'How should I know?'

Tubbs and Géricault glanced at one another again, then Tubbs collected up the photos, announced he was leaving the room then quickly departed. Leaving me and Géricault alone.

They've got nothing. Remember that.

She clacked her dwindling mint and studied me, as though comparing paint swatches. Like she couldn't decide which way to go.

'Your father Tommy was your hero, wasn't he?'

'Dads are most little girls' heroes, aren't they? I expect yours was too.'

'Did Tommy teach you to box?'

'He taught me how to throw a punch, yeah. In case I ever needed to.'

'*Have* you ever needed to?'

'Once or twice at school.'

'At Julia Kidner?'

Ooh she's got you on the ropes now, Mummy.

'No, like I told you, I barely knew the woman.'

'What did you do with her fingers?'

I laughed. Hooted. 'Seriously? You're seriously going down *that* road with me? You said I didn't need a lawyer, that this was an informal chat to take down some evidence. I was providing a witness statement, *you* said.'

Géricault switched off the tape. 'Where did you keep Julia Kidner?'

'I don't know what you mean. What happened to your fingers?' A eyebat.

'What did you do with *her* fingers?'

342

'Are you deaf?'

'How many times did you visit Lana Rowntree in the weeks before her death, goading her, enabling her, drugging her food?'

'I had nothing to do with Lana's untimely death.'

She sat back. The mint had gone. Her colleague had gone. It was her and me, a staring competition. And she blinked first.

Yay, go Mummy.

Gathering her papers, she pushed back her chair and stood up, exiting the room. I heard voices in the corridor – too faint to work out. A full half an hour later one of them returned but it wasn't Géricault.

'You're free to go, thanks for your time,' said Tubbs. 'I'll have one of the squad cars run you back.'

'You better,' I said, gathering up my things.

Sunday, 2nd December
– 30 weeks exactly

It's Dad's birthday today. He would have been fifty-seven. I still light a candle for him on this day. I can't find any today. I think all the Yankee Candles from the flat have gone into storage. Got to go out and buy one.

Pregnancy continues to be a never-ending cavalcade of delights. Today it's time for the listlessness and achy lower back symptoms to shine. Another crap night's sleep and a kick-fest that went on for two and half hours.

I had a dream about the fortune teller. She was on the clifftop outside the Well House. She had the baby in her arms and she was telling me to *Go*. That's all she kept saying. *Go. Go. Go.* And then I was in the water. Awake but face down. And my body kept smashing into the rocks again and again.

I don't like going to sleep anymore. I don't feel safe in my own head.

I'm supposed to be starting antenatal classes this week. Two hours a week for the rest of my gestation. I'm supposed to be learning all about diet and exercise, breathing techniques, coping with labour, breastfeeding and aftercare, which hole it comes

out of, that kind of thing. Pretty sure it'll be a waste of time though. I can probably Google most of it.

*

I can't do anything about the bad dreams or the achy lower back but I decided to do something about the listlessness. My walk into town this morning to buy a candle took me instead to the church. I decided to light a candle in there instead. The Sunday service had emptied out but two of the WOMBATs – Poll Potts and Bea Moore the Colossal Bore – lurked, tidying up the hymn books. I lingered near the children's area at the back. The last time I'd got stuck talking to that interminable giblet Bea Moore on the coach to Cardiff, she'd bored my ear off about the picture book she was writing – *Pip the Glow Worm and the No Fucking Hope of Getting Published Whatsoever*. Elaine had told her I had written a book myself and worked in journalism so knew what I was talking about.

The children's art boards were better illustrated. Jesus's face on paper plates. Interpretations of *What God Looks Like* on A4 card. Decorated paper puzzle pieces with the heading *We are each a piece in God's great plan* with coloured-in lolly stick crosses decorating the edges.

I headed towards the green-clothed altar, next to which stood a table with a display of lit tea lights, each one a memory of a passed loved one. I lit one for Dad.

'Hello,' said the vicar, a sweet-faced young man who appeared from the vestry like an apparition.

'Sorry, is it all right to come in and light up?'

'Of course.'

'It's for my dad. It would have been his birthday today.'

He nodded. 'He'll feel the warmth of its glow. You can be sure of that. Did you enjoy the service today?'

'I didn't go. Sorry.'

'That's all right.'

'I do like the Bible; I've been reading it.'

He smiled. 'Any particular passages?'

'Yes lots.'

I contemplated telling him about the ones I'd underlined but I thought better of it and went for the safer 'I like Noah's Ark' option.

'Yes that's one of my favourites, too.'

'Is it all right if I sit and talk to Him? He hasn't clocked off, has he?'

He laughed. 'No, He's always here for you.'

Bea and Poll had finished – the hymn books all stacked neatly on the ends of the pews, the kneelers upright, the organ off, the flowers changed over. The dust had stilled, the air had cooled, and I was alone. I started up the central aisle towards the gold eagle lectern. I sat down in the front pew staring up at the saints on the three stained glass windows at the front of the church. The middle window was a mother and child. Mary and Jesus.

'Dad?' I said. 'You might not even be up there – wherever "there" is – I don't know. What do I do? I need signs. I know I'm probably going the other way when my time comes but if anyone can point me in the right direction now, it's you. Keston says he can get me away from here but can I trust him? Where do I go? And... is there any point anyway? Does the world need me in it? I don't want to die. But at the same time, I don't know how to live.'

Silence. The window seemed to glitter in the morning light. The eagle lectern glared at me, all sharp and beaky.

'Seren said I thought you were some kind of god. I think she was right. I worshipped you. I still do. You're always in my dreams. You're always the hand that pulls me out of the pit. The arms I fall into. The voice saying everything will be all right. You're my Man in the Moon now. And I need a sign. Tell me what to do. Where do I go? Will the baby be all right?'

I looked down at my kneeler – blank blue and scratchy. The kneeler next to it had a picture cross-stitched into the wool – a boat.

Still the silence. The candle flickered in its holder.

'Is that it?' I said. 'A boat? Is that supposed to mean something? Do I find the answer on a boat? Which boat?'

More silence. The candle flickered again. Dust motes floated up as I patted the kneeler and checked underneath it for a written note or something, anything. 'Technically that's not my kneeler though. Mine's blank. What am I supposed to read into that? Are you telling me I need to get on a boat? Can you be more specific please? Give me a definitive sign – do I find the answer on a boat or do I get on a boat? What does the boat mean?'

The candle flickered. Then went out altogether, as I was looking at it. 'Noah's Ark, is it? You were agreeing with the vicar, were you?'

The candle came back on. I blinked. I didn't see that. That did not happen. 'Dad? Are you fucking around with me or what?'

*

Elaine did us a nice roast for Sunday lunch – sweet potato pie for me but with all the trimmings. And then we had blueberry

crumble (vile) and we all sat down to watch *Sister Act 2: Back in the Habit*. I didn't even mind that they talked the whole way through it. I curled up with Tink on the sofa and nodded off thinking about what I'm going to get them for Christmas. I'm going to get Tink her usual – stocking full of treats and a few bulls' cocks. I'm thinking of getting Jim and Elaine something substantial – like a holiday.

Or a cruise maybe. I can hear the Man in the Moon laughing at me, somewhere beyond the clouds.

Wednesday, 5ᵗʰ December
– 30 weeks, 3 days

1. *People who give Baylis and Harding gift sets as presents.*
2. *People who tell pregnant women that 'if it's a ten or eleven pounder, you're going to struggle cos you've only got narrow hips'.*
3. *People who constantly eyeball me for eating chocolate.*
4. *People who say 'your bump is huge but your breasts haven't grown'.*
5. *Elaine – who is responsible for the above listings.*

I decided to go round and see Marnie and Tim this evening. Thought I'd give the old Nazi the benefit of the doubt. Besides which, I just wanted to see my friend, even if she didn't want to see me. I missed her smile and her smell. I missed her being in the room; her atmosphere, you know? You know that feeling when you want to be near someone? I bought the largest pizza they had on offer in Tesco, a bagged salad (I didn't intend on eating any anyway) and a bottle of White Zinfandel – Marnie's favourite.

Tim opened the door.

'Oh hey, Tim, how are you?'

'Oh Rhiannon, hi,' he said, buttoning up his white shirt. There were wet patches below his moobs. 'Yeah good, thanks. How are you?'

'Fine thanks. Sorry, I didn't disturb you, did I?'

'No, I just got out the shower. You okay?'

'Well I was a bit bored actually. Thought I'd pop by and see how Marnie's doing. I tried texting her but she's not answering. Is she okay?'

'Yeah, she's fine.' He pulled the door open a little wider and Marnie was standing at the end of the hallway in her leggings and vest, holding a sleeping Raphael against her shoulder.

'Rhiannon? What are you doing here?'

'Hiya. I just came to see how you were. I was saying to Tim that I haven't been able to get you on your phone.'

'Oh. Must have been switched off.'

'For two weeks?'

She looked at Tim. Tim looked at me. I looked at Tim, then her, then held up my carrier bag. 'I brought pizza and dough balls?'

'We were going to get a takeaway tonight weren't we?' she said, coming to the door to form a triple human barrier against my entry.

'No need to now, is there?' I said, practically barging them aside.

'I'll stick the oven on,' said Tim.

Marnie laughed. 'Yeah, of course. Do you mind taking your shoes off? We've just had the carpets cleaned.' She stood aside as I de-shoed and shuffled behind her and Tim into the kitchen.

The first thing I noticed was the mess – there wasn't any. At all. No leftover plates or mugs or crumbs, nothing. It was like a

show-home kitchen with a bassinet in the corner by the French windows. All the utensils were perpendicular on the immaculate black granite worktops. The giant American fridge looked like it'd just come out of its box. Highly disturbing.

'Are you selling up?'

'No,' said Tim, flicking the oven on. 'Why d'you say that?'

'It's so tidy.'

'That's all me,' he said. 'Comes from my army days. I like things in their right places.'

I handed Tim the pizza as Marnie took the wine from me and put it in the fridge. If there's one place you can be messy in your house it's the fridge, right? Not here. Top shelf jars, next dairy, next veg, then meat. All stacked. Labels outwards. No drips. No overhanging packets. Quite extraordinary.

'Blimey.'

'What?' she said, turning to face me.

'Your fridge is immaculate. Ours looks like a Jihadi's gone off in it.'

Neither of them spoke. I wondered if they had known someone killed in a bombing. Or if it was just a bad time. Or maybe it was that I was an uninvited guest. I saw it on *Saved By the Bell* once – Zac and Screech turned up at the muscly one's house with a pizza and he was so pleased to see them. I thought Marnie would be pleased to see me. I don't think she was.

'Ribena?' she asked.

'Yeah, please.'

She knew I was a murderer. Did Tim know as well now, hence the awks? Had they seen me coming up the drive? Had she already given Géricault a witness statement about Fuckboy Troy? Were they on their way to arrest me?

'I'm sorry to turn up unannounced, Marnie, but like I said I couldn't get an answer when I called.'

'Oh?' she said, making for her phone, charging on the sideboard. She clicked it on. 'There's no missed calls or anything. Must be a bad signal.'

'I've sent texts too,' I said. 'And WhatsApped. They all delivered.'

'Something wrong with it, Marn?' asked Tim, unwrapping the dough balls from their plastic box.

She frowned and clicked open her messages. 'Nope, nothing here. Are you sure you've got my number, right?'

The oven came up to temperature and Tim turned to put the pizza in. I mouthed *Bullshit* to Marnie – she looked away. She was skittish; her hand was shaking slightly as she poured me out a tumbler of Ribena. She diluted it, handed it to me and watched me drink.

'Nice,' I said, amidst all the awks. I stood there, half a glass to go. I could sense her watching me. Looking at the oven clock. Watching me again. 'Am I on a timer or something?'

She laughed. 'God, no.'

'So have you heard from the Pudding Club since the barbecue, Rhiannon?' asked Tim, leaning back against the sink.

'No, not at all. I don't think I was cut out for that kind of crap anyway.'

'What, barbecues?'

'No, friends. Not those sorts of friends anyway. Too cliquey. And I didn't agree with a lot their ideologies. Like, we're supposed to be feminists and build up our sisters and support them come what may but what if your sister's a cunt? What then? Do you just lie about it?'

352

Tim cleared his throat and threw a glance at Marnie as she rocked Raph in her arms, watching the rain pitter-pattering on the patio doors.

'I always say less is more anyway. One good friend is worth a thousand acquaintances and all that.'

The second my empty glass hit the sideboard, Marnie put Raph in the bassinet and walked over to wash it up. I don't think the Ribena had hit my oesophagus before the glass was dry and back in its place in the cupboard.

She and Tim both stood there, not offering any further conversation.

'Is everything okay?' I asked.

Tim folded his arms. He seemed larger in this house than he had in Pin's massive garden – like a bear at the mouth of an immaculately clean cave.

'I'm not great with hints this is a bad time, isn't it?'

Tim turned to me. 'Marnie told me all about Cardiff. And I don't think you're a good influence, Rhiannon. There, I said it to her face now. That make you happy?' Marnie was suddenly crying like the tears had been hiding backstage and he had just torn down the curtain.

'Told you what exactly?'

'About you and her going out. Drinking all night, even though *you're* six months pregnant and *she's* breastfeeding. It's disgusting. You encourage her.'

'Encourage *her*?'

'Marnie has a problem with drink.'

'Yeah, she wants to drink and *you* won't let her.'

'No, this is all *you*,' he snipped, pointing a stubby finger my way. 'Anything could have happened to her in that state.'

I turned my head slowly to Marnie. She had one hand on the bassinet, staring out into the garden.

'I don't want you seeing her anymore.'

'Wow. Well, I'm shook, I don't mind telling you, Tim.'

'Shame on you. You are free to do whatever you want with your body but that baby isn't. And nor is my wife.'

'Your wife isn't free to do what she wants with her own body?'

'Of course she's not. Not when it's feeding our son.'

I looked at his face the way Tink looks at me sometimes – tilting left to right. 'What's wrong with you, Tim?'

'I beg your pardon?'

'Why does it threaten you that your wife might have a mind of her own?'

'I won't be spoken to like this in my own home.'

'Let's go outside then, Adolf, I'll do it in the street.'

Marnie stepped back towards the bassinet and gripped the edge, as though Raph was her shield. Mr Aryan Nation stepped towards me. 'Better watch your mouth, Rhiannon. I don't take kindly to people calling me names.'

'What, Adolf? I've called you worse. Haven't I, Marn?'

He whipped his head round to look at her.

Marnie shook her head. 'Rhiannon, please go now.'

He towered over me by a clear foot. 'What else have you called me?'

For God's sake, you're going to get me killed here.

'Goebbels. Heil Husband. Timmler. And plain old The Cunt.'

His nostrils inflated. I prepared myself for flames but I did not stand back. I would not. I thought of Julia – the way she was at school. I thought of Grandad. I thought of Antony Blackstone

at Priory Gardens. Same eyes – blue. Same smile – thin. Same breath – rank. Same meaty fists ready to pound.

'Do your worst,' I said. 'Don't mind the pregnancy thing. Go for it. Hit me. Choke me. I want you to.'

'Tim, no!' cried Marnie somewhere in the blurry distance.

But he did. He choked me right there in the kitchen, underneath the family wall calendar. 'Show me… who you really are,' I spluttered. He tightened his grip. 'Give it… to me, baby.'

He put his face right next to mine so I could feel the heat from his skin, taste the salt. 'Get. Out. Of. My. Fucking. House. You. Skanky. Bitch.'

Then he let go, and I bent over and coughed my airways clear. I rose up, face all hot, and smiled at him. 'Not. Without. My. Fucking. Pizza. Bitch.'

It was the smile that did it. He flung open the oven door, ripping the pizza out with no gloves on and threw it in my face. Then he grabbed the bagged salad and tore it open, sprinkling it over my head. Dough ball after dough ball came flying at me as hard as bullets. Well, of course not as hard as bullets but they were frozen so they were still pretty hard.

'There. You. Go. Have. Your. Pizza. And. Don't. You. Ever. Come Near. Me. Or. My. Wife. Or. My. Son. Again.'

Each of those full stops represents a dough ball, by the way. That'll teach me to buy the bigger pack.

He pushed me out on to the Welcome mat and slammed the door behind me.

I waited on the doorstep, still plucking pieces of Lollo Rosso out of my hair. I could hear both of them shouting – Marnie giving as good as she got. *F'ing this. F'ing you. F'ing Rhiannon. Bitch. Whore.* Slamming. This guttural Mel Gibson-esque

shouting from him. This high-pitched twittering from her. The baby was crying.

I got to the bottom of the road when I looked back at the house. Marnie was upstairs. Bedroom window, pulling the curtains. She saw me. I waited. The curtains closed and she was gone.

When I got back, there was an episode of *Kitchen Nightmares* on that seemed to sum up my sitch. The son was driving the business into the ground while the parents had health issues and were on the verge of bankruptcy. Gordon tried everything. Got the guy counselling for his alcoholism, gave their restaurant a makeover, devised a whole new menu, even bought them new cash registers. But things didn't change. The son got worse. The dad had a heart attack. Customers complained about slow service. And in the end, Gordon just walked away.

Sometimes you have to I guess.

Saturday, 8ᵗʰ December
– 30 weeks, 6 days

God is playing the comedian. He has sent me boats – lots of boats – about a hundred in all – in the form of the Monks Bay Christmas Flotilla, an annual event that takes place when the sun goes down one Saturday each December. Every boat in the harbour is adorned with fairy lights, and sails around honking horns and blasting out Noddy Holder.

The Flotilla was clearly the highlight of the year for Monks Bay's residents. Everyone came out to enjoy it. A real family event.

Probably why I felt so utterly out of place.

Along the harbour side was a Christmas market. Fish and chip shacks transformed into chestnut and eggnog stalls as chefs turned sausages on sizzling grills and flipped crepes and span sugar in copper barrels. There was a pop up ice rink, glow-in-the-dark mini golf and a giant inflatable snow globe filled with paper snow that people were having their pictures taken in. Mum, Dad, sisters, the dog. The WOMBAT choir sang carols and rattled charity buckets. I donated generously to the animal and homeless ones but try as I might I just can't find a shit to give about the closure of the town pool.

The foetus is now the size of a coconut and oddly enough, the thirty-one-week mark seems to be the point at which I can no longer stand up for more than twenty minutes. Everything starts to buckle. I'm as heavy as a baby elephant and I have backache like I've been lugging boxes for a week.

When I thought my feet were going to burst into flames, I sat down on a mooring post on the jetty and rubbed my aching bump.

'You all right, Love?' asked Elaine. 'Have you got any pains?'

'Just one. Right in my backside.'

We each sat on a different mooring post and watched the ships bob and glide in the fishy water. Tink jumped up on my lap but jumped down again when there was no room for her and the bump. She jumped on Jim instead.

'Here's to a good Christmas and a better new year for all of us,' he announced, toasting us both with his eggnog.

'I don't want to think about next year,' Elaine sighed, sipping her eggnog, before tipping it into the harbour. 'Urgh, that's curdled. Don't drink it, Rhiannon.' She took my cup off me and threw mine away too.

'Let's not think about next year then,' I said. 'Let's focus on Now, not Next.'

'Well said,' smiled Jim, raising his cup. 'To living in the moment.' Elaine patted my bump and sort of steeled herself to say something else, but then just exhaled.

'Right, well I want to do a bit of shopping,' I said.

'Oh, I'll come with you.'

'I need to be on my own, Elaine,' I said. 'You know, surprises.'

She beamed. 'Oh, I see. All right then, love, we'll see you at home.'

Let's focus on Now, not Next – my own words swirled round as I walked through the town. 'Now' I tried stepping into Christmas. 'Now' I tried eating candy floss. 'Now' I walked along the harbour edge and watched boats bobbing, people on board clinking glasses and watching fireworks go up on the jetty. 'Now' I stood and listened to WOMBAT tunelessly murdering 'I Saw Three Ships' and 'Mary's Boy Child'.

I tried so hard to feel contentment; to feel that this was normal and it was enough. That the deafening forced jollity of jingle bells and Shakin' Stevens booming out of every damn shop was what I wanted to hear. That the sight of my friend Marnie walking along with Tim, hand in hand like something in chains, didn't make me want to scream.

But there was only heartburn and aching feet. And the woman in the mustard jumper who didn't hold open the door for me in Boots. The man in the brown jacket who pushed past. The man in the fudge shop who didn't offer me a bag. And the paedophile Sandra Huggins eating a toffee apple and watching the flotilla – eyes dazzled by the lights. Jigging along to Elton John. New handbag. Smiling with her friend – and the friend's child.

The friend's child. The friend's child. She was allowed around children. After what she did. Did the friend know what she was? Did she know what that woman had done in a previous life?

No, not a previous life. *This* fucking life.

You gotta accentuate the positive, eliminate the negative, latch on to the affirmative, don't mess with Mrs Inbetween.

Why was the choir singing that? That's not a Christmas song.

I nipped into the next door travel agent, ten minutes from closing, and got a good armful of brochures for Jim and Elaine's Christmas present. All-inclusive Europe. Australia

on a shoestring. Cruises. I'll go through them all later and pick something out. California perhaps. I want Jim to see the Superbloom. I can just see his face.

*

Keston finally answered his phone – I must have tried him seventeen times since I saw him at the Well House. He didn't seem eager to chat.

'Rhiannon, you've got to trust me on this. Let me get on with it.'

'I need to know what's happening. What's going on with Géricault? Where are my new documents? Did the pictures come out ok? I know the wig's a bit ropey but it was the best one I could find.'

'Yeah yeah it's all being processed, I told you it takes time.'

'I saw Sandra Huggins at the flotilla. She was with a child.'

'On her own?'

'No, with her friend. It was the friend's child I think. Even so.'

'Don't go near her. I mean it.'

'She looked happy. What right does she have, hmmm?'

'Leave it, Rhiannon, please. Only call me in an emergency, all right? I'll be in touch when I know more. Sit tight.'

I couldn't ignore the nagging doubt I had about Keston. Yeah he knew Dad and they were mates and they'd done bad things, but he was still a *detective*. And I was a mass murderer. If I was him, I'd want to nab me. I'd want that adoration. Perhaps he was playing softly softly, catchy mummy.

He still had friends in the force. He took that oath thing they all take to protect and to serve and all that – or is that just *Police Academy*?

I don't know. And bloody baby brain means I can't think straight. Help me out here why don't you? Throw me a bone.

How can I help? What do you want me to do? I'm just a coconut.

'Should I trust Keston Hoyle?'

Maybe. Maybe not.

'Helpful. Thanks.'

All I can think about is that fudge in your handbag. You cracking it out again any time soon?

Thursday, 13ᵗʰ December
– 31 weeks, 4 days

1. *Lorry drivers who drive in the middle lane and go as slow as the guy in the inside lane so you can't overtake.*
2. *People who respond to a Like or a Favourite with a conversation.*
3. *People who run ultra-marathons – when did running more than one marathon in a lifetime become a thing?*

I feel like Keston and DI Géricault are laughing at me today, somewhere in this town. I can hear laughter wherever I go. It follows me around. It's in the shower drain when I got down to pluck the stray hair out. It's in the crash of the waves on the shore. It's in the swaying of the bare branches in Jim's garden. Keston's told me not to phone him, he says everything's in hand but no news is bad news. No news means 'something's up'. No news means the cancer's come back and it's gone to his brain.

'Dad, send me a sign! Where are you?'

I'd asked Keston what was happening with Géricault but he skirted around the answer. He told me to stay clean away from Huggins – *Don't go near her. I mean it.* Why? Why would he care about Huggins? He hates paedophiles as much as I do. He'd spent half his career targeting them and getting together with

his mates to bump them off and then conveniently sweeping the police investigations under the carpet.

Maybe he's trying to protect you from yourself?

Maybe Dad *did* send him for me and he *is* just looking out for me, like he said. But I can't live on maybes. I still can't fully trust him. I can't take the risk. The only person I know I can trust is myself.

Oh well that's reassuring.

Had another scan this afternoon – my bump had been measuring small for the last few midwife appointments and she just wanted to check everything was okay. All is well and the placenta appears to be in the right position now, where it wasn't before. She checked my blood pressure and piss again – all fine – and the baby's heartbeats are as strong as a horse's hooves clopping along. For some reason, her kicks are becoming much more prominent now, like tiny electric shocks at any moment. It's like transporting Karate Kid around with me. She looked huge on the scan too – a proper person now.

'That's scary,' I said.

'No, it's your baby,' said Bitch Midwife. 'She's a fifth engaged now.'

'What does that mean?'

'It means she's almost in the right position.'

'Right position for what?'

'To come out.'

'COME OUT?' I cried. 'She can't come out yet. I'm not due until February. It's too early. She'll die.'

'No it's perfectly normal for the head to engage this early on, we see it all the time, don't worry. How are your antenatal classes going, by the way?'

'Oh yeah. Terrific,' I said. 'Learning so much.'

'Now's the time to put your feet up as much as you can. Try not to exhaust yourself. She needs to bake for a little bit longer if possible.'

'What; if I do something strenuous will she fall out?'

'I don't know about falling out but you might bring on labour,' the bitch laughed. 'You'll get some warning though, at least!'

'How much warning?'

'Try not to stress about it. Have you picked your birth partner?'

'Uh, yeah. My friend Marnie I expect. She's got a baby of her own. I was going to ask her, seeing as she knows what to do.'

'Good idea.'

Of course I couldn't ask Marnie. She was gone from my life as quickly as she'd arrived. I had no one. I left the hospital through a side door and there were these big windows I walked past and there it was – the full on lean-back preggo waddle, like you've shit yourself, in all its ugly glory. Hideous. Wretched.

My ribs ache today. My back still aches but not as much as my ribs. And my bra hurts. Bitch Midwife says I 'need better bras with no under wiring' so I've bought a load of maternity ones in Marks. She also recommended I 'try eating more blueberries'.

Bought some baby bath stuff in Boots, too. Lavender-scented, because it was on offer, and some cream for my itchy bump – apparently that's a thing too, Itchy Bump Syndrome. And I saw this cute pink flopsy rabbit with a rattle in one foot and shiny pink stitching reading 'Happy Bunny' on the other. I held it to my nose – it was soft and smelled of lavender. I chucked that in the basket as well. At least she'll have one cuddly toy that wasn't Elaine-selected and approved. An old woman recognised me from some news item a month ago.

'Starting to nest I see?' She grinned, nosing her colossal beak into my basket.

'Oh no, this was on offer, that's all.'

She peered into my basket where the Marks bag of bras was. 'Oh I think you are. So exciting getting everything ready, isn't it? I remember it well. Will your husband be out of prison for the birth?'

For three seconds I allowed myself to live inside her mind – inside her mind where I was pregnant with Craig's baby and we were married, like we planned. Like he was going to be free any minute to come home and move to Honey Cottage with me, like we'd planned.

'He's not my husband,' I said eventually. She looked down again at my bump. For one moment I felt the blood rush to my hands when I thought she might rub it. If she had, I may have torn the papery skin from her flesh and worn it as a scarf but, luckily, she kept her arthritic digits to herself.

'Oh, well best of luck to you.' She smiled toothily. 'Being a mother is the most important job a woman can do.' I didn't reply but she had already shuffled off in the direction of the Tena Ladys anyway.

A business card fell out of my purse when I was paying. I had to stand like a giraffe to pick it up. It was the one Heather had given me – Wherryman & Armfield Solicitors. And a golden gondola etched on one side.

I called her the moment I got back. She answered on the first ring.

'Heather – it's Rhiannon Lewis. Are you busy? I need you.'

'Name it,' she said.

Tuesday, 18th December
– 32 weeks, 2 days

1. *People who park craply.*
2. *People who hunt animals for sport.*
3. *People who call you 'Mummy' when you're pregnant (i.e. Jim).*
4. *Those Nicole Scherzinger yoghurt ads.*
5. *People who make yoghurt.*

Seren called today. It wasn't a long conversation.

'So, Cody was Googling Craig's building firm today. To find out a bit more about him,' she said, her voice ever so slightly on the wobble.

'Oh, right.'

'He found out… that Craig's in prison. For multiple murder.' Her breath caught.

'Oh, right.'

Silence.

Her breath caught again. 'What the fuck have you done, Rhiannon?'

Thursday, 20th December
– 32 weeks, 4 days

Today Jim and Elaine got the decorations down from the loft and then we trimmed up. They have certain traditions in the Wilkins household when it comes to trimming up/Christmas in general. One of them is that Elaine likes to put a cuddly toy in the corner of every step on the staircase and wrap the bannisters with holly and ivy intertwined, fresh from the garden. Another is that they like to eat the first mince pie of the season with a glass of sherry as they 'toast' the angel on top of the tree – the angel Craig made aged seven.

They also like a certain Christmas film on when they're trimming up – a terrible Seventies made-for-TV version of *A Christmas Carol*. The irony of the movie wasn't lost on me. Perhaps being visited by the ghosts of all the people I've killed is all I need to see the light. Perhaps my dreams of AJ are trying to tell me the same. Maybe seeing my own grave is all I need to change for good.

Or maybe life isn't that straightforward.

Tink came scurrying in with a decorative stair Santa in her mouth and refused to give it back to Elaine, who chased her around the house for it.

'I'd let her have that one, E,' laughed Jim, as Tink scampered out of the room. It was the first time I'd seen Elaine laugh in months.

There was a gnawing in the middle of my body – I initially thought it was the return of the bad heartburn from the first trimester but it wasn't that. It was knowing that in that parallel universe I'm always thinking about, this *was* my life. These were my parents-in-law for real, that this was a Christmas trim-up like any other, that any minute now Craig would come in and pick up Tink and hold her up and tickle her ribs like she loved him doing. And then he'd come over to me and rub the bump and we'd all cuddle in and sit down to watch *Jingle All the Way* or some such other piece of shit Christmas movie that everyone pretends isn't completely and utterly awful.

Fake. That's what this scene is. Fake. Plastic. Bullshit.

It wears me out thinking about the parallel universe thing all the time because I know it's a billion miles away from this reality.

The Overfriendly Troll Erica popped round briefly while we were mid-trim to thank me for all my advice with *Pip the Glow Worm* and to tell me rather excitedly and with far too much touching of my right forearm that she was 'poised to sign with a publisher'.

I remained remarkably composed and said all the right things – all the *Well done*s and the *So happy for you*s, as my brain sizzled like it was on a hot brick. I had a string of tinsel in my hands and by the time we'd said our goodbyes it was quite bald.

I watched Erica walk back down the garden path, noticing DI Géricault sitting on the sea wall, watching me. She was wearing the same skirt she'd had on the last time she visited but

this time, her handbag was different. Dark green and bedecked in little padlocks. I don't know if that's important but the only information I could read about her was from what she was wearing. She gave me nothing else. I pulled the door to.

'You're back again?' I asked as I crossed the road. 'This is becoming infatuation, Detective Inspector.'

'I won't keep you long.'

'Fine, but can we keep walking?' I said. 'My mother-in-law is more than likely watching us through the bay window and I don't want to be responsible for another meltdown this close to Christmas.'

'Of course,' she replied, walking in step. 'I thought you'd like to know – I've been taken off your case for the time being. A complaint has been made and it's being followed up.'

'Who complained?'

'I don't know.'

I fought to breathe against the strong wind that had whipped up around us. 'You came all the way here to tell me this?'

She stopped walking and leant against the wall, looking out to sea. It was a languid pose – normally she was so upright and uptight. It didn't suit her. 'I hold all killers in the lowest possible esteem, Rhiannon. Whatever reasons they give for what they do. They're not the ones who have to tell the mothers, husbands, children of their victims that their loved one isn't coming home. They bestow that hideous responsibility on me.'

'And?'

'I *will* be back on this case after Christmas and I *will* prove Craig Wilkins' innocence.' She stood up straight and dead-eyed me. 'I know you have friends in high places but nothing stays buried forever. Sooner or later, something will start to stink.'

'You're not supposed to talk to me then, presumably?' I said, turning to face her. 'If you've been taken off the case?'

'I wanted you to hear it from my mouth that we – you and me – are not over.'

'You could have called.'

She shook her head and a strange smile appeared. 'I know what you are. And if it takes me the rest of my natural life, I will prove it.'

'Presumably you'd get into a lot of trouble if anyone knew you were down here threatening me like this? Threatening a heavily *pregnant* woman, with a hitherto unblemished record?'

'I'm not threatening you, Rhiannon. I'm promising you.'

'Promising me what?'

'That I will be there when that cell door closes on you. I will hear that click if it's the last thing I ever hear.'

I stood up straight and dead-eyed her back. 'No, you won't. The last thing *you'll* ever hear will be my voice. Laughing.'

'I'll get you like they got your dad.'

'My family are waiting to start our Christmas now,' I said, turning and walking back in the direction of Jim and Elaine's. 'I'm sure yours are too?'

She smiled that strange smile again. 'Make the most of it, Rhiannon.'

'You too, Detective.' I called back. 'Merry Christmas.'

Sunday, 23rd December
– 33 weeks exactly

1. *Woman in red Honda at the crossing who, apropos of nothing, swore out of her window at me. She clearly has a huge problem with braking. And Chihuahuas. And people who cross roads.*
2. *Men who cat-call women from cars – why don't you annunciate? Do I have a 'nice dog', a 'nice bra', or a 'nice ass'? I need to know before I can continue my life.*
3. *People who bring their babies to Christingle services, stand in the pew in front of me and allow them to stare at me over their shoulder throughout.*

You know that bit in that film *Nine Months* when Hugh Grant finally realises he's been a colossal wang and starts taking care of Julianne Moore and his unborn child? And she sees the nursery he's decorated and it's all pristine and stuffed with cuddly toys and there's this magical twinkly music playing and she's all teary-eyed and love-struck and thankful? Jim and Elaine unveiled my baby's nursery today. And it wasn't like that at all.

They'd gone for lemon and white as a theme. All the Elaine-approved cuddly toys lined the Elaine-approved cot under the Elaine-approved mobile. The window was festooned with

ruched lemon curtains and Elaine-approved safety cord, and in the corner was a lemon and white Gingham rocking chair for me to nurse. It was all very nice, don't get me wrong – Jim had made a bespoke chest of drawers and a changing unit under the window, and all the stuff me and Elaine had bought at Baby World had been sorted into neat units and boxes and labelled by her using her QVC-bought label maker.

It didn't feel like mine.

And I knew there never would be a baby in there.

I forced my face into elation and managed a tear or two when I hugged them, which they seemed to accept in payment. I put the pink flopsy bunny rabbit with the rattle in its foot in the cot but Elaine didn't think it matched.

'Keep that one in her pram perhaps,' she said, handing it back to me.

My stomach turned over.

Guilt, that's what you're feeling. They've been good to you and you're going to hurt them in the worst way.

I resolved to put the Well House listing live on Airbnb that afternoon. There were two booking enquiries within the first twenty minutes – one for the end of January and one for next Easter. Some people would jump in your damn grave as quick.

*

Me and Jim and Tink went to the WOMBAT Christingle service around tea time. It was pay on the door, so WOMBAT couldn't stop me from going, but Elaine couldn't face them yet so she stayed home and made shortbread tree decorations. Everyone was handed a homemade Christingle orange with a lit candle in it, and I made a beeline for the end of the pew nearest the organ

so I could linger near Big Headed Edna and give her evils every time she turned the page on her libretto. I made sure my voice was the one she could hear above all the rest.

Marnie and Tim and Raph were there. I waved to her when Tim was bending over to adjust his kneeler, but predictably, I got blanked. She pretended she was looking around for someone else. I still don't hate her for it though, strangely. If anyone else was doing this to me I'd be mentally slicing off some limb or baking them in a pie, but with Marnie that feeling wasn't there. She looked smaller this evening.

The sermon was all about how the Christingle orange represents the world, the red ribbon around the middle being Jesus's blood, sweets on the cocktail sticks representing the fruits of the earth and the lit candle being Christ the light himself.

'Christ is symbolising the hope of light in the darkness,' said the vicar. I evilled Edna who was suddenly quite taken with a stain in her skirt.

Kids from a local primary school sang 'Away in a Manger' and the vicar talked about 'the true meaning of Christmas'. Then after the longest version of 'Silent Night' ever, everyone filed out along the central aisle, allowing the light of the Christingles to 'travel out into the world'.

We said The Lord's Prayer. We thanked the vicar for a wonderful service. We filed out, absolved of all sin.

Outside the church, Jim met up with some guy called Len from the bowling club who he hadn't seen since his knee operation, so I was left standing alone like a spare one, until from nowhere someone gripped my elbow and pulled me into the shadows behind the church.

It was Marnie.

'Oh you're talking to me now?' I said, stumbling after her in the grass towards a dark corner. We came to a stop behind a large headstone dedicated to an old rector of the parish called Erasmus Percival Blenkinsop.

'I only have a moment. He's talking to someone from football.' She gave me a wrapped gift tied with ribbon. 'Don't open it now, wait 'til the day.'

'I didn't get you anything. I didn't think we were friends anymore.'

She shook her head. 'It's okay, I didn't expect anything back. I wanted you to have this. And I wanted you to know… '

She stopped talking. Her face was barely lit by the candles meandering all around the churchyard. She breathed softly, stutteringly like she was crying. Then pulled me into the strongest hug I'd ever received.

'What is it?'

'I know what you did. In Cardiff. And I know about Craig. I know it wasn't him who did all those things.'

'Oh.'

'You like doing it, don't you?'

I nodded.

'You like doing it to bad people.'

I nodded again.

'But what gives you the right to decide who lives and who dies?'

'Nothing,' I said. 'It's just who I am. I'd never have hurt you though.'

She pulled back from me. Studied me. Her chin was wobbling. 'When I saw Tim choking you in our kitchen, I saw him through your eyes. You stood up to him when I couldn't.'

'You can stand up to him too, Marnie.'

She shook her head, hesitating for a second before pulling me close and hugging me completely and totally. And somehow I knew it was for the last time. We held each other until the voice called out in the night. She stiffened and moved away.

'Are you going to the police?' I asked.

She shook her head, her conker-brown eyes watery. 'Maybe the world needs you, maybe it doesn't. I don't know. But there's more to you than what you've done.' She looked down briefly at my bump then stepped away. 'I need to go now.'

'Where?'

She backed away from me, dissolving into the churchyard air like she'd never existed at all.

*

When me and Jim got home, Elaine was in a state. Craig had called.

'I called and called both your mobiles but neither of you answered! I left so many messages. Why didn't you answer? Where were you?'

'We were at the Christingle, love, like we said. Remember? You said you wanted to finish icing your Madeira,' said Jim, holding her elbows in an attempt to stop her flailing her arms around like a windmill. I picked up Tink and cuddled her in. She was out of sorts too – Elaine had clearly had one of her head fits and frightened her. She shook in my arms.

'We told you where we were going, Elaine,' I said.

'He called here. I heard him.'

'What did he say?'

I could barely understand her through her sobs but the basic

upshot was that no cats had been let out of any bags, that he missed his mum and Jim, and that he wished them a merry Christmas.

'He wanted to speak to you, Rhiannon.' She sniffed as Jim settled her in front of *Celebrity Blind Date* with her tea and pills.

'Oh, did he?' I said.

'He's going to call again.'

Jim rubbed Elaine's back as he sat beside her on the armrest. It was the first time she'd spoken to him since his arrest. 'What did you feel like, talking to him, E?'

She shook her head. 'His voice! I've missed him so much!'

So while she was continuing to have a breakdown in the lounge and Jim was doing the elbow-holding and Tink was chewing her bull's cock on the kitchen lino, I went upstairs and awaited the second coming of Craig on the landline. I waited around half an hour. I didn't think he'd have the balls to speak to me. But then he rang.

'Craig?'

'Are Mum and Dad in the room?'

'No, I'm upstairs. What do you want?'

'Did you kill Lana?'

'She committed suicide, Craig. Couldn't handle her scandal.'

I had to wait an age for him to regain his composure. I got into my PJs while he was sobbing. 'Was there anything else?'

'Did you… ' His voice hushed down. 'Plant the jars?'

'No, I didn't.'

'But you said—'

'Why would a "psycho bunny boiler" do *you* any favours?'

I heard a thumping thump, possibly a fist against a wall.

Lots of breaths. 'I've told the police it was her. Like you said. What do I do now?'

'Rot?' I shrugged.

'If I mean anything to you as the father of your child, you'll do the right thing. Go to the police. Please. I beg you. Tell them everything. Get me out. Otherwise, I'm going to do something.'

'Like what?'

'Top myself.'

'Oh, stop. You'll be out by the New Year.'

'Rhiannon, I'm not joking.'

'Neither am I. I will tell the truth, the whole truth and nothing but the truth, so help me God.'

Silence. 'I'm not falling for it.'

'Have you suffered in there, Craig?'

'What do you think?'

'Yes or no, Craig? Have you suffered?'

'Of course I've suffered. I'm in Hell, you bitch.'

'Say "Yes, Rhiannon, I've suffered."'

I heard the sigh. 'Yes, Rhiannon, I've fucking suffered.'

'Say "Yes, Rhiannon, I trust you."'

'Yes, Rhiannon, I trust you.'

'Say "I will leave it to you to get me out of here, Rhiannon cos I know my parents are in trouble if I don't."'

'I will leave it to you to get me out of here, Rhiannon, cos I know my parents are in trouble if I don't.'

'Say "The baby isn't mine."'

Silence. 'What?'

'"The baby isn't mine." Say it.'

'But it is.'

'No, it isn't yours. Say it.'

'The baby… isn't mine?'

'"But my parents are still in trouble so I'll be a good boy."'

'My parents… still in trouble… a good boy.'

'Now hang up the phone.'

Monday, 24th December
– 33 weeks, 2 days

1. *People who send Christmas cards to people who live in the same house (e.g. Elaine).*
2. *People who send Christmas cards To the Bump, From the Dog or To the Postman (e.g. Elaine).*
3. *People who tell their kids Santa doesn't exist (Helen posted rant on Facebook today) – just let them believe in the shiny stuff for a bit longer.*

The more I try not to think about Marnie, the more I do. If she didn't have Tim, I could imagine us setting up home in the Well House together, like Doris Day and that maid in *Calamity Jane*. Bringing up our kids together. Cleaning the house together. In a parallel universe, perhaps we are.

Santa Claus came early this morning – an A4 white envelope landed on the mat. The writing on the envelope was indecipherable. After much thinning of eyes and mouthing the words – Frog Rainbows, Foot Bananas, Flat Lebanon – I deduced that it read 'FAO Rhiannon' and opened it up.

Keston had come through for me. I had all my new documents – my new passport, banking details, spare photos of me in my Sally Bowes wig, plus the details of an account where I

was to deposit the forger's fee. I'd also been given my new name which I didn't like but I guess killing off Rhiannon Lewis is the main thing. I had to keep telling myself that anyway.

'What's that you've had?' asked Elaine, coming down the stairs.

'Just a Christmas card from my sister,' I said, filing it back inside the envelope. 'I'm going to nip into town in a minute, get some last minute bits and pieces. Do you want anything?'

Elaine gave me a list as long as her arm of her last minute bits and pieces – all the veg for tomorrow, plus condiments, potato salad, coleslaw, eggs and 'four pints of milk to see us through' like we were going down into a bunker or something. I insisted I didn't need any help carrying it all back.

So I waddled into town – *waddle waddle scratch scratch waddle waddle* – and did my last bit of Christmas preparation before everything closed. I stopped at the Post Office to post my last two parcels – one for Seren's kids, the other for Freddie.

'I'm afraid you've missed the Christmas post, my love,' said the old lady behind the desk. 'These won't arrive 'til the New Year now.'

'Perfect,' I said.

On the way home I hit the travel agent's as planned, and it took less time than I thought to make all the arrangements. I walked back with a cinnamon spiced latte from Costa and a renewed spring in my step. Coffee tastes good again. Making plans feels good again. There's still a Marnie-shaped hole in everything but maybe I can work around it. I'm good at that.

Talking of whom, I got back and was barely through the front gate when I had the coffee ripped out of my hands by an extremely irate Nazi.

'WHERE IS SHE?' Tim yelled at me, pulling me through the gate and sending me crashing forwards onto the front lawn.

'What the fuh?' I said, dazed, as he pulled me to my feet in one single movement and grabbed hold of my coat lapels and shook them as though by some miracle his answer would come trickling out of me.

'WHERE. IS. MY. WIFE?'

'I don't know, do I?'

'WHERE'S MARNIE?'

'I don't bloody know!'

'You must do, she tells you everything.'

'She's left you?' I laughed. 'Wow, I didn't think she had it in her.'

'She's taken my son with her!' he cried. 'She's taken my son!'

'Well she would, wouldn't she?'

His breath still stank of garlic. Did he ever brush his teeth? Not good for an ex-Army man. That's a drop-and-give-me-fifty offence if ever I saw one.

'Tell me where she is or I swear to god I will make you regret it.' His knuckles were cold and hard under my chin.

'Oi, what's going on out here?'

My knight in shining Pringle – Jim – was already marching down the front steps towards us, rolling up his cashmere sleeves. Following closely behind was Tink, yapping and scrabbling along the parquet hallway.

Tim released my lapels and I ran into Jim's arms again, like when he saved me from that evil lady detective who was always hounding me. Mein Fuhrer totally switched on the old charm then of course.

'Sir, my wife is missing. I'm sorry to cause such a scene on

Christmas Eve and I hope you can please see my side of this but I have to find her. She's not in her right mind and she's got my son.'

Tink yapped at Tim's trouser hems and was swiftly kicked away by the toe of his jackboot. She took no notice and went back for some yappy more.

'Well Rhiannon clearly doesn't know anything so I suggest you get off my property now before I call the police.' Jim was holding me in a hard embrace and rubbing my arms to keep me warm.

Tim held up his hands. 'I'm going.' He stared me out then carried on walking back towards the garden gate. 'If you know, you better tell me or else.'

'She doesn't have to say anything,' Jim called out. 'Now bugger off.'

Tim closed the gate behind him and disappeared.

When Jim had escorted me safely inside and I'd done a bit of dramatic breathing to further illustrate my trauma, he went upstairs to change and I went into the lounge. Through the bay windows I saw Tim sitting on the seafront bench opposite. I could have left him to stew. To wallow. To carry on suffering, wondering where his wife had gone. It was torment enough.

But he had kicked my dog. And nobody does that and lives for long.

I quietly opened the front door and slipped back outside, bracing myself in the freezing air. I crossed the road and stood before him, underneath the gloomy street lamp and fairy lights swinging on a salty Christmas breeze.

'I'm not leaving until I know,' he said. 'I'll stay out here all

night if I have to. You have to understand, I am desperate. My son, Rhiannon. I need him'.

'I do understand,' I said. 'Why do you think I'm out here?'

'Has she gone abroad? Her passport's gone. She told you where she was going, didn't she? She must have said—'

'Do you know the Well House? Up on the Cliff Road?' I asked.

He frowned. 'The one right at the top? Yeah. Why?'

'If you meet me there at midnight I'll take you straight to her.'

'Why there? Why midnight?'

'You'll find out, I promise you. Don't be late.'

Tuesday, 25th December
– 33 weeks, 3 days

1. *Old people who moan at young people 'always being on their phones'.*
2. *Big Headed Edna at WOMBAT – I'd tell her to go fuck herself if she could find it under all the flab.*
3. *The doctor on Web MD who says baby kicks 'aren't that painful'.*
4. *People who wear flip-flops in winter.*
5. *The entire royal family.*

Updated AJ's Facebook as soon as I woke up – Happy Christmas from China guys! That's me on the Great Wall! It's got thirty-three Likes already.

Today was nice. Not Christmassy, despite all the tinsel and lights and cranberries forced down my neck, but nice. Just me, Jim, Elaine and Tink. We opened our presents together – I got Jim a model boat kit, aftershave, a new kneeler for his gardening, and a hardback war book he'd been on about.

'Oh that's fantastic, what a kind thought. Thank you, darling!'

Elaine had a jumper, some perfume and matching hand cream, and a set of Yankee Candles.

'Aww, Rhiannon you must have spent a fortune. We're so lucky!'

They got me the Applewood Cottage set, complete with vegetable patch, garden furniture *and* panda family (good), a blouse (hideous), books (two New Mummy ones, one Baby's First Year and a Sylvanians page-to-a-day diary), perfume that made me rashy, a Pandora bracelet that didn't fit and some DVDs of films I'd never expressed an interest in seeing.

'Thanks guys. This is all… rather lovely.'

Then came the obligatory roast dinner, stomach ache, fart fest, beachy dog walk and marathon TV watch, followed by a stare down the barrel of a whole week with only chronic indigestion and each other for company.

I didn't give them their joint present until they were both in their pyjamas.

'Hey, I forgot this other present I was meant to give you, sorry. I just found it down the side of the sofa.' I produced the white envelope with a flourish and handed it to Jim.

'Another one?' he yawned. 'You've got us enough, Rhiannon.'

'Oh, it's not much, honestly. Go on, open it.' I lifted up Tink to watch them quizzically peel back the gum on the envelope.

Elaine frowned. She looked at Jim, looked back to the tickets and looked at me. 'For us?'

'Yeah. You're both booked on the sleeper tomorrow morning.'

Jim laughed. 'It's a week in Scotland, love. We'll be there for Hogmanay! Oh Rhiannon, this is too much.'

'No, it's not. It's a thank you for looking after me and Tink so well. It's the least I can do.'

Elaine started crying. 'But tomorrow? I won't be ready. I haven't packed. Look at the state of the kitchen.'

''We can pack now, love,' said Jim.

'Yeah, and I can tidy all this up, that's no bother,' I said.

She was still putting up hurdles. 'How are we going to get to the train station? Where will we leave the car? It's such short notice.'

'It's *meant* to be short notice, it's a surprise, Elaine,' I said. 'I'll take you both to the station in the morning so you don't have to worry about parking. It's all arranged. I've booked you a five-star hotel in Edinburgh and everything.'

Elaine stroked Tink's head. 'When are we back?'

'New Year's Day.'

'What about you? What about Tink? Who's going to look after you?'

'I can look after myself. I have friends here I can call on if I need anyone. And do you want to take her with you like you did to the Lakes?'

'Shall we do that, love?' asked Jim, practically jumping on the spot.

'I can't walk her as often as you guys do,' I added. 'Take her to Scotland, show her the sights. She's allowed on the sleeper.'

'Yes,' said Elaine, snuggling Tink against her face. Tink licked her nose. 'We could do that.'

Jim looked at me as Elaine stared down at the tickets in her hands. 'What is it, love?'

'New Year's Day is next year. I didn't want to think about next year yet. We've got it all to come, haven't we? The trial.'

'That's next year,' said Jim. 'Let's just think about this one for now.'

She choked with tears. 'I've always wanted to go up for New Year's. Thank you, Rhiannon.' She leaned over for a hug which

Tink pre-empted and jumped from my arms into hers. 'Are you sure we can take her?'

'Of course.'

I opened Marnie's present last of all while Jim was tidying up the wrapping paper and smoothing it out to use again next year, and Elaine was rooting around in the laundry basket to put a late wash on. It was a book – a scruffy old copy of *The Wind in the Willows* with childish writing inside the front cover.

Property of Marnie Gallo, Year 3

The only writing inside the book was a single line that had been underlined in red ink on page twenty-three:

This day was only the first of many similar ones for the emancipated Mole...

I was smiling about that all afternoon.

*

Once I was sure both Jim and Elaine were sleeping, I snuck out and drove up to the Well House. I unlocked the back door, unfastened the bolts on the Perspex lid and made myself a cup of tea. Then I walked through to the lounge and just waited. By 12.03 am my rat was in the trap squeling his head off.

'Get me out of here!' came the pained echo from the open hole. 'I've broken my fucking leg! Please!'

'You'll be fine,' I called down. 'There'll be people renting this place out at the end of January. I'm sure they'll want you out before they can settle in.' I threw him down a Selection Box. 'I'd try and eke it out if I were you.'

Tim began to sob and the sobs echoed around the hole, punctuated by his short breaths.

'Oh, stop being so dramatic.'

'I'm… I'll fucking kill you, fucking bitch!'

'Not if I kill you first.'

*

I took Tink up to bed with me tonight for one last time. I thought she would do what she used to and sleep curled up in a nook of my arm but she didn't. Half an hour after lying down, she heard Jim having a coughing fit and ran out of my room and into his. I heard her jump up onto his bed instead. She stayed there all night.

Wednesday, 26ᵗʰ December
– 33 weeks, 4 days

1. *Petrol station pump hogs – get petrol, pay for petrol,*
   leave. Don't start buying lattes and sacks of charcoal.
   Get a damn move on.

Got Jim and Elaine to the train station without a hitch.

'Are you sure you're going to be all right?' asked Jim, loading
Tink's bed and bag of toys into the boot of the Focus. 'You're
not going to be lonely?'

'I'll be A-Okay, I promise,' I said, jangling their keys. 'I'm
meeting the Pudding Club later for their Christmas party and
parlour games. I promise I'll be fine.'

Of course I had draped a tissue of lies over my deeds. I had
nothing planned and nobody to see. All of my bridges had been
burned – no WOMBAT, no Pudding Club, no antenatal buddies,
no Tink and no family. It was just me and my enormous bump,
walking in the rain.

It was hard saying goodbye to Tink at the station, but she
didn't seem at all bothered. My throat hurt as I rubbed my
cheek on her velvety ear but she was more concerned with
getting back into Jim's arms, near his glasses pocket with the
chicken bites inside.

Had a text from Keston on my return – All sorted for NYE. Will pick up at 5pm. Flight leaves 7.45pm. Don't text back. Ditch your phone ASAP.

So that was about as reassuring as aromatherapy on a cancer ward and therefore I was stressed for the rest of the morning.

The Pudding Club have put a picture of them all on Instagram, wearing Christmas knits and paper hats, sitting before an enormous professionally-decorated tree in Pin's living room. The kids are running amok in tutus and onesies and Helen has a right face on her, like she's just discovered her mince pie isn't Fair Trade. Pin's husband Clive's wearing his apron and brandishing a massive turkey baster like he's about to impregnate the world. They have a couple of new preggos in the throng; all blonde and white bread smiley and accepting of their bullshit. Much more their type of parents, I'm sure.

I went for a walk after lunch – through the side streets and all along the seafront. It was strange walking without a dog beside me. Strangely freeing. I didn't have to break my stride as Tink stopped to sniff lampposts or chew dewy grass. I could walk and walk. Aside from some clusters of families farting out their Christmas roasts on the beach, there weren't many people around and no shops were open, save the newsagent's and a café which was closing early. I bought a paper – front page was yet another Hollywood star caught with his cock out. The funicular railway was closed until New Year, same as the Temperley ferry. I wondered where me and the baby would be when they opened up again.

I don't want to leave.

I walked around the churchyard. Nobody about. Well, I mean there were *bodies* about, but none living. WOMBAT

390

were always moaning about the graveyard because the council wouldn't let them tidy it up – there was always litter collected in the corners or dog mess and some of the stone crosses on the larger graves had to be laid down, rather than standing upright, because 'one headstone had collapsed on someone in the Seventies'. It looked unsightly but I guess needs must when people will sue for anything nowadays.

I must have walked around that graveyard a dozen times since I'd been living in Monks Bay but I'd never read the graves before – never thought about what the inscriptions meant. A grave is a grave, right? There were lots of *In Loving Memory* dedications, a few instances of *Here lies my beloved wife*, and *Fond and tender memories* of our precious sister. The Talbots – a man and wife who died one day apart in their eighties at the turn of the century – '*I heard the voice of Jesus say Come unto me and rest.*'

Are you listening to me? I said I don't want to leave. We can't just go. What about Jim and Elaine? What about Tink? You haven't even left them a note.

And babies. Lots of graves for babies. Millicent Ogden – *called to the higher life aged one month*; Cecil William Hames, *born asleep 1853*; Sarah Mary McTavish, *died aged twenty-six hours. Our darling Jane Counsell, taken with her mother Bella in childbirth, 1903.* And the twins – Catherine and John – who died '*after only a few breaths*'.

My bump ached and tightened. I kept on walking around. One of the headstones was of a sea captain lost in the First World War – his body was never recovered but they buried his uniform there as a lasting tribute. On the top of the stone was a clump of ivy and hidden beneath it were two little ships engraved and

some writing – *They that go down to the sea in ships, that do business in great waters; These see the works of the Lord… He maketh the storm a calm, so that the waves thereof are still. Then are they glad because they be quiet; so he bringeth them unto their desired haven.*

Bloody boats again. 'Yeah all right,' I said. 'I've got the hint now. You can stop with the boats.'

I'm not going. I'm not leaving. You can't make me.

Everyone in that graveyard was much loved or much missed or had taken with them a piece of someone's heart. There were no murderers, no paedophiles. No one had left a tombstone engraved with 'He was a massive cock and deserved the pain he felt in his last days', nothing like that. Not that the council would let anyone put that, I suppose.

There were fresh flowers on some of the graves, going back to the Fifties and Sixties. People still remembered them.

Who would miss me? Where would my grave be? Who would stand at *my* grave and weep? I suppose I'll be dead anyway so what will I care?

All the benches were rain-spackled so I sat down on the cross-less plinth of Oswald Faustinus Garland who had *'entered into eternal rest'* in 1895. He was nineteen. Same as AJ. Aside from my still-growling stomach, I felt rested. I always do when I'm around death. It's like nothing else matters. The plug is pulled and all the shit drains away – it's just me and my maker, thinking things through.

'We'll be okay,' I said aloud. 'Wherever we end up, we will be fine. We can start anew. New name. No more killing, not if you don't want me to. I'll give it up. I'll find happiness some other way.'

392

Nothing.

'You not talking to me now? Why are you hurting me?'

Nothing.

'We have to go. It's too risky to wait any longer. God you ache today.'

I felt a movement in my peripheral vision – an old woman with a Christmas wreath – ivy, red roses, pine cones, sprigs of holly, dried orange slices and cinnamon stick bundles. It was Elephant Vadge Madge from WOMBAT. She normally didn't like confrontation but I knew what she was going to say, even how she would say it.

'Who are you talking to, Rhiannon?'

'God,' I said, quick as a blink. She seemed contented with that answer.

'I see. I talk to Him myself sometimes, when I need some answers or some guidance. Did you have a good Christmas?'

'So so.'

'You know you're not meant to sit on the graves,' said Madge.

'All the benches are wet,' I said, an arrow of pain shooting through my bump from my ass. 'Not that comfortable anyway.' I struggled to my feet, shooting pains up both thighs. She offered me her gloved hand and helped me up. I nodded towards the wreath. 'Are you on the flower rota today?'

'No, I've come to see Stan. I come every year on Boxing Day. Eleven years today he passed over. It's important to me to keep coming.'

We walked in the direction of Stan's plot – a small black marble headstone that looked brand new – recessed gold lettering bearing the name of Stanley Lawrence Pugh, Beloved Husband of Margaret, Father of Andrew and Josephine. *For we*

believe that Jesus died and rose again, and so we believe that
God will bring with Jesus those who have fallen asleep in him.

Madge lay her wreath on the rectangle of disturbed earth where Stan's body lay. 'Are you visiting someone here as well?'

'No. I just came out for a walk.'

'On your own?'

'Yeah. I need to be on my own sometimes. I'm not good around others.'

'You should come back to WOMBAT. Pay no attention to Edna and Doreen and Nancy. Nobody likes them anyway, we just put up with them.' She nudged my elbow and cheeky-grinned.

'Why are you being nice? I barely said two words to you at WOMBAT.'

'"Let all bitterness and wrath and anger be put away from you. Be kind to one another, forgiving one another, as God in Christ forgave you."'

'Proverbs?'

'Ephesians Four, if my memory serves me correctly.'

'You live by the Bible don't you?'

'Got to live by something in this world. Got to have something to hold on to. We all have to be anchored to something.' Bloody boats again.

God forgives everything if you love Him enough, that seems the constant refrain. But I'm not buying it. I'd like to, but I can't. I'd like to live in a world where it's that simple; where we do something bad but it's wiped out with a prayer. Where the people we love are waiting for us on a cloud. But they're not. As far as I'm concerned, all bets are off.

Forgive us our trespasses as we forgive those who trespass against us.

Well I do not forgive.

And lead us not into temptation.

Even as those around us would be tempted?

But deliver us from evil.

Deliver me towards it.

For *mine* is the kingdom.

The power *and* the glory.

Forever and ever.

Amen.

I slowly moved away from Madge. The ache in my back swelled and began to stab. 'Happy Christmas to you and yours.'

'Same to you, love, and your little one. God bless you both.'

I didn't move away from her because the tangy scent of her unwashed creases were getting to me. Or because the folds of her corpulent arm kept rubbing against me. I moved away instinctively because I didn't want her to know what was happening and I didn't want her to help me.

I'm getting out of here.

I'd barely reached the cemetery gates when I felt the warm gush down both of my legs.

Thursday, December 27th – 33 weeks, 5 days

I'm in fucking labour. I'm in fucking hospital. And fucking Bitch Midwife is on duty. I wanted Mishti with her soft hands and kind eyes and genuine concern. Instead I get this pass-ag tattooed harpy who looks like she's just been lifted out of a fucking mosh pit. Soo perb.

Confusion? Intense pain? Irritation? It me.

*

It was first the gush, and then the searing stabbing pain, cutting and slashing through my body at regular intervals.

'How often are the contractions?' the voice kept saying.

'I DON'T KNOW. PRETTY FUCKING OFTEN,' I seethed. The voice was a random woman on the seafront walking her dog. Her dog was sniffing at the drips from my hems.

The ambulance took forever but when it came, events progressed mercifully quickly. I didn't take too much notice of anything until the doors of the ambulance swung open and I was stretchered down a ramp and into the main hospital. Two drunks were having a fight in the corridor. A security guard was pulling them apart. Slamming doors. Flashing lights. The reek

of hand-sanitiser and coffee. Porters wheeling beds. Long-ass corridors. Where are my trousers? Where's my shoes?

I didn't realise we'd arrived in the delivery suite at Southampton General until I saw Bitch Midwife standing at the basin, washing her hands.

'Hey Rhiannon, you're early, babes!'

'No shit… ' I could not remember the guy's name. Warlock? No shit Warlock? That didn't sound right. 'Ugh, stop this pain please!'

I threw up – the paramedic caught it in an egg box thing.

'Is there anyone we can call for you?'

'No. There's no one.' The pain seemed to radiate out from my lower spine – like my skin was splitting open. 'Holy shit I can't take hours of this.'

'Might not *be* hours, Rhiannon,' said Bitch Midwife. 'You're crowning.'

'CROWNING?'

They kept asking and asking me if there was someone I'd like to call. I kept saying no but none of them believed me. 'You all know where the father is, he's in prison. I'm on my own!'

I've never felt pain like it. It was taking every single thought and emotion I had and snatching it up. Chewing it. Twisting it. I couldn't think about anything else other than the agony. The nearest description I can get to it is the world's worst period pain, accompanied by Anthony Joshua repeatedly thumping me in the back.

My ass burned too. A tube appeared in front of my face. I sucked on it before I was told to, wrenched it out of Bitch Midwife's hands. Such nice air. The nicest air I've ever had, in

fact. I sucked it in deep and out again and in and in and out and in and I couldn't get enough of it.

'Nice and slow,' said Curly Hair. 'Calm breaths, easy breaths.'

'Am I sitting on fire?' I kept asking. 'My ass is on fire!'

'Nice and steady, you're doing so well.'

'Am I?' Nice air kept coming. Burning ass was washed with cool water from a mountain spring. Heaven. Briefly. So briefly before the wave of pain came crashing back over me.

'Looks like she doesn't want to wait,' said Bitch Midwife, appearing from underneath the white sheet they'd draped over my nethers. 'Okay, deep breaths now. Every exhale, imagine the pain flowing out of you. You can do this, Rhiannon. Say it with me, "I can do this." Exhale, "I can do this."'

'Inhale I can't do this. Exhale I can't do this.'

'Come on, Rhiannon, work with me now.'

'No. You do it. Please don't make me. I don't want this kid.'

I imagined Craig sitting there in the chair next to the bed, holding my hand, wiping my hair back. He'd have been useless – going out for a smoke every five minutes and calling his dad. But he wouldn't have missed it. The empty chair was all I could focus on.

'Okay come on, Rhiannon, the baby needs you to do this now. She can't stay in there forever. She needs you to help her.'

I tried to remember every film I'd ever seen where a woman was giving birth – the deep breathing, the pushing, trying to get into the headspace of a mother – *Nine Months*, *Parenthood*, *What to Expect When Everyone's a Bland Superhot American Actor and You Can Never Think of Their Names*.

'Why's she coming so early? She's not due 'til February!'

'That's pregnancy for you,' said Bitch Midwife. Cue Porky Pig laugh.

'Helpful.'

It actually felt good to finally push. My body wanted me to push because it knew it was pushing the pain out.

'Okay, nice deep breaths, deep diaphragmatic breathing. Push down right into your bottom.'

My body is working on its own, doing things I haven't asked it to. I'm just going with it – pushing myself inside out. Sweating, tearing pain.

'This is horrible,' I cried. 'I want to die.'

I sucked too hard on the gas and puked on someone's hair. Not Bitch Midwife, unfortunately, one of the other midwives who'd come in to have a rummage about in my nethers. That'll teach her.

Bitch Midwife keeps yelling at me. 'Push, that's it, we're nearly there, Rhiannon. One more big push and she'll be out.'

I push something out but it isn't a baby. 'That's good, we can clean that up. Now one more big push.'

It felt like everything was going to come out – womb, lungs, ribs and baby – the whole damn lot all joined up by umbilical cord bunting.

'One more, come on, nice big push.'

'You keep saying one more one more, I've done about fifty of these!'

'We need a really big one, Rhiannon. We need her shoulders out now and then the rest of her will follow. One big push, come on! Good girl.'

And so I did. I pushed with all my might. I knew that if I didn't, she might get stuck – she might die up there between my legs and that's no place for anyone to die, believe me. So I pushed to save her life. That's what I did for her. I did it for her.

And everything seemed to give way – she was out of me and in their arms. And lots of high voices were saying 'Well done' and 'Good girl' but they were all the adult voices. The voice I wanted to hear wasn't there – the little cry of freedom. There was silence. And one of the midwives and two of the doctors took her over to the corner of the room onto a little flat bed.

'What are they doing?'

'They're helping her to start breathing,' said Curly Hair, snapping off her gloves.

'Why isn't she breathing?'

'She will in a second, don't worry. Give her a moment.'

I lay there still panting, legs akimbo, pushing out the placenta into the midwives' hands. They busied around my nethers, tearing strips of tissue and tidying away empty packets and collecting up surgical equipment. And I still lay there, numb, still watching the corner, waiting for the cry.

And then it came – a squawk. Like a tiny sparrow.

And my body gave like a tidal wave.

'There she is,' said Bitch Midwife. 'See? Told you she was all right. She's a bit shocked, that's all. It's quite normal.'

I wasn't in the least bit prepared for that feeling. I didn't know I was capable of that feeling. Bitch Midwife brought her back to me and she was all I could look at – this little squawky bundle, all purple and wriggly and ugly with pasty white shit all over her little scrunched up angry face.

Just like her mother.

'She's beautiful,' said Bitch Midwife as she placed the wriggly fish on my chest. She stopped crying instantly.

'There you go. She wanted her mummy, didn't you, darling?'

I looked down at her – my daughter – her tiny hands pushed

up to her chin – fingers splayed like her face was the centre of a flower. This little girl who had grown inside me, against my will, forcing me to feel things I didn't want to, didn't think I could. She was part of me. Built of my skin, my bones, my hairs, my nails. She was wound up so tightly within me, I couldn't untie her now if I wanted to.

'Have you got a name for her yet?'

No names had seemed appropriate until now. 'Ivy,' I said. 'She's Ivy.'

'Ahh that's nice. Is that a family name?'

'No, after the plant.'

Bitch Midwife nodded. 'Lovely. She'll need to go to neonatal for a little while so we can get some nutrients into her. Need to fatten you up a bit, don't we, darling? We weren't expecting you yet.'

Ivy nuzzled into me because she was her own woman now and she didn't have to put up with all that patronising shit. I was empty and there she was. Warm. Real. Little chest pulsing. I was shaking from head to toe.

'It's the adrenalin,' said Bitch Midwife. 'Quite normal.'

Ivy opened her eyes and it freaked me completely and totally out.

'Woah! I didn't know they could open their eyes so early!'

'Oh yeah, look at those,' said Bitch who was down at the goal end, cleaning me up, not that I could feel anything. 'Beautiful.'

'She's got her father's eyes,' I said. And the tears came again.

Of course Bitch Midwife still thought it was Craig's baby, like the rest of the world apart from Claudia. 'Does he want to be involved?'

I didn't answer and Ivy started to cry in my arms. I knew what she was thinking – *My real daddy is dead. She killed him.*

Marnie had said it would all fall into place. Click, all of a sudden. That I'd know what I had wanted all along the moment I saw my baby for the first time. But it didn't. The moment she started crying, all I felt was pain. Shocking, terrifying pain in my head and my chest. And all I heard was screaming. Crying. Glass smashing.

I was back at Priory Gardens.

A vase crashing to a hardwood floor.

The sound of blood dripping from a cot mattress.

The creak of the eaves as the rope swung back and forth.

My dead friends. All babies.

Heartburn clutched my throat. 'I think I'm going to be sick again.'

I handed Ivy to the midwife. 'Can you take her now, please?' I grabbed the empty egg box from the side locker.

'You can have her for a bit longer if you want?'

'No, it's fine,' I said, clutching my egg box with shaking hands. 'You said she has to go to neonatal.'

'Yeah, we need to keep an eye on her for a bit. She'll be monitored twenty-four-seven, I assure you. She's in the safest hands. Are you sure there isn't anyone you want me to call?'

Ivy was still crying. She wouldn't tell me why – was it me? Was it the midwife? Was she thinking about her daddy? I needed her gone, I needed her out of there.

'Claudia. You can call Claudia.' I reached for my handbag on the armchair and she scurried around and pulled out my phone, handing it to me. I found the number and handed it

back to her. 'She's the baby's godmother. Can you take her away now, please?'

'She's a good weight, Rhiannon, five pound two ounces. A good sign.'

'Thank you.'

'You're welcome.'

My heartburn didn't start to go until Ivy had gone with the midwife, out of the door and up the corridor. I could still hear her wailing right until she was through the second set of double doors. Then there was peace. Then there was silence. And my head returned to normal. And I no longer heard the sounds. I sat up in bed alone and in complete silence.

Until I began crying my fucking eyes out.

*

When I woke up, surrounded by rough, starchy sheets and the smell of disinfectant, I was no longer shaking. Nor was I alone.

There was a blonde blur sitting in the armchair beside me: Claudia.

'Hey there, Sweetpea, how are you feeling?'

'Bit grim,' I replied.

'She decided to come early then?'

'Yeah. No holding her back. She's a bit small.' I rubbed my face all over to force wakefulness. I had a hospital bracelet on my right wrist that I didn't know who had put there – my name and date of birth were on it.

Claudia had brought with her a pink balloon and a large bunch of flowers – gerberas and roses. 'Where is she, neonatal?'

'Yeah. Don't you have to be at work today?'

'Time off in lieu. The midwife said you did it on your own.'

'Yeah I did.'

'What about Craig's parents?'

'They're away 'til the New Year.'

'You should have called me sooner, I could have been here for you.'

'You're here now.'

'Yes, and I packed a bag. I can stay here as long as you need.'

I nodded. 'Thanks. Might be some time.'

Friday, December 28th
– 1 day post-partum

1. *Sandra Huggins*.

MORNING – 10.00 a.m. – 9 hours 'til DEPARTURE
Mmm, so post-partum pooing is a nightmare then. Thanks everyone for warning me about that little sunny delight. It was like pushing out The Houses of Parliament. At one point I thought I was giving birth again. It came with a full sweat and a rush of blood but Bitch Midwife assured me it was 'all part and parcel of the wonder of pregnancy'.

'Yeah yeah, just get me an ice pack and a rubber ring,' I said, trying desperately not to twat-slap her to Mars.

I'm still waiting for maternal instinct to kick in so that kind of shit doesn't bother me anymore but so far, so bad. Everything is annoying me. The amount of blood on every single pad I wear seconds after changing it. My tap-like tits. The crying babies in the other delivery suites. The gaggle of midwives standing about the nurses' station laughing and drinking tea from mismatched mugs and talking about last night's TV. Doctors milling about looking all sexy and knowledgeable. Where are all the endorphins that were supposed to have kicked in by now? Did they come out with the baby?

All dressing-gowned up and looking like Fifty Shades of Shit, I walked along to neonatal this morning to see Ivy. There were several babies in their plastic boxes, all attached to tubes and wires, all with worried mums and dads and grannies sitting beside them or cuddling them in armchairs. I spotted Ivy instantly. She had her head against the bunny. I put my hand through the hole in the box and felt her breaths through her tiny white romper suit. I used to do the same with Tink when she was a puppy.

She was all tiny tubes and a woolly hat like an egg cosy. The on duty midwife said she was 'a good weight but she'll have to stay in for a bit'.

'Can't I take her home and feed her there?' I asked.

'No,' said the midwife. 'She needs to be in there for a while.'

'How long?'

'Difficult to say but she's a bit early so usually around a week.'

'A week? I can't wait that long.'

'It really is the best place for her. Would you like to try breastfeeding?'

'With people watching?'

'Does that make you uncomfortable?'

'I don't want to do it here.'

'We can arrange for—'

'I don't want to do it. I don't want to do it at all.'

'That's fine, no problem.'

Ivy looked so much like AJ it was shocking. She was a small, wriggling guilt trip. Her face wrinkled up like she was about to cry and I made to leave but she settled and went to sleep again. I put my face next to the box, so only she could hear me.

'I'm sorry you didn't get to meet your dad. I am sorry about him.'

I stroked her tiny hand – her fingers as soft as petals, her skin as smooth as catmint. 'I don't know what my future looks like, Ivy. But I know I don't want it to be *your* future. I don't want you running and hiding. I want you to have four walls and a big garden. And toys. And friends. If they catch me, they'll put me in a tiny room. I need fresh air. I need a garden. And I need to kill. I know you don't like it but that's me. All those people who would hurt you. I need to cause them pain. Lots of pain. That's not the kind of mother you need. You need better than me.'

I guess that was the moment I knew – I *was* a mother. And I only wanted the best for her.

The tears came. 'I can't take you with me. I want you to be with someone who puts you at the centre of their world. Because however hard I try, I can't make you the centre of mine. That fortune teller was right about me. She could see it – a baby covered in blood. That would be you. And I can't handle that.'

I reached in and picked out the pink bunny I'd bought her. I held it to my nose and inhaled. It smelled of her. She started crying – this stark, repetitive roar that felt like being grated from the inside out.

'I can't handle it when you cry either.'

'I think she's hungry,' said the midwife, bustling over in her white plastic apron and clumpy platforms. 'Why don't you try feeding her now? I can take her off again if you're in the least bit unsure?'

'I don't want to,' I said, getting up, putting as much space as I could between me and the noise. I wiped my eyes and pocketed

the bunny in my jogging bottoms. Ivy screamed louder. 'I don't want her anywhere near me.'

LUNCHTIME – 1.00 p.m. – 6 hours 'til DEPARTURE
Heather and I had finished going through the forms. I was getting changed back into my freshly-laundered clothes, courtesy of the NHS – when Claudia walked back in, fresh from lunch and seeing Ivy.

'Oh Rhiannon, she's gorgeous. I couldn't stop looking at her. Ivy is the perfect name, too – I love it. She looks so much like her daddy, it's uncanny – not discharging you already, are they?'

'This is Heather Wherryman. She's a family law solicitor.'

They shook hands. Claudia looked at me. 'What do you need your solicitor here for?'

'She's going to help you.'

'Help me do what?' It was then that she clocked the fact my shoes were on. And I was putting on my coat too. 'Are you discharging yourself? What's going on?'

'I need to leave, Claudia. I can't take Ivy with me. Heather's prepared all the forms I need to make it all official.'

'What?' Claudia looked from me to Heather in quick succession. 'I don't understand.'

'Ivy's your baby now,' I said, putting my arms through my coat sleeves and buttoning the front. 'I've set up an account for her. Heather will explain everything else.'

'Rhiannon, what on earth? Make what official?'

'Do you want a baby or not, Claudia?'

'What? Wha— but… ' She stepped forward, her eyes full of tears. She cupped my cheek and put her face next to mine. 'Don't leave her, Rhiannon.'

'I have to go.'

'She'll be out of here in a week and then we can take her home, you and me together, you don't have to leave her.'

'I can't.'

'You can both live with me, it'll be fine. Don't do this. Your body's still in shock from the birth. We can raise her together, you and me. You and Ivy can have your own rooms.'

'No,' I said, squeezing past her towards the door.

'You can't just go,' she cried, pulling on my arm. 'She needs you as well. She needs her mum, Rhiannon.'

I pulled my arm away from her. 'I'm sorry. She needs a better mum than me. She needs *you*.'

EVENING – 5.05 p.m. – 2 hrs 'til DEPARTURE

No little voice.

No one stopping me.

Eyes wet.

Arse sore.

Tits leaking.

Chaining paracetamol.

Nothing to lose now. Nothing standing in my way.

Did a couple of BuzzFeed quizzes in the car outside the Farm Shop. I discovered which Spongebob Squarepants character I am most like (Mr Krabs), which member of Little Mix should be my best friend (Jesy), and that I'd definitely be first to be eliminated on *RuPaul's Drag Race*. As I suspected.

Events happened quicker than I could process them after that.

Five to five, I could see Sandra moving about inside the shop. Turning off lights. Turning over the sign. Loping back to the cloakroom.

I got out of the car, striding towards the front door. My rules had all gone out the window – I didn't care who saw, I didn't care about covering my tracks, I didn't care that the place was monitored by CCTV, or that my trainers had Velcro on them. They would link this irrevocably to me and for the first time in my life, I didn't give one shit.

Stopping at the log pile. Pulling the axe from the stack. I tried the door handle. In I went.

Mariah Carey was blasting from the speakers. She'd been having a little dance around while she was locking up.

'Sorry, love, we're closing,' came the voice as the music lowered slightly. I didn't see her at first. Then there she was, behind the till, in the near-darkness. *Clicks* as she turned off the Christmas lights displays – one after the other – until just the background music and the glaring light of a neon Father Christmas illuminating her tired, hangdog face remained.

All.

I.

Want.

For.

Christmas.

Is.

You.

Sandra slung her handbag over her shoulder – the red handbag with the saggy mouth.

'Hey Sandra,' I said, sliding the bolt across.

She looked over at me. 'Sorry you've got the wrong person.' She looked away. Tidied a display of Lindt reindeer that didn't need tidying. 'We're closing up now.'

'We?' I said. 'You're on your own.'

'No I'm not. Colin's in the back, I can get him for you.'

'Colin leaves at four-thirty p.m. On the dot. Every single day. I've been watching you for some time.'

I must have looked quite the scary sight, looming towards her in the darkness with only Mariah Carey at her shrillest to lighten the effect. 'It's just you, me and Mariah. I've locked the door.'

I walked towards her, twirling my axe like a sadistic majorette. I had her cornered behind the till. 'Got your kids back from social services yet?'

'No, get back, get back,' she said, grabbing a can of fake snow from the cash register and aiming it at me.

'What are you going to do with that, pray tell?' I laughed.

She gasped for breath, crouching down. 'Please no, please, no, help me! God help me!'

'God won't save you. He's working for me now. Mmm, now what was it the judge said in that court report? You told the seven-year-old boy to get on his knees and... help me out here, Sandra, my memory is shot.'

'No, please. Get away, AWAY from me!'

'Get on your knees and... open your mouth, that was it, wasn't it?'

'No, no, I'll do anything, please, take the money... '

'I don't want money.'

'What do you want? Why are you doing this?'

'It's what I do. I kill paedophiles. I kill people like you.'

She cowered lower, trying to make herself small enough so I couldn't see her. Fat chance. She sank against the wall. Knocked the Christmas rota off the board. It fluttered to the straw-strewn floor. 'It wasn't me, it was *them*!'

'They told you to do it. You took those photos.'

'Yes but...'

'You had a choice. You *chose* to take those photos. Those children screamed and cried and you. Took. Photos.'

'I'll do anything. Take anything you want, please.'

'Anything?'

'Yes, yes.'

'Anything at all?'

'Yes please. Here.' She fumbled open the till and threw ten pound note after twenty pound note straight at me. They each fell to the floor and skittered away. 'Take it.'

'I said I don't want it, Sandra. Now get on your fucking knees.'

*

Think of the happiest you've ever been. Might have been during that childhood game of Tig. Or your wedding day. Maybe the time you first locked eyes on your newborn or injected heroin. That moment – times it by a thousand and wrap it in the best chocolate you ever ate and put it on the fastest rollercoaster and you're still nowhere near as happy as I felt leaving that shop, having hacked Sandra Huggins to pieces.

And I do mean pieces.

I don't know how long it took the axe to tear her up but it wasn't long. Wet slap after whooming crack after squelching hack, I kept going and going until the screams stopped and there was nothing left of the woman who had once been Sandra Huggins. Looking at the landscape of blood when I had finished, a strange sort of warmth flooded my body from my heart outwards. This was it. This was bliss.

And I felt the click in my mind.

The sight of it – the diabolical red poetry before me – brought tears. Exquisite, ecstatic tears. In my feverish trance, the sight of the sugarplum and gingerbread displays dripping with her innards was just so damn funny.

Deck the Halls with Sandra's insides, Fa la la la la la la la la.

One part of her was still throbbing.

Every every ache disappeared. Nothing else mattered. Just me and the axe in that beautiful moment that I had given birth to.

The only thing I left intact was her head. I carried it around the store– showing it around like it was new in town. Holding it up for the CCTV. Swinging it around by the hair left on it. I removed the neon Santa head and replaced it with Huggins's own.

Sandra Claus is coming to town…

I laughed all the way home – my car seat is soaked. I just left it.

The house phone was ringing when I got in. I went straight upstairs for a shower. I put my contacts in and didn't bother to dry my hair, I tucked it wet underneath my wig. The phone rang again as I was leaving.

'Rhiannon? Thank god.' A man's voice. The line was distant. Scratchy.

'Keston?' He was on a car phone.

'Rhee, have you seen the news?'

'No, why?' They can't have found Sandra already.

'I'm on my way to pick you up, allright? I'm two hours away but I'm gunning it so sit tight, all right? I'm coming.'

'What news, Keston?'

'There's been a new development. The house – your mum and dad's. They've found bones in the woods.'

'What bones?'

'Whose bones do you think? Pete McMahon's. The white tent's right over the spot where we put him.'

'How would they know he is buried in those woods, Keston?'

'I don't know. They haven't identified him yet but this is why we need to get you out of here now—'

'There are only three people in this world who knew that body was there. Me, you and Dad. And Dad's dead.'

'Rhiannon, I swear I never told anyone. I'd be in the shit as much as you would. You *know* I wouldn't do that to Tommy.'

'Do I?'

'Of course. Why would I be busting my balls to get down there and get you as far away from Géricault as possible? Huh? Talk sense, Rhiannon.' His voice was breaking up. I could hear rain against the car windows. 'This ricochets off me as well as you. They start looking into those woods they're gonna find more than McMahon. Just be ready, I'm going as fast as I can.'

I picked up my bag and Jim's car keys. Checked my tickets and passport were in my coat pocket. And I left the house.

It was quiet on the roads. It wasn't until I was on the clattering blue and white Park and Ride bus heading to the main terminal that I realised my mistake. It wasn't Keston who'd told Géricault what was buried in those woods – I had omitted to remember the other person who knew what had happened that night. Who knew what I'd done. Who'd seen me and Dad walking back across the lawn afterwards with our shovels. It wasn't just the Man in the Moon who'd witnessed our dastardly deeds from after.

Seren had too.

The sister I'd killed for twice – one being our own grandfather.

Two being Pete McMahon himself – the yellow-toothed trickster who hadn't taken no for an answer, whose naked back was riddled with red slits when I'd finished with him.

The sister who had watched the Perseid meteor showers with me as we lay on hay bales in the fields.

The sister who'd helped me walk again, talk again, use my fine motor skills, played Sylvanians with me, taught me how to roller skate and pirouette and lace my shoes, how to roll my tongue and cartwheel and spell Inconsequential, and French plait my hair, who'd spent hours designing outfits for me on the Fashion Wheel she'd got me for Christmas.

The sister who'd helped me bury the toys in the garden to save them from the charity shop.

The sister who'd sobered up in time to see me and Dad coming through the kitchen door, his khaki trousers covered in bloodstains, my hands covered in mud. This kind of burial was where she drew the line.

Seren had not just thrown me under the bus – she'd put the bus in reverse and run over my fucking head. Twice.

My own sister. My own Judas.

*

I was one of the last twenty passengers to board. I'd left it to the last hour to check in. The guy checking my documents and passport said I was 'very wise to leave it until the end of the day', because of the long queues that had built up that morning. I passed through the X-ray and got my bags scanned, and then my bigger bags went off with a porter to my cabin. The security wasn't as stringent as it is at the airport, though there were some raised eyebrows about the pink rabbit in my coat pocket

and the knapsack of Sylvanians – I chose to ignore them. New me and all that.

I didn't miss Ivy until I saw the couple with the baby. Cooing over it in the pushchair. Mum feeding her raisins. Dad making faces. I felt the pull but I pushed it away. Might as well get in the habit now.

Had an interminable conversation with Gloria and Ken from Yorkshire in the queue behind me – this is their tenth cruise. He collects antique vacuum cleaners – she does sugar craft and has had four new hips. Ken talked me through the different excursions and what food to avoid on the buffet. Gloria had a squeaky, doll-like voice and she was already in holiday mode with the fake tan, white pedal pushers, strappy gold sandals and firebox red toenails even though the boat hadn't left dock yet.

'Is there much to do on board?' I asked them.

They both laughed. 'Do?' Ken chuckled and he began counting them all off on his fingers. 'They got cabaret every night, live music, comedy shows, casinos, picture house—'

'And beauty salons and keep fit classes and loads of shops,' squeaked Gloria. 'You won't be bored on here, no danger.'

'Any gardening facilities?' I asked. They both looked at me blankly.

'There might be a flower arranging group you could join, if that floats your boat,' Ken laughed. 'You've no need to be lonely at any rate, my love. You can pal around with us if you want to. We can show you what's what.'

'Yeah, course you can, babe!' said Gloria. 'Just until you meet your husband in the next port.'

'That's so kind of you, thanks ever so,' I said, smiling sweetly, like a sweet pea would.

I had to spin them a yarn of course, because people travelling alone always seem to garner questions. New me, new act.

I was then directed to a huge carpeted lobby with roped-off lines, and my line was the shortest – it being for occupants of executive class cabins. That impressed the hell out of Ken and Gloria. I got given my boarding card-cum-room key plus a map of the ship —

The *Flor de la Mer*.

It was bloody enormous – like a huge towering white shopping mall but with Christmas lights and bunting draped around the upper decks and water lapping the sides. I had to stop and pose for a picture beside the life ring on the springy metal gangway – I gave it the full peace sign and kicked up heel which seemed to tickle Gloria's fancy. When in Rome…

Inside the sleek and sparkly main atrium, passengers filed into lifts and swarmed staircases – some people already dressed for dinner. Buffet tables with complimentary snacks and drinks had been laid out in the glitzy gold and cream dining room, but because I was so late boarding, most of the good stuff had gone. I took a highly-polished green apple from a fruit basket and a few cereal bars. I couldn't remember the last time I'd eaten.

The ship was about to leave dock and all the passengers gathered on the top deck to wave off their families and friends below. There was quite a big turnout. People with happy, smiling faces, some crying, waving, balloons buffeting in the cold evening breeze. Somewhere behind me a speaker was trilling out a pan pipes version of 'Across the Universe'.

I'd already eaten half the apple when I saw the middle was brown with rot. I slung it overboard, waiting for the pleasing splash but it didn't come. There was too much other noise.

The sea breeze lifted the fringe of my wig as I stared out to sea, feeling the ship move beneath my feet. My t-shirt felt cold where my tits had started leaking again. I pulled my coat tighter around me.

Craig would be back home by the end of January – a free man.

Jim and Elaine would get their son back. And their car.

Tink would get her daddy back. She's missed him.

Claudia would know what I was sorry for. And why AJ wasn't calling.

DI Géricault would be fuming that she'd had me so close before I'd slipped through the few remaining fingers she had.

Ivy would have a warm, safe home, and a bed, and someone who loved her more than anything else in the universe.

And in the New Year, Freddie would receive the parcel containing my full confession. And then the whole world would know about Sweetpea.

The ship's horn boomed one long blast as the humungous vessel eased out of dock. People cheered below and on deck. Gold balloons floated up into the starry black. Then three more blasts as it hit the open sea. Rhiannon Lewis was dead. I had to be someone else now. Died and rose again. Died and rose again. Died and rose again. And rose again.

I stayed on deck, staring – an abyss horizon with an abyss tomorrow on my mind. I didn't want to go down to my cabin yet. It felt too small in there. Like a prison cell. Somewhere on the ship, party poppers snapped.

A couple in evening wear walked past me, hand in hand.

Grey-haired ladies in sequins and block heels clomped along smoking cigarettes and chattering in foreign accents.

Groups of men in dinner suits sauntered past with glasses of wine.

I was on my own and the endless cold night hung over me like a shroud. The world looked huge from the middle of the sea. I inhaled until my lungs were sore. I bit my nails down until they throbbed. The taste of blood lingered in my mouth – I didn't know whose. Somewhere on board a child wailed. My empty belly throbbed. I felt the wetness of my t-shirt. She was still with me in some ways, her tendrils had got in and clung to me tightly. I cried my own sea on that deck.

I reached into my handbag and pulled out my phone. I scrolled through my contacts until I hit the right name. It dialled. I waited.

Finally, a click. 'Hello?' A man's voice. 'Who is it, please?'

I waited. I breathed.

'Rhiannon?' A woman's voice then. *Seren's* voice. 'Rhiannon, is that you? Speak to me.' Heavy breaths. Fear. 'Rhiannon, I did it for you. And the baby. Craig doesn't deserve this. Someone had to do something.'

My silence seemed to be unnerving her far more than any words I could have punctuated it with. I continued to listen – protestations of 'having no other choice' and 'wrestling with my conscience for days'.

'You have to do the right thing,' she sobbed. 'You've caused so much damage, taken so many lives.'

I waited. The ship boomed out another long low note.

'Rhiannon, where are you? You need to face up to what you've done now. It's not fair. Look what you've done to Craig. What kind of mother are you going to be to that child? Rhiannon? PLEASE? Say something. Just say something, please!'

419

I removed my phone from my ear and threw it as far as I could out into the sea – my sister's frantic screams growing more distant as it soared and plunged down into the black waves. The Man in the Moon was the only person who saw me do it. That's why he was smiling.

Seren didn't know when I was coming for her, but she knew beyond any doubt that I was. Tomorrow or the next day or maybe the day after that. She just couldn't be sure.

ONE PLACE. MANY STORIES

Bold, innovative and
empowering publishing.

FOLLOW US ON:

@HQStories